TAPPED BY FATE

GHOST SHOP PARANORMAL MYSTERY/SUSPENSE SERIES BOOK 1

HEATHER AMES

WELL OF IDEAS PRESS

CHAPTER ONE

Sunny Kingston watched Tina Mason shake crumbs from her sandwich wrapper onto the ground. Two sparrows swooped in to peck up the impromptu meal inches from Tina's feet. Overhead, clouds billowed in from the Coast Range, threatening Salem, Oregon with an end to the unseasonably warm mid-March weather. Sunny shivered as a cold breeze slithered through Bush's Pasture Park.

Ignoring predictions of a midday storm bringing soaking rain, possible hail and the risk of lightning, Sunny's stubborn best friend had not only insisted on going to the park, she had adamantly refused to accept a lift from Sunny, driving in from Portland for their impromptu picnic. Tina had arrived on her bicycle, and was wearing a short-sleeved white blouse, colorful peasant skirt and sandals. Sunny wondered whether clairvoyant Tina had consulted alternate sources for information on the weather forecast. If so, then those sources were definitely defective and misinformed, she thought, as she heard thunder in the distance.

The cold breeze lifted Sunny's blonde hair from her shoulders and slid under her denim jacket. She hastily fastened it, glanced up and noticed the sky had darkened toward the west. Gunmetal grey clouds were advancing at a rapid pace.

"Chilly?" Tina's dark eyebrows arched. She grabbed the empty take-out bag before a gust of wind whisked it away to litter the picturesque rhododendron hillside nearby. She crammed her empty sandwich wrapper inside before offering the bag to her friend.

"Not just chilly…cold to my bones." Sunny pressed her own sandwich wrapper into a neat square.

Tina shook the bag. "Trash? Or are you making origami?" She smiled, her blue eyes twinkling with amusement.

"Yeah, right. The day I take up any kind of craft, hell will definitely freeze over." Sunny returned Tina's smile. A louder thunder-clap made her glance up at the sky again. The clouds had increased, both in volume and speed. "We'd better go." She took the bag and shoved the remains of her meal into it.

Tina stood up and stretched both arms above her head. She yawned. "I'm so glad we came here instead of a restaurant. But now I'm well-fed, I feel lazy." She checked her watch. "Almost two. Armenta will say it's too late for her lunch break. That'll make me feel really guilty about leaving her alone in the shop." She smiled. "But we had a lot of catching up to do."

"We did," Sunny agreed, "but mostly we talked about what a mess I've made of *my* life." She got up and looked around for a trash can. "How's yours, especially the business?"

Tina had opened her metaphysical shop the previous year and struggled financially ever since. "The shop's doing okay," she said.

"Really?" Sunny spotted a can hiding behind a nearby tree and took the bag to it. Branches swayed in the oak trees as the breeze turned into a gusting wind.

"Yes, really," Tina said. She seemed fascinated by a couple walking their dog along the trail surrounding the park.

Sunny knew pushing Tina for information would be fruitless. "After I get back from my cruise, let's chat about me helping you with marketing," she suggested, keeping her tone light. "Don't say you can't afford my rates, because I won't be charging you. Pro bono work will look really good on my resume, and it'll fill the unemployment gap."

Tina sighed. "You're hard to refuse." She gave a half-smile. "Okay, I'll think about it."

"Good." Sunny picked up her purse and keys. "I should get on the road before the traffic builds up going back to Portland," she told Tina. "I still have to pack the last of my boxes, too."

"You don't need to do that today, do you?" Tina brushed a few remaining crumbs from her skirt. The sparrows moved in fast, pecking around her feet in a flurry of brown feathers and eager chirps. "You've still got a week left on your lease."

"I know." Sunny plastered on the fake smile she'd been showing everyone who exhibited concern over her giving up her apartment and moving all her possessions into storage. "I really don't need that extra time. My furniture's being picked up the day after tomorrow. I've scheduled a cleaning company for the day after that, and I'll stay at a hotel until my Alaskan cruise."

"And when that's over, where are you going to live?" Tina frowned.

Sunny tried to sound upbeat as she jiggled her keys. "I'll think about that while I'm cruising."

Her friend's dark brows arched again, but instead of commenting further, Tina put on her backpack and picked up her helmet.

Sunny had tried without success to envision moving forward with her life after returning from her trip. Her divorce was final. Mark was no longer her treasured other half. A painful ache ignited inside her, as it always did when she thought how disastrous their second year of marriage had been. Their life together had deteriorated into daily spats over what to eat for supper and why Mark insisted on spending longer and longer hours at the office. His career as a sales executive for a Portland marketing firm, he told her, had moved onto a fast track that demanded his dedication.

To Sunny, his profession had become more meaningful to him than his homelife. Until she found out that her supposedly-workaholic husband had found time for an affair. All while she'd been unsuccessfully trying to conceive a child.

She fought off recollections that threatened to ruin what had been a pleasant interlude with her best friend. Tina had brought laughter back as they shared silly childhood memories, followed by stories about the often strange and off-beat clientele that frequented Tina's metaphysical shop in northeast Salem.

"Maybe I'll move to Eugene when the cruise is over," Sunny said as they walked toward her car, Tina wheeling her bicycle. "I don't think I can go back to my marketing career in Portland. I'd probably run into Mark on a regular basis."

"Why don't you move to Salem?" Tina suggested. "I bet you'd find a really good job in local government."

"Politics? Me? I don't think so." Sunny grimaced.

"There are a lot of businesses here. It's not *all* about what goes on at the Capitol." Tina shook her head.

The wind blew even harder. Dust kicked up on the trail. A couple of joggers glanced up at the sky and went from jogging to outright running.

Sunny shivered. "Why don't you throw your bike in the trunk and I'll give you a ride?"

Tina shrugged off her friend's concern. "No thanks. I'll be fine."

They reached Sunny's Subaru Forester, parked head-in at the edge of the park. An even stronger gust whipped around them, ruffling the collar of Tina's white blouse. Her brightly-colored peasant skirt billowed out, flashing a glimpse of long, bare legs. A passing cyclist slowed to whistle appreciatively.

Tina laughed, waved to him and patted down her skirt. "Keep your eyes on the road," she called out.

The cyclist gave her a thumbs-up. At the end of the road, he turned right and began pedaling in a leisurely manner down the long slope that ended with a traffic light at High Street's intersection with Mission.

"Men." Tina rolled her eyes, but her smile looked more than a little self-satisfied. "He was kind of cute, though."

After they hugged, Sunny watched Tina strap on her helmet, settle onto the bicycle seat and adjust her backpack. "Say hi to Armenta for me," she said.

"I'll give her your love." Tina winked.

"That'll be the day." Sunny had to laugh. "Your assistant, the fortune-teller."

"My assistant, the seer," Tina corrected. "She told you the truth the last time you were at the shop. You should have listened to her."

"I suppose so," Sunny admitted. "At least when she warned me I was going to have a big career change coming up. But then she tossed that other prophesy at me like a hand grenade. A live one, with the pin out."

"She told me afterward the revelation was such a shock, she couldn't stop herself." Tina sighed. "Sometimes, predictions come in a less-than-gentle way. It's not always possible to control the delivery."

"She read my cards without my permission."

The memory still annoyed Sunny. Tina had apologized several times, but Armenta had refused to do so. She said she was never sorry for being a vessel for truth.

"She told me someone very close to me had to die before I found my true calling." Sunny opened her door and threw her purse onto the seat. "I thought it was Mark, but it couldn't be. He's out of my life now."

"I *know.*" Tina looked pale in the sallowing light as the sun gave up its struggle against a sky now filled with clouds so black, night seemed poised to swoop in. She put one foot on a pedal. "I have to go; it's late."

Dead leaves clustered around the perimeter of the parking area rustled angrily as they scudded across the narrow street into the yard of a neighboring home.

"Armenta has a gift she doesn't always like. Me, too. Before you can fully realize your own psychic potential, you're going to have to stop being such a skeptic."

"This is one subject you and I will never agree on." Sunny tried her best not to sound irritated.

"Your aura's dark today." Tina started to cycle away. "You need to think positive thoughts," she said over her shoulder.

"I will. As soon as I'm cruising," Sunny responded, wondering whether her friend was still within hearing range.

Tina circled back. "Everything will work out," she said, her voice as soft and soothing as a breath of warm air. She stopped in front of Sunny. "I want you to remember this...everyone can find what they seek inside my shop. You, included. But until now, you've refused to open your mind to the possibilities."

Sunny didn't want disagreements lingering between them. She told the dark aura to trouble someone else. "I'll try to do that the next time I'm in there," she said, knowing she sounded flip, but unable to stop herself.

"I hope you *do* remember." Tina's blue eyes held sadness.

Sunny's heart contracted painfully. An icy blanket seemed to drape itself over her. "I *will* try, I promise," she assured her friend.

Some of the sadness left Tina. The cold weight lifted. Sunny thought the wind must have shifted.

"Now, I'm really leaving. For good, this time." Tina blew a kiss. "Goodbye, my friend. Be *good* to yourself." She didn't glance back.

Sunny followed one of her psychologist's tips for coping with stressful situations by taking a few deep, cleansing breaths before getting into her car. A strong, earthy smell saturated the air. Rainfall was definitely imminent.

A man walking a panting beagle nodded to her as he passed by. Thunder rumbled again, almost overhead. Ears flapping, the dog bolted. The man shouted a command to slow down, which the animal totally ignored. They ran across the street, the beagle leading the charge for shelter.

By the time Sunny turned her Forester onto High Street, Tina was coasting toward a red light at the bottom of the hill. Rain spattered the windshield, and Sunny turned on her wipers.

The light changed from red to green as a sudden squall brought a deluge of hail. Tina peddled furiously. Sunny turned her wipers to their highest setting and tapped her brakes. Even that didn't clear the hail fast enough. Visibility decreased dangerously as icy pellets pounded the windshield.

She watched in horror as the light turned red but Tina continued pedaling into the intersection. The blurred outline of a car came into view on Mission. Brakes screeched. The vehicle hit Tina and her bicycle so hard, the impact threw them into the air. They landed at the very edge of the park. The hail abruptly ceased, and the squall passed over.

Sunny careened her Subaru onto the curb and scrambled out. She ran frantically, weaving her way around people standing on the trail like frozen statues. But although she reached Tina almost as quickly as the driver of the car that had hit her, neither of them could do anything. Her neck broken, Tina resembled a rag doll that had been thrown onto the sidewalk. Police and paramedics arrived swiftly, but neither they, nor a pastor from one of the nearby churches could comfort Sunny in her grief.

Later that evening, as she thought back to Tina's last words, Sunny found them strangely prophetic.

Sunny and Armenta were the only mourners at Tina's funeral. With no close relatives, Tina had made her best friend the sole beneficiary of her will. Along with The House of Serenity and all its peculiar contents, Sunny inherited the little apartment attached to the back of the shop. Even as she grieved, she knew what she needed to do. She cancelled her cruise, moved to Salem, and assumed full responsibility for Armenta the seer's financial future as well as her own.

She told herself it was only until she found a buyer who would treat Tina's dream with the respect it deserved. She had no idea how much her own life was going to be impacted by her friend's untimely death. But she had a distinct, unsettling feeling that Tina had known and accepted her fate even before she insisted on a picnic at the park.

CHAPTER TWO

ASH HAINES SLIPPED and slithered along an embankment leading down to the slow-flowing Willamette River in Salem's Riverfront Park.

"Careful, Detective," yelled a homeless man from his nearby encampment.

"Yeah, yeah, Pete." Ash turned his head and waved toward the man who, over the past three months, had watched Ash's weekly pilgrimages to where his youngest daughter, Amy, had fallen into five feet of water and drowned.

Ash's foot hit a patch of mud. Instead of going home to change, he'd decided to go straight from the cemetery to the park, which turned out to be a big mistake. He slid in his dress shoes and went down, sprawling flat on his back in his best suit. Ash stared up at spindly saplings reaching toward a heavily-overcast sky that promised more rain.

"Ya need help?" Pete sounded concerned.

"Nope, I'm good." Ash got to his feet. Thick mud covered both his hands. Cursing under his breath, he picked up a twig and began scraping goop from his left palm. Something glinted.

He stopped to see what he had inadvertently picked up. It looked like an earring. He rubbed it on his pants and held it up to the meagre daylight. Oval in shape, it had what looked like a pentacle design wrought in silver.

"You find something?" Pete was lumbering over to investigate.

"My cuff link." Ash jammed the earring into his pocket. "Nothing you need to worry about."

He hoped Pete's knowledge of men's dress shirts was lacking. No one wore cuff links anymore, except his father, who still attended formal dinners in a tuxedo. His mother had sent photos, despite their lingering estrangement.

"Oh, okay." Pete stopped a few feet away. "Got any change? I sure could do with a cheeseburger and coffee."

Pete smelled strongly of body odor and cheap booze. Ash dug out his wallet. "Here." He held out a five-dollar bill. Anything to get rid of Pete and have some peace.

"Thanks, Detective." Pete took the money.

They had played the same scene too many times already, and Ash was tired of being a steady source of income. But he reminded himself he could have taken the wrong path in life, too, and that he also drank too much, especially after Amy died.

"You're welcome, Pete." He fought to keep irritation from his voice. "Do me a favor and visit with your buddies at the picnic table for a while, would you?"

"Sure." Pete nodded.

Predictably, he then saluted for no reason Ash could ever fathom, before trudging away. Ash sighed with relief. He gingerly picked his way down to the water's edge.

No matter how many times he stood only a step from the river, he could never understand how Amy had managed to wander away from a supervised school outing to the carousel and sternwheeler at Riverfront Park. The students always held onto a length of rope. Their teacher walked at the front of them, and a teaching assistant was always at the back of the little students.

But somehow, Amy had left the group, walked down the steep embankment and fallen into the water. No one had seen her go or heard her call out, scream or frantically splash, despite a well-traveled footpath between the carousel and the sternwheeler.

Ash looked at the water. Even if Amy was too small to stand up in the river, she had been taught not to panic if she inadvertently fell into any body of water. She knew how to tread water if something prevented her from swimming, and how to call out for help. So did her older sister, Katie. His ex-wife's family had a house on the coast at Lincoln City, and they had made sure both girls were as safe as possible on trips to the ocean as well as swimming pools.

But Amy's death had been ruled an accident. The investigators determined she had slid down the steep river bank, just as her father had done only minutes before, and been either too shocked or too frightened to save herself once she landed in the water. Ash refused to accept their findings. For him, Amy's case remained open. An unsolved crime. His ex, Caroline, was struggling to come to terms with the verdict. So was her mother, Maxine.

They all did their best to hide lingering doubts from Katie. Grieving was muted by their attempts to return her to a normal life. Ash wondered whether that was a healthy response, but he was firmly told by both his ex-wife and his ex-mother-in-law to mourn in private. He respected their wishes, but kept in touch with Brad Schilling, the Salem detective assigned to Amy's case. Schilling still harbored doubts of his own

Amy had been six years old. She knew not to wander away from her classmates. She knew the rules and always abided by them. She was to stay away from water unless accompanied by an adult. And she had been told repeatedly, by both parents and grandmother, that she was never to lose sight of Ms. Ramey, her teacher, on a field trip.

Cold and dampness seeped through to Ash's skin and took him away from his painful introspection. The threat of rain had turned into a reality. Icy droplets landed on his uncovered head. The moment of reflection he'd hoped for on the riverbank was too elusive that afternoon. He turned and plodded back to the bike and pedestrian path that led to the old decommissioned Union Street railroad bridge that spanned the river and connected parks in downtown with those in West Salem.

He'd take the earring home. Clean it up after he showered and changed clothes. Local police had done a thorough investigation, including combing over the area where they believed Amy had initially fallen into the water. They had found no clues other than mildly-disturbed vegetation.

Ash wondered whether divine providence had sent him crashing to the ground so he could unearth evidence that had remained hidden from the vigilant eyes of the crime scene investigators. He might finally have found something more concrete than his own misgivings.

But he had to have more than an earring to present to Schilling. If it had been sold at any of the local metaphysical shops, they might have a record of the transaction. For the first time in three months, he felt a renewed sense of purpose and a glimmer of hope.

CHAPTER THREE

Sunny stood behind the counter at the House of Serenity and watched Armenta shuffle a deck of tarot cards.

All around her lurked crystal balls, trays of assorted crystalline rocks, books on the occult and various objects d'art of a decidedly odd nature. Aromas of sandalwood and patchouli wafted from small boxes of incense cones piled beside the register for last-minute impulse buys. The more pungent odors of white sage, lavender and sagewort, which was supposed to ward off headaches but seemed to be triggering one in Sunny, emanated from smudge sticks she needed to move to a more distant location.

"It's so slow," Sunny complained. "It hasn't stopped raining for days."

A bell over the front door tinkled. A pair of long-haired teens wearing tight black t-shirts with the words METALLICA and THE WORLD-WIRED TOUR emblazoned across them, shuffled down one aisle to the music section and began leafing through old CDs. Sunny wondered what they could possibly find that would interest them, and even if they did, what they planned to play a CD on, unless they had an older-model car parked somewhere out of sight or a grandparent with a stereo.

She returned to watching Armenta. Her assistant laid out a half-moon of cards, closed her eyes and moved her hand above the deck, pausing intermittently over one card or another. "The days of mourning are over," she said. "A big change is coming."

The teens dropped merchandise with a loud clatter. Sunny jumped. A constant, drizzling rain intermittently sprayed the front window and shop door whenever a gust of wind carried it under the faded awning. A gunmetal gray sky, visible through a grimy skylight above the cash register, held clouds as low as Sunny's mood.

"It had *better* be a big one," she told Armenta.

She'd opened the invoice from Portland Gas & Electric that morning. If business didn't pick up soon, the power would be cut off, leaving the shop and her attached apartment in darkness.

It had been a month since the accident that had taken Tina's life. A very *long* month, Sunny thought, leaning her elbows on the counter. She had decided to keep her friend's dream alive through spring and summer while she reviewed her options. Once fall arrived, she'd start sending out her resume to prospective employers wherever she was going to relocate. San Diego had always been one of her favorite cities, and many miles away from any possibility of running into Mark. She felt she could make a fresh start there.

She had placed a small sign in the shop's front window to notify regular customers of Tina's death. Then she began learning what she thought was marginally necessary to run a metaphysical shop. She quickly realized that what she thought was needed, and what was actually needed, were two completely different things. She had to rely on Armenta more than she could ever have imagined.

Depressed and demoralized by the events of the past few months, Sunny wondered what she was trying to accomplish by keeping the shop open. Despite her aversion to all things mystical, she was now spending eight hours a day learning from Armenta, and most evenings staring at her laptop while she studied the many uses for all those smudge sticks, amulets and crystals.

The bell over the door tinkled again. A young girl with curly brown hair and wide blue eyes stepped slowly inside. She cast a worried look toward the teens, who had started flipping through a pile of used albums in a bargain basket on the floor. Although their voices were muffled, their comments were interspersed with audible swearing as they discussed the merits of one artist over another. Sunny was tempted to tell them they could take everything away for ten bucks. She couldn't understand why Tina had wanted music in her inventory.

The boys' long, stringy hair mingled as their heads bent to their task. "That's a fuckin' great CD," one said, shaking the cover in his friend's face. "There's all sorts of subliminal shit on it."

Sunny cringed. The girl hesitated beside a rack of deeply-discounted Halloween costumes, her expression troubled, her widening eyes shifting from the teens to Sunny before fixing on Armenta.

Seated at a black lacquered table under a canopy of ragged burgundy and black velvet curtains, Armenta was dwarfed by her enormous wing-back chair. Faded burgundy velvet upholstery had split in several places, tufts of wiry horsehair protruding from the worn arms and rising in a crown above her head. Armenta's tiny body barely made a dent in the seat, but her dark eyes peered sharp and clear from the little arbor. Her flashy gold jewelry and brightly-colored clothing contrasted sharply with the overall gloom.

The girl drifted over to the arbor, as though drawn by invisible strings. "I…I need my…my palm read," she blurted. "I only have twenty dollars. Is that enough?"

Armenta crooked one bony, ring-encrusted finger, drawing the girl under the canopy. She motioned for her client to sit on a folding chair at the other side of the table.

Sunny's preoccupation with Armenta and her customer broke when the metal-heads ambled up to the counter with their purchases, which added up to a grand total of $4.75. That wasn't going to pay to keep the lights on, Sunny thought while she bagged two CDs and the album one teen had waved at the other. But she heaved a sigh of relief as she watched them slouch out the door, knowing Armenta's jumpy client wouldn't get spooked any more by the teens crashing around and cussing.

She wasn't being much of a shopkeeper, she told herself after the door closed and a sense of tranquility returned to the aisles. She decided to dust and rearrange the window display. As soon as the rain stopped, she'd clean the window outside, too. As she walked to the back of the shop, where the cleaning materials were kept in a broom closet next to the refrigerator, she wondered whether it was worth climbing onto Tina's rickety ladder to clean the light fixtures. Maybe she could find a couple of cheap table or floor lamps at a thrift store, instead, and use them to highlight the displays she planned to set up.

It was time to put her marketing skills to good use. Perhaps a couple of signs could be placed curbside, advertising the palm and card reading. Special sales announced by colorful signs in the window, proclaiming discounts on the smelly smudge sticks and incense cones. She should put everything on sale, she thought, surveying the crowded, dusty displays while she walked down the center aisle. If the inventory got depleted, new merchandise might possibly look better and smell fresher.

She pushed aside a heavy brocade curtain dividing the shop from the small storage area and came face to face with what remained of Tina's belongings. Although she had boxed and moved them out of the apartment, she hadn't found the courage to dispose of Tina's clothes and jewelry. Her loss was still too raw. While those boxes remained, Sunny felt a small part of Tina remained, too.

Glass cleaner in hand, she stopped to polish the counter first. Armenta's wavering voice interrupted her work.

"You will find love very soon. Very soon indeed," the fortune-teller intoned, stabbing her customer's palm with the same hoary finger she'd used to lure the girl into the arbor. "It awaits you outside this shop."

The girl burst into tears, covering her face with her hands. "I can't believe it," she sobbed. "When I lost my husband in a car accident last year, I thought I'd never find love again. Are you sure? I came here to find out if I should move back to live with my parents in Nebraska,."

Armenta grabbed the girl's right hand and stared at it. "You do *not* belong in Nebraska. This man will mean everything to you," she grated.

The girl wailed louder.

"Armenta!" Sunny grabbed a box of tissues. She had wondered why tissues sat beside the register. Now she knew. Tina had probably dealt with similar reactions to some of Armenta's predictions.

The seer raised her voice. "You are disturbing my concentration!" she quavered, her eyes glittering as she watched Sunny striding toward them.

"You are *not* to upset people." Sunny put the box of tissues in front of the weeping girl.

Armenta's chin jutted out, and a deep frown appeared between her brows, but before she could speak, the bell tinkled frantically over a wide-open shop door, and a stream of seniors swarmed into the narrow aisles. Multi-colored windbreakers and chattering voices brightened the interior like an influx of tropical birds. Delighted squeals and exclamations of horror echoed around the shop.

"Take *that* for your concentration," Sunny muttered in Armenta's direction.

Catching a glimpse of a small tour bus straddling all four parking spaces outside, she hurried back behind the counter.

"I absolutely *adore* crystals." A woman wearing a jaunty yellow raincoat with matching hat smiled as she emptied two handfuls of glittering stones onto the fraying black velvet mat Sunny had almost thrown away. "Do you have any amulets?"

Sunny caught Armenta's smirk as she scrambled to pull out a tray filled with scarabs, tourmaline, tiger's eye and silver, all on black cords. They had been hidden by the mat. Another marketing mistake she planned to rectify as soon as the group left.

She hoped the woman wouldn't ask her any questions about the benefits of one amulet over another, and wondered if the rows of little velvet pouches on the tray beneath the one she had pulled out were filled with more amulets or something more sinister, like dried bat wings.

Over the woman's shoulder, she saw Armenta's customer leaving the shop. A ray of sunlight pierced the gloom outside, and Sunny turned to watch incredulously as the girl walked straight into a young, handsome UPS deliveryman with a package under his arm.

"See," Armenta muttered, pausing on her way past the counter. "I *told* her he'd be right outside."

Sunny hoped her mouth was closed and that she wasn't staring like an idiot.

Armenta winked and tapped the counter with one long red nail. "The lady might also like the amulet in the dark blue velvet pouch," she suggested. "It wards off evil spirits. Or perhaps your own favorite, in the turquoise pouch, which brings luck in love."

Sunny scrambled to pull out the lower tray and placed her hand on the dark blue pouch. A tingling sensation shot up her arm. "I'm sorry, but another customer already paid for that," she told the customer. "I was just about to take it out of the case to hold it for her." The woman pouted her disappointment. "But I'm sure you'll like this one." Sunny picked up the turquoise pouch, opened the drawstring and gently shook a beautiful rose quartz heart onto the mat.

"Oh, that is absolutely beautiful." The customer looked up at Sunny with tears shining in her eyes. "I want that for my granddaughter. Her eighteenth birthday's coming up in a couple of months."

While Sunny rang up the purchases before wrapping them in tissue paper, she realized she had been left alone with a formidable line of customers. "Armenta, some help here, please," she called, hoping she didn't sound as irritated as she felt.

"Back in a moment." Armenta's gravely tones carried clearly from the front of the shop. "That deliveryman should have my order of herbs. I checked the tracking number on the UPS website this morning, He's usually here around eleven." A cackle rang out before the bell tinkled again, and Armenta joined the two young people outside.

Sunny kept her head down while she completed a credit card transaction for three hundred dollars. She wasn't sure what her expression would have said about Armenta's extremely timely prophecies.

Charlatan or seer?

Maybe a bit of both.

CHAPTER FOUR

ASH THREW his keys onto the coffee table. He took a beer from the refrigerator and opened the French doors to the deck at the back of his northeast Salem cottage. A breeze carrying scents of pine and freshly-mown grass touched his face. He walked across the deck and stepped down onto the lawn, making his way over to four red Adirondack chairs grouped around a table under the shade of an old apple tree. He sat in the one facing a bird feeder and watched a couple of small birds swoop in to peck at the last of the food before taking a drink from the birdbath nestled between a couple of azaleas.

If Katie saw how he had neglected his weekday job of replenishing the seeds, she would be upset with him. She was working diligently on an assignment to identify as many local species of garden birds as she could entice into their yard. Ash's job was to supply the seeds and fill the feeder, which was too high for Katie or the neighborhood cats to reach.

He placed his bottle on the glass-topped iron table while he pulled out pack of cigarettes and lit up. Misty rain began drifting onto the furniture, rapidly covering everything with a sheen of moisture. He thought about taking his cigarette indoors, but he'd promised Katie and Amy he was going to quit. To prove his sincerity, he'd placed a hand on his chest.

"And hope to die," Amy had solemnly added.

A chill that had nothing to do with the weather passed through him. He retreated to the covered patio and stubbed out his cigarette in a half-filled ashtray. Although he'd kept his promise not to smoke inside the house, he hadn't been able to quit. Not after Amy died. The drinking he'd thought he had under control had become another crutch. He drained the beer bottle and thought about getting another, but doubted it would ease the misery inside him. That afternoon, he needed something stronger.

A deep and painful yearning surged through Ash. It almost took his breath away. He longed to hold both his daughters and feel their softness, their sweetness. He closed his eyes and raised his head toward the sullen skies, attempting to draw energy from the elements to rebuild his strength. He reminded himself he had to go on for Katie's sake. He slouched down in the chair.

Moments later, Ash realized the wind had changed direction and was now bathing his face with drizzle. He retreated to the living room and heard his cell ringing on the kitchen counter. Hurriedly closing the doors before rain blew into the house, he rushed over to snatch up his phone.

"Got your voicemail, Ash." Detective Schilling sounded tired.

Ash would take that reaction over annoyed or disinterested any day of the week. He checked his watch. Three o'clock. "Can I bring the earring to you?" He took it out of his pocket and laid it on the counter.

"Why don't I drop by your house tomorrow morning instead? Say eight forty-five, and I bring you a large coffee and one of those bagels you like?"

Ash wondered whether Schilling's actual purpose was to keep him away from the police department. He figured he'd probably been classified as a nuisance by then. He'd dropped by so many times to offer possible clues, suspects or scenarios, Schilling had gently but firmly told him his superiors didn't want Ash to continue shadow-boxing someone who didn't exist. Amy's death had been ruled accidental. That ruling wasn't going to change.

But Schilling hadn't unofficially closed Amy's case. Something about her supposed accident bothered him, too. He'd kept in touch with Ash on an informal level, and Ash began to realize they were becoming somewhat unlikely friends. Schilling wasn't averse to having one beer here and there when they met at one of the local bars, but he stopped at that one drink, and he definitely didn't smoke. He and Ash not only shared their years in law enforcement. Schilling was the father of two girls close in age to Katie and Amy. Ash figured his loss struck a nerve with the younger detective.

Ash placed his cell back on the counter and shrugged out of his jacket. He tried not to be disappointed by Schilling's slow response to a possible clue. He loosened his tie and walked around the breakfast bar into the kitchen, where he had stowed bottles of bourbon and whisky behind several empty coffee cans on a high shelf, far above the reach of his children.

He took down the open bottle of bourbon and forced himself to stop pouring when the shot glass was only half-full. If Schilling was going to drag his feet, Ash decided he'd begin his own investigation into the earring's origin. He upended the shot glass, savoring the bite of his favorite liquor before swallowing. Fire lit his gut.

He gave himself a refill before returning the bottle to its hiding place, but left it untouched on the counter and started a pot of coffee before changing clothes. He opted for jeans, boots and a roll-necked sweater. No sense in getting cold and wet traipsing between metaphysical stores before they closed for the evening. He opened his laptop and printed a short list of likely places to find similar earrings to the one he'd found. After a short debate, he emptied the shot glass into the sink, drank a mug of coffee, and brushed his teeth and tongue before leaving.

Drinking and smoking had been the only things to get him through the all-too-frequent arguments with Caroline, followed by their contentious divorce. She'd blindsided him with complaints he'd been a neglectful and verbally-abusive husband and father who drank to excess. Ash counted himself lucky he'd come out of the proceedings with two unsupervised weekends a month.

Rubbing a hand over his face, the rasp of stubble against his fingers told him a speed shower and shave would have been a good idea. But he'd wasted too much time feeling sorry for himself and indulging in vices he should be giving up if he wanted to be around for all of Katie's milestones. The way he was burning through his life, he'd be lucky to attend her high school and college graduations, much less walk her down the aisle and hold her children in his arms.

He ran a comb through his hair, carefully washed off the earring and dried it with a paper towel before sealing it in a snack bag. Glancing outside, he saw the misting rain had turned into a downpour. He put on a raincoat and hat before heading to the first shop on his list.

CHAPTER FIVE

S<small>UNNY HAD MADE</small> cleaning and rearranging a dust-covered display of gargoyles one of her priorities for the day. Of all the merchandise, she liked them best, although she couldn't figure out why. They were ugly creatures with talons, wings, scales and a lot of long, jagged teeth. And they never sold, Armenta said.. Probably because they were hidden away on a top shelf, Sunny thought. The first step in making them more visible would be to place them within view of all but the smallest customers. She doubted children would find them as appealing as dinosaurs, and neither would their parents.

With one foot on a rickety ladder and the other foot on a shelf, she reached out to grab the largest gargoyle, whose head resembled a raptor's. He glowered at her, and she found herself reassuring him in an undertone that she wasn't going to drop him, which made her feel really silly. It was 2:00 PM, and the shop was deserted except for Armenta, polishing fragile crystal balls and faeries on a display close to her arbor.

As Sunny pulled the gargoyle forward, she saw that although he had the raptor's appearance at the front and small wings folded on his back, the rest of him was a lion, complete with long tail and large paws. She knew enough about heraldry to realize he was actually a gryphon. Her fingers curled around his neck. An exquisitely painful sensation knifed through her. She cried out and clutched the ladder for support, but it tipped and she fell backward, landing on a thick pile of prayer shawls she had stacked in front of an enormous rattan basket filled with books on the occult. The ladder crashed to the floor, and the gryphon flew out of her hand.

Dazed and breathless, Sunny blinked up at the ceiling and thanked her lucky stars she had moved those shawls. As she struggled up onto her elbows, a floating sensation made her head spin. She closed her eyes and sank back onto the shawls, but that only made the sensation worse. She heard boards creaking under Armenta's rapidly approaching feet.

As she watched a kaleidoscope of multicolored stars fan out around her head, nausea swept over her. The aura intensified. Quivering and shimmering, it broadened and deepened until it completely obliterated her surroundings. Frightened she was going to completely lose her grip on reality, Sunny grabbed a handful of the silky shawls beneath her.

The air thickened. Expanded. Contracted. Then wrapped around her like gauze. It pressed against her face. Blinding her. Slowing her breathing.

A claustrophobic panic swept over her. She felt herself slipping away into a dark void.

The logical part of her brain told her she must be dying, while the irrational part whispered for her to open her mind. She tried...

A terrible image materialized. A man's face, contorted with anger, his eyes filled with hate.

Desperately attempting to distance herself from the apparition, Sunny slipped and slid on the material beneath her as she fought to sit up. The fog became a heavy weight pressing down on her. She gasped for air and told herself that what she was experiencing wasn't anything like the tales of dying people floating above their bodies while feeling completely free and unburdened.

Suddenly, someone was shaking her. Speaking to her from a great distance. Calling her name, over and over.

The weight on her chest subsided, like a wave rolling back from the shore. The terrifying image of the man's face melted away. The voice calling her name grew louder. A woman's voice. It had to be Armenta. Sunny struggled to answer, but her voice stayed in her throat.

She watched another image slowly materialize, shimmering around the edges. A deeply furrowed brow. Dark wavy hair, graying at the temples, and an unshaven chin. Sad, haunted eyes. Sunny felt the impact of the man's profound grief as though it was her own. She reached for him, but the apparition faded.

Armenta broke the trancelike episode, shaking Sunny like a rag doll. "Come on," she commanded. "Come back. *Breathe!*"

Sunny finally managed to open her mouth. She took it great gulps of musty air, weighed down by odors of sage and patchouli. The floating sensation subsided. The detachment left. She felt like she had been dropped from a great distance. Her head swam, as though some invisible force had pulled out a large plug in her head.

"Are you all right?" The lines on Amenta's dark face seemed to have multiplied and deepened. "For a minute, I thought you were dying."

"I thought I was, too." Sunny felt exhausted. Completely spent. As though she had run the last leg of a triathlon. She tried to draw in a deep breath, but a strange whistling came from her chest.

"You sound like you're having an asthmatic attack," Armenta said. "You want me to call an ambulance?"

"No, I'm not asthmatic." Sunny tried another deep breath. The whistling had subsided. "Better," she said.

"Well, thank goodness for that. Let's get you up."

With surprising strength, Armenta pulled Sunny into a sitting position. She had really wanted to stay where she was for a while, despite the fusty odor wafting into her nostrils, but Armenta kept tugging, and resistance became painful.

"Up," Armenta commanded. "You can pull yourself together in the apartment. I'll make tea."

Sunny felt pain in her right temple. Tentatively, she touched the sore spot and found a small lump. She winced. "Ouch! I must have hit my head on the way down."

The bell above the shop door tinkled softly, and a draft blew through the shop.

"Come on," Armenta urged. "You need tea and an ice pack."

Sunny looked over Armenta's shoulder. Curious faces peered down at her. "Customers," she muttered.

Armenta glanced back. "Out!" she yelled. "All of you!" She straightened up and began shooing the group toward the door like a collie herding sheep. "Come back in an hour," she told them. "We're rearranging stock."

The customers scurried out as though pursued by the Devil himself. Sunny wished she was one of them. Armenta's shouting had turned up the volume on her headache.

She scrambled to her feet as her assistant locked the door and flipped the 'Open' sign to 'Closed.' Armenta waved at the group on the other side of the glass before turning off the lights. They waved back. The shop plunged into semi-darkness.

CHAPTER SIX

ARMENTA MIGHT LOOK FRAIL, but the strength she exhibited as she helped Sunny to the apartment and pushed her down on the sofa confirmed looks could be deceiving. Grateful for somewhere private to rest, Sunny leaned back. The ceiling spun in circles. Nausea made a come-back. She sat upright as an ice pack landed in her lap.

"Use that on your head," Armenta commanded.

"I think I may have a concussion," Sunny ventured.

Armenta clucked disapproval. "I saw you fall. You hit your head on that big rattan basket. You're just shaken up. You'll be fine in a few minutes." She bustled off to the tiny kitchen.

Sunny heard water running into the stainless-steel tea kettle as loudly as rain onto a tin roof. The sound pulsated through her head. She leaned back against the couch and gingerly placed the ice pack on her bruise. "I still think I hit my head on one of the shelves."

Armenta, humming tunelessly as she clattered china, ignored her. *What a day,* Sunny thought, closing her eyes. *And what the hell was that nightmare of a waking dream?*

She came back to reality with a jolt as an incredibly strong smell roared up her nostrils.

Her headache accelerated from a dull ache to a knifelike stabbing. Through tears, she saw Armenta holding a small glass bottle.

"My God." Sunny made a grab for the bottle, but missed. "That absolutely *stinks*. What is it?"

"Smelling salts," Armenta said. "Glad to see they still work. I've had them for years."

"Ugh. They smell like it." Sunny thought she might have passed out after all. Instead of sitting up, she was lying flat on the couch. Her head throbbed, and her stomach churned. The room began turning in circles. She struggled up and put both feet on the floor. Thankfully, the circles slowed, then stopped.

"I was resting my eyes," she protested. "At least, I think I was."

"Nonsense," Armenta held out a delicate china cup filled to the brim with green liquid. "Your eyes had rolled up into your head. Drink this."

The tea smelled a lot better than it looked. A fragrance reminiscent of a meadow on a warm summer day wafted up. Sunny was relieved she could smell anything. Her nostrils felt singed from the ammonia.

She wanted to disagree with Armenta about her eyes rolling, but it had been a strange afternoon, and truthfully, she couldn't remember much after being pushed onto the sofa. She really couldn't swear if she had been awake, asleep or passed out before Armenta brought those evil-smelling salts under her nose.

"I might want something stronger than this," she said after sipping the tea and finding it fairly bland.

"You lost your balance and fell off a ladder," Armenta said. "You'll be fine." She touched Sunny's temple with a gentle, but very cold finger. "You've got a lump, so maybe you *did* hit a shelf."

Sunny placed the cup and saucer on the coffee table, next to a stack of books. The top one was titled *Northern Mysteries and Magick. Runes and Feminine Powers*. She laid the ice pack against her bruise. "Right now," she told Armenta, "I feel more like a truck ran over me."

"You'll be even more sore tomorrow," Armenta predicted. "Maybe we'd better stay closed so you can rest. I'll do more dusting and reorganizing."

Sunny didn't want Armenta making a lot of changes they hadn't discussed. "Like you said, I'll be fine tomorrow. But I'll rest this afternoon. You'll be busy with those customers you told to come back. They looked too curious not to return. After they leave, you can close up and go home early for a change." She scooted to the edge of the sofa. "I'll take a Tylenol."

She tried to stand, but her knees buckled. She fell back onto the couch. One foot came up and kicked The Northern Mysteries onto the floor. Sunny found herself staring at another tome titled *Pharmako Poeia. Plant Powers, Poisons, and Herbcraft.* She didn't remember any books being on the coffee table that morning.

"Are these yours, or were they Tina's?" she asked, pointing to the stack.

"Tina's." Armenta scooped up the Mysteries tome and put it back on the table. "Finish your tea. It's got medicinal benefits."

Sunny dubiously eyed the remaining tea. Its color had deepened to a vivid emerald. A froth of bubbles floated at one side. "Did you brew bat wings or toad parts?" she asked. "This tea certainly isn't plain old English Breakfast."

Armenta chuckled. "I can brew English Breakfast if you're really that squeamish." She plumped a pillow she had taken from Sunny's bed and laid it on one end of the couch, along with a crocheted comforter. "I didn't grow this tea. I ordered loose leaves through a health food website. It's a blend of natural homeopathic herbs."

Sunny felt rightly chastened, despite Armenta's bantering tone. "It's fine." She hurriedly took a sip and smacked her lips, trying to project enthusiasm. "In fact, it's pretty tasty."

Armenta smiled. She patted Sunny's shoulder. "It'll make you feel better quickly," she proclaimed.

"I'm not so sure about that." Sunny took a deep breath. "But not because of the tea," she added quickly, when a slight frown appeared between Armenta's gray-flecked brows. "I saw and felt something while I was on the ladder. Something really..." she struggled for words, "well... *strange.*" She shuddered, the memory of those sensations way too close and powerful.

Suddenly, the whole room spun. It felt like one horrible night back in college, when she had gone to a frat party with her boyfriend and drank Crème de Menthe after two glasses of wine and a beer. She'd never gone near cordials again.

"You had a vision," Armenta said.

CHAPTER SEVEN

SUNNY SLOWLY MOVED her head side to side. Unexpectedly, the spinning stopped.

Her bizarre afternoon had taken a preposterous turn. How had she gone from marriage and a successful marketing career to owning a metaphysical shop, drinking green tea with a fortune-teller and having a conversation that included the word 'vision?'

"Did I fall down a rabbit hole?" she asked Armenta. "I don't have visions. I'm a normal person. An everyday non-believer. Earthbound, Tina called me." She put down her empty cup and gently rubbed the temple that wasn't bruised. "This is a nightmare."

Belatedly, she realized the gryphon was on the table, right next to her cup, and he was staring at her. She turned his face toward the shop's entrance. How had he gotten onto the table? She'd heard him rolling across the floor after she landed on the prayer shawls. Why would Armenta have brought him from the shop?

"You *did* have a vision," Armenta said. "I can tell by your expression. I've seen that look before."

Sunny felt too exhausted to argue. Random thoughts drifted around inside her head before rising above her in a shimmering mist. *What was in that damned tea?* She needed to get up and look at the ingredients listed on the package, but she couldn't seem to find the energy to move.

"Even Tina didn't have visions," she said, finding her voice still worked, even if nothing else about her did. "She told me she was an empath, right from childhood."

Suddenly, Sunny's thoughts were transported to a day when she and Tina were playing dress-up in her mother's closet. She could actually feel the big high-heeled shoes on her feet. She saw Tina, giggling and dwarfed by yards of material that pooled around her, wearing Sunny's mother's favorite red and white polka-dotted summer dress, a red purse over her arm. Perched on her head was a ridiculously large hat decorated with a red rose. The image was so vivid, Sunny smelled the gardenia perfume her mother always wore.

And then, the memory of her grandfather's illness came to her in a rush: *the light on all night, because he didn't want to be in the dark. Her mother's quiet strength and small acts of infinite kindness, even when he was angry from the pain and the weakness.*

"Telepathic Tina was, more than empathic," Armenta said. "She knew she was going to die more than a week before it happened."

Sunny jerked back to reality, like she had been caught inside a balloon that had suddenly popped. "She *knew?* Why didn't she tell me? Why wouldn't she share that with me?" Anger replaced the warm memories. "Why didn't she *do* something about it? Why didn't *you?"*

Armenta shook her head. "You don't understand, but you point fingers. And you always ask too many questions." She sighed. "You want cut and dried answers to events over which we have no control."

Her sharp features seemed to elongate as a shadow passed across the room. Rattled, Sunny glanced up to see a cloud crossing the skylight above their heads. She looked back at Armenta. Her face had returned to normal.

"Tina knew there was nothing she could do but prepare." Armenta nodded, like she fully understood the inevitability. "Fate's fate. It's not going to be cheated."

Sunny felt tears running down her face. It was the first time she had cried since cradling Tina's lifeless body at the accident site. Her last memories were of Tina lying so still, her face covered with blood from a head wound. Sunny mentally shut the door on that graphic movie strip before it could roll through her mind again, like it had too many times since Tina's death.

"How could she listen to me whining about my troubles when she felt she was facing imminent death?" she asked Armenta. "We were best friends, regardless of how much our beliefs, or in my case, non-beliefs conflicted." Sunny stumbled along, trying to make sense out of what was, to her, nonsense. "She was so serene. Like she...like she..."

And then suddenly, as though a switch had been thrown, understanding came to her.

"She knew I wasn't ready to accept it."

Armenta nodded again and offered a box of tissues. "She did."

Sunny took a tissue and wiped her eyes. "I'm still not." She dabbed her cheeks. "Maybe I never will be ready for that."

"She'd made her peace." Armenta's voice was uncharacteristically gentle. "When you *do* choose to accept the truth, you'll be ready to cope with what goes along with it." She leaned forward, her voice lowering, as though addressing a co-conspirator. "Psychics learn to live with their gifts."

"Being clairvoyant wouldn't be a gift; it'd be a nightmare." Sunny tried to will away her vision, but the more she tried, the more vivid the two men's faces became. Unlike the flashback of Tina's accident, they refused to be shut off by sheer willpower.

"Why don't you tell me what you saw?" Armenta prompted, as though she knew exactly what images had reappeared in Sunny's mind. "I can help you translate it. I've got more experience, although I don't see as clearly as Tina did, or maybe as well as you do, either."

"I don't want to think about it ever again." Sunny grimaced, then regretted even that small movement as pain shot across her forehead. She felt as though she was slipping in and out of reality, which was completely unnerving.

She saw her cup was full of green tea again. When had Armenta refilled it? She decided not to ask. Instead, she picked up the cup. But when she glanced down before taking a sip, she saw tea leaves circling rhythmically around the bottom for absolutely no reason. Hands shaking, she set the cup down, but not before tea slopped onto her pants and the rag rug beneath the kitchen table. Since when had she moved from the couch to the table?

Armenta tore several paper towels from a roll hanging next to the sink. She handed one to Sunny before dropping the rest onto the floor and tamping them down with her foot.

"Listen," Sunny said, "there's some mistake being made here." She dabbed the green stain on her pants with the paper towel. "I'm not a psychic. I'm an out-of-work marketing professional who happens to be *temporarily*," she stressed, "managing her best friend's business. If this was meant to be fate, then the wrong person got tapped for the job. I'm not dealing with visions of any sort, and that's final."

She glanced defiantly around the apartment. Let the spirits take that kick in their ectoplasmic pants. Beyond a sliver of light spilling into a small area at the back of the shop, The House of Serenity seemed spookily quiet and watchful. Sunny wished Armenta had closed the curtain that divided the shop from the apartment. "I'm only here out of respect for Tina," she continued when Armenta stayed silent.

Sunny decided to close the curtain herself. Apart from her headache, the weakness and disconnected feelings were beginning to subside. Maybe the tea had helped after all. Encouraged, she got to her feet, felt stable enough to walk, and drew the curtain without glancing into the shop.

"If there was even a chance of selling this place for a profit, I'd do it," she told Armenta, who was sipping a large cup of what looked like plain black tea.

Feeling she was carrying on a one-sided conversation, Sunny took her own cup to the sink and added it to the dishes already there. She turned on the faucet, squirted soap and watched bubbles cover the china. She raised her voice over the running water.

"Three realtors have already told me in no uncertain terms this property isn't marketable. That old saying, 'Location, location, location' doesn't apply to this cluttered, dark little shop with limited parking and no other retail within a comfortable walking distance. One of those realtors advised me to pack all the merchandise into boxes and donate every-thing. He told me to drop them off after hours and drive away quickly, before anyone realized what I was trying to get rid of."

Armenta snorted. "Another unbeliever. He had no idea how valuable the stock is. And trying to sell now? Very unwise. The markets are too slow. If you did get an offer, it would be ridiculously low."

"When did you start studying the markets?" Sunny couldn't help smiling at the thought of Armenta perusing *The Wall Street Journal*. "Can you make predictions based on tarot card readings, or do you use a crystal ball?"

"Keep laughing." Armenta had finished her tea. She put the comforter and pillow back onto Sunny's bed. "Today you got a little taste of your power. It frightened you, so you react by poking fun at me. But remember, when you do that, you disrespect Tina and the trust she had in you, bequeathing you her beloved store."

Sunny didn't feel like laughing anymore. "I'm sorry. You're right. I *was* frightened." She glanced toward the doorway. The curtain was wide open again. "I still am," she added. "Things are happening that I don't understand." She looked at the table. The gryphon was sitting on top of the neatly stacked books. "Did you move him?" she asked.

"Move who?" Armenta looked around like she had no idea what Sunny was talking about.

"The gargoyle." Sunny pointed toward the table. The gryphon was gone.

"What...oh, him?" Armenta shrugged. "No. Things do move around here sometimes. You'll get used to it."

"Things? Plural?" Water splashed her feet. Sunny jumped back, real-ized the sink was overflowing and turned off the faucet.

"Oh, dear. I should have told you about that." Armenta opened the broom closet and brought out a mop and bucket. "Always watch how much water you're putting into the sink. The washbowl acts like a drain plug."

"It definitely does." Sunny took the mop from Armenta. "What a day. It just keeps getting better and better. Is it time to close, already?"

"Not even close." Armenta snickered. "How about a late lunch?" She opened the refrigerator. "You've got ham and cheese slices, and I think there's a loaf of whole wheat in the freezer. I'll make you a sandwich."

"How about making two? One for you; one for me?"

"I brought my lunch." Armenta pointed to a black lunch pail, sitting next to her oversized purse on the small desk next to the TV stand. "But I could eat that for dinner."

"I'll wash the dishes now I've washed the floor." Suddenly, Sunny saw humor in the situation. "And my feet," she added, and then found herself laughing.

Armenta joined in before they both settled in to their tasks. For the first time, Sunny felt like they were on the same side, instead of being slightly adversarial. Armenta must have resented Tina leaving the store to a non-believing friend instead of her trusted and faithful assistant, Sunny thought, not for the first time. But she didn't know how to broach the subject without potentially upsetting Armenta.

As she rinsed the last dish and added it to the rack, she heard Armenta humming somewhat tunelessly under her breath. The sound seemed to trigger a return of the billowing fog that had brought Sunny's vision.

"Stop that." She turned around and swayed, dizzy. "Please." She leaned back against the sink for support.

Armenta peered at her. "Stop what? I just finished making the sandwiches. Don't you want yours now?"

"No...I mean yes. Yes, on the sandwich. No, on the humming." Sunny pushed away from the sink and took two very shaky steps toward the table. Armenta helped her to a chair.

"I was humming?" Armenta's eyebrows rose. "I don't know why."

"You were. At least, I think it was you." Goosebumps rose on Sunny's arms. She felt a draft and shivered. "There's no one else in here, is there?" The doorway to the shop seemed empty, but it was difficult to see through the shifting mist. "There's something wrong with me," she said. "I can't see properly."

"You've probably got low blood sugar." Armenta slid one of the plated sandwiches in front of Sunny. "Eat this. I'll brew more tea."

Sunny tried to ignore the shifting, swirling mist and took several bites from her sandwich before Armenta brought cups and a pot of chamomile tea to the table. After eating and drinking, Sunny felt able to relate what she had experienced while on the ladder, but when she came to describing the faces, she faltered.

"I can't," she said. "I'm afraid to let the images return."

"They may never have left," Armenta said. "That's probably why you're experiencing residual effects."

"How do I get rid of them?" Sunny realized she had finished her tea. She felt relieved the bottom of her cup was devoid of leaves.

Armenta had left her seat. Her bony hand came down on Sunny's shoulder. Ice cold, it sent sparks of pain shooting through her. The faces returned, as clear as though both men were right in front of her.

A stench of death emanated from the first man. Sunny could barely breathe. The smell overpowered her. She felt smothered. Nauseated. She flailed her arms. "Get them away from me!" And then she opened her mouth wide and screamed, the sound raw and deafening, making her ears ring.

Armenta released her grip.

Sunny wanted to run away. Right through the apartment, out the shop, and into her car. She'd head for I-5 South and keep going until she ran out of gas.

But when she stood, it took all her energy to stagger over to the couch, where she fell onto her back and lay staring up at the skylight.

As she watched, the gloom subsided. Sunlight beamed down. She shielded her eyes against the glare and listened to the blood pounding through her veins. Her heart surged like a stallion at a full gallop. Utterly exhausted and scared out of her wits, she felt tears rolling down her face.

"I was going to ask you to describe the men," Armenta said, pulling a couple of tissues from the box and handing them to Sunny. "But maybe we should wait a while."

"Yes, please. I can't handle anything more." She blew her nose and wiped her eyes.

"More tea?" Armenta had something in her hand.

"No, and you'd better not be holding those awful smelling salts, either." Sunny made a concentrated effort to pull herself together, even though she felt like she was shattering into a million pieces.

"Tina kept something hidden that might be better than either of those options." Armenta shoved the tissue box into Sunny's hands before going into the kitchen. She drew the stool over next to the refrigerator so she could stand on tiptoe and pull a bottle from the very back of the cupboard.

She returned with brandy and a couple of glasses, poured generous servings into each, held one out to Sunny and raised hers. "Bottoms up," she said.

They both drank. Sunny wondered how aged the liquor was, because it burned brightly all the way down. She gasped. "Good grief, that's strong."

"Tina said if you buy the best, then you don't need much." Armenta took a tissue and patted it against her lips. "Now, can you tell me what those men looked like? The customers I told to come back in an hour will be standing outside."

After Armenta plied her with another shot of brandy, Sunny managed to give a her a thumbnail sketch of each man without a return of either the mists or the vertigo. Indeed, afterward, she felt well enough to go back to work. When they returned to the shop, a line had formed outside. Customers spilled through the door immediately Armenta opened it.

The rush ended abruptly thirty minutes later, and a state of calm settled over Sunny. She knew Armenta felt it, too.

"We should clean and rearrange the amulets, don't you think?" Armenta said. "I can teach you some of the properties while we work."

"Sounds like a plan." Sunny had temporarily blocked off the new and still unfinished gargoyle display with the stepladder. She had no stomach for finishing it at that moment, breaking her own rule of cleaning up before closing at the end of the day.

CHAPTER EIGHT

WHILE ASH VISITED two metaphysical shops, heavy showers turned to continuous rain. The first shop held a wealth of candles and incense. A young woman behind the counter told him she was filling in for the owner, spending the day at home with two sick children.

"They've all got the flu or something," she pronounced, buffing her nails while smacking gum. "What do you need?" She gave him a frank once-over. "You want to get rid of evil spirits in your house?" She pointed to a basket at one side of the counter. "Smudge sticks'll do it."

"Really?" Ash didn't like her manner. "You've had success with those, have you?"

"Customers like you swear by them," she retorted, going over to the basket. She poked around the contents. A distinctly herbal aroma wafted up. "Bay leaves or something." She pulled up a paper sign that had slid down inside the box. "Oh, well, make that sage. They're all about the same. You light them and throw them in the sink so they don't burn your house down."

Her bright blue hair blended with three bells hanging on a wind chime over the smudge sticks. She thrust the bundle at him.

Ash refused to take it at first, but seeing her annoyance, he relented.

If he completely alienated her, he felt sure she'd refuse to tell him anything. "Do you sell jewelry?" he asked.

"Nah." She smacked the gum again. "This place specializes in candles and incense and herbal stuff. What you see, this is it." She brushed her hand across the smudge sticks, provoking another strong herbal smell.

"Thank you." Ash beat a hasty retreat before he started sneezing.

The owner of the second shop told Ash that although he sold amulets, he didn't stock earrings. "Too easy for shoplifters to pocket," he explained. "I've already got trouble with people stealing the stones." He gestured toward a table holding bowls loaded with loose stones of many colors and textures. "But customers do love earrings. You might try The House of Serenity. It closed for a couple of weeks after the owner passed away, but recently reopened." He scowled. "My customers tell me the new woman doesn't know much about what's she's selling, but they keep going back because her assistant knows everything there is to know about the spiritual realm. Armenta's been working there since the shop opened. She'll know all about the inventory. If they don't sell anything similar to your earring, she might be able to tell you who does. Be easier on you than traipsing around from shop to shop." He grinned. "You don't look like you believe in any of this."

"I don't." Ash dropped the earring into its little plastic bag and tucked it back into his pocket. "Thanks for your time."

"You bet." The owner leaned on the counter. "Have a good day, now, and don't get too wet." He smirked, like he thought Ash should get soaked for wasting his valuable time and not giving his merchandise the respect it deserved.

Ash left that shop with even less enthusiasm for his mission. He made a dash for his Range Rover, sat behind the wheel and watched rivulets of water travel down the windshield. He wavered between giving up for the day, or making one more stop. He was probably going to make a fruitless visit to another dingy shop filled with stuff no one in their right mind would buy.

He looked at the smudge stick lying on the passenger's seat. Why would that blue-haired woman think he'd light that and throw it into his kitchen sink? Would the smell of burning sage clear the sorrow from his home? Ash decided a mountain of smudge sticks couldn't accomplish that.

He checked the next shop's location. It was less than a mile, and not even much of a detour from his home. Even if the earring hadn't been sold there, maybe that supposedly-knowledgeable assistant would be able to tell him if it was a local piece or something made in China and sold in bulk all over the U.S.

If that was the outcome, then he might as well toss the earring into the garbage and move on. But to what? He had no other leads to follow. No other clues. He had found no witnesses, even among the homeless living on the riverbank or hanging out all day in the park.

While he drove, Ash told himself the earring could have been lost by one of those visitors. Assuming it belonged to Amy's abductor was a long-shot.

He checked the dashboard clock: 5:30 PM. He only had 30 minutes to get to The House of Serenity before it closed, and he was in the middle of rush hour traffic.

Once out of the shop's parking lot, he stepped on the gas and hoped he wouldn't get pulled over for speeding through the downtown core. A need for something a lot stronger than soda swept over him as he passed several bars. He definitely had a drinking problem, but wasn't sure he had any desire to curb it, even for Katie's sake.

His girls had begged him to adopt a pet from a local shelter. Caroline had always maintained she was allergic to both cats and dogs. Ash told Katie and Amy that his cottage, with French doors leading to the patio, didn't have easy access for a dog door, and he wasn't fond of cats. Two disappointed little faces stared up at him when he described cats as strange creatures with independent natures and well-deserved reputations for ignoring their owners. He knew if Katie asked him again the next time he saw her, he'd immediately adopt any animal she took a liking to, regardless of the inconvenience. Anything to make her smile again.

Whenever Caro and her mother, Maxine, decided he could resume taking Katie for weekends, he reminded himself, anger surging through him. Katie had been suffering from nightmares since her sister's death.

She'd taken to sleepwalking. Caroline had reminded him he was a very sound sleeper. She and Maxine were concerned he wouldn't hear Katie wandering around. She could get hurt, even leave the cottage, and Ash might not hear her.

He told them he'd get a baby monitor and make sure all outside doors had bolts too high for Katie to reach without standing on a chair. Caroline brought up his drinking, and all further discussion stopped before they really starting insulting each other. It had been on the tip of Ash's tongue to tell her he knew about her liaisons with clients to clinch a lucrative real estate deal.

Traffic slowed due to the downpour. Ash decided to give Caroline one more week before demanding he got his weekends with Katie restored. If she still refused, he'd remind her of their custodial agreement and involve his attorney. He made a pact with himself to cut down his drinking. At least he'd managed to limit his smoking to a cigarette after lunch and one with a drink on the patio before dinner. One vice at a time, he told himself as he drove down Capitol.

He needed a concrete lead. But even if that woman remembered selling earrings like the one in his pocket, would a shop like that keep good records? What if, instead of paying with a credit card, the person used cash, and they didn't give a receipt?

While he pondered the many shaky aspects of finding the earring's purchaser, rain pounded the roof and obscured his view. Ash turned the wipers on high. He'd left the downtown core behind. Surrounding buildings changed from large office blocks to single family homes, interspersed with clusters of professional medical offices, marijuana dispensaries, and small retail stores. He tried reading numbers on signs he passed, but visibility had narrowed so drastically, he could barely see the red tail lights on vehicles ahead.

He hit his brakes hard as a cyclist materialized, head down and slicker pulled over his face, pedaling at a fast rate across a busy intersection as the light turned from green to red. Ash peered through the gloom as he waited for the light to change again and noticed a flashing neon sign in a shop window to his left. An arrow on a sandwich board next to the sidewalk pointed to The House of Serenity. He made a fast turn into the small parking lot. A startled driver laid on his horn.

Ash parked in front of the metaphysical shop. He put on his hat, turned down the brim and stepped out of his car as a bus lumbered by, cruising through a huge puddle. A torrent of filthy water missed him by inches.

"Son of a bitch!" He annunciated each syllable clearly as he watched red lights on the large, cheerfully-lit blue and white vehicle disappear behind swirling rain and mist before he made a dash for the shop door.

CHAPTER NINE

SUNNY STARED AT THE GRYPHON. It stared right back, head forward, talons appearing to curl over the edge of the counter. The effect was definitely unsettling, like the gargoyle was about to spread its wings and take off.

Sunny decided she needed to quit locking gazes with it and put it onto the highest shelf in the darkest corner, where customers wouldn't get startled by it. Not only customers, she admitted, shuddering. The shop felt cold, its contents alien, as though more eyes than the gryphon's silently watched her. She felt like she was being tested. Would she step into Tina's shoes and get control of the shop and its contents, or would she leave defeated and vanquished, while disembodied forces laughed her out the door?

Stop it, she told herself. Tina had been sure of her best friend's adaptability to take command of her dream. Armenta hadn't laughed at her yet, although sometimes Sunny thought her assistant might be rolling her eyes theatrically behind the new owner's back and commiserating with the occupants of the shelves.

The gryphon had somehow been transported from the shop floor to the apartment's coffee table. It should still be sitting there. But it wasn't. Instead, it was right next to the cash register. *Had it flown on granite wings?* Sunny broke eye contact with the gryphon to look up at the ceiling. Strip lighting and stout wooden joists were the only things over her head. At least nothing else was circling.

She returned her attention to the gargoyle. Was his mobility a lingering result of her visions? She reached out a hesitant hand. Her fingers touched his back. He felt as cold, hard and inanimate as he looked. No ethers swirled, and she didn't feel faint, although she knew if she continued breathing shallowly, she soon would. She took a deep breath, then picked up the gryphon.

He felt as heavy and inanimate as he looked. She had to hold him against her chest with both arms to carry him through the shop. By the time she reached the shelves where she'd placed the other gargoyles, her arms ached and her back was telling her she needed to put the gryphon down. She swore he had become heavier as she walked, and what she felt beneath her hands at that moment was far more pliable than stone.

She slid him onto the lowest shelf and took a moment to rest. She refused to look at him. What if he suddenly sprouted real feathers and flew? She looked at the ladder. Getting him down hadn't been easy. Tired and sore from her fall, lifting him above her head would be even more difficult.

Sunny didn't want to risk falling again, and she knew customers might never see him on the top shelf. Better to leave him where he was and group the rest of his cohorts around him in a grotesque display that would have made the medieval architects of Notre Dame happy.

The gryphon glared as she carefully climbed past him. "I don't care if you don't like it there," she told him. "I'm giving you a chance to go to a new home. One where you'll get dusted regularly and see daylight, if you're lucky."

She brought down other far lighter and smaller gargoyles, clustering them around their large companion. She stood back and studied her new display. It was still too dark in that secluded corner. They needed a spotlight to show them off. Perhaps colored to accentuate their grotesque features, she thought, tilting her head slowly side to side. *Blue or green? Not red. Too grotesque.*

She imagined a red light illuminating the gryphon's hooked beak or shining down on his talons, which were now curling around the edge of the shelf. Instead of remaining in the middle of the display, where he had been placed, he was at the front of it. Poised in front, like he was about to take off...

"How are you doing?" Armenta asked from behind.

Sunny jumped. "Don't do that." She felt weak in the knees, and her accelerated heart rate was making her head spin. She found it difficult to turn away from the gryphon.

"Did I spook you?" Armenta's cackle sounded like dry leaves scraping across a sidewalk. "I finished polishing the crystals, but it's too dark to see them clearly. We should get a spotlight on them. These, too."

"That's just what I was thinking," Sunny said.

Armenta looked around. "None of the merchandise sells back here. Probably because no one can see any of it."

Sunny didn't want to ask Armenta if she had ever seen the gryphon move. *What if she said she had? What then?*

"I...I hope there are wall plugs somewhere close," she muttered, trying hard to look like she had no random, disturbing thoughts in her head. "We don't want customers tripping over extension cords. Cord covers and rugs can only do so much to keep people safe."

"Tina had more plugs put in a couple of months ago. She was talking about moving some of the merchandise around, too." Armenta smiled and patted Sunny's arm. "See? You're on the same track."

Sunny found both the remark and the pat comforting. It sounded like her friend had known the store had shortcomings.

Armenta pulled a penlight from a pocket in her skirt. "I think there's a plug over here." She illuminated a wall plug right beside the shelves. "I'll look to see if there's another close to the crystal display. Otherwise we may have to move that."

"I hope not. You put a lot of work into it. Thank you." Sunny took a final glance at her afternoon's handiwork before closing the ladder. She needed a change of scenery for a while.

After she returned to the counter, she didn't feel watched anymore. She spent the next hour under Armenta's tutelage, familiarizing herself with more of the amulets while dusting and rearranging them. Silver chains, knotted cords, velvet pouches, twinkling stones. Sunny learned the properties of rose quartz, citrine, peridot, amethyst, and many others. So many, she became confused and frustrated.

Armenta smiled at her new boss's frustration. "You'll learn. It takes time." She returned the last tray to its location in the glass case. "Let's wait until tomorrow to start on the engraved pewters."

"There's so much. So many." Sunny swept her hand across the glass. "How long did it take you?"

"A lifetime." Armenta smiled. "And I'm still learning. I take weekly instruction from a shaman."

"What would I do without you?"

The question may have been rhetorical, but without Armenta's wealth of knowledge, Sunny knew she would be floundering every time a customer asked her a more in-depth question than where the dream-catchers could be found, or how much it would cost for a palm-reading versus a face-reading.

Armenta shrugged her thin shoulders, dismissing Sunny's concern. "Why don't I make tea? I've pushed enough information into your head this afternoon, and it looks like customers don't want to brave the rain."

Sunny turned to look out the front window. Below the street lights, dark outlines of vehicles hurried past beyond the empty parking lot. "That sounds really good." She massaged her temples. "I've still got a slight headache."

"Chamomile, then." Armenta walked away, her long skirt rustling softly.

Sunny checked the forecast for the following day, a Saturday, and traditionally the busiest day of the week. Intermittent showers, heavy at times, would probably mean a lot of customers. Regulars combined with browsers searching for a new hobby to break the monotony of yet another gloomy day. Armenta had said she'd come in early, and Sunny wasn't about to argue against it.

"Would you like a warm scone with your tea?" Armenta called. "I baked a batch before work."

"Sounds wonderful." Sunny felt the remaining tension slide from her shoulders.

With muffled traffic noises and thundering rain the only sounds in the shop, she decided she should finish bringing down the remaining gargoyles. With a little luck and no further interruptions, the display would be finished in a few minutes. She'd run out to a hardware store after they closed, pick up some lighting and make the new displays really stand out.

Usually, Sunny was no fan of daylight-saving time, but she didn't like being in the shop after dark, even with all the lights on and Armenta sitting in her arbor. She was convinced she heard things moving around after the sun went down. More than once, she'd seen the long black tail of a cat, and a shifting mist sometimes drifted around at floor level.

As she brought down one gargoyle at a time so she could keep a hand on the ladder, she wondered whether rodents could be responsible for the cat's visits. She refused to believe he was anything but a feral who had found a hole large enough to squeeze through. But if he was coming in through a hole large enough to accommodate him, then raccoons or possums could get into the shop, too. Sunny paused to glance around, listening intently. She heard nothing but rain and muted traffic sounds.

From her vantage point, she could tell the reorganization was paying off. New stock occupied the front of the store and lined both sides of the center aisle. With the gargoyles brought down to eye level, most of the more-desirable merchandise would be invitingly displayed instead of tucked into murky corners.

Sunny checked her watch, and was pleasantly surprised to find that in only 15 minutes, she could take off her shoes and relax. She had six more gargoyles to relocate before putting the ladder away.

She spotted a couple of capes on the floor. Half the book rack was spread out on a small table designed to hold an ornate mirror she had found packed away in a box close to the back of the storeroom. Next to the table, a selection of witches' hats hung. Sunny hated the capes and hats. She thought them tasteless. But Armenta had told her they sold very well not only at Halloween but year-round. Tina's sales book backed up that assertion with strong figures. Sunny had made a notation to reorder as soon as stock dwindled.

She heard something moving close to the bottom of the ladder, and that time, she actually saw what was causing it. A long black tail swished as the cat sidled between the supports holding Sunny suspended above the wooden floor. Something drifted into her eye, and she rubbed it away with a finger. When she glanced down again, the cat was gone. She looked at her finger and swore she saw a long black hair. She blinked, and it was gone. Sunny decided she'd had more than enough hallucinations for one day, and was ready to close a few minutes early.

As she started down the ladder, the front door opened and in walked the metalheads, wearing those same Metallica tour shirts under ripped and grubby gray sweatshirts. They always smelled funky, and other customers avoided whichever aisle they chose to hang out.

She thought the teens were shoplifters, but had never been able to catch them in the act. She was also leery of them. Who knew what they might be carrying in those grimy sweatshirt pockets? She watched them slouch down the center aisle, stopping here and there before heading for the music section yet again. They had started coming in right before closing, while Sunny was busy tidying up and Armenta frequently dozed in her arbor.

Two middle-aged women who came in regularly to check out new merchandise quickly browsed their way right out the door. Remaining alert for a possible return of the cat, Sunny made a rapid descent.

Standing in front of her new display, she realized it looked too crowded with the big gryphon dominating it. Against her better judgment, she would have to move him back to the counter. She could face him away from her while she tended the register, so she wouldn't have to deal with his glare. He might also sell quicker if he was more visible.

An old man came in and shuffled toward the prayer shawls. Sunny breathed a sigh of relief. He might look like walking was an effort, and absolutely would not be able to give her any protection unless he was a Jedi knight in disguise, but at least she was no longer alone with the scruffy teens and her overactive imagination while Armenta was apparently making and baking the scone she had offered.

The door opened again. The place was becoming a hot-spot of activity ten minutes before closing. Sunny cleared a space on the table holding the mirror and temporarily placed the gryphon there. She brought a demon with wings and a long, forked tail to the front of her new display. Finally, Armenta re-emerged from the apartment. Sunny felt overwhelming relief, disproportionate to Armenta's size and age. Worse than being the only person in the shop was being in the shop with an old man and those two metalheads. She couldn't see anyone else, and wondered why the shop door had opened a third time.

Armenta brought a cup of tea and a plated scone over to the little table and placed them next to the gryphon. She patted him on the head.

"Sorry that took so long," she said. "The scones I brought with me had fallen apart, so I baked another batch." She took two sugar packets and one sweetener out of her pocket and placed them next to the mug. "I wasn't sure if you needed sweetening." With a soft cackle, she walked over to her arbor, ducked under the canopy and sat. She started shuffling cards.

Sunny decided it was time to ring up any final purchases, shoo out the customers and bolt the door. As she picked up her cup and plate, she heard merchandise clatter to the floor. Definitely time to close, she thought, wincing at the thought of having to eject the metalheads. She walked back to the counter.

The front door opened for the fourth time in less than five minutes, and a stocky man in a wet raincoat stepped inside. He closed the door, gazed around until he spied Sunny, and strode purposefully toward her. A battered hat hid most of his face, but she noticed a dark shadow covered his chin.

Armenta was blowing softly across the surface of a steaming cup of tea. Without turning to look at the new customer, she placed her cup back on the table and picked up her tarot deck. The cards snapped crisply against each other as she shuffled.

The man barely glanced Armenta's way before his attention shifted to the metalheads, visible only as two dark humps bent over whatever had fallen onto the floor.

"Don't even think about pocketing any more of those or anything else," the man rasped. He sounded like he smoked at least two packs of unfiltered cigarettes a day and shouted way too much.

"Get over to the counter and empty your pockets," he commanded. "Then pull out the goddamned CDs you just stuffed down your pants."

The metalheads gawked at him. They slowly got to their feet, glanced at each other, then at the door.

"You want me to crack your heads, try running. You want me to cuff you both and take you in, fine with me. I'm in no mood to dick around with either of you. You're not ripping these people off." The newcomer planted himself between the teens and their way out of the shop. "After you're done, get the hell out of here and don't come back. You do, I'll break your noses."

The teens hesitated.

The stranger pushed back one side of his coat.

They ran toward the counter. Sunny watched one of them bounce off a display cabinet and stop momentarily to steady it before following his companion. As she passed them to stand behind the register, they hurriedly pulled an assortment of items out of several pockets to build a pile on the counter. The last to land in front of Sunny were the CDs, pulled out of low-slung jeans.

The stranger, who Sunny thought must be an off-duty police officer, sauntered over to the door. He opened it for the metalheads to tear past him. Sunny watched them run through the parking lot without looking back. She breathed a long, deep sigh of relief.

"You ready to close up?" the man asked.

"Yes."

She watched him unplug the neon sign in the window and flip the plastic one on the door. The old man dropped the prayer shawl he was holding and scurried out a lot faster than he'd come into the shop. The man locked the door behind him and turned to face Sunny. She wasn't sure she liked that. He'd effectively dispatched a couple of shoplifters with verbal threats and was very possibly carrying a firearm.

"Are you the manager?" He walked over to her and took off his hat, his face coming into full view.

Sunny found herself incapable of speaking or moving.

"I asked if you're the manager." He frowned.

Sunny felt so shocked, she couldn't open her mouth.

"What are you…deaf?" He looked at Armenta. "Well?" he asked. "Is she?"

Armenta stayed silent.

"Are you *both* deaf?" the man asked, looking from Armenta to Sunny. "Or maybe neither of you speaks English?"

Sunny was shaking so hard, her legs threatened to buckle. She'd seen his face before, only a couple of hours earlier, when she'd held the gryphon.

The grieving man from her vision stared at her with the same sadness in his dark eyes. "Are you okay?" His sharp voice had softened and filled with concern. "You don't look so good."

Those were the last words Sunny heard as the room started spinning faster than Armenta's toad-green tea. *Not again,* she thought as she began falling in slow motion. She reached out for the counter and missed. Everything went black.

CHAPTER TEN

"SHE'LL BE fine in a few minutes," Armenta's reedy voice proclaimed. "She had a similar spell earlier today. We skipped lunch, and my herbal tea might have been too strong for her."

Sunny wanted to protest, but she had no strength. She felt disembodied yet wretchedly sore from the two falls.

"Is there somewhere I can take her that's more comfortable?" asked a deep male voice. "I hate to see her lying on that hard floor."

Not only was his face familiar, his voice was, too. Sunny struggled into a seated position.

"There…see? She's coming around." Armenta pushed the man aside.

Suddenly, Sunny's nostrils were on fire. Armenta was brandished her smelling salts again. "My god, Armenta!" She pushed the vial aside. "Get that away from me."

Nose running and eyes smarting, Sunny struggled onto her hands and knees. "I'm fine," she assured them. She sneezed violently, pain shooting through her head. "I'm getting up," she announced, trying to convince herself as well as them. But when she tried, her legs gave out.

Strong hands helped her sit back down. "You should stay still a couple more minutes," the man said.

"I'm sure she'd recover faster if you carry her into the apartment."
Armenta sounded like she was commanding a troop exercise. "It's behind
that curtain at the back of the shop. I'll close up before I join you."

The last thing Sunny wanted was to be carried into Tina's little apartment by a large man in a wet raincoat. But when he easily picked her up,
she was relieved to find he smelled only of damp fabric and a hint of
cologne. Thinking she should act more cooperatively, she put an arm
around his neck.

Instantly, her body tingled and her mind buzzed, like she had touched
a live wire. She wanted to break the disturbing connection, but she was
powerless. Her arm stayed locked around his neck, and her fingers felt
his collarbone moving beneath them. The bond between them was
intense. She wondered whether he felt the same connection, but when
she glanced up at him, he was intently looked straight ahead as he strode
through the shop.

He elbowed the curtain aside and stepped into the apartment. "Where
do you want me to put you? The couch or the bed?"

"The couch. Thank you."

She could barely catch her breath when their eyes met as he gently
lowered her. Sunny had the distinct feeling they were far from strangers,
but why she felt that way, she had no idea. He felt so damned familiar.
Surely her vision couldn't account for that, could it? Her arm slid from
his neck. He stood back up.

She wanted to lie back against the cushions, but didn't want to risk a
repeat performance of her earlier waking dreams. She watched the man
take off his raincoat and drape it over the back of one kitchen chair, then
hang his hat on the other.

He brought her a glass of water and sank onto the other end of the
couch. Sunny didn't like his close proximity, but asking him to move to
one of the chairs felt rude after his help. She was still having trouble
drawing more than shallow breaths as she watched part of her vision
come to life. A shudder moved through her at the thought that he might
have been drawn to the shop. He got up, brought the afghan from the end
of the bed and draped it over her.

"Thank you." Her voice quivered. She wished Armenta would hurry up. How long did it take to turn out a few lights?

"I'm Ash Haines," he said, pulling a card out of a jacket pocket and handing it to her. "I recently retired from Portland Police Bureau. You can call the number on the bottom of this card to verify I'm telling the truth."

She read the plain black print. His full first name was Ashton, and he had evidently been a detective in the robbery division. She ran her fingers over the script. Something flashed at the back of her mind. She quickly laid the card onto the cushion between them.

"I'm sorry I scared you," he said. "I'm unarmed. I flapped my coat to scare those two idiots."

"You didn't...um...really scare me." She searched for the right phrasing. He *had* scared her. Scared the living daylights out of her. But she couldn't tell him why. It sounded completely absurd. *"I saw you in a vision,"* didn't exactly make a good starting point for any reasonable conversation.

Armenta bustled in, all calmness and affability. "Tea," she pronounced, heading for the kitchen.

"We just had some," Sunny protested.

Armenta ran water into the kettle. "That was an hour ago."

"An hour?" Sunny checked her watch. With disbelief, she saw it was seven o'clock.

"You were out a while longer this time." A cabinet door creaked. China rattled. "Ash was quite concerned." Armenta sounded so matter-of-fact, like there was nothing unusual about a woman lying unresponsive on the floor for an entire hour.

"I wanted to call an ambulance," Ash Haines said. "But Armenta told me this happens when you have visions. I didn't find that very reassuring, but she was insistent. She pointed out you own a metaphysical shop, so why wouldn't I think you have visions?"

"Oh, my god. She told you *that?"* Sunny covered her face with her hands. Now he undoubtedly thought she was crazy.

"I did." Armenta sounded indignant. "He needed to know you weren't having a seizure."

"He didn't need to know anything of the sort," Sunny said. "It's none of his business. He's a retired detective, Armenta. He must think I'm completely *nuts.*"

"Hey, I'm still here," Ash said. "Don't talk about me in third person."

"Sorry," Sunny muttered, although she didn't feel at all apologetic. "But Armenta shouldn't have told you that. It's not her place."

"It made sense to me." He shrugged and looked a little sheepish. "Well, kind of. Having visions might be something you two think is normal."

"Visions aren't normal anywhere," Sunny said. "Including The House of Serenity. Armenta's trying to convince me they are, but they're *not.*" She glared defiantly in the direction of her assistant, who appeared to be engrossed with putting cups on a tray and measuring tea into a large china teapot decorated with violets. The kettle began to sing softly in the background. "I don't need a cup," she told Armenta. "I'm not drinking any more toad tea."

Out the corner of her eye, she saw Ash Haines' startled reaction.

"It's nothing of the sort. It's not even herbal," Armenta admonished as she brought the tray from the kitchen.

Ash jumped up. "Let me take that from you."

Sunny and Armenta cleared the books from the coffee table. Ash deposited the tray, loaded with cups, plates, a large tin, and little dishes filled with various additives for tea.

Armenta opened the tin. Ash sniffed appreciatively as enticing aromas wafted out.

"Chocolate chip with macadamia," she announced, placing the tin on the table. She handed their visitor a plate. "Do help yourself, Ash," she told him. "Sunny's being sarcastic," she added. "She thinks my tea is responsible for her visions, which is ridiculous. She had the last one before I even brewed a pot." The kettle whistled loudly and Armenta left to pour boiling water into the teapot.

Sunny watched Ash from the corner of her eye while she listened to Armenta energetically clanging a metal spoon around the inside of the china pot. He looked suspiciously like he was trying hard not to laugh. Sunny decided she might grow to like one of the men from her visions.

Armenta returned with the pot and poured a cup. She handed it to Ash, who looked at his drink with suspicion. "This looks like dishwater," he said.

Armenta smiled. She took the cup from him. "You'll like it more after it steeps a few minutes," she said, giving Sunny a slight smirk. "As you can clearly see, it's not green."

"Armenta…" Sunny began.

Armenta held up one hand in a gesture that plainly said 'Enough.' "Before you ask, Sunny, it's English Breakfast. Completely harmless." She turned, her skirt rustling angrily, and stalked back to the kitchen, Ash's cup in her other hand. "I'll pour this down the drain."

"I'm bringing a chair over for myself," he said. "Armenta, you should sit on the comfortable couch after your long day at work." He smiled at Sunny. "I'm so glad I decided to drop by before you closed up shop." Then he winked before turning away to fetch the chair.

Sunny almost cracked a smile, too. His unexpected calmness in the midst of what most people would class a very unusual turn of events, was infectious.

Without asking Sunny if she wanted to play hostess, Armenta poured the tea. "Would you like lemon or milk, Ash? Brown sugar or honey?"

"Lemon, thanks." Ash glanced into the cup she handed him. "Ah, a much better color." The hint of a smile touched the corners of his mouth. "And definitely not green."

Armenta offered a small plate of lemon slices. Ash took one and dropped it carefully into his cup. Sunny watched. No tea spilled over the edge. His large hands held the delicate china like it wasn't the first time he'd been invited to a tea party. His cup had forget-me-nots on it, which she thought looked a little ridiculous. Maybe Tina's collection didn't have anything more manly. But what china teacup ever looked manly? she asked herself.

"Sunny?" Armenta was holding a cup and saucer covered with delicate pink roses. "Would you like honey, too?"

"Yes, thank you." She watched Armenta squeeze the honey into her tea before handing it to her. She found a thin lemon slice nestling inside.

"I added extra honey," Armenta said. "It's excellent for restoring strength."

Sunny sipped her tea and waited. She felt sure retired detective Ash Haines hadn't walked into The House of Serenity to buy a couple of sticks of Lotus Blossom incense or get one of Armenta's palm readings.

And then, belatedly, she realized who he was. "You're the detective whose daughter was drowned in that horrible accident at Riverfront Park," she said. "I'm so sorry for your loss," she added.

He nodded. "Yes. I'm *that* detective." His hand shook slightly, and the china cup rattled on its saucer before he placed them on the coffee table. "My daughter died a month after I moved from Portland to Salem to be closer to both my girls." He stared intently at his unsteady hands before placing them on his knees. "My other daughter, Katie, is nine. It's been very hard on all of us...my ex-wife and her own mother..." He trailed off.

"I'm sure it has," Sunny said, after Armenta didn't add her own condolences. Sunny felt very awkward. Ash seemed to be trying to regain control of his emotions, while Armenta sat intently watching them both.

"Would you like more tea, Ash?" Armenta asked into the silence. She lifted the pot. "And do have a cookie."

Ash Haines seemed to shake himself out of whatever particular sorrowful place he had wandered off to in his head. "Yes, please." He watched Armenta refill his cup, add a slice of lemon and then offer him the tin. He took one cookie. Armenta continued to hold out the tin. He took another. "Thank you," he said.

The enormity of his loss covered Sunny like a tsunami. She quickly set down her own cup before she dropped it.

Ash took a bite of his cookie. "It's very good."

"Armenta's a phenomenal baker," Sunny said.

Armenta inclined her head. "It's my hobby." She was perched on the edge of the couch.

Sunny realized her assistant was closely scrutinizing their guest. She wondered how to bridge another awkward silence that was developing, and how long after he finished both cookies would she need to wait before gently suggesting Ash return the following day to do his shopping.

"So, what can we do for you?" Armenta asked. "I'm sure you didn't come here on a whim."

Well, Sunny thought, that certainly got to the heart of whatever matter had brought him into the shop.

"You're right; I didn't." He reached into his pocket and pulled out a small plastic bag. He shook an earring into the palm of his hand and held it out so they could both see it clearly. "Do you recognize this as something you might have sold?"

"Armenta's much more familiar with our merchandise," Sunny said. "I only inherited the shop a couple of months ago."

Armenta peered at the earring and grunted. "May I pick it up?"

Haines shrugged. "I suppose so. I found it in mud on the riverbank, so I doubt fingerprints or DNA are an issue at this point."

Armenta pulled a pair of glasses from her cavernous bag, resting beside the couch. She placed bifocals on the end of her long nose and carefully scooped the earring out of Ash's palm. She rolled it around between her fingers.

"I don't think it's one of ours," she said. "But Tina took several items on consignment a month or so before she died, including jewelry. Mostly necklaces and bracelets." She held out the earring to Sunny. "Why don't you look at it closer, too? You've been rearranging the jewelry. Maybe you noticed something similar."

Sunny doubted Armenta missed anything, but she held out her hand.

As soon as the earring dropped into her palm, a searing pain burned through Sunny's hand and shot up her arm. She bit back a scream and dropped the jewelry. It landed, not on the floor, but in the bottom of her teacup, which Sunny, holding her burning hand against her chest, felt sure was no act of sheer chance.

CHAPTER ELEVEN

ASH SAW the alarm on Sunny's face after the earring hit her palm. When she dropped it and it landed in her cup, even Armenta looked startled.

"I have to get out of here." Sunny jumped to her feet.

She bolted, pushing aside the curtain and dashing into the darkened shop. Ash scooped the earring into its plastic bag, put on his hat and shrugged into his raincoat.

Armenta thrust a woman's purse and coat at him. "Take these. Her keys are in the purse. I'm locking up and going home."

Ash took them and hurried after Sunny. He thought he'd catch up with her easily, but by the time he reached the parking lot, she was already at the far end. He followed, splashing through puddles, his feet drenched in seconds. Sunny veered off to the right and ran down a heavily pitted and uneven sidewalk. Ash followed at a slower pace while he wished he'd already quit smoking and taken up regular exercise instead of finding excuses.

Ahead, cars flashed through an intersection, headlights briefly illuminating a crosswalk. As Sunny approached, the traffic light turned from red to green. She ran across. Immediately she reached the other side, the light flipped back to red.

Ash pressed the crosswalk button and took a moment to orient himself while catching his breath. He found himself standing on the corner of Shipping and Summer. He knew a long residential block followed. After that, Sunny would come to Fairgrounds Road, an even busier street than Summer. In pouring rain, with traffic rounding a sharp curve and without a crosswalk for at least another block, she could be struck and killed.

With that disturbing thought in mind, the light finally changed and he ran on. Rain pounded the sidewalk. It fell from the trees and spewed from downspouts in the quiet residential area. A car turned from a side street, its headlights briefly illuminating Sunny's flying figure.

Ash's lungs were on fire. His breath seared his throat as he pushed himself to take longer strides. Sunny's purse and coat hampered him, but he wasn't ready to leave them behind. He *would* catch her, he assured himself, and when he did, she'd need them.

Thankfully, as she approached Fairgrounds, Ash watched her steps falter. He shouted her name, but his words became lost in the pounding rain. Desperate to stop her, he dropped her purse and coat, made one last desperate sprint, lunged as she stepped off the curb, and grabbed her arm.

"Let me go!" Teeth chattering, she clawed at him.

"Sunny," he shouted. "It's Ash. Stop!" He got a better hold and pulled her back from the street. "Sunny, it's Ash." He turned her to face him and shook her hard. "You've got to wake up."

Sunny stopped tearing at his hands. "Ash?" She blinked. Looked around. Looked at him. Shivered uncontrollably. "Where are we?"

She sagged. Ash caught her. Pushed strands of wet hair from her face.

"Are you okay?" he asked.

"I...I think so." She made an effort to stand upright. "What happened?"

"You're safe," Ash told her. "You ran off without your coat, but I've got it." Belatedly, he remembered leaving it somewhere. He noticed a covered doorway and brought her to its meager shelter.

"I'm absolutely freezing." She clung to him. "Where are we? The last thing I remember was needing to get out of the shop."

"We'll talk about that when we're out of this rain." He was afraid to leave her, but her teeth were chattering. "Don't move. I'm going to get your coat."

"I won't," she promised, shivering.

Ash grabbed the coat and shook water from it as he brought it to her, the purse over his arm.

Sunny slipped her arms into the sleeves, but her shaky hands couldn't button the coat.

"Here." Ash fastened it for her and handed her the pink purse. He felt really awkward. "Is that better?"

"A little. Thanks." She looked around again. "I don't know where I am. Can you tell me how to get back to the shop?" She sounded on the verge of tears.

Ash didn't know if he could cope with anyone else crying. He'd seen and done too much of it over the months since Amy's death. "We've got to get you warmed up and dried off," he said. "My house is closer than the shop." He felt as well as saw her hesitation. "I swear it'll be safe."

She looked intently at him. "Something's telling me to trust you. You'd better not let me down."

"Come on." He offered his arm. "We're both soaking wet, and my feet hurt. Let's get moving."

"I'm so sorry about everything.." Sunny looked genuinely anguished as well as bedraggled. "You must think I'm crazy. I can't believe you came to rescue me." She took his arm.

"You needed help, and Armenta doesn't look like she could run fast enough to catch you." They turned away from Fairgrounds to walk down a quiet street. The rain subsided.

"Armenta's stronger than she looks," Sunny said. "Don't underestimate her."

"Good to know." He slowed his pace as the pressure of her hand on his arm increased. "Tired?" he asked.

"Very." Her voice sounded weak.

"Not much further," he assured her. "Do you have any idea where you were headed?"

"No." Sunny brushed wet hair from her face. "I wish I did."

"Maybe it'll come back to you when you've had a chance to rest and warm up."

"Maybe." She didn't sound like she had much faith in that happening. "I feel spaced out as well." She sighed heavily.

Ash felt damned tired, too. The thought of trekking back to Capitol to pick up his car didn't sound at all appealing.

"I'm really hungry," Sunny said. "That may be why I've got no energy."

"Armenta said you both skipped lunch. You do need food." Ash thought about what he had to offer from his kitchen. Not much. "I'll get take-out. You like pizza? There's a good place close to here, and they deliver."

"I love pizza." She looked up at him. "Do you like pepperoni? It's my favorite." She gave him a weak smile.

"I'm more of a Canadian Bacon kind of guy. "I'll order two mediums. You want extra cheese with your pepperoni?"

"That would be wonderful." She squeezed his arm. "Do you have coffee?"

"I'll brew a pot as soon as we get in the door," he promised.

Ash was hesitant to ask Sunny any other questions at that moment. They walked in companionable silence down dimly-lit streets empty of either pedestrians or traffic until they came to his vintage cottage behind its white picket fence.

Ash had never liked coming home to a dark house. He had lamps on timers inside the living room and his small office. The porch light spilled a welcoming yellow glow onto three front steps. He opened a gate in the fence and motioned Sunny to go ahead of him.

"Oh," she said. "Your home's lovely. I've always thought the cottages around here are *so* charming."

"Thanks. Me, too. I like older homes with character." The security lights popped on, illuminating a small yard with a Japanese maple and shrubs under the windows. He followed her along the flagstone path, up the steps and onto his porch, with its swing at one end and a bistro set at the other.

He deactivated the security system, opened the door and stepped inside, turning on more lights. "Let me take your coat. I'll hang it up to dry."

Sunny laid her purse on a bench in the entryway, unbuttoned her coat and handed it to him. As he took hangers from a closet beside the front door, Ash watched her walk slowly into the living room. She was trying hard not to shiver, but her shoulders were shaking.

He quickly hung up the coats. "I'll light the fire. I had it converted to gas. Much less trouble than the old wood-burner that was here when I bought the place." He knew he was babbling, but he was on edge and wanted her to feel be comfortable. When he ignited the gas, flames danced, and his face warmed.

Sunny reached both hands toward the fire. "That feels really good."

"I'll bring you a towel." Ash got up quickly and left her standing in front of the fireplace. He wanted to tell her to go into the bathroom and take a hot shower while he made coffee, but what could he give her to wear while her clothes dried?

"Could I use your bathroom?" she asked, echoing his thoughts.

"Of course." Ash turned on more lights as she followed him to the small bathroom with its claw-footed tub.

"Can I use that?" She pointed to the terrycloth robe hanging on a hook. "I could dry my clothes in front of the fire."

"I've got a clothes dryer and a hair dryer," Ash said. "Use anything you like. I'd offer some of my clothes, but they would definitely be too big."

"What about you?" she asked. "You're as wet as I am."

"I'll change after I get coffee going and order pizza," he said.

She stepped into the bathroom. "Thanks, Ash." She closed the door.

He made coffee and ordered take-out while the shower ran. Right after he hung up, the water stopped. Sunny came out a couple of minutes later, a towel wrapped around her head like a turban, and his bathrobe firmly girded around her waist. She held a bundle of clothes.

Ash showed her the dryer in the tiny laundry room off the kitchen. "Coffee's about done," he said. "I paid for the pizzas, so if the doorbell rings before I finish changing, make sure it's the delivery guy." He pointed to folded bills on the kitchen counter. "There's the tip."

"You should shower, too," Sunny said. "I feel so much better. Take your time...I've got this." Her smile touched her eyes.

She looked at ease. Ash allowed himself to relax. He took her advice, showering before putting on jeans and a sweatshirt. By the time he came back to the living room, Sunny was seated on the couch with a throw wrapped around her and a coffee mug cradled in both hands. Two pizza boxes sat on the coffee table with plates and napkins. The dryer hummed quietly in the background.

"I made myself at home. I hope you don't mind." She brought one foot out from under the throw and showed him a thick gray sock. "I found a pair in the basket on top of the dryer."

Ash sank onto his favorite chair with its optimal view of the 50" TV he had watched mindlessly far too much over the last three months. He wanted beer with his pizza, but wasn't sure whether that would make Sunny uncomfortable again.

"I bet you feel a lot better, too," she said.

"Definitely." He watched her upend the mug before setting it on the coffee table.

"That really hit the spot, Ash," she said. "Don't you want to go outside to smoke?"

Ash didn't think his clothes smelled of tobacco. "No, I've cut down," he said. "Almost quit. You really are a psychic."

"Nothing so exotic." She grinned. "When I went looking for coffee cups, I saw an ashtray on one of the shelves."

Ash decided he *did* need a drink. He stood up. "You want a soda?"

The dryer stopped cycling and the timer buzzed. "Soda's good." Sunny pushed the throw aside. "I'll get dressed."

"I only have Sprite or orange soda," he warned as he opened the refrigerator. "Katie's mom won't allow cola because of the caffeine."

"Sprite, then." Sunny took her clothes out of the dryer and went back into the bathroom.

By the time she reappeared, Ash had placed mats under their plates, coasters under their drinks, and had light jazz playing in the background.

"I hope you don't mind," he said. "Music relaxes me, and today was a difficult day for me, too. I visited my daughter's grave."

"I'm so sorry. I can't believe you've been so kind to me." As Sunny sat, her blonde hair slid across her shoulders and the lamplight accentuated her pale face. "I love music. Is that David Sanborn?"

"It is." Ash knew he was watching her a little too long. He quickly opened both pizza boxes. "Dig in. And don't keep apologizing. Getting involved with your problems today took the focus off my own. Amy died a week after I'd retired and moved to Salem. Since then, I've had trouble finding interest in anything outside making sure Katie, my older daughter, feels supported and loved."

He didn't know why he was confiding in a complete stranger, but it felt good. Cathartic. Like telling Sunny about the chaos in his life since Amy's death was easing the burden. "I stopped off at the riverbank today, too." He took a deep breath. "Where she drowned. I slipped and fell in the mud. That's when I found the earring."

"That explains why I thought you looked disheveled." Sunny's eyes were bright with unshed tears. "You've had a terrible day. No wonder you drink." She picked up her napkin and covered her mouth. "Oh, my god. I can't believe I said that."

Ash was stunned. How far back in the top of his cupboards had she looked?

"I don't know why I said you drink." Sunny took the napkin away from her mouth. She ran it nervously between her fingers and avoided eye contact. "I think bourbon's your drink of choice." She paused, her teeth worrying her bottom lip.

Ash still didn't have anything pertinent to say, so he waited her out.

"Something's telling me you've been using it a lot to dull the pain of your daughter's death" she said. "That you don't believe what happened to her was an accident."

Ash wasn't sure if he had turned as pale as she looked, but either she was truly psychic, or she had read more about Amy's death that she had let on when she mentioned it during Armenta's impromptu tea party.

"Are you playing some sort of game?" he asked.

CHAPTER TWELVE

SUNNY'S HAZEL EYES WIDENED. "What kind of a person do you think I am?"

"I don't know." Ash settled back in his chair and folded his arms across his chest. "Why don't you tell me? Concrete facts. Let's see if they line up with what Armenta said while you were recovering from your blackout spell or whatever you call it."

"I don't call it anything," she snapped. "I have no idea what happened to me today," she added, eyes narrowed, mouth drawn in a tight line.

She sounded like she wanted answers as much as he did…if she was really telling the truth. But why would she lie about something so completely odd and frankly, frightening for anyone? Ash asked himself.

Sunny cleared her throat. "You want to hear the entire sorry story? I'll fill you in."

While Ash listened with interrupting, she told him about her best friend, Tina, who was an empath from childhood. How Tina had embraced her gift, while Sunny chose to deny they shared anything more in common than their lifelong friendship. Despite their differences, he learned, they had remained close, even while their paths through life diverged.

He watched Sunny's body language, her animated facial expressions and the fluctuating tone of her voice as she told the story of Tina using a small inheritance from her mother to open The House of Serenity. How hard Tina had tried to make the store a success with no experience in sales and without a prime location. Sunny had attended college, graduated with an MBA, and with her mind set on owning her own marketing firm in a big city, took a position with one of Portland's premier companies, where she was mentored by a top executive. She had offered to help Tina grow her business, but Tina was stubborn and refused to make necessary changes.

Sunny's voice softened when she spoke about falling in love and marrying a similarly-ambitious young executive she had met at a convention. But it hardened when she told Ash the marriage had fallen apart before their second anniversary. He didn't need a crystal ball to empathize with her distress. He'd had a couple of failed marriages, himself.

When she'd finished telling him about the disturbing visions she'd had that afternoon, Ash found himself struggling not only to absorb what she had told him, but to determine how gullible he felt when it came to paranormal experiences. Sunny didn't sound or look like she was unhinged. Although Armenta definitely had the appearance of someone he'd expect to find hovering over a crystal ball in a circus sideshow, she hadn't come across as any less rational.

"Okay, I have to tell you, I'm baffled," he said.

"That makes two of us." She eyed the pizzas.

"Maybe we should eat while I try to get my head around some of the things you've told me?" he suggested.

"I agree." She took a slice. "Thanks, again, Ash."

Both pizzas didn't look very hot. Ash poked at his Canadian Bacon. It stuck to the cheese and felt barely warm. "You want yours nuked?"

Sunny shook her head, her mouth full. "Too hungry," she told him.

"Me, too," he decided.

She finished her pizza one slice ahead of him. "Ah, so much better." She wiped her mouth and her fingers on a napkin before curling her legs back under the throw.

"Cold?" Ash asked. "I can turn up the heat."

"Oh, no thanks." She ran her hands through her hair and yawned. "Do you still want to give me the third degree, or did I answer enough questions for tonight?"

"It's too late for interrogations," he said. "I've already had a lot to digest, and I'm not talking about food." He closed both empty pizza boxes. "One thing *is* troubling me, though," he added. "Are you *sure* you don't know why you saw me or the other man in your visions?"

"Really sure." Sunny pulled the blanket up to her chin. "When I saw you, I didn't feel at all frightened. But that other man's face terrified me."

"Is anything coming back to you about where you were running?"

She took a moment to consider that question, then shook her head. "No. It's still blank."

Ash had his own theories, but didn't share them. Her run had taken her only three streets away from his house. When she faltered at Fairgrounds, he'd initially thought some safety mechanism had alerted her to the danger of crossing that busy street. But if she'd continued running, she'd have needed Olympic stamina to reach Riverfront Park, and more than that, a guardian angel to prevent her from being killed by the heavy traffic she'd have encountered.

He'd seen the light turn for her when she crossed Summer, but that could have been sheer luck. He hadn't spared a thought to whether it wasn't, and whether the same phenomena could have repeated itself at Broadway or any other downtown intersections.

Ash decided he'd had enough weirdness for one day. He took the empty boxes to the trash and brought a tray into the living room.

"You want me to try holding the earring again? See if I get that same sense of urgency?" Sunny asked. She helped him clear the table and pile everything onto the tray.

Ash took the tray back to the kitchen. "Let's leave that for tomorrow," he said. He opened the dishwasher, already filled with dirty dishes, and added the plates and glasses.

"I should help you clean up." Her voice sounded faint and filled with sleep. "And then we'd better walk back to the shop. You need to pick up your car."

"Not much to clean," Ash said. He added soap to the dishwasher before starting it and threw away the napkins. He wiped off the tray and put it back into the pantry.

When he returned to the living room, Sunny was asleep. He told himself that waking her would be unnecessarily cruel. He also told himself his decision had nothing to do with a reluctance to put shoes on his aching feet and walk back to Capitol to pick up the Range Rover. The sound of rain pounding the patio gave him an even better reason to leave Sunny undisturbed.

He turned off the gas fireplace, brought a blanket from the linen closet and carefully placed it over her before arming the security system and dimming the living room lights. If she awakened in the night, he wanted her to know where she was, and that she was safe.

He took his laptop into his bedroom, where he learned all he could about Sunny Kingston's professional and personal lives. He called in a couple of favors, one from a former colleague, another from a private investigator, for background checks on both Sunny and Armenta before setting his watch to vibrate so he could catch a few hours of sleep before trekking back to The House of Serenity.

CHAPTER THIRTEEN

SUNNY AWOKE to the smell of coffee. Something felt different about her bed. She opened her eyes to find herself lying on a couch and covered with an unfamiliar blanket. A quick glance at the fireplace and the recliner facing the big TV told her she was still at Ash's home, and it must be him she could hear quietly moving around the kitchen.

She sat up. "Good morning. I thought we were going to walk back to the shop last night. You should have woken me up."

"Good morning." The refrigerator opened. "You looked too peaceful, and it was raining hard." His voice sounded muffled. "How do you take your coffee? I've got milk and creamer."

"Creamer, please." Sunny threw off the blanket and turned to look at him.

Ash's hair looked damp and freshly combed. He was holding a carton of creamer. "You want sugar? I don't like the artificial stuff, so if you're into that, you're out of luck." He closed the refrigerator.

"Sugar's fine." Sunny stood up. She felt stiff and dry-mouthed. "You don't have a spare toothbrush, do you?" She walked over to the counter.

"I think I do." Ash put down the carton and went into the bathroom. He rummaged around in the medicine cabinet for a moment. "Yep. Here's one." He held up a toothbrush in plastic packaging.

When she took it from him, she saw Disney princesses on the handle.

"Amy used to drop her toothbrush all the time," Ash said, his voice slightly unsteady. "On the floor, in the tub…or worse." He looked at the toilet. "I had to remind her to put the lid down." He closed the medicine cabinet, glanced at his reflection and quickly averted his eyes.

"Thanks." Sunny felt the heavy mantle of grief that weighed him down. "I was really bad about brushing my teeth when I was little," she told him, hurriedly finding a way to fill the silence. "I discovered there were worse things than using a toothbrush regularly when I had to get fillings in my teeth."

"Life's little lessons." Ash gave her a half-smile. "It's seven o'clock. You want breakfast? I've got eggs and toast or frozen waffles."

"Thanks, coffee's fine. I should get back to the shop, so I can change clothes and put on makeup before Armenta arrives. I don't want to look like I could model some of those discounted Halloween costumes I need to pack up and send to a thrift store."

"I should have reminded you to call last night. To let her know you were okay." Ash looked stricken.

"Not your fault, Ash. I did text her while you were in the shower, so she knew I was safe. But I didn't tell her I was here at your house."

"Okay." Ash nodded and left, closing the door behind himself.

Sunny wondered whether she should ask him not to tell Armenta about the sleep-over, then decided she didn't care if he did. After brushing her teeth and washing her face and hands, she gave her reflection a hard look. She not only had a spectacular bed-head, but dark circles around her eyes and a pinched look to her mouth. It was going to take a lot more makeup than usual to look perky that day.

She worked on her hair with a brush she thankfully found in her purse, drank her coffee and folded the blanket. They left the house at 7:30 AM and walked briskly back to the shop. The morning was crisp but dry and pleasantly warm; a welcome change from the seemingly-endless bands of rain that had persisted during the first four months of the year.

"About that earring," she said, as they neared Capitol. "Saturday is our busiest day at the shop. I know I said I'd hold it again today…"

"It's okay," Ash interrupted. "I saw what happened yesterday. I wasn't going to ask you to risk that this morning. Katie will be staying with me tonight. Could you do it after I drop her at her mother's tomorrow?"

"We close at six. I can do it after that. Will that work for you?" They walked past the darkened insurance office, closed for the weekend, and approached The House of Serenity.

"That'll work." He nodded. "Thanks for agreeing to do that."

Sunny almost took his arm, but resisted the urge. Something drew her to him. Not physical attraction, she thought, giving him a quick glance to make sure she wasn't lying to herself. No, she thought, Ash Haines definitely wasn't her type. Not that choosing her type had worked so well for her, if Mark was an example, she thought, ruefully.

"I'll ask Armenta to stay, in case I go into another trance," she told him.

Ash shoved his right hand into his raincoat pocket and pulled out his keys. "I'll understand if you change your mind. Call or text, and I promise I won't bother you again." He walked over to the Range Rover without looking back.

"I won't change my mind," she called before unlocking the door. She waved to Ash before stepping inside the shop, deactivating the alarm and on turning on the lights.

The gryphon was back on the counter.

"Why did Armenta put you there?" She put down her purse. "I don't want you scaring the customers." She tried to pick him up, but he wouldn't budge. Deciding he must be stuck to the counter, she glared at him.

He glared right back.

"Stay there, then," she said. "But I'm warning you, I'm going to cover you with one of the capes."

She turned on the wall heater in the apartment, brewed coffee and ate a scone she found in the refrigerator. After changing clothes, she carefully applied makeup to minimize her goth-like appearance.

Back in the shop at 8:45 AM, she spotted Armenta walking across the parking lot from the bus stop. The gryphon was no longer on the counter. He had returned to the topmost shelf in the darkest corner.

CHAPTER FOURTEEN

THE WEEKEND FLEW BY. The shop was busier than usual, and nothing else strange happened. Even the gryphon stayed put. If he wanted to stay in the rafters, then she'd leave him there. She avoiding saying anything to Armenta about him changing locations, and told herself she'd experienced residual effects from the visions.

She did tell Armenta she'd been unable to learn anything useful for Ash. She nonchalantly added that she'd fallen asleep on Ash's couch after dinner and stayed there overnight. Armenta looked like she thought there was more to the story, but to Sunny's relief, didn't ask for more information.

Sunday afternoon, as Sunny wrapped purchases and placed them into paper bags with hemp handles and the shop's logo on front, she smiled and chatted with the customers, all of whom seemed to be in a good mood. Nobody returned merchandise. Nobody complained the shop didn't have what they were looking for. In fact, Sunny began to wonder whether Armenta had put some sort of spell over the entire place before locking up Friday evening. Maybe her assistant had fairy dust hidden in that big purse of hers as well as her lunch and endless tins of cookies.

At 4:00 PM, Ash called the shop's landline. Sunny answered. "Are you still available after six?" he asked.

Armenta strolled up to the counter. "Why don't you take a break?" she suggested. "I don't have anybody else waiting for readings."

"Give me a minute," Sunny told Ash. "I'll take this call in my apartment."

Walking briskly through the shop, she noticed the crowd had thinned. When she picked up the extension, she sat for the first time since noon. Her feet ached, and she rested them on the kitchen stool. The receiver in the shop clicked quietly. Evidently, Armenta wasn't into eavesdropping.

"Hi, Ash," she said. "Yes, you can still come at six."

"I'd like to buy dinner," he said. "Do you and Armenta like Chinese food?"

"That's very kind of you," Sunny said. "I love Chinese, but I don't know whether Armenta does."

"Ask her when you've got a minute. If she likes it, the menu for China Palace is online, and you can text me your choices. I'll pick up the order on the way over to the shop."

"Thank you. We've been so busy today; I know we'll both be ready for a meal. But before you bring the food here, I've been thinking about my visions. Maybe I wouldn't have them if I wasn't in this building. Could we come to your house, instead?"

"Of course, if you think the shop could be influencing you in any way."

A sudden chill slid across Sunny's shoulders. She looked around. The door to the alleyway was closed and bolted. There were no windows in the apartment. She looked up at the sealed skylight. Charcoal gray clouds sailed past.

"I'll pick you both up," Ash said. "After we eat, you can hold the earring."

"Okay," she said, shaking off a sudden feeling she shouldn't get anywhere near the earring again. "I'd better get back to the shop. Armenta needs her afternoon break."

She filled the kettle, set it over a low flame and returned to her post behind the counter. Two more clients for palm readings came in after Armenta's break, but the overall number of customers continued to dwindle. Sunny felt a mixture of anticipation and anxiety about the upcoming experiment. As they prepared to lock up, she told Armenta about the plan to use Ash's home instead of him coming to the shop.

Armenta said she'd read Ash's face, and he could be trusted, which Sunny found reassuring. At 5:59 PM, Armenta patted Sunny on the arm before announcing she wouldn't be needed at Ash's home. She picked up her purse and walked out the front door.

Sunny ran after her. "What if I go into a trance and he can't get me out of it?"

"He'll manage." Armenta smiled. "He will always manage where you're concerned. Now go back inside and wait for him. I have a bus to catch."

Sunny did as she was told, but she decided she would make sure Ash had Armenta's phone number before she touched the earring.

CHAPTER FIFTEEN

SUNNY WAS TOO anxious to eat much of the Chinese food, but she finished a full glass of white wine.

Ash told her he loved the wineries in the scenic Dundee Hills. He had become friendly with the staff at one of them, which led to a well-stocked wine fridge in his unfinished basement. He never had to worry about Katie exploring that cold, murky space. She was convinced the furnace was a monster. Sunny wondered how often Ash needed to replenish his supplies, but he only drank one glass of wine before asking if she was finished with her meal and offering to make coffee.

After they had chatted companionably over their coffees, he shook the earring into her palm and she reluctantly closed her fingers over it. As soon as she did, a tingling started, but unlike the first time, pain did not shoot up her arm. When the mist developed, she fought off fear and allowed it to cover her.

It swirled around her, lifting her and drawing her forward. Her feet no longer felt the floor beneath them, and she became completely disoriented. Her hands grasped nothing but air. The swirling became faster and faster. Her stomach threatened to toss out what little she had eaten of her Moo Goo Gai Pan.

And then, as suddenly as the swirling had begun, it stopped. Sunny's feet came into contact with solid ground. She found herself standing in a dark place. Leaves rustled around her. Branches touched her face and entangled themselves in her hair. She stretched her arms out to push aside thick vegetation. The path was so narrow, she could feel plants brushing her bare legs.

A cool breeze stirred. It wrapped around her, chilling her skin. She shivered, and discovered she was wearing a thin, sleeveless cotton gown, the skirt bordered with a whisper of lace. The gown was short. Too short. The plants brushing against her legs became thorny. They caught her skin and scratched her.

Sunny tried to keep her feet closer together, but the path kept narrowing, and overhead branches hung lower, their twigs scraping her scalp and digging into her face. She cradled her head in her arms for protection. As she stumbled along, she wondered where was she going, and why she couldn't stop.

"Hello," said a voice right beside her ear.

Sunny jumped and whirled around. She saw no one.

"I'm here," said the voice, from over her right shoulder.

She turned, but saw only darkness.

"Where?" she asked. "Stop moving, so I can see you."

"You can't see me," the voice said. "I'm invisible."

"Why am I here?" she asked.

"To talk to me," the voice said.

She couldn't determine whether it belonged to a man, a woman or a child. It whispered into her ear but held no audible sound.

"What do you want to tell me?" she asked.

"My story," it said.

"What if I don't want to hear it?"

"That would make me very disappointed," the voice said. It sounded angry.

Sunny became afraid. She wanted out of the dark place where the voice lived.

"Go away," she said. She began to run.

Trees whispered around her. The gentle breeze turned into a wind that howled through the thick canopy above. Sunny ran as hard as she could, searching for a way out of the undergrowth and the deep, dark woods. She followed the path as it weaved around rocks and tree trunks, looming up suddenly in the twilight. Her feet splashed through an ice-cold stream, water clasping her ankles like frozen fingers.

Where was she? How could she get away?

Unease turned to panic.

She sensed a presence behind her.

The panic became terror.

She ran harder, but didn't seem to be going anywhere. Indeed, the rocks and tree trunks began to look more and more familiar. Convinced she must be running in circles, she stopped, panting and exhausted. Her heart pounded so loudly, she could no longer distinguish the sounds of the woods.

"I thought you came here for answers." The voice was in front of her.

Impossible. She had left it behind her, and the path was too narrow for anyone to have passed by.

She refused to give in to fear. If she did, she knew she wouldn't learn anything. "I want to talk to Amy," she said, striving for a firm but unconfrontational tone.

"That's not fair." The voice sounded annoyed, whiny, and more distant. "No one ever listens to me, and I was here first."

Suddenly, Sunny had trouble sensing the presence she assumed was associated with the voice. She wondered whether it had become too angry and left.

The howling wind had abated, but a strong breeze slipped through the trees. It blew through the undergrowth to curl its icy draft around her. Sunny shivered as goosebumps covered her.

"Hello?" she called. "Are you still there?"

"I'm here." The voice drifted to her on the wind.

Relief flooded her. "I'm glad you didn't leave," she said. "Where *is* this, exactly?"

"I don't remember." The voice sounded regretful. "I think I've been here a long time. No one ever gets out of here, and we can't see each other."

Sunny turned toward the voice. "There are others? Can you see them? Can you see *me*?"

"I can see you a little," it said. "You make a lot of noise. A lot more than the rest of us. We've learned to keep as quiet as possible."

The voice was behind her again. She turned more slowly that time and tried not to stir up the leaves beneath her feet. "I suppose I do," she said. "Where are the others? You said there are more people here."

"They're not people. They are more voices."

"Oh. I see," Sunny said, although she didn't. She didn't seem to be getting anything useful out of whoever or whatever she was communicating with, either. Was it another hallucination, or something more sinister?

A disturbing thought popped into her mind. *What if it was a demon, and she became trapped there?*

"Don't you get frightened sometimes?" she asked. "Or lonely?"

"Less than I used to. I missed my momma a lot, at first."

"You're a child." Sunny felt intense sorrow. Who would abandon a child in those woods?

"I'm ten." The child sounded defensive. "I'll be eleven soon. At least I think I will."

Sunny wondered how long the child had been ten if it didn't remember how long it had been in that place. "What's your name?" she asked.

"Everyone calls me Buddy."

"That's your nickname." She tried to make her tone friendlier. "Don't you have a given name?"

"I never used it." Buddy's voice had become fainter. "I don't think I can remember it."

"What about your last name, then?" she asked, hurriedly. "Can you tell me that?"

Leaves rustled. Branches creaked. The cold breeze caressed her shoulders, brushed against her back, and slid through her hair. Buddy didn't answer. The cold breeze became an icy wind again, and the twilight turned darker, as though night had come to the woods.

Sunny barely dared to breathe. Was she truly alone? What if she couldn't find a way out? Would she remain trapped there like Buddy, and apparently, countless others? She wrapped her arms around herself for comfort and to reassure herself she was not losing her own solid form.

What if, instead of a wind encircling her, disembodied souls were creating the air flow? She clenched her jaw to prevent her teeth chattering. It had become bone-chillingly cold.

Ash had promised to protect her. But how could he do that if he didn't even know where she had gone?

"I think my given name is Peter," Buddy said, his voice no more than a whisper.

Sunny jumped. For a moment, she felt lightheaded with relief. He hadn't disappeared after all, but she had to strain to hear his voice.

"Or maybe Paul." His voice was a sigh on the wind. "Something with a P."

"Where's Amy?" Sunny called. "Can Amy hear me?"

"She can't." The sound caressed her ears, slid along the rippling length of her hair and disappeared into the air.

"Buddy?" Sunny peered around. "Where are you? Please come back."

Branches swayed wildly above her head. Twigs snapped and cascaded down around her. She cowered. Dry leaves swirled up from the ground to scrape her flesh with the sharpness of knives. The air crackled with an intensity similar to an approaching storm.

Sunny sensed another presence approaching through the woods. Foreboding washed over her. Maybe that's why Buddy had disappeared, she thought, edging away. The path ahead seemed to have become completely overgrown. She tried to turn back, but the trail was covered with a nest of thorny, twisted branches.

She had to get out of there fast, but how? Ash's protection was only good if she could communicate with him. "Help," she cried, as loudly as she could. "I need help. I don't know what to do or where to go."

The presence loomed larger and closer. An overwhelming sense of dread filled Sunny. The sounds of the woods had suddenly stilled, but the ground beneath her feet felt disturbed by a great force. She had to get away, but even as she tried to push through the dense vegetation, her dress caught on thorns and branches barred her way. She was trapped.

Suddenly, someone's hands were on her shoulders, and she was being shaken, harder and harder. As the presence approached with gathering speed, she had a sensation of being pulled backwards through a long, dark tunnel.

The shaking became even more forceful. Painful. She needed it to stop.

"I can't take any more," she gasped, the effort taking all the air from her lungs.

CHAPTER SIXTEEN

"Wake up, damn it!"

Ash was leaning over her. He sounded really panicked. Sunny tried to tell him he was hurting her, but she didn't have the energy to speak.

He released her and stood up. Ran a hand through his hair. "What the hell am I going to do? I shouldn't have pushed her." He strode away, muttering under his breath.

Sunny heard water running. Ash reappeared with a cloth in one hand. He dabbed her face. *Oh, God, the cloth was so cold!*

"What if she doesn't come out of it?" He sounded agonized. "Armenta, I should never have asked her to go into a trance again." He groaned. "It's all my fault." He started shaking Sunny again, his fingers digging into her upper arms. "Sunny, for Christ's sake, will you please wake up?"

"Ash!"

Sunny heard Armenta's voice.

"Ash, listen to me. I'm sure she's okay. She must have gone deeply into the trance again. It took her a while to come around last time. You mustn't panic."

"You're not here. She's so pale!"

"Don't send me another picture of her." Armenta's voice was a strange mixture of sympathetic but commanding. "You've shown me what she looks like more than once. Her color's actually improving."

"I know you don't want to come over here, but I'll pay for the car service."

Ash sounded both irritated and pleading. Sunny was surprised to hear him so out of control, but then, he was intermittently shaking her until her teeth threatened to start rattling.

"I don't need to come over to your house," Armenta assured him. "You can handle this. Brew some tea. She'll need it when she comes back. Do you have any honey?"

"Honey? Yes, I think so."

"Plenty of honey in the tea."

Armenta's calm voice on speaker-phone brought Sunny farther away from the black void. She was able to take deeper breaths and move her fingers.

"Sunny!" Relief flooded Ash's deep voice. "Armenta, she's beginning to stir."

"Tea," Armenta repeated. "With lots of honey."

Feeling like her brain was shaken around as well as the rest of her, Sunny finally found her voice. "I can hear both of you. Please take that cloth off my forehead, Ash. I'm freezing."

Ash looked as relieved as if he'd given her CPR and brought her back to life. "Thank God." He threw the cloth onto the table and laid a warm hand over hers. "You *are* freezing."

He jumped up and strode away again, returning with a pink comforter covered in unicorns and rainbows, which he tucked around Sunny as though he was tucking one of his children into bed.

She was very relieved to feel nothing but warmth emanating from the comforter. "Is that Katie's?" she asked.

Ash nodded. "It is." His face was creased with worry.

"Thank you. I feel much warmer, already." She managed to smile.

He looked slightly less stressed. "Thank goodness. I thought you were dying for a moment."

"Ash?" Armenta's voice floated up from the phone on the coffee table. "Tea! I'll see you both tomorrow." She hung up.

Ash picked up the cloth and hurried off to the kitchen. Sunny heard water running again. "I hope you're putting water on to boil for tea," she called. "Please don't put anything else cold on my face."

"No worries. Tea, it is." Gas roared, then was turned down. Cupboards opened and closed. "I have English Breakfast. Is that okay?"

"I'm sure it is. Armenta didn't specify anything except honey." Sunny felt strong enough to swing her legs off the couch and sit, but she kept the comforter tightly wrapped around her.

Ash came back to light the gas fire. He lingered, even while a kettle sang in the kitchen. "I hate to ask, but did you get anything?"

Sunny saw expectancy on his face. "I did, but nothing I think would be useful for you, I'm afraid."

Ash broke eye contact. The lines around his mouth deepened. "That's damn disappointing." His voice was gruff. He turned away. "You should lie down until the tea's ready," he said as he walked back to the kitchen. "You still look pale."

"I'm sure I do." She leaned her head against the back of the couch. "I feel completely drained."

He brought her a cup of tea a few minutes later. Sunny had begun to warm up, but she still lacked strength. Even holding the cup was an effort. Ash perched his large frame on the arm of the couch, as though he wasn't sure he wanted to be any closer to her.

Sunny wondered whether he was afraid some of her weakness would migrate, or even some of her psychic instability.

He cleared his throat. "I usually drink coffee when I'm alone. Katie likes tea. Her mother's not at all happy about her drinking that instead of hot chocolate, but you can't keep a kid away from everything she likes." He shrugged. "I'm a bit of a failure as a father."

"I doubt that." Sunny held up a corner of the comforter. "This is way too girlie for your taste."

"I do my best," Ash said. "Amy was into princesses. I had to remember who liked what when I bought them anything new, or I'd get a lecture. They had both learned that from their mother, unfortunately." He looked away again. "Do you need me to turn up the heat?"

"No, thanks. I'm warming up nicely." Sunny managed a wider smile she hoped would help put him at ease. "You know, if Katie's mom doesn't like her drinking black tea, there's herbal. Chamomile is supposed to be soothing. Armenta gave me some earlier, and it was pretty good."

A beep from the kitchen startled her. She jumped and spilled tea on the comforter. "Oh, Ash, I'm so sorry." She quickly put her cup on the coffee table and struggled to unwrap herself so she could get up. "I think the stain will come out in cold water."

"Don't worry about it. The comforter's been in the washing machine several times, and I've got stain-remover in the laundry room." He stood. "Relax. You want more tea, or do you want to switch to coffee? The noise that startled you was the coffeemaker."

"I'm not relaxing until this comforter gets into the washer." Sunny finally freed herself.

"Here, give it to me." Ash held out his hand.

"You get us coffee; I'll take care of this." Sunny tried her best to sound like she was back to normal, but when she tried to stand, she lost her balance and grabbed him. He pulled her to her feet and watched her sway as she gathered up the comforter. "I'm fine," she reiterated. "You don't need to hover."

"Good." He slowly backed away, but didn't leave. "I'm not much good at hovering."

"I'm not going to fall over," she assured him. "I'm sure I'll do better if I move around."

"Okay." He didn't sound like he entirely believed her, but he went back to the kitchen.

Sunny took a couple of tentative steps before deciding she wasn't going to sink to the floor. Relieved, she returned to Ash's little laundry room. As she sprayed the tea stains, then gently rubbed them, she inhaled scents of soap and shampoo from the comforter along with something else...the faint and distinctive odor of a child. Something she hadn't smelled since she'd lifted a friend's toddler to see the bride throw her bouquet at a wedding. As the child clung to her neck, then squealed with delight when several young women vied for the prize, Sunny remembered wondering whether she and Mark would ever have a child of their own. Tears flooded her eyes. Sunny wasn't sure whether she was crying for Ash's lost daughter, for Buddy, lost and wandering in the woods, or the lost opportunity to have a child of her own.

"Are you doing okay?" Ash called.

Sunny blinked the tears away. "Yes, I'm fine." She pushed the comforter into the machine. Added soap and started the gentle cycle before pasting what she hoped was a pleasant expression on her face to join him in the kitchen.

Ash had creamer, a sugar canister and a spoon waiting for her on the counter beside a mug filled with coffee. She sniffed appreciatively. "Thank you. That smells *so* good."

"Did Armenta really serve you toad tea?" he asked.

"She did. At least it looked like toad tea. The chamomile came later. She said the green tea was some blend of lemongrass and myrtle. It kept swirling around." She stopped speaking as a vivid image of that strange tea popped into her head.

"You mean after she stirred it?" Ash was reaching into the top shelf of a cabinet, his back turned.

"No, when it was in my cup. It kept swirling faster and faster. It made me nauseated."

"Okay, enough of *that* memory." Ash placed a half-empty bottle of bourbon on the counter. "You want some of this in your coffee? It'll warm you up and steady your nerves."

"Okay, but only a splash."

He slid the bottle over to her. "Here, add it yourself. My splash might be a lot bigger than yours."

"Probably." She added a small amount to her mug and stirred. The pleasant aroma wafted up her nostrils as she took a sip. "Mmm, that's good."

Ash smiled. "I wonder if all psychics are like you."

"Hopefully, you won't ever have to find out." Sunny lifted her mug in a toast. "I never thanked you for running after me the other day and taking me in. I don't want to think about what might have happened if you hadn't caught up with me."

"Better not to dwell on that, either." He added a more generous amount of bourbon to his own mug and slowly stirred, his attention focused on the task.

When he looked at her again, his expression was so serious, Sunny wondered uneasily what he was about to say.

"I'm not sure what I'm getting myself into with you," he said. "I've never found myself in a situation like I've experienced since meeting you and Armenta."

"Ash, I'm so sorry…"

He waved away her concern and ushered her back to the living room. Sunny sat on the couch, and he took a seat in the recliner

"No apologies," he said. "I'm open to finding out, however bizarre a ride this turns out to be. I've got a weird feeling you can help me find answers to Amy's death. I'm not going to fight that or ignore it." He broke eye contact and looked down at his shoes. "My feet still hurt. I forgot to take off my shoes. Do you mind?"

"Of course not. It's your house. I'm just an unexpected guest."

"Unexpected, but definitely not unwanted." Ash pulled off his shoes and took them over to the hall closet. He threw them inside and closed the door. "Ah, that's better. You want more coffee?"

"No thanks. I'm good."

Sunny rested her head against the couch and heard Ash moving around the kitchen. Something went into the garbage before he sat back down and wiggled his toes in his socks. "I put a few miles on these puppies today." He told her he'd visited Riverfront Park again before driving over to the shop.

"That must have been really difficult for you," Sunny said. "How are you doing? Really?"

"Not good." He sighed and rubbed a hand over his face. "I'm trying to hold myself together for Caroline and Katie. Mostly for Katie. She's older than Amy by three years. They were so close. They always wanted to share a room, and they never fought over anything."

"Katie must be devastated."

"I don't know if Amy's loss has really sunk in yet." Ash put down his cup. "I wonder whether Katie's trying to hold herself together because she sees her parents falling apart. Maybe we're all hiding our feelings. That would be ironic. Probably self-destructive, too."

Sunny wasn't going to ask whether the Haines family had been to counseling. Not her place. "Katie sounds like a wonderful little girl," she said. Tears welled into her eyes. As much as the loss of her best friend pained her, she couldn't even imagine what Ash and his family were going through.

"Are you ready to talk about what you saw?" he asked.

Sunny heard the emotion in his voice. He wasn't ready to share more of his own thoughts. She appreciated the space he'd given her to recover from her disturbing vision.

"Yes," she said. "I can do that now."

"Do you want something stronger to drink?"

"No. You've only got scotch left, and I hate that stuff."

"You saw me finishing the bourbon in the kitchen?" His eyebrows rose. "Could you see through the couch?"

"No. I saw you looking at the bottle before we left the kitchen. When you didn't put it back into the cabinet, I figured you were going to finish it."

Ash frowned. "I'm not sure I buy that explanation, but I'll let it slide. I do have a bottle of scotch, but it's stashed at the top of a cabinet I haven't opened since you got here."

Sunny had no better answer for him. She had no idea how she knew about the scotch.

"Let's move on," he said. "I'd rather hear about what you saw while you were in the trance than you try to tell me how you know about the contents of my kitchen cabinets."

"I can go for that."

Over more coffee, she told him about the child she had encountered in her vision. "It was so cold there. I got the impression we were some-where in the mountains, but not in Oregon. I don't know why I feel that way."

"You must have some idea, Sunny. Was it the height of the mountains?"

"No, I couldn't see them clearly. The woods were too thick. But the air was thin, and I felt like I was somewhere near the snow line."

"Maybe it was Washington?" Ash suggested.

She closed her eyes and tried to remember details. "The wind howled and the trees bent. There were leaves on the ground, not pine needles. There was an icy stream. I waded through it. The trail was so narrow, plants and vines kept touching my legs. Then brambles tore my flesh." She looked at her ankles, unblemished in the reality of her waking life.

"Do you have any idea of the time? Present day or sometime in the past? Maybe even the future?"

"No." She ran a hand over her aching forehead. Tried to stop frowning. "The boy said he was invisible. He was always just out of sight. The child wasn't evil. He was lost and lonely. He said his name began with a 'P' but it had been so long since he'd used it, he'd forgotten whether it was Peter or Paul. He called himself Buddy. He remembered that nickname, so he must always have been called that, don't you think?"

"Sounds like it," Ash agreed. He had pulled out his cell phone. He made a call, identified himself, then listened for a moment. "Yeah, good to talk to you, too, Beale. I'm doing okay. Yes, Katie and her mom are, too." He grimaced. "Yes, thank you. I know...we know...how much you all keep us in your thoughts." He listened again for a moment. "Look, Beale, can you look into something for me?"

He asked Beale to check for missing boys around ten years of age. "First name beginning with 'P.' Maybe Peter or Paul, but who went by Buddy." He looked at Sunny. "Try Washington, Oregon and Northern California to start. If that gets no results, could you widen the search?" He listened again. "A tip I got. Could be nothing, but I'd really appreciate anything you can do. Thanks." He hung up.

"Someone you worked with?" Sunny asked.

Ash nodded. "In Portland. If that gets any hits, I'll think about involving the lead detective on Amy's case in Salem. I've burned enough bridges already not to call him with what he'd think was another wild goose chase."

"Yes, if you told him you got a tip from a brand-new psychic, you'd really lose credence."

"Believe me, I've already lost that, Sunny." He grimaced again. "But Schilling, the Salem detective, told me he still has reservations about the accidental drowning verdict. I wish you'd gotten something that was even remotely tied to Amy's case, but from what you've told me, her name meant nothing to Buddy."

"All he said was there were a lot of people in those woods." Her headache had worsened. She rubbed her temples. "I wish I could help you more, Ash, but I've got no control over what I'm seeing in these visions."

"I believe you." He placed the empty cup he'd been nursing onto the coffee table and leaned forward, forearms on thighs, hands clasped. He stared at her, sorrow etched on his face, sadness in his eyes. "You've been through a lot, too, from what you and Armenta have told me. Your friend's death may have triggered a gift you don't want, but I think it might help me find the truth about my daughter's death. I'm hoping we get a hit on that missing child."

"If you get a hit on Buddy, then we can both be freaked out." Sunny drew her legs onto the couch, wrapped her arms around herself and shivered. Suddenly, the room had turned cold again. She looked over at the gas fireplace. The flame was so low, it was almost out.

"Well, that's weird." Ash stood up. "What's up with that?" He went over to the fireplace. The flame reignited with a roar.

"You'd better stay right where you are tonight," Ash said.

"I'm not going to put up any objections." Sunny felt a sense of relief. She didn't want to go back to the shop until daylight. "I forgot to put the comforter in the dryer," she said.

"I've got a spare blanket in the linen closet." He stood up and grabbed both the empty cups. "I'll get it for you. You left the spare toothbrush in the holder, if you want to brush."

Sunny made a quick trip to the bathroom while he tidied up the kitchen. When she returned to the living room, he had already placed a blanket and pillow on the couch. She settled down, the gas fire adjusted to a gentle heat that didn't fluctuate before she fell asleep.

CHAPTER SEVENTEEN

CAROLINE BARLOW WESTMONT HAINES gazed distractedly at her wet car, sitting alone in Superior Realty's parking lot, and suppressed a sigh of frustration as the client's voice droned on. She clamped the phone between her ear and shoulder while she shuffled papers and slid them into their various folders.

She had spent the last hour scrutinizing older listings. The result was disheartening. Owners needed to lower their prices, but none of them had reached that sad reality. The house on Gardner had great curb appeal but a postage stamp-sized back yard overlooked by an apartment building's second floor balconies. A large brick owned by an elderly couple hadn't been updated in 20 years. Although the high-priced condo in a new building overlooked the picturesque Willamette River, it was a studio packed with oversized, dark furniture and a kayak the owner refused to store anywhere but the entryway.

At the thought of the condo, Caroline's mind drifted to Ash. She wondered if he missed his own view of the Willamette from his Sellwood condo, and whether he was coping any better with their daughter, Amy's death. The last time they'd been together for any length of time, he'd reeked of cigarettes and alcohol. Caroline shoved the folders into the bottom drawer of her desk. She'd had more than enough of real estate for a Monday afternoon.

The complaining client finally paused for breath. Caroline seized the opening. "Look, Mr. Hensen, I've personally shown your home eight times over the past month. Other agents through the multiple listing service added six more. Your price is too high for the current market. Please consider dropping it at least five thousand dollars. Preferably eight to ten. I assure you interest in the property will be renewed, and you'll dramatically increase your chances of finding a buyer."

Hensen told her his home was worth far more than the current asking price. He wondered what was wrong with the people viewing it. Couldn't they see the beautiful deck? The pleasing sage green wall-to-wall carpet? The new vanity in the master bathroom? Wasn't she pointing out those features? Did he need to find another listing agent?

"I understand both your reluctance to lower your price and your pride of ownership," Caroline told him, eyeing the cup of cold latte congealing on her desk. "But the economy's still weak, and people are demanding more for their money. A lot more. Sometimes unreasonably. You have to be patient…"

She paused, reorganizing her thoughts and reminding herself not to raise her voice. At the other end of the line, a snort and indrawn breath warned her she'd better find some soothing words before he jumped back into his tirade. Her usually long, tireless patience had worn pitifully thin since Amy's death, and she worried she could lose some of the higher maintenance clients she could ill-afford to send packing if she wanted to maintain her *Top Producer* title.

"I'm sure the right buyer will come along," she said, falling back onto stock reassurances. "But I also know that dropping the price again, even marginally, will renew interest," she added, knowing she had to continue planting that seed despite the client's present mood. "Please think about it and call me again tomorrow morning." She quickly checked her schedule. "Let's say ten o'clock." She heard another sigh that sounded like it was sliding through clenched teeth. "I have to leave now to meet another client."

She crossed her fingers under the desk to ward off any evil spirits waiting to pounce on her little white lie. She had no other appointments for the rest of the day.

Caroline wanted to go home, although it now lacked Amy's rambunctious enthusiasm for life. Her sister, Katie was a quiet, introspective child, much like her father, and preferred to spend most of her time in her room. Caroline felt abandoned, and her large home seemed empty. She promised herself she'd make up for her shortened workday later in the week if any motivated buyers suddenly materialized.

The disgruntled client grudgingly agreed to the date and time. Caroline gratefully hung up and forwarded the lines to the answering service. Her partner, Clarice Newman, was on a photographic safari somewhere in Africa.

"Lucky Clarice," Caroline said aloud. "I'd give practically anything for two weeks away from this office right now."

She wished she could have transferred the whining client's call to her more tactful and nurturing partner instead of having to deal with him herself. Or *not* deal with him, she admitted as she poured the latte down the sink in the little kitchenette. Instead, she had only delayed the inevitable, and at that moment, she had no idea how she was going to find enough sugar-coating for Hensen to agree with the price-reduction.

Beyond the window, another heavy shower threatened. Caroline wondered if the street lamps would pop on, even though it was only one-thirty in the afternoon. When she turned off her desk lamp, shadows lengthened inside the office.

She decided to pick up Katie a little early instead of hanging around outside the school to return calls and make appointments. Envisioning changing into her favorite black velvet pants and turquoise sweater, lighting the gas fireplace and pouring herself a large glass of Chablis, she made sure the back-exit door was locked and turned off the neon sign in the front window.

She'd order pizza for an easy dinner and try to convince Katie to watch a movie with her. But unlike Amy, strange little Katie didn't like cartoons or musicals. And Caroline didn't think documentaries or fictionalized accounts of true stories were suitable for a nine-year-old. Maybe they'd skip TV or a movie altogether and play a game. She threw the empty cup into the trash while she tried to decide whether Monopoly was a better choice than Checkers, because it might last longer. She didn't enjoy being a divorced, single mother. Not for the first time, she thought about convincing her mother to move with them to the coast at Lincoln City. But she knew that would upset Ash, who had retired and moved away from friends and coworkers to see his girls more frequently.

Caroline decided to tell the school secretary she had forgotten Katie had a dental appointment. Another white lie. An uncomfortably cold sensation passed through her. She crossed her fingers again before taking her coat from its peg and checked the automatic thermostat, which seemed to be functioning normally.

She bumped her knee against Clarice's desk on her way back to her own. It really was becoming increasingly dark outside. She turned her lamp back on. Its cheery glow made the shadows recede. Caroline felt less chilled and unsettled as she drew on her pale blue wool coat, took her purse from the desk drawer and walked out, locking the door behind her.

She noted the parking spaces on both sides of her black Lexus were empty. Her spirit lifted a little. Frequently, the busy dry cleaners next door kept all spaces filled and she had to squeeze behind the wheel with her coat dragging the ground.

Large raindrops peppered the blacktop. Holding her purse over her head, she jogged over to her car and hurriedly got into the driver's seat. Her phone rang. She let the call go to voicemail.

Caroline checked her side mirrors, pulled down her visor and surveyed her reflection with a critical eye. The dark circles and bags beneath both eyes alarmed her. Either she was going to have to add another layer of concealer or try harder to leave her sadness behind. Otherwise, a face-lift could be in her future, and she didn't have the time or the energy.

Grimacing, she flipped up the visor. A sale would brighten everything, especially if it was one of those listings she had relegated to the bottom drawer of her desk. Caroline took a moment to consider her choices. Hensen had looked at her legs while they were going over comps. She thought he might be a candidate for her own brand of TLC, which she kept a secret from Clarice. If reasoning with him at the office in the morning didn't produce results, she was going to make sure she did another walk-through of his home, with emphasis on the master bedroom.

A cold chill encircled her legs immediately after she made the decision to bend the definition of a full-service agency to suit her purposes. She hurriedly checked her rearview mirror and started the engine to warm up the car. Instantly, she received a warning that her door was open. She realized the hem of her coat was caught in it. After hauling her wet and muddy coat inside, she took a moment to appreciate the shapeliness of her legs as the heater warmed them.

Ash had always complained her work outfits were too tight, the necklines too low, and the skirts too short. He could be such a prude sometimes, Caroline thought with a spark of anger. But not *all* the time, she thought, remembering their last encounter soon after Amy's death, when they had both needed confirmation that life still existed. A flush ran up her neck.

Ash had always made her feel desirable, even when they were fighting, she thought, nostalgia bringing tears of regret. But there was no repairing what had already been broken. If it hadn't been for Katie, she knew they would not have remained in contact with each other after Amy's funeral. Caroline pulled a tissue out of the box she kept in the back seat and carefully dabbed away her tears. The weird, unsettled feeling that had been with her since she began to close up the office lingered. She told herself she had to stop dwelling on things she couldn't change, as they always cycled back to her grief.

She gazed through the rain-splattered windshield at the lamp glowing on her desk and hoped she would feel more like working the following day. One thing was certain, she thought, searching for a radio station to accompany her drive to Katie's school; she had no problems attracting men, despite approaching her thirty-eighth birthday. But while she told herself she was willing to use all the powers of persuasion she possessed to convince Hensen to lower the price of his home, unsettling memories of their previous encounters came to mind. He had a habit of sniffing and wiping his nose frequently with the tip of his thumb. If he needed the

TLC visit to secure the deal, she was going to make sure she left herself time to go home and shower before her next appointment.

A text came in. She reluctantly checked it. A client wanted her to go over details of the contract he had already signed. There was no reason for him to make that request. He suggested she go to his home.

"Not today, honey," she told the phone as she waited for him to pick up. When he did, she told him she was driving and suggested they meet at the office in the morning. She had an opening at 10:15 AM.Although he sounded less than enthusiastic, he agreed.

Tossing her phone into her purse, Caroline put her Lexus into reverse. A delivery van had squeezed into the space next to hers. She eased back carefully. The other vehicle began to back up, too. Caroline tapped her horn to alert the driver, but the van didn't stop. Indeed, it gathered momentum as it rolled down the sloped parking lot toward the street.

Alarm bells sounded in Caroline's head. The other vehicle was going to roll into oncoming traffic and cause a wreck. She peered up at the cab as it slid past, but couldn't see the driver. She stomped on her brake.

Horns sounded, tires screeched, metal crunched. Caroline only had a moment's warning before a garbage truck slammed into the delivery van and both vehicles careened into hers. Her last thoughts were for her daughter and her mother as the airbags deployed.

CHAPTER EIGHTEEN

Loud ringing awakened Sunny. Groggy and disoriented, she groped around for her cell before realizing the sound was coming from Ash's office. She listened as his recording told the caller to leave a message. A moment later, a muted but definitely agitated female voice could be heard, demanding Ash pick up the phone.

Sunny pushed hair out of her eyes and sat up. A note propped on the coffee table told her Ash had left to pick up food. She glanced at her watch and was dismayed to see she had slept until 2:30 PM. Why hadn't Armenta called? As she checked her phone for messages, Ash's caller hung up. Armenta had left a text, telling her not to worry about coming in late. One of their regular customers had volunteered to help out, and business was slow.

Sunny got halfway to the bathroom before Ash's landline rang again. The same caller shouted Ash's name. The woman sounded frantic. Sunny decided she had better answer.

She picked up the receiver and interrupted more shouted demands Ash come to the phone. "Hello?"

"Hello?" The woman sounded surprised. "Who is this?"

"A friend of Ash's," Sunny said. "He's out running an errand. He'll be back soon."

"A friend, huh?" The woman snorted loudly. "Ash doesn't have women friends. He has *girlfriends*. I suppose you're the latest. When's he coming back?"

Sunny decided disagreeing with the caller would open her to more verbal abuse. "I'm not sure," she said, trying to keep the irritation from her voice. "Do you have his cell phone number?"

"I do not. This is an emergency. Are you *sure* he's not there?"

"I'm sure." Sunny wished she hadn't picked up. "Would you like to leave a message?" She took a pen from a cup with the Portland Police Bureau logo and saw there was no paper on the desk. She didn't want to invade Ash's privacy by opening drawers.

"Young woman, I told you this is an emergency. Now, you tell Ash he needs to call Maxine immediately."

"Yes, ma'am." Sunny dutifully jotted Maxine's name on her palm. "Would you like to leave me your number, too?"

"He's got it." Maxine slammed down the phone.

Sunny called Ash's cell immediately. She heard it ringing and found his phone on the kitchen counter, next to the pad of paper he must have used to write the note he'd left for her. She wrote a brief note for him, but wasn't sure where to put it. Would he go straight into the kitchen if she was still in the bathroom when he returned?

She decided to leave it prominently displayed on the breakfast bar. While she was brushing her hair, she heard the front door open and close. He was already on his cell when she left the bathroom, and she watched him listening intently, a frown on his face as he paced back and forth in the living room. On the table, two cups nestled in a cardboard tray beside a paper bag.

Ash glanced at her. "On my way," he told the caller. He hung up and waved his cell. "What a day to leave this behind." He jammed the phone into his coat pocket. "Can you be ready in a couple of minutes? My ex-wife's been in a wreck. That was her mother. Maxine needs me to pick my daughter up from school."

"I'm ready now." Sunny slid her feet into her shoes. "I'm sorry I picked up your phone, but she sounded really upset."

"She always sounds like that." Ash scowled. "This time, she's got reason." He held out Sunny's coat.

She put it on and grabbed her purse. "I'll walk back to the shop," she told him as he tried to hand her the tray of cups and the bag.

"I want to ask you a big favor." He ushered her onto the porch, set the alarm and locked up. "I need to check on Maxine and Caroline. Can you watch Katie for a couple of hours? She won't be any trouble. She can watch TV after she does her homework."

Sunny had no hesitation. "Of course."

"Thank you. She's usually with me afternoons if Caroline's still working when school gets out. We stopped sending Katie to an after-school program..." He trailed off, averted his eyes and guided Sunny across a brick path to where his Range Rover sat in the driveway.

"We'll make sure Katie's okay," Sunny assured him after he got behind the wheel. "Armenta texted me. Business is slow, and one of our regular customers is helping out in the shop." She still felt guilty about sleeping through the morning. "But I should have gone home last night," she added.

"If you had, I would have been begging the director of the after-school program to take Katie back while I go the hospital," Ash said. "She made it clear she didn't feel it was a good idea to change Katie's routine." His fingers tapped the steering wheel as he drove through downtown, with its 25-mph speed limit. "I wasn't very polite when I told her what I thought of her opinion." He shrugged. "I could have used more tact, but that's not my specialty. Neither's eating crow."

"Well, at least for today, you won't have to face that possibility." Sunny watched as they joined traffic flowing along Commercial Street in the direction of Salem's south side. "You must really be trusting your gut feelings when it comes to Armenta and me," she said. "You don't know us very well."

"As long as you don't let Katie hang out in the shop, which she'll think looks like Aladdin's cave, and Armenta doesn't teach Katie to read tarot cards, I think she'll be fine." Ash's smile looked a little strained.

"I'll do my best to keep Katie in the apartment," Sunny promised.

"And I'll ask Armenta not to take her into the arbor. She's got all sorts of fun stuff in there, including a crystal ball."

Ash shook his head as he turned off Commercial and approached a school zone sign with a flashing yellow light. "I can only hope you keep that promise."

Sunny clung to their cooling cups as he drove over a couple of speed bumps. Coffee seeped out through holes in the plastic lids and ran into the cardboard container.

The Range Rover slowed. "I really don't want her messing around in the shop, Sunny," Ash said. "While I was carrying you to your apartment, I saw snakes and lizards in jars and a sign that said Dragon's Blood."

Sunny had to laugh. Lukewarm coffee spilled onto her pants. "That's dragon blood sage," she explained. "It's very popular. We have a big basket of it."

"Oh." He sounded a little taken-aback. "Well, I still saw jars with snakes and lizards."

"We have those," she acknowledged. "I haven't been able to phase them out. Tourists love them."

"God." He sounded tortured.

"I'll stay in the apartment with her," Sunny promised. "Armenta and the customer can handle the store until you come back, otherwise we'll close early. I'm not a total stickler on hours, which Armenta keeps lecturing me isn't good business practice."

"I don't want you losing sales because of me and my problems." Ash pulled over to the curb. "I'll pay you for looking after Katie. She's very mature for her age. She won't be any trouble."

Sunny saw a sprawling single-story building ahead with a line of cars edging into a pick-up zone. "You're not going to pay me for babysitting your daughter a couple of hours. You've been more than kind to me since you walked into my shop."

"Thanks." He sounded relieved.

"My pleasure. Really."

"She'll listen to you," he said. "I'll make sure she knows that before I leave."

"Don't scare her." Sunny smiled when his eyebrows raised. "I doubt she's ever seen the inside of a metaphysical shop, and we do have a lot of unique merchandise she'll see as she walks through."

"Noted." He turned off the ignition, then looked intently at her. "Has Armenta ever told your fortune?"

"No," Sunny said. "Why? Are you thinking of having her tell yours? I wouldn't recommend it. She frequently shocks people."

"Having her read my palm hadn't even occurred to me," Ash said. "But I'll keep the shock part in mind if I suddenly have the urge to sit in her tent."

Sunny didn't try to correct him about the name for Armenta's corner of the shop.

The school's double doors opened and children spilled out onto the steps. They swarmed around, laughing and talking in multicolored jackets, backpacks slung over shoulders or dangling from hands. They quickly flooded the area, running along sidewalks, climbing into cars, or marching across the road under the direction of a crossing guard.

Ash looked around. "I don't see Katie. She usually waits next to the front steps. I wonder if Maxine called and they've kept her inside?" He checked his mirrors before cautiously opening his door. "Stay here," he told Sunny. "If I miss her, she may recognize my car, but she won't get in even if you tell her you're a friend. Ask her to use her phone to call me." He closed his door and hastened away, his coat flapping.

A moment later, Sunny swore a little voice whispered in her ear. Unsettled, she glanced into the back seat, finding it empty except for a child's booster seat. She told herself the voice must have been outside the car. She found a bottle of Tylenol in her purse and took one.

She moved their drinks to the cup holders, opened the door and shook cold coffee from the tray onto the grass easement. She stowed the wilted cardboard container on the floor behind Ash's seat, where it joined several empty cups and fast-food wrappers.

Her stomach growled. Sunny opened the bag and found two neatly-wrapped bagels. Letters written on the paper told her one was a cinnamon raisin with cream cheese. The other was smoked salmon on pumpernickel. She took half the cinnamon raisin to go with her coffee.

After drinking most of the lukewarm coffee and finishing the bagel, she leaned back and closed her eyes. She wished visions weren't so exhausting. And she hadn't found out anything useful for Ash. She fervently wished she had better control of her so-called gift.

Her heart ached for Buddy, the lost little boy. He'd been so frightened when he left. He must have sensed the presence approaching through the woods. A disturbing chill stole over her, and she felt herself slipping away from reality.

Alarmed, she jerked back from a swirling vortex, opened her eyes and reassured herself her feet were firmly planted on the floormat inside Ash's SUV. A large group of chattering students passed by. Suddenly, the door behind her seat opened. A backpack landed on the floor. She turned to watch a child clamber into the vehicle.

"Yuk, Daddy; it's dirty back here," Katie complained, braids swinging as she pushed cups and bags away with her feet.

"I wasn't expecting company today." Ash sounded tense. "Katie, this is Sunny. Sunny, this is my daughter, Katie."

Sunny forced a smile as she looked at the little girl wearing an unfastened coat over a severely-pressed school uniform. Katie's braids had begun to unravel, wisps of blonde hair floating around a serious, pale face. A large-brimmed hat hung low over her eyebrows, but vivid blue eyes shone with curiosity as they regarded the strange woman in her father's car.

"Who's Sunny?" Katie's brow furrowed beneath the hat brim.

Without answering, Ash closed the door, walked around the back of the Range Rover and got into his seat. Sunny wondered whether he was going to ignore Katie's question.

Ash started the Range Rover, adjusted the rearview mirror and directed a stern look at his daughter. "Is your seatbelt fastened?"

Sunny heard a click.

"Yes," Katie mumbled.

Glancing over at Ash, Sunny watched his stern expression soften before he cautiously eased the SUV into traffic.

"Sunny's helping me with an investigation, Katie," he said. "She's a psychic."

There. The secret was out. Sunny had a label in Ash's life. Very matter of fact. Nothing she thought he wouldn't share with Caroline, Maxine or anyone else, since he'd told his daughter.

"Like on TV?" Katie asked.

"Better," Ash said. "Those psychics on TV are actors delivering lines they memorized. Sunny's the real thing. And she's going to be your sitter for the afternoon."

"Cool," Katie said.

Sunny liked Ash's daughter already. She gave Katie the rest of the cinnamon raisin bagel.

CHAPTER NINETEEN

"WELCOME, WELCOME." Armenta smiled broadly, her gold tooth glinting, as Sunny, Katie and Ash trooped into The House of Serenity.

"Hi, Armenta," Sunny said. "We have a visitor for a couple of hours this afternoon. This is Ash's daughter, Katie. We're going straight through to the apartment."

"Hello, Katie. Nice to see you again, Ash. A good time for my break." Armenta rubbed her bony hands together. "We're closing for thirty minutes," she shouted. "A late lunch. Bring all purchases to the register."

Sunny's first thought was that potential sales could be lost if shoppers were rushed out the door. She paused to observe the customers' reactions. Katie ran right into her back. Hard-tipped shoes struck Sunny's ankles. She bit back a yelp.

The deadline actually appeared to galvanize the shoppers. They loaded handfuls of merchandise into their baskets on their way to the counter and formed an orderly line without a murmur of complaint. Sunny decided she should stop second-guessing Armenta's unorthodox sales techniques.

Katie tugged on Sunny's sleeve. "Sorry," she whispered. "I didn't mean to walk into you."

"It's okay." Sunny put her arm around the little girl, guided her through the shop and behind the curtain. "This is my apartment. You can eat a snack and do your homework at the table."

Katie nodded her approval. "I like your home, Sunny. It's really pretty." She walked over to the sleeping alcove, gently drew aside the gauzy drapery that separated the niche from the rest of the apartment and peeked behind it. "Oh, I like your bedroom. Do you think I could take a nap in there after I finish my homework?"

"You can, if you'd like."

Sunny felt touched by the little girl's response to what had to be yet another abrupt change in her schedule. She wondered if her own nine-year-old self could have responded with the same level of maturity. Katie slid her backpack off her shoulders, took off her coat and handed it to Sunny to be hung on the row of wooden pegs too high for her to reach.

Sunny slipped off her shoes and pushed her feet into slippers. Katie took off her shoes and put them beside Sunny's. Ash placed the bagel bag on the table and strode into the kitchen.

He brandished the kettle. "Tea?"

"Lovely," Sunny said.

Katie took a couple of books out of her backpack and got to work. A moment later, her legs swung rhythmically below the chair and her brow furrowed in concentration. Sunny decided procrastination wasn't a fault in the Haines family.

Ash sat down at the table with his daughter. "You listen to Sunny and Armenta," he instructed. "If you don't want to take a nap, and it's okay with them, you can watch TV after you finish your homework."

"Either will be fine with us," Sunny said.

Katie nodded without raising her head from her work. Her legs continued their rhythmic swing. "Yes, Daddy. Thank you, Sunny and Armenta."

"Do you have milk?" Ash asked Sunny.

"Yes." She started toward the refrigerator.

"I'll get it. You sit and relax." Ash opened the refrigerator and took out the milk.

Sunny didn't feel like relaxing. In fact, she felt more than a little tense about taking responsibility for keeping Ash's child safe for the next couple of hours. She reluctantly perched on the arm of the couch while Ash poured a small glass of milk and set it in front of Katie's books.

"Thank you, Daddy." Katie took a drink and smiled up at him with a milk moustache. "I'll be good, I promise."

Ash shook the remaining bagel and a pile of napkins out of the paper bag. He used one of the napkins to gently dab away Katie's moustache. "Are you still hungry?" he asked her. "I don't remember...do you like smoked salmon?"

Sunny felt like an intruder. She stopped perching and sat down on the couch, but she couldn't stop watching them.

Katie wrinkled up her nose. "I definitely *don't* like smoked salmon." She watched her father return to the kitchen. "Daddy, where's Mama?"

Ash brought a tea canister to the table and carefully took the lid off the china teapot before sitting next to his daughter and taking the hand that wasn't gripping a pen. "Mama had a car accident leaving work today."

Katie's eyes widened. Her grip on the pen whitened her knuckles, but she said nothing.

"She's okay, Katie."

Ash's voice was so gentle and soothing, it calmed Sunny's anxiety about being a successful babysitter. Suddenly aware of how tense she had become, she worked to relax the tightness in her back.

"Then why couldn't I go home?" Katie asked.

"Your mother had to go to the hospital to get treatment for a broken leg. Grammy's with her. I'm going over to check on them both. That's why I want you to stay with Sunny."

"Oh." Katie sat like a statue. Tears glistened on her face.

"Your mother may have to stay in the hospital for a few days. If she does, I'll take you there as soon as the doctor says you can visit." Ash blotted away his daughter's tears.

Katie carefully put down the pen, took the napkin from him and blew her nose. "Can you take her some flowers?"

Sunny felt tears sliding down her own cheeks. She discretely wiped them away.

"I'll buy a bouquet from the gift shop as soon as I get to the hospital," Ash promised. "Roses? Are they still her favorite?"

"They are." Katie nodded once, definitively. "She always wants red, but I'd like her to have pink...Amy's favorite color." She sniffed and picked up her pen.

The kettle started to sing.

"You're the best, Katie." Ash stood up, cradled her face in his hands and kissed both her cheeks. "Time for tea," he said. "Sunny, how many spoonfuls do you put in this pot?"

Sunny brushed away her own tears and got to her feet. "I'll make it. Armenta read on the Internet that tea tastes better if the pot's warmed before the leaves go in. She says tea enthusiasts swear it enhances the flavor. What did you pick?"

"I'm not sure. The first one I grabbed." He turned the canister around. "I don't see a label."

As she picked up the pot, Sunny watched Ash take the lid off the tea canister and hold it up to his nose. He grimaced and held it out to her.

Sunny took one whiff and closed the lid. "That's the green tea."

She exchanged it for a canister she knew held Darjeeling. While Ash sat at the table and watched, she warmed the pot, added five spoonfuls of leaves and poured boiling water over them. She put the lid back on, added a cozy, and placed the pot on a trivet to steep.

"Was that the one?" Ash didn't elaborate.

Sunny knew he meant the toad tea. "Probably. There's a wide selection of teas in this kitchen. I should ask Armenta to label them. Some are pretty strong and have medicinal benefits. And then there are those, like the specialty green tea I told you about, that she brews up and tries to convince me drink. I've learned to ask before I taste."

"Can I have some of that?" Katie asked, using her pen as a pointer. "I really like tea, Sunny. Daddy has it at home."

"He told me." Sunny wasn't sure Ash would approve.

"No caffeine late in the day," Ash said.

Katie looked disappointed. "Do you have cookies?" she asked Sunny.

"Perhaps. Armenta's the baker. Sometimes she brings really delicious cookies from home"

Katie glanced toward the shop. "Can I ask her if she made cookies?" She slid to the edge of her chair.

"Only when she comes back here," Ash said. "I don't want you in the shop."

"Why?" Katie asked. "I saw so much interesting stuff in there. I would love to explore."

"No exploring!" Ash's voice was uncharacteristically harsh.

Katie's eyes widened. "Daddy, you sound angry."

"Sorry, sweetheart." He patted her shoulder. "A lot of things in the shop are very expensive. If you broke something, I'd have to pay for it."

"I see." Katie's brow creased. "Sunny, why do you live at the back of that weird shop?"

"Katie..." Ash warned.

"It's okay, Ash," Sunny reassured him. "Katie, I own the shop. A very good friend gave it to me."

"Oh." Katie tapped the end of her pen against her front teeth as she processed that nugget of information.

Sunny decided the tea had steeped long enough, even though it was probably still weak. She poured two cups. Not the best, she thought, but definitely drinkable. "Milk and sugar?" she asked Ash.

"I'll get them. Where's the sugar?" He stood up.

"It's already on the table." Sunny pointed toward a rose-patterned china bowl with a spoon handle jutting through the lid.

"Is Armenta the lady who's wearing the Halloween costume?" Katie asked.

"Katie!" Ash looked horrified. He almost dropped the milk carton before setting it on the table.

Sunny couldn't help laughing. "Katie, those are her regular clothes. She tells fortunes as well as helping the customers with purchases, and she always dresses like that. It's...well...it's..."

"It's a tradition," Ash broke in. "Like the ladies you saw wearing costumes at the tulip festival last year."

Katie's mouth formed an oval of surprise. "Oh. That's really cool."

Sunny breathed another sigh of relief. Ash was very good at providing rational explanations.

"I like it here." Katie patted Ash's hand, mimicking his own gesture of comfort. "Don't worry, Daddy, I'll be okay. And you don't have to hurry back to pick me up."

"Oh, god," Ash said. "What have I done? I've normalized this place." He ran a hand over his face and checked his watch. "I should go. I'll have to take a raincheck on the tea. I'll call as soon as I have more news about your mom," he told Katie. "Stay out of the shop. Sunny..."

"We'll be fine," she assured him.

He didn't look convinced, but he kissed the top of Katie's head.

"Daddy, you know I hate that." She squirmed.

"I know." He smiled down at her. "Sometimes, dads have to be annoying. There's a law or something."

"There is *not.*" She tried to frown, but the attempt failed. She returned his smile.

"Is, too." He turned away. But as he passed Sunny, his hand lightly touched her shoulder. "You *do* realize I'm trusting you with my daughter," he said, his expression grave.

"We'll take good care of her," Sunny assured him.

She tried not to react to his touch. His hand not only felt warm and strong, but somehow familiar. A not-unpleasant tingle radiated through her shoulder. "I should promise she won't sit in the arbor with Armenta or play with the crystals," she said. "But I think we both know that could end up happening, regardless how good my intentions are at this moment."

"Daddy," Katie interrupted. "I'm not tired, and the shop looks *so* interesting. I promise I won't touch *anything.*"

"Katie, you and I both know your promises don't hold up well when you see something you really like. Remember the store at Disneyland?"

"I do." Katie nodded like an ancient sage. "But I was younger then. And you're always telling me how bad TV is for me."

Ash gave a long, theatrical sigh. "Katie, you're wheedling."

"I only have a little homework," she said. "And you told Sunny you didn't want her to lose money because she's looking after me. If she owns the shop, doesn't she need to be in it?"

Ash threw up his hands. "There's so much wrong with me leaving you here, I don't even want to think about what your mother and grand-mother are going to say when they find out. Sunny will decide what you can or can't do this afternoon."

The look he gave Sunny made her want to cringe. She imagined he had used the same technique very effectively on suspects in interrogation rooms.

He strode away, but paused to give the occupants of the table another piercing look before pulling back the curtain. "Whatever you decide, you know my wishes."

The curtain rose and fell. Ash could be heard briefly conversing with Armenta, but the words between them were muffled and indistin-guishable.

"Do you ever do anything he doesn't want you to do?" Sunny asked Katie.

"I do, but I try not to confess it to him." Katie suddenly grinned. "He's more into threatening than punishing. Most of the time, I have to go to my room and think about what I did wrong. Then he comes in and we sit on the bed and talk about what I could have done better, or why I thought what I did was okay."

"That's pretty advanced for your age," Sunny said. "Do you think it works?"

"Most of the time." Katie picked up her pen. "I should do my homework."

"You should," Sunny agreed.

She hoped Katie took a long time to complete it. She didn't want to be confronted with making a choice between Katie watching TV or wandering around all corners of the shop. Like Ash, she didn't even want to consider all the ramifications of Katie being watched over by two women who worked with the macabre and the occult.

Armenta bustled into the apartment, took a circular tin from her big purse, sitting next to the TV, and removed the lid. Aromas of cinnamon and sugar filled the air. She looked at the tea pot, steam curling lazily up from its spout. "Oh, good."

She rubbed her hands together, rings sparkling from every finger, bracelets jangling on both wrists and smiled, all benevolence and sweetness, as she slid the tin toward Katie. "Here, dear. Have a Snickerdoodle."

Katie's face lit up as though Armenta had offered her a gift with enormous possibilities. She chose a cookie and took a big bite. "Mmm," she mumbled.

"Have another one." Armenta lightly shook the tin.

Her mouth full, Katie selected a second cookie.

Armenta laid a fresh paper napkin next to Katie's books. Katie became completely absorbed with eating and writing. Armenta smiled her approval. She went over to her bag and drew out a second, much smaller tin, which she placed on the coffee table.

Sunny took the hint. She loaded the tea-pot and accoutrements onto a tray and took them into the living room.

"Now," Armenta said. "Let's have tea and cookies while you tell me everything that happened since you left the shop with Ash yesterday afternoon." She took the lid off the small cookie tin, which was filled with ginger snaps.

It was going to be a very long afternoon, Sunny thought, watching Katie munching as Armenta poured two cups of tea. Tea that had a distinctly green tint to it, and didn't look at all like Darjeeling. A very long afternoon, indeed.

But the potential interrogation was suddenly interrupted when the bell over the front door tinkled loudly.

"I thought you locked up," Sunny said.

"I did." Armenta put down the pot. "At least, I thought I did."

CHAPTER TWENTY

INSIDE THE SHOP, something crashed to the floor. Wild flapping followed.

Sunny shot to her feet and pointed at Katie. "You," she hissed, motioning toward the sleeping alcove.

Katie quickly disappeared behind the curtain and Sunny heard rustling. Either the little girl had managed to squeeze under the low bed or had gotten beneath the comforter.

Sunny wasn't sure where or how to hide Armenta, but quickly realized her assistant was more of the confrontational type of person. Armenta had grabbed a skillet, wielding it in one hand while holding pepper spray in the other. Sunny flipped all the shop lights back on and cautiously pulled the heavy curtain divider back a few inches. The first thing she saw was a lot of broken glass from the panel in the front door. Then she saw a figure running away across the parking lot.

She ran to look out the front window with Armenta right behind her. She caught another glimpse of what looked like a man, black hoodie flapping in the wind as he ran across the street, dodging traffic. She couldn't see his face, but he was tall and wearing black pants and shoes. Capitol was heavily traveled, and not easy to cross. She figured the man must be in his teens or twenties to display that much agility.

"Well, well." Armenta rested the skillet on top of an empty pedestal beside the front door and tapped her foot against a brick lying on the floor. "I wonder why the alarm didn't ring?"

"I don't know." Sunny looked at the pedestal. The gryphon had been sitting on top of it when she walked into the shop with Ash and Katie. "Where's the gargoyle?"

"I have no idea," Armenta gazed around. "I wonder where he took off to?"

"You talk like it's got the ability to fly, Armenta." Sunny had no more patience for weirdness. "He absolutely can't do that. His wings are far too small." She tried a sarcastic laugh, which came out sounding more like a nervous giggle. Despite her denial, she wasn't sure that couldn't have been happening already, unless he was transporting himself around the shop and the apartment, too. And she'd seen him flap his wings one time, already. Big wings, when fully extended.

Armenta gave a harrumph, took up her skillet and started checking around, like she was ready to bat the gryphon if it flew out at her from the depths of the shop.

"Katie, it's okay to come out," Sunny called. "Okay as it ever is around here," she added under her breath.

"I'll get a broom and clean up the glass," said the ever-practical Armenta. "We don't want customers cutting themselves and suing you for damages."

"While you do that, I'll call the police and report the attempted burglary." Sunny walked to the back of the counter and picked up the landline's receiver. "Then I'll have to figure out who to call about replacing the glass. There's not enough damage for insurance to cover the cost." She stifled a sigh as Katie ran in from the apartment, her shoes clattering across the wooden floor.

"We had an attempted break-in a year ago and had to get the panel fixed," Armenta said. "Capitol Glass was very reasonable."

"Did you lose anything that time?" Sunny asked.

Armenta shook her head. "Whoever it was cut their hand trying to reach inside. Must have deterred them."

"Served them right." Sunny hoped that person had a big scar. Something easily identifiable.

Tina had a short-list of numbers taped under the glass next to the register. The non-emergency information for Salem Police Department was first. As she punched the numbers, Sunny saw Katie walking toward her with a Snickerdoodle in one hand and a cell phone in the other.

"Do you have my phone?" Sunny asked.

"Uh-uh...Daddy gave it to me." Katie waved the phone. "It's a burner." She took a bite of her cookie.

"You've been watching far too many cop shows," Sunny admonished. "That's called a pre-paid phone in everyday life."

"My daddy used to be a detective," Katie said. "He told me drug dealers call these burner phones." She looked very serious. "I can call 911 for you. I know how."

It took a lot of effort not to laugh. "That's okay, Katie," Sunny said, striving for a serious tone. "This isn't an emergency. I have to call another number."

Armenta clapped her hands. "Smart girl." She winked at Sunny over Katie's head. "I'll use my cell to call about the glass replacement. If the burglar comes back, you let me know. I'm armed." She pulled pepper spray out of a skirt pocket before walking away, skillet in hand.

Sunny saw the gryphon sitting on the end of the counter, close to the front door. "What in the world is he doing there?" She couldn't believe her eyes. "Armenta..."

Armenta was nowhere to be seen, but the curtain at the back of shop was dropping back into place. Sunny wasn't sure whether she felt more disturbed by the speed her assistant had walked through the shop or the fact that the gryphon definitely did seem capable of moving at will.

"Ooh. He's really cool." Katie ran over and reached up, stroking the gryphon's chest. "What's his name?"

"I don't know." Sunny felt like she was on the wrong side of the counter to protect Katie if the gryphon fell on her. She left the phone and rushed over to them. "He's hard to pin down."

"Can I name him?" Katie was stroking his talons.

Sunny thought his head was lower than before, like he was leaning over to watch Katie. "His name is Watcher," she blurted.

Katie looked up, her eyes very much like Ash's in their intensity. "You said you didn't know his name."

Sunny felt flustered. "I...I forgot for a moment." She heard the defensiveness in her voice. "He watches over the shop," she said.

It was a reasonable explanation. Really reasonable, she decided, looking at the gryphon again. She must be learning from Ash. She swore Watcher was looking at her from the corner of his eye while his head remained attentive to Katie.

"And us," Katie said. "He watches over us, too."

"He does." Sunny was reluctant to leave Katie near the door. "Why don't you come closer to the register? I don't want you to step on broken glass."

Armenta returned with a dustpan and broom. "Capitol Glass is sending someone right over. I'll get this mess swept up."

"Thanks, Armenta," Sunny said. "What a day this has turned out to be."

"That it has." Armenta nodded her agreement.

"You could call my daddy." Katie ran her hand along the counter as she sidled closer to Sunny. "He used to work in Robbery. He would know what to do."

"That wouldn't work, Katie. Your daddy worked for Portland Police Bureau. I have to call Salem Police." Sunny kept moving back toward the phone, monitoring both Katie's progress and Watcher, in case he suddenly flew off.

"Oh, that's right. Daddy told me it's a different police department." Katie backed away from the counter.

Armenta took the trash can from behind the counter and emptied the contents of the dustpan into it. "All done," she said. "I'm going to take my break now. If you need me, just holler." She gave a dry little cackle before returning to the apartment.

"I'll go finish my milk and do some coloring with Armenta." Katie skipped away. "She said she has a coloring book and crayons in her purse."

Sunny wondered why Armenta's purse would be holding things a nine-year-old would like. She also wondered how she could take a peek into that purse without being downright nosy. The inside of it sounded like a magical realm.

As she waited on hold to speak with whoever answered the phone at the non-emergency number, Sunny marveled at Katie's resilience. Either Katie was exceptional, or kids had really toughened up since she was one.

A crisp, authoritative voice answered Sunny's call. While she talked, she watched the gryphon sitting stoically on the counter as though he belonged there. She decided he did.

She made sure Armenta had cleaned up all the broken glass, including any that might have fallen into the window display, then checked her watch. It was close to 4:00 PM, and they still hadn't reopened. She decided to cover the broken window with cardboard, but as she brought a box from storage along with tape and a box-cutter, a truck with the Capitol Glass logo on its side turned into the parking lot.

Armenta came back into the shop as though on cue, walked to the front and waved to the driver. A patrol car rolled to a stop alongside the truck. Sunny stowed her makeshift repair kit behind the counter.

"This is *so* exciting." Katie had evidently forgotten her father's strict instructions about staying in the apartment and returned to the scene of the crime. "I wish I could come here every day. I hate after-school care. *So* boring. Daddy told me he wants to take care of me in the afternoons, but Mama and Grammy won't let him. Mama told me he's irresponsible and dirty." She grimaced. "I want Daddy to take better care of himself. He's really a nice man." She gave Sunny a very direct look. "You'd like him a lot if he was all cleaned up."

Sunny gave her a reassuring smile. "I like him already, Katie. He's been nothing but nice to me. Armenta, too."

"Good." Katie wore her sage-like expression again.

CHAPTER TWENTY-ONE

ARMENTA CHATTED with Winston the glazier while he worked on the broken panel. After giving a brief report to the police about the attempted burglary, Sunny managed to convince Katie that finishing her homework and eating a peanut butter and jelly sandwich was a better idea than over-seeing the glass repair as a chill wind circulated around Winston's work area.

"If I got a cold, Daddy would worry about me even more," Katie said as Sunny brought bread, grape jelly and a jar of peanut butter to the table. "And I think Mama and Grammy would be angry because he left me here instead of the after-school program. I hope he doesn't tell them." She looked up at Sunny, worry plainly visible on her little face. "I've had such a good time. I hope you and Daddy let me come back."

"I'd love you to come again," Sunny assured her. "But only if it's okay with your daddy."

Katie nodded. "I won't wheedle. He hates when I do that."

"Yes, I remember him saying that." Sunny took a knife from the drying rack. "Would you like jelly or a sliced banana with your peanut butter? I have both."

"I'll like whatever you make," Katie said. "I can take Armenta and Winston's sandwiches to them before we eat."

Sunny hadn't planned on making more than a sandwich for Katie. Ash's daughter was filled with surprises, she thought. Pleasant ones. "I'll make some of each," she decided. She took four plates out of a cabinet.

The burner phone rang, musical tones announcing it was a small world after all. Katie picked it up. "Oh, hello, Daddy. Yes, I'm fine. Sunny and Armenta are taking very good care of me. How's Mama?"

Sunny continued her sandwich-making, but watched a little frown crease Katie's brow as she nodded, like Ash could see her.

"So you're coming to pick me up right now?" She nodded again. "I will. Do you want to speak to Sunny? We had such an exciting afternoon, Daddy. Armenta was going to have tea, but then someone tried to break into the shop. And Sunny's gargoyle flew, Daddy. From a table near the door onto the counter. His name's Watcher. I really like it here. You don't have to worry about me."

Sunny cringed. She could only imagine Ash's horror. Katie had seen Watcher fly. What was the use of denying it, either to Katie or to herself? That gryphon had been moving all over the shop and the apartment for at least two days. That was concrete fact.

Sunny winced. Very concrete, she told herself. Granite, probably. She knew without even opening a debate that trying to convince Katie she hadn't seen the gargoyle fly was a lost cause. Katie's eyes shone while she listened to her father.

"It's okay, Daddy, really it is," she said. "No, I didn't sniff anything in the shop." She nodded again. "Yes, I will. I love you, too." She pulled the phone away from her ear. "Here's Sunny." She held the phone up.

Sunny had a sudden desire to run. She forced herself to put down the knife and take the phone instead. "I'm so sorry, Ash," she told him, before he could say a word. "It's not as bad as it sounds."

"I sincerely hope not." Ash's voice was very matter-of-fact, like flying gargoyles were a natural part of anyone's day. "Was there really an attempted break-in?"

"Well, either that or vandalism. We had just closed for a late lunch when someone broke a glass panel in the front door."

"I'll be there in fifteen minutes," Ash said. "Please don't let Katie go into the shop again."

"I won't," Sunny promised, hoping he was taking the news as calmly as he sounded. "It's too drafty in there. But the window's almost repaired, and I filed a police report."

"I'll see you all soon," Ash said. "Tell Katie I love her."

"I will." Sunny found herself talking to empty air. "He sends his love," she told Katie.

Katie got the milk carton out of the refrigerator. "He'll be okay. By the time he gets here, he'll be as cool a cucumber." She set the carton on the table. "Are we all drinking milk? I can't reach the glasses."

"No, I'll make tea, too." Sunny decided a tea party was the best way to greet Ash. He might not start yelling immediately, especially if Winston was still with them. "Can you find out what Winston would like to drink with his sandwich? He might not like tea or milk. I think I still have a couple of sodas in the refrigerator, or there's water."

"Okay. And I'll see if the policeman wants to join us, if he's still out in the parking lot." Katie skipped off at high speed.

"Don't…" Sunny found herself talking to empty air again. She heard Katie's piping voice inviting Armenta and Winston into the apartment for a snack.

The expression 'going to hell in a hand-basket' came to mind. Sunny filled the kettle, set it on the stove and lit a flame under it. Turning back to the sandwiches, she began spreading peanut butter.

CHAPTER TWENTY-TWO

"I DON'T THINK this was random," Ash said.

He drew Katie onto his lap as he sat at the table with Sunny and Armenta. Winston had enthusiastically accepted a can of soda and a sandwich to eat on the way to another job site.

"As I told Sunny, the same thing happened last year." Armenta bit into a thick sandwich filled with sliced banana and peanut butter.

Katie's effort to grab another cookie almost toppled her milk. Sunny quickly righted it.

"Oops, sorry." Katie looked up at her father.

"Careful," Ash admonished. "How many cookies have you had?"

"Two or three." She gave Armenta a sideways glance.

"Four," Armenta said. "Two large, two small, plus a sandwich."

"Where have you put it all?" Ash asked, eyes wide. "Do you have a hollow leg?"

Katie giggled. "No, Daddy, of course not. You always ask me that."

"I think you've had enough food for now," he told her. "Drink your milk. I have a few more questions for Armenta and Sunny before we go home. Did you finish your homework?"

"I did." Katie vigorously nodded her head.

"Maybe you could finish coloring that picture we started together?" Armenta suggested. "I'd love to see it when it's done."

"Okay." Katie slid off Ash's lap and took the coloring book and crayons over to the coffee table.

"I have a few questions, myself," Sunny said. "Starting with asking why anyone would try to break into the shop during business hours?"

"I'd turned off all the lights and the sign in the window said we were closed for lunch," Armenta said.

"But he brought a brick, so he must have intended to break in. It's not like we leave one outside with a note attached, inviting people to throw it through the window."

"He couldn't have gotten inside unless he had a key to the deadbolt. And I had bolted the door top and bottom like I always do when I'm eating lunch back here."

"Then it was vandalism," Sunny said. "Someone has a grudge against the shop. That's scary."

"Let's go back to the routine for locking up," Ash said. "What happens when you close for the day?"

"I bolt the front door after Armenta leaves," Sunny said. "If I go out in the evening, I use the back door." She pointed to the door between the bathroom and the kitchen.

"Where does that go?" Ash asked.

"The alley. There are four dedicated parking spaces for owners and staff of this shop and the insurance office next door."

"That's not very safe, Sunny." Ash sounded concerned.

"It's fairly well lit, but no, I don't like going out there at night," Sunny said. "Tina didn't have a car. She rode her bicycle, and she kept that on a rack in the storeroom. She probably never used this door."

"Maybe I can take a look tomorrow and see if I can figure out a way to improve your safety." Ash glanced toward his daughter, intently coloring. "I should get Katie home." He picked up her backpack, leaning against a table leg next to his chair. "I really appreciate both of you taking care of her on short notice." He looked at his watch. "You're not going to reopen the shop, are you?"

"No." Sunny pushed her plate and cup aside. "I think we've had enough excitement for today."

"A little too much," Ash said. "Are you sure you're both okay?" He looked from Sunny to Armenta, quietly sipping tea and eating a ginger snap from the smaller of the two tins.

Sunny shrugged. "A little shaken up, but now the glass is fixed, pretty much okay."

"Me, too," Armenta said.

"I can't believe you're both so calm." Ash laid the backpack across his knees. "Most people I encountered on the job after they witnessed an attempted break-in were more than a little upset."

"Armenta and Sunny were great!" Katie abandoned her coloring to come back to the table. "But Watcher frightened the man. We all heard his wings flapping. He scared away the burglar." She took her backpack from Ash and tugged his hand. "You have to meet him, Daddy. He's right there in the shop."

Ash looked momentarily startled, but he recovered quickly and gave Katie's hand a squeeze. "Why don't you sit back on the couch a few more minutes? Finish your coloring."

Katie let out a loud sigh. "I did finish. Two pictures." She went over to the couch and held up the book. "See?"

"Those are lovely," Armenta said. "You're a talented artist, Katie."

Katie wasn't into platitudes. "I'm done coloring," she announced. She put down the book and picked up the remote. "Can I watch TV?"

It was Ash's turn to sigh. "Okay. But no news programs or cop shows."

"I know." Katie had already found the onscreen menu. "I'll look for a nature program. I like those better than kids' shows. Those are really boring."

Ash rubbed a hand over his chin. "Children these days are much tougher TV critics than I ever remember being."

He sounded tired. Sunny felt really sorry for him, and was appalled at her self-centeredness since he'd arrived. She hadn't even asked how everything had gone at the hospital.

"So your ex…" she whispered, stumbling over the woman's name.

Armenta leaned toward her. "Caroline," she hissed.

"Oh…ah," Sunny took a quick look at Katie, lying on the couch with the afghan pulled over her, "is Caroline going to be okay?"

Ash's weary eyes spoke volumes about the stress he must have been under that afternoon. "She'll stay in the hospital a few days before being transferred to a rehab center. With a fractured right ankle and a hairline crack in her pelvis, the orthopedist decided she'd need a few days of in-patient therapy before going home. Maxine told him she's got back trouble and wouldn't be any help to Caroline." He rolled his eyes. "Maxine's never had back trouble in her life."

"Maxine is Caroline's mother, huh?" Armenta asked.

"Yeah." Ash's voice had hardened. "I told both Maxine and the doc I wasn't taking care of Caro, either. They'll have to hire a caregiver if she can't manage after discharge. Maxine grudgingly agreed to make the arrangements." He looked over at Katie, who appeared to have fallen asleep. "At first she was reluctant to let me take Katie until Caroline's well enough to cope at home, but then she thought better of it. She didn't want to tie herself down to driving Katie to school and picking her up from the after-school program." His smile was fleeting. "One ray of sunshine in an otherwise sad and difficult time."

Sunny heard china grating and saw Armenta pick up Ash's cup and peer into it.

"You've had a difficult time with your ex-wife and her mother," Armenta intoned. "That will continue. I see strife and conflict. The leaves never lie."

CHAPTER TWENTY-THREE

"You PROMISED you wouldn't read his fortune." Sunny made a dive for Ash's teacup.

"I said I wouldn't read his cards." Armenta clutched the cup to her chest and leaned back, evidently forgetting she was sitting on an upturned packing crate topped with a satin cushion. She slid, her head coming dangerously close to the refrigerator.

Sunny shouted and sprang to her feet. Ash grabbed Armenta. The table screeched across the wooden floor. Katie rolled off the couch.

"Oh my god." Sunny wasn't sure what to do first.

"That was close." Armenta smiled up at Ash. "Thank you. Look, I didn't even drop the cup."

"You're welcome." He pulled her to her feet. "Here, take my seat."

Katie had recovered without adult intervention. She scampered over and hugged Armenta. "I'm so glad you're okay."

"She's fine," Ash reassured Katie. "Let her sit down."

Armenta managed to fix her lopsided topknot back into place with a large bobby pin while maintaining her grip on his cup.

Ash ran a hand across his brow. "Life here is never dull, is it?"

"No, it certainly isn't," Sunny agreed, pushing the table back into place. "I'm going to buy another chair. No one else is going to sit on that crate."

"There's a stool hidden up somewhere in the back of the storage room that would be perfect for extra seating," Armenta said. "It would fit under the table so it doesn't make moving around this little kitchen even more difficult."

"Please give that cup back to Ash, Armenta," Sunny said. "I shouldn't have tried to grab it from you. That was rude of me."

"It's okay, Sunny." Ash shrugged. "I doubt tea leaves are going to reveal anything about my future. You know I don't believe in fortune-telling." He looked at Armenta. "Sorry if that offends you."

Armenta waved the cup. "Another non-believer who needs convincing."

Katie had taken a seat on the packing crate. She slid across to be closer to Armenta. "Can I see?" she asked, leaning forward.

"I've had enough of the paranormal for one day," Sunny decided. "I'm going to make sure the shop's closed up for the night and count the till. You can all leave through the back door when you're ready to go. No rush." She had to stifle a sudden yawn. "Sorry. I didn't get enough sleep last night."

"My fault," Ash said.

Armenta's eyes narrowed as she slowly gazed from one of them to the other. "I see." Her tone radiated disapproval.

"No, you don't," Ash told her. "I kept Sunny up talking way too late. She fell asleep on my couch."

Katie completely lost interest in the tea leaves. "Sunny slept at your house? Mama won't like that." She folded her arms across her chest and stared at him. "Grammy won't, either."

"I don't like tattling, Katie, remember? Please go do some coloring."

The stern tone in Ash's voice made Sunny want to take up coloring. Katie's mouth drew into a firm line. She left the table, but not until she had given her father a mutinous glare. At the coffee table, she took out a blue crayon and began coloring so vigorously, the paper ripped.

An awkward silence ensued. The incessant scraping of crayon on paper was suddenly interrupted by a whirring sound from a large clock mounted over the back door. It chimed five times in rapid succession, each chime reverberating until it mingled with the next.

Sunny had never heard the clock strike the hour. In fact, she had thought it broken. After the echo of the chimes died away, loud ticking could be heard, and the second hand moved relentlessly around the clock-face.

Armenta frowned as she stared up at the clock. "Katie, why don't you help me clean up the dishes before you go home?" she suggested.

Katie put down the crayon. "Okay." She came back to the table and took her empty glass and plate to the sink.

Sunny left the kitchen. She realized Ash was right behind her when his hand grabbed the heavy curtain and held it out of the way.

"I'll make sure the front door's locked," he said, squeezing past her. He strode down the center aisle.

Sunny turned on several of the overhead lights before following Ash. She discovered Watcher had moved again. He was crouching close to the cash register, which put him face-to-face with anyone coming to pay for their purchases. Fearing his presence would intimidate her customers, Sunny cupped her hands around his body and tried to lift him, but he wouldn't move.

She tried tipping him. The heavy bird instantly slid across the counter at an alarming speed. If he fell, he was going to break the glass top of the display case. She grabbed him, and he leaned against her. Relieved, but feeling the weight of the gryphon biting into her shoulder, Sunny held him tightly as she straightened him. He glared at her.

"You are one pesky bird," she told him. "I wish you'd stay on that high shelf."

She tapped his talons. A warmth spread through her hands and radiated up her forearms. Sunny, her head bent close to the bird's, swore she felt Watcher's breath on her cheek.

"You want that put somewhere else?" Ash came up behind her. "I should do that. It looks heavy." He placed a hand on the gryphon's back. "You'll have to let go, Sunny. I don't want to drop it on your feet." When she moved aside, his other hand slid around Watcher's neck.

"Don't do that; he won't like it." The words were out of her mouth before she could stop herself.

"He's stone, Sunny. He's not going to feel it." Ash tried to pick him up. "Damn, he really *is* heavy. How did he get over here? I saw him with the other gargoyles when I came yesterday. I swear he was looking at me." Ash let go of Watcher. He stepped back a pace and stared intently at the gryphon. "That's weird the way his eyes seem to follow you."

"I don't think he wants to be moved," Sunny said.

"He's not a sentient being," Ash said. "He's an ugly statue that belongs in someone's yard." He stepped back. "Not mine," he added.

"He's a gargoyle, Ash, not a garden gnome." Sunny wondered why she felt irritated by Ash's rank dismissal of the gryphon.

"You want me to tell him I'm sorry?" Ash's eyebrows rose. "This is ridiculous. He has to be stuck to the counter. If you didn't move him, the only other person who would have carried him here was Armenta. He can't be as heavy as he feels, or she couldn't have lifted him."

Sunny watched Ash straining to pick Watcher up and wondered how she had carried him down the ladder without help. "Don't strain your-self," she warned when Ash grunted. His cheeks were flushed. "I only wanted to move him to the side a little more," she added.

Wiping sweat from his brow, Ash gave an unexpected chuckle. "He shouldn't stay where he is. You don't want him spying on you when you're pilfering from the till, do you?"

"Very funny." Sunny had to smile. "Not much to pilfer today, I bet." She opened the till and pulled up the tray. The fifty-dollar bill she had tucked under it that morning had stayed solo. She counted the twenties. Only two more. The five-dollar bills had increased, so had the ones, but not enough to justify even turning on the lights. "Definitely not," she said.

"Which is mostly my fault," Ash said. "I kept you up late, let you oversleep, and then asked you for a big favor. The shop's been closed most of the afternoon. I'm so sorry. Let me make up for some of it." He pulled out his billfold. "Katie!"

Shoes clattered. The curtain drew aside. "Yes, Daddy?"

"Pick out a few things," he told her. "I'll have to vet them," he added as she rushed up to him. "No dried lizards or bat wings."

Katie's face lit up. "Really?" She spun around, her plaid school uniform skirt rippling around her thin legs.

"I mean it. Nothing grotesque," he warned.

Katie giggled. "You know I *love* grotesque stuff." She pointed toward Watcher. "Can I have him?" she asked Sunny. "Is he even for sale?"

Watcher's head had turned. His glower was directed at Sunny.

"No," she said. "He's not."

"Then can I have one of his friends?" Katie skipped over to the gargoyles' display. "I would really like one to watch over me when I'm home. Watcher makes me feel so safe."

Ash looked at the gargoyles and grimaced. "I suppose so. If you feel drawn to one of them, you can have it." He gave Katie a mock shudder. "They give me the creeps."

Armenta had come into the shop. She picked something up from the pedestal Watcher had once occupied and brought it to the counter. "What do you want to do with this brick?" She laid it next to Watcher's feet. "The police officer didn't want to take it as evidence."

Sunny successfully scooted Watcher to where she wanted him. With one hand on his back, she picked up the brick. Suddenly, the mist descended, thick and swirling. Sunny dropped the brick. It crashed to the floor, narrowly missing both the glass counter and her feet. She grabbed Ash's arm for support.

A terrible realization came to her. "He took the wrong child," she told him.

CHAPTER TWENTY-FOUR

"ARE you sure you can't remember anything else?" Armenta placed a cup of green tea in front of Sunny as she sat at the kitchen table.

"That was all I got." Sunny took a small, cautious sip of her tea. It tasted slightly acrid, but not unpleasant. Deciding Armenta's brew might be beneficial, she took a bigger sip.

"Maybe you need to touch those things again." Armenta sat and poured herself a cup of tea. Steam rose, partially obscuring her face.

Sunny wasn't quite sure how she had gotten to the table. She saw Ash watching TV in the living room, Katie sleeping beside him.

"Maybe I do." Sunny reluctantly stood, unsure whether the weakness that had accompanied her previous visions would return. It did not. Wondering whether that was because of Armenta's tea, she hastily drained her cup.

The audio on the TV lowered. "Are you okay?" Ash asked, worry in his eyes. "You don't look very steady."

"I'm a little tired, that's all," Sunny hastened to reassure him. "I'm going back to the shop."

Although she hadn't fainted, she still felt off-kilter. She was sure Amy had been taken by mistake, but why? If only she hadn't resisted that mist, she berated herself. If she hadn't been such a coward, perhaps she'd have more answers. But giving up all control could mean a return to that dark wood, where lost souls cried out to her, and a terrifying presence lurked. Sunny wasn't at all sure she was ready for that experience again. She pushed back the curtain and turned on all the lights. The silent shop felt benign and peaceful. As she walked toward the counter, Armenta close behind, Sunny saw Watcher with his head lowered, like he was contemplating the brick beside his feet.

"I wish I could control this gift," she told Armenta. "When I see the swirling mist, I want to get as far away from it as possible. I'm so frightened I'll get lost…that I won't find my way back." Tears welled, blurring her vision. "How can I get over that?"

Armenta took a moment to respond, nodding slowly. "I believe you'll gain more control with time. You have to be patient. This is like improving any new skill. The only way to gain knowledge is to practice." She urged Sunny forward with gentle hands. "Take your time. If you don't get anything when you touch Watcher's talons, try stroking his head or his wings. Don't be hesitant. Be in control. Fear is a negative reaction. It throws up walls, which could trigger an even stronger response.

The gryphon, head lowered, continued to stare at the brick.

"Breathe deeply," Armenta coached. "Release the fear."

Sunny did her best to follow Armenta's instructions as her assistant's reassuring hands left her waist. She placed one hand on the brick, finding it firm and slightly warm. Nothing happened. She took several more deep breaths before placing her other hand on Watcher's talons and closing her eyes.

Again, nothing happened. She rubbed the brick. She rubbed Watcher's feet, his chest, his head, and finally, his back. No mist swirled. No dark aperture opened. She didn't fly off into a dark wood filled with thorns and decay.

Well, damn, what an anticlimax!

Sunny couldn't decide if she was relieved or disappointed. "I'm getting nothing." She picked up the brick, hefted it, and rubbed her hand up and down Watcher's cold, stone back. "Still nothing." She turned to face Armenta.

"You can't *force* visions," Armenta said. "I'm sure of that."

"Which is so frustrating." Sunny leaned back against the counter and tried rubbing the tension from her face, but her hands were too cold. "I feel hollow, like part of me is missing. It's a really weird sensation."

Armenta patted Sunny's arm. "I'll tell Ash we have to go home so you can rest."

Sunny thought of Armenta standing alone at the bus stop with a brick-throwing hoodlum possibly still in the neighborhood.

Armenta gave her a reassuring smile. "I see you frowning. Don't worry; I'll ask Ash to drop me off at my apartment."

Solitude and rest sounded both welcome and frightening to Sunny. "I don't know if I want to be alone here or not," she hedged.

Armenta tossed her head, her topknot flopping around. "Nonsense. With the alarm set, you're safer here than a lot of other places."

Sunny thought her assistant looked more like a comic book character than a wise seer at that moment. "You'd make a lousy spokeswoman for a security company," she said. "I can think of a lot of other places far safer than this."

Armenta gave a hearty dry-leaves chuckle, which reassured Sunny even less as it echoed around the rafters.

"Nonsense. This place is a fortress." Armenta placed a strong, sinewy arm around Sunny's waist and propelled her in the direction of the apartment. "You just haven't allowed yourself to believe that, yet."

"What about all the supernatural things that could be circulating around the shop?" Sunny protested, resisting. "None of them trip any alarms."

Armenta stopped forcing her reluctant employer forward. "Don't be silly, dear. They won't hurt you; they like you. Look how well Watcher did his job today." She waved her arms in an arc, the fringes on her colorful shawl swinging rhythmically. "I'll brew chamomile tea before I leave. Guaranteed to make you sleep like a baby.."

"If I drink any more tea, I won't sleep at all," Sunny complained. "I'll be spending most of the night in the bathroom."

"Suit yourself, dear." Armenta drew the curtain aside and strode into the living room ahead of Sunny. "No more revelations," she said, when

Ash looked up, startled. "I'll wash the dishes. Ash, would you be kind enough to take me home after that?" The curtain dropped behind her.

Sunny became enveloped in heavy damask. Heavy, dusty damask. She pushed it away to find Katie still sleeping on the couch, but Ash already washing dishes, his jacket off and sleeves rolled up. A kettle sang on the stove, and Armenta had packed the tins into her purse, which sat bulging to overflowing on a stool that had miraculously made its way from the storeroom.

Sunny wondered what time warp she had been in while enveloped by damask. She decided to ignore yet another weird moment at The House of Serenity. "I'll finish cleaning up the kitchen," she told them. "Ash needs to get Katie into her own bed. She's got school in the morning."

"Katie isn't going back to school until we're sure your vision was of some other kid," Ash said. "We'll be back in the morning, after I talk to the principal at Katie's school. My daughter's going to be home-schooled until I'm convinced she's in no further danger." He picked up Katie's backpack and took their coats from the rack. "I'll check your existing alarm system and see what I can do to make you safer getting in and out of your car in that back parking area."

Sunny was about to remind him she was on a strict budget that didn't allow for expensive security modifications when he stopped to take a deep breath.

"I'm sorry," he said. "That sounded dictatorial. Let me start over. I'd like to bring Katie with me tomorrow while I check those things out and see what can be done to make you and Armenta safer. Your merchandise, too. If that's okay with you, of course, Sunny. You're the boss around here."

"I am, for better or worse," Sunny agreed. "I'd welcome your expert opinion. Just remember this shop is currently running in the red."

"That's going to change very shortly. I've read the cards." Armenta put on her coat. "Are you sure you don't mind taking me home, Ash?" She glanced up at the clock. "The bus will be here in a couple of minutes." She picked up her purse.

"I'm happy to take you anywhere you want," Ash assured her. He turned to Sunny. "Thank you for trying again. I'm beginning to realize how hard it is for you to do whatever it is you do."

"I want to help," she said. "I really do. But I don't seem to have any control over what happens when I have one of these visions, and it scares me."

Ash gave her arm a gentle squeeze before he took his and Katie's coats from the rack. "Believe me, when you were at my house, I was scared, too."

Armenta gave an unladylike snort. "So, you're both scared. But you're going to have to get past that if you want results." She looked from one of them to the other. "That's the way it is. I've consulted others about this. But help can come from unexpected and unusual sources. That's what my shaman told me."

"I'm going to ask Katie about where she's been and who she's seen over the last few weeks," Ash said, his voice lowered. He glanced toward the couch. "I can't do it tonight, but I'll find the right time tomorrow." He grimaced. "She's not going to be happy about being home-schooled. She had several weeks away from her classmates after Amy's death, and she was just getting back into a routine. Between this revelation of yours, Sunny, and Caroline's accident, that routine will go right out the window again."

"But when I said he took the wrong child, I don't know if I was talking about Amy and Katie," Sunny said, feeling anguished about potentially turning Katie into a prisoner for an unknown amount of time.

"I know, or at least, the rational part of me understands that. But where Katie's concerned, I can only react as a parent. I'm terrified of losing Katie, too." His voice faltered. "She's the only reason I get up in the morning and go through the day."

"Bring her here," Armenta said. "We'll help with the home-school-ing, won't we, Sunny?"

"Of course. You're both welcome to come here whenever you want, and stay as long as you want. Who knows, maybe we'll all turn into believers." She watched the worry on his face recede, to be replaced by a faint smile.

"That, my friend, will be the day," Ash said. "All right. Give me a minute to get Katie up and into her coat, and we'll be out of here, Armenta." He pulled on his coat and started to take Sunny's comforter off Katie, who stirred in protest.

"Daddy?" She blinked up at him.

"We're going home," he told her, gently pulling away the comforter. He helped Katie into her coat. She yawned and placed her arms around his neck when he picked her up.

"I'll bring her backpack." Armenta already had it over one shoulder. She went over to the curtain and pulled it aside.

Ash stopped before walking into the shop and jerked his head at the curtain. "This is another example of poor safety."

"I know." Sunny took the curtain from Armenta. "We can talk about it tomorrow. Yes, I'll lock up after you leave. Yes, I'll check every door and make sure the alarm system is set. Now, go home, all of you."

But Ash paused again before joining Armenta in the parking lot. "If you need reassurance in the middle of the night, call," he told Sunny. "I'm a light sleeper. Most cops are."

"I hope I don't need to do that, but thanks for the offer." His genuine concern enfolded her like a security blanket. Suddenly, she didn't feel as jittery. A cold breeze swirled around her legs and stirred the wind chimes, setting off a gentle ripple of sound.

"Call me if anything makes you uncomfortable," Ash reiterated. He looked at Watcher, sitting stoically on the counter. "I don't care how weird you think it sounds."

"Anything might happen in here," Sunny agreed. "Did you remember to take Katie's purchases?"

"Already in her backpack. The creepy gargoyle you two picked out, the necklace Armenta suggested and the incense. I think there's a smudge stick in there, too."

"Dragon's blood sage, of course." Sunny patted his arm. "Go home, Ash. Don't worry about me. I'll be fine."

"If you hear or see anything that isn't spooky tonight, call 911 immediately," he told her.

"You'd better call me for advice on the spooky stuff," Armenta called. "I'll tell you whether you can ignore it and go back to sleep. You know, if things are materializing or flying around." Her snicker carried on the breeze to ruffle Sunny's hair.

"I'll get you back for that remark," Sunny promised. "Somehow, some day, when you're least expecting it, Armenta Kaslov."

For once, Armenta's cackle felt reassuring.

After waving them away and securing both shop and apartment, Sunny noticed a teapot in the middle of the coffee table, a cup and saucer covered with Forget-Me-Nots beside it. Armenta had brewed the tea.

Reading in bed with a cup of chamomile sounded far more relaxing than watching TV. Sunny undressed, poured her tea and snuggled under the comforter with an Agatha Christie novel she had found under the bed. *Ten Little Indians.* She wondered whether Tina had been reading it or it belonged to Armenta.

The tea didn't taste like chamomile. It had a deeper yellow hue than the tea Armenta had brewed before, but it was warm and soothing. After reading the same page three times, Sunny admitted she couldn't focus. She drained her cup, turned out the light and stared up at the skylight. A full moon illuminated the bed.

She tried to relax, breathe deeply, and stop the questions drifting around in her head. Could she really see into the future? But if so, why were the messages so garbled? Did the frightening vision she'd had of being lost in the woods have anything to do with her telling Ash an abductor had taken the wrong child? Was Amy the wrong child? And if she was, did that mean the person who threw the brick was trying to break into the shop to abduct Katie?

Perhaps, Sunny reasoned, she wasn't able to see the future at all. Perhaps she was seeing the past. Buddy said he had been in the woods so long, he couldn't remember his given name. And she had told Ash the wrong child been taken, not given him a prediction about something happening in the future. Feeling as tight as an over-wound timepiece, she listened to the kitchen clock's loud, rhythmical ticking.

She tried to relax and allow the mists to gather, but Armenta was right...the more she concentrated, the less detached she felt. Abandoning her attempt, she tried to find a comfortable position to sleep, first on her left side, then on her right. Neither felt right. She turned onto her back. Moonlight penetrated her eyelids. She covered her eyes with a pillow.

Her cell phone rang on the nightstand, startlingly loud and insistent. Sunny threw off the pillow and sat up. Her book fell to the floor. She checked the caller ID and was relieved to see Ash's name.

"Are you and Katie okay?" she asked.

"Katie, yes. Me, not so much…I'm in a cold sweat." His voice sounded shaky around the edges. "After I tucked Katie into bed, I sat on the couch to watch the news and dozed off. I dreamed she got abducted and thrown into the river at the same place Amy drowned."

"Oh, Ash. I'm so sorry. I tried to have another vision, but it wouldn't come. I've been lying here tossing and turning. I think I'm too afraid I'll go somewhere I can't get back from."

"I've been pushing you too hard, and the sad part is, I don't even believe in clairvoyance, or whatever you want to call these visions." He sighed deeply. "At least, I didn't believe before I walked into your shop with that earring. Now I'm not so sure of anything. What I said earlier, that was a lie."

"I refused to listen when Tina tried to tell me I had a psychic gift. Now it's too late. She died and left me this shop, where every day I see more evidence that I was a stubborn idiot not to listen and learn from her and Armenta."

"The flying gryphon," Ash said, softly. "Please tell me it's a mechanized toy that Armenta operates with a remote control."

"I wish I could. I don't know what Katie saw, but I heard wings flapping, and the person who was trying to break in took off like…well…a bat out of hell. Armenta was with us while that happened. She was making tea."

Ash didn't respond immediately. Sunny wondered whether he had hung up on her or was thinking of a diplomatic way to tell her he'd decided never to visit the shop again.

"The House of Serenity is a special place," Sunny said. "I've had to open my mind to things I thought were pure fiction. I used to think Armenta was, at best, eccentric. Now I realize she's so much more than that. I completely depend on her guidance and wisdom."

"You must have been very good at marketing," Ash said, a hint of humor in his voice. "You've almost sold me, and my feet are firmly planted on the ground. Detectives are very analytical in their approach to life in general. I've always said there's a logical explanation for everything. Since I walked into your shop, I've developed strong doubts."

"Does that mean you haven't changed your mind about coming here tomorrow and bringing Katie with you?" Sunny crossed her fingers. "Armenta and I would really miss you both if you decided we might be a bad influence. I swear we'll try to keep things as normal as they get around here."

Ash actually chuckled. "I'd like to see that."

Sunny noticed a long black tail sashaying around the bed in the moonlight. "I can't make any guarantees, though."

"Fair enough. I'll text you when we're ready to come. Katie can do her schoolwork in the kitchen. I may be able to install solar lights at the back door. Those are a cheap and easy fix that would make your parking area safer."

Sunny's tension floated away with the cat's tail, which left the pool of moonlight and disappeared. "Thank you," she said. "You're so understanding."

"Goes both ways," he said. He hesitated a moment before continuing, as though he was trying to organize his thoughts. "Look, Sunny, I don't think either of us understands what's happening in our lives right now, but when I'm with you and Armenta, I feel at peace, regardless of the strange things going on around you."

"I feel strength from you, too," she said. "And support. Sometimes, Armenta's version of tough love makes me really nervous."

"Yeah...she made me sweat the evening she left us to cope with getting you back from that vision," Ash said. "Christ, I was scared."

"Me, too. But I think she was testing us. She's funny that way." *Funny a lot of ways,* Sunny thought. *But an ally they both needed.*

"I'm beginning to see that." He sighed deeply. "I've got a confession to make. When Katie told me she saw that damned granite gargoyle fly, I didn't think it was because of some elaborate remote control device Armenta had rigged up. I believed Katie was telling the truth."

Sunny wondered whether she should try to convince him otherwise. To have him buy into Watcher flying around the shop was to leave the realm of grounded reality. She didn't even know if *she* was ready for that, regardless of how many times she felt eyes on her, Watcher flapped his wings, or that black feline sashayed around.

"Ash," she began, trying to decide whether he'd believe Armenta had hidden behind the counter and flown Watcher around as a prank. "Er…"

"Don't try to lie," he interrupted. "I know when someone's feeding me a line. One of the best attributes for a detective."

"I'm sure you've very astute," she muttered, pushing the hair back from her face and closing her eyes to shut out strong moonlight concentrated on her bed.

"The fact that I didn't question Katie's statement graphically illustrates how far I have traveled into the land of the bizarre and unnatural," Ash said, his voice calm and authoritative. "But I need to know, and I want you be truthful…is Armenta feeding us hash cookies and hallucinogenic tea?"

CHAPTER TWENTY-FIVE

SUNNY TRIED to embrace the possibility that everything they had experienced was because Armenta had been drugging them. But why would she do that? she asked herself as she watched clouds scudding across the moon. Shadows deepened around her, and she heard gentle rustling at the foot of the bed. The hairs at the back of her neck stood to attention.

She slowly sat up in bed. "I hadn't even considered that."

"I'm assuming you're not involved, because you seem to be as freaked out by all of this as I am."

"I'm not involved. But I don't believe Armenta is, either. I refuse to believe she'd drug me. Tina's will stipulated that if the shop ever leaves my ownership, any profits from the sale will go to charity. Armenta wouldn't benefit from losing her job, and I genuinely feel she's a good person."

"I could take samples and get them analyzed," Ash said.

Sunny carefully swung her legs off the bed and jammed her feet into her slippers. She peered into the darkness. A shadow passed through a patch of moonlight. It had a long black tail and moved swiftly. She stood up and reached for a flashlight she'd placed on the nightstand.

"Don't do that," she told Ash. "Please," she added. "How about an experiment, instead? I'll buy English Breakfast and hide it from

Armenta. We won't drink any of the tea she brews or eat her cookies for…say…three days. If I have another vision during that time or we see Watcher flying, then we'll know Armenta's not to blame."

As she turned on the flashlight, she saw the edge of the heavy brocade curtain move. She took a moment to turn on the bedside lamp before taking the phone with her to the doorway and pulling the curtain aside. The bedside clock told her it was 1:15 AM.

"Fair enough," Ash said. "What are you doing? Are you walking around?"

"I'm checking the shop again before I try to sleep," she said as she directed the flashlight's beam down the center aisle. A tail swished close to the counter before disappearing behind a display rack.

"And why are you doing that?" Ash asked. "Did you hear something?"

"No." She jogged to the front of the shop. "Because I *saw* something." She swept the beam around. Nothing moved. Watcher sat on the counter, his head erect. "There's this cat that keeps showing up and then disappearing. There has to be a hole somewhere in a wall that I haven't found. Armenta said the cat comes and goes. I thought I might be able to follow it, but now it's disappeared again."

"Go back to bed," Ash said. "Looking for holes in walls sounds like a great job for Katie. She'll love to do that, and since she's shorter, she'll be able to search around the baseboards a lot easier."

"That's true." Sunny went over to Watcher. She had a sudden desire to run her hand over his head and pat his talons. He felt very cold. She saw his long tail was neatly curled around his bird ankles, and then wondered if birds actually had ankles. Directing the flashlight, she realized he only had talons at the front. His back legs were those of a lion. In the flashlight's beam, he looked even more menacing.

"We'll talk tomorrow," Ash promised. "I'll pick up the tea and bring us all a sandwich lunch after the meeting at Katie's school wraps up. "

"Thanks, Ash." Sunny walked back to her bed. *"If,* and it's a very big *if,* I'm right about Amy being abducted by mistake, then why did the abductor get your children mixed up and take the wrong one?"

He grunted. "That's a big part of what's keeping me awake. I've got to talk to Caroline. See where she took Katie and Amy the last month of Amy's life. Who they met." His voice trailed off.

Sunny looked at her rumpled bed before sitting on it and taking off her slippers. She wondered whether she'd get any sleep that night. "I saw the news reports on TV, but I'm sorry, I don't remember whether Amy and Katie resembled each other. Did they?"

"Kind of," he said. "Although Amy was three years younger than Katie, she was almost as tall as her sister. She'd gotten her height from my side of the family. Caro's side, they're shrimps, and Katie got that gene. Curly blonde hair. Shoulder length. Amy didn't like anything but barrettes. Katie likes braids or a pony tail. Similar builds, but Katie has Caroline's skinny legs. I think they both got their mother's high metabolism. Appetites like a pair of horses." His voice had softened. "Katie's the quiet one. Amy was always in motion. Always inquisitive." His voice broke.

A lump had formed in Sunny's throat. She swallowed hard. "I wish I hadn't asked."

"You had to." Ash's voice sounded choked. He coughed. "The mere thought that this nightmare we've all gone through could be prolonged, could be even worse than we ever dreamed...well, it's..."

"Don't go there yet," Sunny begged. "I could be completely wrong. Who knows why I said what I did?"

"Do you remember where Amy was found?" he asked.

"The river. But not the exact spot."

"And yet you were heading for downtown when you ran the other evening. You'd have had a long run, but the way you were going, I think you'd have made it as long as you didn't get hit by a car. She was at Riverfront Park."

A sudden flash of a riverbank streaked through Sunny's mind. Water, sunlight glinting across it. Muted traffic sounds...

...and then it all vanished, and she was lying flat on her back and staring up at the moonlit skylight.

"Are you still there?" Ash yawned. "I must have fallen asleep."

"Me, too, I guess." Sunny looked at the bedside clock. It was 3:15 AM.

"Goodnight," Ash said. "See you tomorrow."

She avoided pointing out it was already the next day. "Goodnight, Ash," she said to empty air. He had already hung up.

Sunny felt sleep stealing over her. She laid the phone and the flashlight on the bedside table and pulled the comforter over her head to shut out the moonlight. She loathed the skylight. If it wasn't so high up, she would have asked Ash to climb the ladder and cover it.

She wondered whether there was tea that would counteract dreams. As she slipped away into welcome nothingness, she decided to find out. If that tea was available, she'd ask for a pot to be brewed every night she spent in that apartment.

CHAPTER TWENTY-SIX

"Principal Grunewald wasn't happy about me being homeschooled again," Katie told Sunny as she deftly handled a delicate snow globe filled with tiny crystals and snowflakes. She grimaced theatrically. "The principal's never happy about anything. We all have to thank her for anything she says or does, even when we don't like it." Katie put the empty box aside and opened the flaps on a new one.

"That's school for you." Sunny took the shimmering globe Katie handed her. Inside, a tiny fairy with turquoise wings hovered over a meadow filled with green grass and delicate, tiny daisies. She gently turned the globe on its side. The meadow shifted, becoming a cascading pale blue sky until the flecks settled back into a carpet of green.

"Oooh," Katie whispered. "That's *so* pretty. I'm going to ask Daddy for an advance on my allowance. I get five dollars. Will that be enough?"

"More than enough," Sunny assured her. She carefully hid the $25 sticker she had been planning to place on the bottom and handed Katie a small white box filled with tissue paper. "Let's tuck it in here for safe-keeping. This one's nicer than the heavy box it was packed in."

Ash came up to them. "It's time for a break."

Sunny checked her watch and saw it was 1:00 PM. "It certainly is. We never ate the brunch you brought."

"Go eat a bagel, both of you," Ash said. "I can finish this up."

Katie cradled her snow globe in its box, got up carefully and walked slowly toward the apartment instead of skipping.

The remaining delicate and expensive snow globes still needed to be unpacked and integrated with the rest of the display. Sunny looked at Ash's large hands. "Thanks, but I'd like to finish this up myself."

"I may not look like it, but I originally majored in art at college," he said. He grinned when Sunny turned to look at him in frank surprise.

She couldn't imagine him painting anything but a wall. "Murals?" she asked.

"Sculpture. Metalwork. My parents finally got through to me that I couldn't support a family with what they considered a hobby."

"You were married?"

"For the first time. And a father, too." Ash shrugged. "We were too young, and she was in love with the illusion of being the wife of a successful artist, not a welder."

"You went from sculpting to welding?"

"My dad's opinion of a career in metalwork. He wanted me to go into the family business...law. I tried that, too, which finally broke up my shaky marriage. After graduating, I practiced briefly, but I didn't like it. Law enforcement made more sense to me. A long story. Much too long for today."

"I agree, although now you've piqued my interest, you know I'll want to know more. But why don't you eat with your daughter while I finish this project?"

"Katie already had breakfast with me, then most of the morning. She's probably ready for a break from me. Give me a chance," he urged. "If you don't like the results, I'll stay in the apartment and drink tea while I supervise Katie's schoolwork."

Sunny thought about their late-night conversation, with voiced concerns over possible tea additives. "That could be hazardous to your health," she pointed out.

"No worries. I brought the English Breakfast. Now, go eat while I take care of these. Trust me. I'm not going to drop anything, I promise."

Her stomach empty, Sunny reluctantly left him to join Katie and Armenta in the apartment.

"Good timing." Armenta rose from the table. "I had an excellent poppyseed bagel with cream cheese. Are you drinking coffee? Ash made a pot. There's still plenty left. Or I could make tea?"

"Coffee's fine," Sunny quickly assured her.

Armenta took her dishes to the sink.

"I'll wash everything when we're finished," Sunny said. "Ash is alone in the shop right now. He's working on a display."

"I'll see if he needs my help." Armenta nodded. "I'm sure you're both quite hungry," she added, seeing Katie eyeing the food in the middle of the table.

"I am." Katie nodded vigorously before climbing onto a chair.

"Help yourself," Sunny encouraged. "But I'll cut the bagel for you."

Katie selected a blueberry bagel. Sunny took a pumpernickel.

"Do you want yours toasted?" she asked Katie after slicing both bagels. Katie shook her head. Sunny slid a plate over to Katie and placed her own bagel in the toaster oven.

"Daddy had a fight with Grammy last night," Katie said. "I heard them arguing after we got home. I wish my family wouldn't fight over me."

"I'm so sorry, Katie." Sunny filled a glass with orange juice from the large container Ash had brought. "I'm sure they all want the best for you, but right now, they're all struggling with their grief over your sister." She took her warmed bagel out of the toaster oven.

"I know." Katie nodded. "It makes them act even less rationally than usual." She sighed.

"Where did you learn to use such big words?" Sunny sat with Katie at the table and spread cream cheese on her pumpernickel before carefully sliding a thin slice of Lox on top.

Katie shrugged. "School. Home. My parents never talk down to us." She put down her bagel. *"Me,"* she said. "I mean they don't talk down to *me."* Tears shimmered in her eyes before spilling onto her cheeks. "There is no *us* anymore."

"Oh, Katie." Sunny dragged her chair over next to the little girl and wrapped her arms around Katie's thin shoulders. "It'll be okay," she whispered. "We're all here for you."

Katie brought her napkin up to her nose and blew gently. "I'm sorry," she said. "I don't want to make a fuss and upset Daddy."

"Is that why you're always so cheerful?" Sunny had wondered how Katie seemed unaffected by her sister's death and the turmoil surrounding it.

"I try not to make Daddy sadder than he is already." Katie sniffed and wiped her face with the napkin. "Mama and Grammy, too. But they have each other. Daddy has no one but me."

Such a huge burden on such tiny shoulders, Sunny thought. She felt tears swimming in her own eyes.

"You and your daddy have Armenta and me, now, too. We'll help both of you, I promise." She gave Katie a quick hug, then drew back to look down at the child's face.

Katie was staring up intently, a little crease between her brows. "Thank you," she said. "That makes me feel much better."

"Good." Sunny nodded. "Now, we should finish our food, otherwise your daddy won't get his meal until close to supper."

Katie's expression cleared. "I did all my schoolwork before I came to help you with the snow globes. Daddy doesn't know that, yet. Can I help in the shop? You could teach me how to use the cash register. I'm very good with money."

"I don't doubt that for a moment." Sunny had to smile. It seemed she had a little genius on her hands.

They quickly finished eating. Sunny made short work of the dishes and brought a mug of coffee with her as she followed Katie into the shop. She found Ash had not only completed the snow globe display, he had set up several others. Customers swarmed around clusters of wind-chimes, an inventive presentation of board games, the globes and the gargoyles, which now had runes scattered around their gnarly feet. Instructive books completed the reorganization.

Armenta manned the register and rang up purchases for a line of people snaking halfway up the center aisle. "I could do with some help," she called.

Katie sprinted over, dodging around baskets.

"I'd like you to take the items from the baskets and tell me the prices," Armenta instructed her diminutive helper, as though Katie was a regular part-timer. "You can stand on the footstool."

Katie nodded, a crease of concentration between her eyebrows. She climbed onto the stool, smiled at the customer, who looked a little dubious about this arrangement, and carefully extracted a delicate snow globe from the basket. Cradling it in her hands, she upended it. "Twenty-five dollars," she pronounced. Her eyes widened, and she looked toward Sunny. "Shouldn't it have a box?"

Sunny thought the widened eyes were because the globe was identical to the one Katie had purchased for five dollars.

"I may have one under the counter," she said as she scooted around the far end, passing Watcher, who was balefully eyeing the customers in front of him.

She saw one woman flinch, take something out of her pocket and place it in her basket. It was a smaller version of the globe with the green meadow.

"That's actually a display item," Sunny said, holding out her hand. "Let me get you another one in a box." She felt tension sweep through her customers. The ones on either side of the woman stared at her. The woman's cheeks reddened.

"My fault." Ash's deep voice resonated from behind all of them. "I didn't label the display items." He strode up to the counter. "Anyone else have an unboxed globe?" he asked the line. Three people raised their hands. "My apologies," Ash said. "Some of us are new at this. You'll have your boxed purchases before you get to the counter."

A murmur of appreciation rippled through the line.

"I'll bag," Sunny said, joining Armenta and Katie. She pulled out tissue paper and bags. As she wrapped, she noticed people looking at the items around them as they waited patiently in line. More merchandise went into baskets.

"Each bag costs ten cents," Armenta reminded waiting customers. "But you want to protect your purchases, and every bag is reusable. It also has the shop's logo on it."

Another ripple of appreciation went through the crowd as Sunny held up one of the bags and shook it open. She had worried that the extra money Tina had spent on those logos would cost them needed income, but by the looks on their customers' faces as they eagerly paid for the bags and swung them from hemp handles as they left the shop, the cost was going to pay off.

When the rush was over, they closed for a short break.

"You brought your own brand of magic to the shop," Sunny told Ash and Katie. Their answering smiles warmed her heart.

Armenta volunteered to color with Katie while Ash made phone calls in his car. Sunny tidied up the shop. When she rearranged the amulets, she found the blue one that had sent tingles up her arm was missing. She swore it had still been in the display case before they closed for their break, and hurried to ask Armenta whether she remembered selling it.

"I sold it to Ash for a dollar," Armenta said. "He needs the protection."

CHAPTER TWENTY-SEVEN

Ash strode back into the shop an hour after he had gone out to his car. Katie and Armenta had moved their coloring to the arbor. Rain had set back in, and customers were scarce. In the last 45 minutes, Sunny had sold only a tarot deck and its instruction book.

Sleepy and leaning on the counter, she was trying to convince herself she should dust and rearrange what they had dubbed the Eastern Corner, where Hindu gods guarded knick-knacks and jewelry. She stifled a yawn. If she had to leave the counter, she would rather brew a pot of coffee and read another chapter of Tina's book on the use of herbs in spells and charms.

Ash momentarily watched Armenta and Katie at the small table, heads almost touching as they worked on their project, before walking over to Sunny. "Can I trust Armenta to take care of Katie while you go somewhere with me?" he asked in an undertone.

"When?" Sunny asked. "They'd be alone in the shop. What if it gets busy?"

"Could you close again for an hour or so? I hate to see you lose potential income, but this is important."

"Armenta always reminds me Wednesdays are slow, but what is so important it can't wait until after we close at six?"

"We have to meet someone. He's available right now."

Armenta looked up. "We'll be fine, won't we, Katie, if your Daddy and Sunny go somewhere for a little while?"

Katie nodded without stopping what she was doing. "Fine," she echoed.

Armenta left the arbor and drifted toward them, her yellow and green striped skirt swishing softly. "If we get busy again, I'll call. How's that?"

"It sounds like a plan, doesn't it?" Ash looked at Sunny. "Well?"

"I suppose that would be okay," she said. "I'm still a bit worried."

"I managed after Tina passed away," Armenta reminded her. "That was a very difficult period, but the customer who helped me the other day was here then, too. Why don't I see if she's available? Would that make you feel better?"

"It would." Sunny nodded. "What's her name?"

"Belinda," Armenta said. "She's been a customer since the store opened. I was thinking of asking you if she could help out on a part-time basis. She's very familiar with our merchandise."

Sunny could sense Ash's impatience and wondered what could possibly make him want to leave Katie behind. He'd been too worried to send her to school, but he was ready to leave her with Armenta.

"You know I can take care of your child, don't you, Ash?" Armenta looked up at him, and the gold hoops in her ears flashed.

Although common sense told Sunny those hoops must have caught reflected light from the neon strips above their heads, she still felt Ash had been given some sort of signal.

His eyes locked with Armenta's. "I do."

"Very well. Now go along, both of you." Armenta made a shooing motion with her hands.

Sunny fetched her coat and purse from the apartment. As she reentered the shop, she saw a shadow, low to the ground, and then a waving black tail disappeared around shelving on the aisle that ended with the gargoyle display.

"There's the cat," she said, running over to that aisle, which held no cat. "Armenta, how does it come and go so quickly?"

Armenta shrugged. "Some things do that around here."

Sunny 's gaze went to Watcher. He was turned toward the gargoyle display. Katie was standing next to him, but how had she managed to move that heavy statue?

Ash broke into her distracted thoughts. "This might be the perfect opportunity to see how it's getting in and out of the store. There must be a hole. Katie, I want you to go around with a flashlight and find it. Then I can patch the drywall."

"Daddy, the cat will die if you get it stuck inside the wall!" Katie sounded horrified.

"I'll make sure that doesn't happen," Ash assured her. "Once we figure out where it's getting in and out, we'll put food down and trap it before I seal up the hole. If it's a stray, we'll take it to the Humane Society or Friends of Felines. You know about both those shelters."

"I do." Katie sidled over to her father and took his hand. "I want a cat, Daddy." She looked up at Ash. "We could adopt him. Then he won't have to go to a shelter."

"Katie, he might be someone's pet." Ash sounded irritated. "Look, I have to take Sunny somewhere. The person who's expecting us can't wait all day."

Katie frowned and dropped his hand. Sunny didn't think it was the time to mention that it might be a phantom feline.

Armenta rustled over to Katie and bent down close to her ear. "After I call Belinda to see if she can help us with the customers, why don't you and I search for the cat, or the hole he's coming through?" she asked in a conspiratorial undertone still audible to Sunny and Ash.

"Okay." Katie's frown cleared. She looked at the counter. "Where's Watcher?"

Sunny spotted him perched next to the cash register. "He's right there, Katie." She pointed to him.

Armenta walked over to the register. She patted Watcher's talons. "Come along, Katie," she said. "Let me make that call, and then we'll hunt for the cat."

"I swear that gargoyle was near the door." Ash sounded downright bewildered.

Katie skipped up to Watcher. "Why did he do that?" she asked Armenta.

"Oh, I don't know, dear." Armenta pulled a little book out of a pocket in her skirt and thumbed through it. "Everything has to find its right place." She found what she was looking for and picked up the store phone.

Ash was digging in his pockets. "Armenta, that amulet you sold me has gone missing."

"No, it hasn't." Katie swung something on the end of a long chain around her neck. "This is it, isn't it, Daddy? You left it on the table, next to my coloring book."

"I did? I couldn't…" Ash's brows drew toward each other. He looked at Armenta. "Should she be wearing it, or should I?"

"It depends." Armenta looked less serene than usual. It took her two attempts to push the little book back into her pocket. "I just remembered Belinda telling me she's unavailable Wednesday afternoons. You two should go on your errand. I doubt we'll have any more customers today. I'll bolt the door behind you and close up. Call me when you get back, and I'll let you in."

Sunny felt a stir of unease at Armenta's sudden change of plan. "You're going to set the alarm?"

"I will. After we finish searching for the cat and wherever he's coming in and out, we'll be in the apartment." Armenta put her arm around Katie's shoulders. "I saw chicken in the refrigerator. I'll cook that."

"Can we have real chicken noodle soup?" Katie asked. "I saw it on a cooking show at Grammy's house last week. It looked really yummy. Much better than what we usually have out of a can." She gave her father a look of frank disapproval.

Ash shrugged. "I'm not much of a cook. Barbequing's more my style."

"I think real chicken noodle soup can be arranged." Armenta smiled down at Katie before ushering Sunny and Ash toward the door. "Off you go."

"Are you sure you still want to do this?" Ash asked, even as Armenta began to physically push him.

"Of course. Nothing to it." Armenta waved away his sudden doubt. "Katie and I are already good friends. After we have a snack, we're going to cook together."

"After we look for the cat's hole." Katie brandished a flashlight she'd brought from behind the counter.

"Of course." Armenta nodded.

"I don't think there are any noodles in the pantry," Sunny said as Armenta shoved her out the door to join Ash in the parking lot. "We should stop off on the way back and pick some up."

"There are noodles." Armenta was already closing the door behind them. "Call when you get back."

Sunny heard bolts sliding into place. She hurried over to where Ash already had his SUV running, the front passenger's side door open for her.

"Where are we going?" she asked when they joined traffic heading south on Capitol.

"I talked to the lead detective on Amy's case," Ash said. "I told him about your visions."

"What?" Sunny felt humiliated. She stared through the windshield as they took a left on Market Street. "Don't you think that'll get around the police department? It can't be very big." Her cheeks burned. "What if I need to make some sort of complaint in the future? Don't you think they'll be skeptical about believing me?"

"Sunny, Brad Schilling's not that way. He won't laugh at you or allow anyone else to poke fun, either. I'm sure of it."

"Oh, right. You and he are such good friends, you know that for a fact." She snorted her disgust and folded her arms across her chest. "Is that an example of the male code we women hear about?"

"No, of course not." Ash accelerated around a slower car, then returned to the right lane. "It's because he also believes Amy's death wasn't an accident. Listen, I showed him the earring and told him what happened when you touched it. He said years ago, he met a detective who used a psychic to help him solve a murder." Ash glanced at her before making a right turn onto 17th Street. "Brad's got an open mind."

"You still shouldn't have told him without asking me first," she said.

"I had a feeling you'd react this way." He reached over and took her fisted hand in his. "I know you're upset, but your gift is too important... to me...to Katie." He stopped, his lips pulling into a tight line. "Schilling asked me to bring you. There's another missing child, and he wants to see if you can pick anything up at a house where they think she might have been held."

Sunny's righteous indignation abated a little. A Salem detective was actually asking for her help? But then doubt set in. What if she got nothing again?

Ash broke into her troubled thoughts. "Without confirmation the child was kept there, Schilling's case is going cold," he told her as he took a left onto a side street a couple of blocks away from Mission Street.

They wound through an old neighborhood, larger Victorian homes giving way to small bungalows with even smaller front yards and spindly sidewalk trees. They drew up at a small white house with peeling paint and the remains of what had once been a picket fence.

"This is it," Ash said.

Sunny felt a cold chill pass through her soul.

CHAPTER TWENTY-EIGHT

ASH KNEW that telling Detective Brad Schilling about Sunny Kingston might have been one of the worst decisions of his life. Schilling hadn't asked whether Ash had paid Sunny for her prognostications, but Ash had tuned in to the emotional detachment in the detective's voice. They'd gone from Schilling gently but firmly telling Ash he couldn't justify having the earring processed by CSI after being encased in mud for who knows how long to a reminder they would need concrete evidence to reopen the investigation. The emphasis Schilling had placed on the word *concrete* graphically conveyed his opinion of a muddy earring and a psychic's predictions. Ash could only be thankful Schilling hadn't yet seen Armenta Kaslov.

As he drove, Ash reminded himself that Schilling had asked him to bring Sunny to the site of an open investigation. Neighbors had reported someone going in and out of a house that had remained empty since the elderly owner passed away and her estate went into probate. It was a flimsy lead in a case that had gone without new information for over six months. The missing 10-year-old girl had disappeared in the middle of a school day. Frantic parents had continued well-organized but fruitless searches. Ash knew Schilling was about to give Sunny a test, and he was willing to bet Brad expected her to fail.

Out of caution, Ash held back all the information from her. If he coached her in any way, he'd taint her first impressions and jeopardize any opportunity to validate her gift. Of course, she might not get anything useful at all...her visions were, at best, erratic and open to interpretation.

He got out of the Range Rover, closed the door and looked at the fence. For every slat still standing, four were either leaning back to be caressed by the long grass or had completely disappeared into it. The abandoned home had faded curtains drawn across two windows to the left of the front door and a matching set to the right, under a small overhang that covered the porch. Overgrown bushes crowded the front steps and touched the eaves. Brad Schilling stood on the porch, a large flashlight in his right hand.

Sunny joined Ash on the sidewalk. "Vacant houses look so sad. I always wonder why no one loves them anymore."

"Some older homes aren't worth saving," he said. "Maybe this one needed too many repairs. It sure looks like a money-pit."

The front gate leaned at a crazy angle by one rusted hinge. Ash guided Sunny past it and up the pitted remains of a concrete walkway. "Hi," he greeted Schilling from the bottom of three worn wooden steps leading to the porch. "This is Ms. Kingston."

"Hi, Ash. Ms. Kingston, thanks for coming." Schilling pointed to the steps. "Watch yourselves. A lot of the boards are rotten. Up here, too." He tapped one with his foot. It creaked loudly.

Sunny's brow furrowed. She stepped off the path. "You go first," she told Ash. "If you don't fall through, I'll follow."

"Very funny." Ash pushed a hanging vine out of his way, carefully mounted the steps and cautiously joined Schilling, who thrust out his free hand. Ash shook it without commenting. The gesture felt awkward.

Sunny was still hovering at the base of the steps. "Come on," Ash said. "If I made it up here, then you should."

Schilling smiled tersely. Ash wondered whether the detective wanted to make a comment about Sunny being able to predict whether she'd fall through the steps, but Schilling turned away to open the front door as she picked her way up to the porch. He stepped over the threshold. "The inside's in better shape, Ms. Kingston," he said. "A forensic team already went through here, so you don't have to worry about not touching anything."

"That's a relief." Sunny came onto the porch. "You'd better move out of my way," she told Ash.

"Me, too?" Schilling asked.

"Probably." She tiptoed quickly across the boards. "It sounds like a lot of people have already been in this house, so I'm warning you both in advance… if I don't get anything useful, that could be a reason." She glanced at Schilling as she passed him.

Once they all stood inside the darkened room, the detective turned on his flashlight, pointed the beam at the floor, and they waited while their eyes adjusted to the gloom. Slowly, hulks of furniture became visible. A couch, a couple of wing-back chairs close to the fireplace, a large china hutch in a dining room that held a table surrounded by six chairs. Beyond an archway at the back of the living room was complete darkness.

They stood in awkward silence. Ash wondered whether Schilling was trying to size Sunny up, intimidate her or was merely waiting for some sort of introduction. "I didn't tell Sunny anything, Brad," he said.

"Good." Schilling nodded. "Let's get this over. The air's stale. There's probably black mold as well as rodents and who knows what else in here." He briefly shone the flashlight around the living room. "I'd like you to go through the house and tell me if you see…hear…whatever it is that you…" He stopped and looked down at her. "I don't know what you get. Ash didn't tell *me* much, either." He shrugged. "I feel really awkward, but we sure could do with any help you can give us."

Sunny grimaced. "That may sum up what you get from me… anything. Ash may have told you my visions are uncontrolled and completely spontaneous. But I'll do my best."

Brad's rigid posture relaxed. Palpable tension eased. Ash wanted to take a deeper breath, but the mention of black mold deterred him. "How about pulling back the curtains?" He suggested, walking over to them.

"Okay, but be gentle." Schilling went into the dining room. "The probate attorney wants the windows covered when we leave, and the drapes are already in shreds."

Ash saw Brad wasn't exaggerating. He drew back dusty blue velvet drapes to reveal stained and yellowed net curtains. Weak sunlight struggled through, hit a threadbare rug and revealed a faded pattern of pink roses.

Sunny slowly toured the living room. She checked out a couple of framed photographs on a side table without touching them, then moved on. "I'm not getting anything," she said.

"Try the dining room," Ash suggested.

"Okay." She didn't sound enthusiastic.

Schilling sneezed so suddenly, and so loudly, Ash involuntarily stepped backward, bumping into an end table. It moved, grating against the wooden floor. Sunny flinched.

"Sorry," Brad said. "Too much dust for my allergies."

As Schilling hurried to light Sunny's way, Ash saw a dark stain on the wall, which he thought must be from a leaky roof. It was probably harboring the black mold, he thought, dismally.

Sunny stopped inside the dining room. "Could you open the blind, too?" she asked.

"Of course." Schilling stepped around her. He extended an arm toward the old metal blind. It clattered to the floor. "What the hell?" He looked at the blind, then at Sunny. "I didn't even touch it."

Light had flooded the room. Sunny was standing beside an upright piano. She sat on the bench in front of it, reached out and placed her hand on the music stand, where an open piece of sheet music sat, its pages yellowed and frayed.

Schilling picked up the blind and attempted to hook it back up. Ash went over to help, but the mounts had fallen, pieces of drywall still attached.

"CSI assured me this place is sound," Schilling said. "But if pulling back the curtains cracked the drywall, then I'm not so sure."

"Yeah. I saw water damage on a wall in the other room." Ash wasn't so sure cracking drywall had brought down the blind, but he wasn't ready to share his suspicions with Brad.

"Damn," Schilling muttered. "The probate attorney isn't gonna like this."

"Don't tell him," Ash suggested. "I doubt he's going to come over here to inspect after we leave."

Schilling grinned. "Yeah. You're probably right."

Suddenly, a tinny sound came from the piano. Music filled the room. The very walls seemed to expand. Ash's scalp tingled. His teeth ached.

In another part of the house, something crashed to the floor.

Ash wasn't sure whether he jumped higher than Brad, but he knew they were way too spooked to respond as cops. His heart pounding, he looked at the detective. Schilling stared back with wide eyes and mouthed: "What the hell?"

Sunny's playing stopped, the chords fading away to silence.

Schilling managed to pull himself together enough to ask: "What in the *hell* dropped back there?" He made no attempt to find out.

A delivery van rattled past outside the house. Above the dining table, prisms on a spindly chandelier tinkled.

"Hadn't we better investigate?" Ash asked as the noise from the van died and the tinkling stopped.

Schilling unfroze. He looked embarrassed. "Yes, of course."

His face covered with sweat, he grabbed his flashlight from the table. Wiping his brow on his sleeve, he strode rapidly into the living room. Ash hurried to catch up.

Trying to ignore an adrenaline surge that told him to get into his car and keep driving until he ran out of gas, he followed the detective down the hallway and into a bedroom. An ornately-carved wooden headboard lorded over a double bed covered with a brightly-colored quilt. The quilt looked fresh and new, in stark contrast to the rest of the décor. On the floor lay a picture frame, face down.

"That's what must have fallen." Schilling crouched beside it.

"Don't touch it," Sunny said. "His fingerprints are on the back of it."

Schilling straightened slowly and turned to face her. "And how do you know this?"

"I just do," she said. "Don't ask me how; I'm new at this, remember?"

Ash decided to rephrase the question. "Sunny, do you know *how* the fingerprints got on the frame?"

She pondered that a moment. "He straightened it," she said, slowly. "The girl was complaining." She looked straight at Brad. "Because she didn't like it being crooked."

Schilling's eyes narrowed. "Why would she complain about something like that?"

"She hated anything being crooked, especially pictures on a wall," Sunny told him.

"Her mother thought she should be tested to see if she had OCD." Schilling's voice was quiet, flat. "Obsessive Compulsive Disorder," he clarified. "How do you know that?"

Sunny frowned. "I don't know how." She walked back to the dining room, the two men following her. She stopped and glanced at Ash. "He played the piano for her." She pointed to the sheet music. "She liked that song. So did his mother, who knew this home's owner when they were both young girls. It was the family home, passed down from mother to daughter. That's how he knew where to come. How to get inside."

"My god." Schilling's face registered shock. "This is incredible. Impossible. You couldn't have known all that before coming here." He directed a penetrating gaze at Ash. "She couldn't, could she?"

Ash shook his head. "No way. I told her nothing about this case, including where we were going when we left the shop."

"You didn't believe I could be psychic, so you set up a test to prove it." Sunny shook her head at Schilling. "I guess you feel pretty silly right now."

"Sunny, did you get anything to tie this missing child to Amy?" Ash broke in.

"No, I don't think so." Her brows drew toward each other. "The information I get isn't organized. I think the best way to tell you what it's like is that it's not like reading a book or watching a movie. Random bits of information spin past me. Some of it seems completely useless, like the episode in the wood that you know about. This time, I got a really strong connection with the woman who used to live here. She gave me all the information. She's still here. She loves this house so much, and she's so sad no one else does."

After Sunny told them the owner's spirit was still in the house, Ash felt a cold draught flow across the back of his neck. He watched Brad Schilling shudder and glance around, like he expected to see a ghost hovering.

"It's cold in here," Brad said. "Why don't we go back outside?"

"Feeling a little less of a non-believer?" Sunny asked.

"Feeling spooked, Ms. Kingston," he said. "I had an aunt who came up with a few random but pretty good predictions. My family called her canny. I know I didn't initially sound like I believed in psychics, but I needed to know if you were going to be a potential help to Ash. Maybe to Salem PD on an informal basis." He stopped at the front door "Very informal," he added. "I'm still wondering how I'm going to justify requesting CSI coming out here again to dust for prints on that frame."

"Talk to the neighbor in the pink house next door," Sunny told him. "I have a feeling she'll verify what I told you about the family. Ask her specifically about the piano and that piece of music. Ask her who learned to play it. I think you'll be able to find out the name of the man that way. The frame?" She shrugged. "You're the detective. You'll have to figure that out one on your own."

"You're amazing," Schilling said. He sounded awed. "Do you want to look around the other rooms?"

"No." Sunny sighed. "No use. I feel really tired, and I'm getting a headache." She rubbed both temples with her index fingers. "Ash, can you take me back to the shop? I'll ask Armenta to brew some chamomile tea, and I'll rest for a while." She swayed.

Ash hurriedly put his arm around her waist. She leaned against him, and he guided her across the porch and down the creaky front steps.

"I'm right behind you," Schilling said. "I'll close the curtains."

"I'm okay now," Sunny told Ash while they waited on the front path.

He reluctantly withdrew his arm, worried she was putting on a brave front, but she smiled up at him.

"Really okay," she said. "I actually got something useful this time."

"Very useful," Ash agreed.

Schilling joined them. "I'll lock up and check in with the neighbor," he said. "Thanking you doesn't seem enough, Ms. Kingston."

They all turned as the home's front door creaked. It closed and locked. The battered screen door clicked into place.

"Shit," Schilling muttered under his breath.

"I'll second that." Ash couldn't wait to leave.

"She won't bother the forensics people," Sunny assured Schilling. "She told me that as I left."

"You'd better have them check the neighbors' trash," Ash said. "I hope the garbage trucks haven't been yet this week. The comforter in the master bedroom looked new."

"I noticed that comforter, too." Schilling took out his cell. "He must have tossed the old one somewhere." He gave Ash a pointed look and offered his hand. "Thanks. I'll be in touch."

Ash shook hands. "Good to see you again."

Schilling turned toward Sunny. "I've a confession to make, Ms. Kingston."

"You were in the shop after Ash spoke to you about me," she said. "You had Armenta read your cards."

"Actually, I didn't," he said. "She read my face before I could stop her. She told me a few things that convinced me she wasn't, well, a…"

"I know what you mean." Sunny smiled. "Armenta's a bit, well…different."

"Do you know what's on the front of that picture?" Ash asked.

"The lab took photos. If I remember correctly, it's a photograph of the home's owner as a young girl," Schilling said. He held out his hand to Sunny. "Thanks again for leaving your business in the middle of the day."

Sunny took his hand but they abruptly broke away. "Don't take your family out in the car this evening," she blurted. "Stay home."

Schilling looked confused. "My son has ball practice. My wife's got class. I'm dropping her off before I take both kids to the field. Her car's in the shop."

"Don't do it," Sunny said.

Schilling looked confused. "What are you trying to tell me?"

Sunny turned away from him. "We need to go," she told Ash.

"Listen to her," Ash told Brad. "Even if you've still got doubts." He helped her into the Range Rover.

Sunny finally spoke again after Ash parked in front of The House of Serenity. "Detective Schilling is going to kill all of them if he doesn't listen to me," she said. "There'll be a crash on I-5. A tanker truck. I saw it when I took his hand." She closed her eyes and tears slid down her cheeks. "I hope he believed me enough to really listen."

Ash's stomach churned. "I hope so, too." He felt like calling Schilling, but the detective had already seen and heard enough of Sunny's psychic power to make his own decision.

Sunny got out of the SUV and waited for Ash to join her. "How are *you* doing?" she asked. "You looked a little pale there for a while."

"I might need something stronger than tea." He opened the shop's front door and guided her inside ahead of him.

"A cup of something Armenta brews may be a better remedy than alcohol," Sunny advised, giving his arm a squeeze.

"You play the piano very well," Ash said.

"You think so?" Sunny looked up at him and frowned. "Until today, I'd never played a piano in my life."

CHAPTER TWENTY-NINE

KATIE COMPLETED her assigned schoolwork at 2:00 PM the following day. Ever the neat and orderly little soul, she packed everything into her schoolbag and took it to her bedroom. Ash had given her the dining table as her temporary school room, enabling him to more easily keep an eye on her progress while he worked in the living room.

"You got done fast," he told her, stretching kinks out of his back muscles. He decided he'd worked long enough, too. He wanted a cigarette in the worst way. Instead, he went into the kitchen to make coffee.

"It's easier to concentrate here." Katie put an empty glass on the counter beside the sink and moved a small dish of fruit from the breakfast bar into the middle of the dining table. "I don't have other kids asking the teacher questions or playing around when we should be completing our assignments."

Ash smothered an indulgent smile he thought Katie might resent. She was firmly convinced her age group should be able to concentrate for extended periods of time, despite the fact her own sister had been a constant source of disruption, both at school and at home. *A good-natured disruption,* Ash reminded himself. Amy hadn't been able to sit quietly anywhere for more than five minutes. Her learning style had been doing rather than absorbing, which had led to frequent parent-teacher conferences.

Katie climbed onto a bar stool and watched him spoon coffee into the filter basket. "You didn't make me take recess, either, Daddy." She smiled. "I think I really *like* home schooling when I can do it here. Mama and Grammy always have so many people going in and out of their houses, and they talk on the phone all the time, too."

"I'm happy you're able to get a lot of work done here, Katie," Ash said, carefully choosing his words. "Even impressed," he added, when Katie began to frown. "But this situation shouldn't continue through the end of the school year. Once your mother's discharged from the hospital, we're all hoping you'll be able to return to her home and go back to school. Maybe you do work better when everything's quiet, but life's not like that. It's full of distractions and interruptions. We all have to learn to deal with them. Besides, you need to be with kids your own age, not adults all the time."

"I know." Katie refused to make eye contact. Her frown remained. "Can we visit Mama today?" she asked, her tone less than enthusiastic.

What she *didn't* say bothered Ash. He knew his answer had disappointed Katie. She wanted to spend more time with him. They had both hoped that would happen after Ash retired and moved to Salem, but Caroline continued to be in complete disagreement with any modifications to the existing custody arrangements.

He knew Katie had wanted him to fight harder to keep his girls with him instead of them being sent to after-school care. Caroline had used the issue of Ash's work interfering with weekends to keep his weekends restricted, despite her own profession frequently taking her away from her children. She had insisted her mother was available to take over for her if she had to work, whereas, Ash had no close family members to take on that role. Ash's retirement and move to Salem made those arguments a moot point, but then Amy died, and he had agreed he wouldn't cause any more disruptions to Katie's life than were absolutely necessary.

"We can't visit your mother today," he said, trying not to sound alarming, despite what Maxine had told him when he called that morning to check on Caroline. "Grammy said your mother was having a difficult day. She said tomorrow might be better."

More like ready to scream her head off, according to Maxine, he thought, remembering their brief conversation. That statement had worried him, but Maxine said Caroline's orthopedist had been contacted, her medications were being adjusted, and she was sleeping peacefully for the first time since the accident. He walked over to the patio doors and opened one to see if it was warm enough to encourage Katie to play outside.

"Okay, then can we see Sunny and Armenta, instead?" Katie asked, legs swinging like they always did when she was either preoccupied or restless. "Please? I'll be really good. I won't go anywhere in the shop you don't want me to, and I promise I won't break anything."

Ash decided that although it was sunny and fairly warm, the ground was still too wet. Katie would get muddy, leading to a bath and a change of clothes. "Sunny and Armenta are working, Katie. They don't need us underfoot during business hours," he said. He closed and locked the patio door.

"But Armenta and I didn't find where the cat's coming in when we looked yesterday." Katie had left the barstool. She walked into the living room and sat on the couch. "And you said you still had to do more to the security system." She peered at his open laptop. "Could you leave your work until tomorrow?"

Ash quickly closed his laptop. He didn't want Katie to see his research on psychics, which had followed another a search through data on crimes with similarities to Amy's abduction.

Suddenly, an afternoon at Sunny's metaphysical shop sounded a lot better than watching movies and eating junk food neither he nor Katie needed. Her teeth would suffer, and if he sat around eating all day, he'd need larger pants.

He took his cell from the coffee table. "I'll call and see if they don't mind."

Katie enthusiastically clapped her hands.

"We don't mind at all," Sunny said when she picked up. "Armenta had such a good time with Katie yesterday."

"She didn't try to teach Katie how to read palms or worse, tarot cards, did she?" Ash asked.

"Not to my knowledge."

"We'll be over in twenty minutes," he said. "Thanks, Sunny."

"No problem." She hung up.

Katie jumped up and skipped around the table while giving an enthusiastic rendition of her phone's jingle. Ash took the laptop back to his office and checked through the mail on his desk. Nothing that couldn't wait, he decided. The singing went on in the background. Ash wished he'd had Katie pick another ringtone when they set up her cell.

They shared a quick snack of banana slices and chopped walnuts mixed into vanilla yogurt, which effectively stopped the singing. Ash gave Katie a bottle of water, bundled her into her outerwear, threw on his coat and locked up. He decided he felt as enthusiastic as his daughter about visiting The House of Serenity.

When they arrived at the shop, another visitor was drinking green tea in the kitchen. Detective Schilling looked like a man who had stared his own mortality in the face. Dark circles ringed his eyes; a day's worth of stubble covered his cheeks and chin.

"Let's go to the arbor, Katie," Armenta suggested. "I made the thumbprint cookies I told you about. With raspberry jam in the center."

"Oooh, good." Katie ran over and threw her arms around Armenta's waist. "I've missed you and Watcher. Do you think we'll see the cat again?"

"I missed you, too, dear." Armenta gave Katie a squeeze, her wrinkled face softened by a wide smile. "We may see the cat. You never know when he'll pop up. Watcher's on the counter, guarding the cash register." Her laugh was the rustle of dry leaves on a crisp fall morning. "I bought a special card deck on the way to work." She winked at Ash. "We're going to play Go Fish."

Ash gave Armenta a nod of thanks. He watched her pick up a cookie tin and leave the apartment, Katie skipping at her heels. "Where's Sunny?" he asked Schilling. "I didn't see her in the shop."

A door opened next to the back exit. Sunny came out, looking like she'd been crying. Ash saw the inside of a small bathroom before the door closed behind her.

"What happened?" A sick feeling churned in the base of his stomach.

"It's what *didn't* happen," Schilling said. "I came to thank Ms. Kingston…Sunny…for what she did for me and my family."

Ash remembered Sunny's prediction. He'd missed the news the previous evening while getting Katie bathed and ready for bed. "The wreck," he said.

Schilling nodded. "I got everyone in the car, and then I heard Sunny's voice, clear as day. I made them all go back in the house. They were all mad at me. My wife said if I wanted to stay home, then that shouldn't stop them going out. She wanted to know what was wrong with me. I said I had been told we mustn't go out. They were all angry, but I didn't care. The kids went to their rooms, and my wife locked me out of our bedroom. I sat on the couch and turned on the TV. The wreck hit the six o'clock news." He looked over at Sunny, sitting opposite him. "My family thinks I'm nuts this morning, but in a good way. Thank you, again. You saved four lives yesterday."

Ash's heart beat heavily in his chest. The last shred of doubt about Sunny's abilities vanished.

"If anyone can help us find out the truth behind your daughter's drowning, it's going to be Sunny," Schilling told Ash. "I'm not going to lie and tell you it'll be easy to convince anyone at Salem PD we need to start working with a psychic, even if Sunny's help leads to an arrest in this other case, but I'm willing to buck them."

CHAPTER THIRTY

ASH NEEDED A MOMENT. Almost four months had passed since Amy's death. Four months of frustration and anger. Four months of feeling his denial was being treated like that of a grieving father unable to accept the truth. Even Schilling's shared doubts had felt token at best. Vindication might be within his grasp, but with its own shades of doubt, denial and ridicule if Sunny became publicly involved.

Warring emotions surged through him. He pulled back the curtain dividing the apartment from the shop and eavesdropped on Katie and Armenta. Seated in the arbor, they were chatting like old friends between admonishments to "Go fish!"

Although he still had reservations about her, he had to admit Armenta's influence on his daughter hadn't been negative. He looked around the shop, brightly lit but completely devoid of customers. He wondered whether it was another slow day before he let the curtain drop back into place. Katie's words about added security weren't wasted on him. He needed to talk Sunny into sealing off her apartment with drywall and a sturdy door she could lock. The glass door to the shop had already been breached. Lives as well as livelihood could be at risk if they continued investigating Amy's death as a possible homicide. He tried to clear his mind as he joined Sunny and Brad at the table.

"I knew I recognized you when we met yesterday," Sunny told Schilling. "I saw you on the news after..." She stopped and glanced at Ash.

"You probably did." Schilling took a sip of his tea. "This tastes weird, but I feel a lot calmer than when I arrived."

"I thought we decided we'd drink the English Breakfast I brought," Ash told Sunny as he pulled the hard wooden stool from under the table and sat. His other choice was the packing crate topped by a pillow, which had been kept there for Katie. Definitely not safe enough to support his weight. Ash decided he'd invest in several fold-up metal chairs for these meetings with an increasing group around Sunny's kitchen table.

"Armenta made the tea while I was in the bathroom," Sunny said. "Do you want me to brew another pot?"

"No. This is fine." Ash didn't want Schilling to think he had been given anything but plain green tea. He poured two cups and placed one in front of Sunny.

"I'm sorry I dropped in without calling first," Schilling told her. "I had to thank you in person. Please call me Brad. I don't think we can remain formal after what you did for me and my family yesterday." He took a card out of his pocket and passed it to her. "Just don't call me Bradford. It brings up memories of being reprimanded by my parents, which happened often. I wasn't a model teenager. Going in the service straightened me out and led me to a career in law enforcement. Kind of going full circle." His smile looked rueful.

"I can relate," Ash said. "Don't ever call me Ashton. My parents used it as a precursor to one of their frequent lectures."

Sunny laughed. "My parents used my full name. 'Sunny Melanie Harris, you get in here right now' was their battle cry."

"I thought I'd never do that to my children, but some family habits die hard," Schilling said. "I find myself doing the same thing whenever I know which child was responsible for whatever infringement."

"More tea?" Sunny asked, wielding the pot.

Ash noticed it was a different pot. This one had a pattern he recognized as Lily of the Valley, his mother's favorite spring flower. Armenta's shrewd face came into his mind. He quickly dismissed any thought that she could possibly know anything about his mother. He pushed his cup toward Sunny and saw Schilling do the same.

"Now, let me give you an update on the picture frame that got dusted for prints," Schilling said.

Ash listened to the background story on the missing 10-year-old. As it unfolded, he watched Sunny's face register a gamut of emotions ranging from interest through disbelief and then, finally, concern. Schilling showed them a map of the area that had already been searched multiple times after various unsubstantiated tips from the hotline. Thanks to the fingerprints on the frame, a potential suspect was now being sought. A man with a history of loitering around primary and middle schools. Parents had complained, but he hadn't been charged with any offenses, only given warnings to stay away from school properties.

"You won't find her alive," Sunny said. "She was lost in those woods with Buddy."

"What wood? Who is Buddy?" Brad Schilling's face creased with anxiety.

"Are you sure?" Ash watched as Sunny slowly nodded, her hands clenched tightly in her lap. "Do you know where he took her after they left the house we were at yesterday?"

"Were you able to get a personal item from the family?" she asked Brad.

He brought a small plastic bag out of his jacket pocket. "I did. Her mother said…"

"Don't coach me." Sunny's voice was uncharacteristically sharp. "Sorry," she said, when Schilling pulled the bag away. "I'm getting strong signals that you could skew whatever information I get." She held out her hand.

Schilling gave her the bag.

Sunny walked into the bed alcove without looking at either man and closed the curtain.

"This is weirder than that tea," Schilling whispered.

"Tell me about it." Ash already had mixed feelings about Schilling involving Sunny in this new case. Sunny hadn't volunteered to go down the embankment to stand beside the river. She hadn't offered to hold the earring again, which Ash continued to carry around in one of his pockets. He wondered whether what he felt was more akin to disappointment and jealousy than relief for the family of the missing girl. He couldn't stay at the table. He didn't want any more green tea. He got up and started a pot of coffee.

Schilling cleared his throat. "I should apologize for involving Sunny in this other case, Ash. But there's a small chance this kid could still be alive. I know I sound callous…" He stopped speaking.

Ash turned and leaned back against the sink. Anguish was plainly visible on the Salem detective's face. Ash felt Brad Schilling's concern showed the extent of his commitment to finding closure for this other family. Perhaps the urgency stemmed from his inability to do the same for Ash, Caroline, Maxine and Katie. Being a homicide detective was the kind of hell Ash hadn't wanted for himself. He'd seen enough emotion-ally-distraught victims during his years working on robberies.

"I understand," he told Schilling. "I don't have to like it, but I get the urgency and the fact you have to prioritize."

"Thanks." Schilling ran a hand over his face. "I couldn't sleep last night. I don't know how to tell my superiors I'm now working with a psychic as well as you. They've already ordered me more than once to drop any further investigation into your daughter's death and move on. I'm reminded we've got plenty of other cases to be solved. Some date back years. The new technologies have brought a lot of unsolved crimes to the forefront again. But they all have to wait right now. The Bigelow kid's abduction is top priority."

"As it has to be." Ash said the words, but his heart wasn't in them. "I'll try to remember that. But you have to remember that I firmly believe my child was murdered, and if Sunny was right when she said Amy's abductor took the wrong child, then another child is in danger right now, and that child could be my other daughter."

The curtain around the bed alcove drew back and Sunny rejoined them at the table. She handed Schilling the plastic bag. "I'm sorry," she said. "I got nothing."

CHAPTER THIRTY-ONE

THE FOLLOWING MONDAY, with the shop closed for the day, Sunny had slept late. As she waited for her coffee to brew, she wondered whether she really had the energy to take a hike through Silver Falls State Park in nearby Silverton. A relaxing day reading a novel sounded far more appealing. Then Ash called.

"Katie's outgrown all her clothes, and Maxine's taking her shopping this morning," he said. They'll have lunch afterwards, and then visit Caro."

"That'll be nice for all of them," Sunny said. "So you've got the day to yourself?"

"Yeah. Kind of." He paused.

She waited, wondering what he was going to say.

"A coworker at PPB is having surgery and asked if I could dog-sit his Lab-mix for a couple of weeks. Jake's a good-natured, laid back kind of dog. Katie's been pressuring me to get a rescue. I thought this would be a good way to see if we're ready for a pet."

Sunny poured her coffee. "That's a good plan. Like trying on new shoes, but not having to wear them out of the store until you're sure you really want them." She added creamer and one spoonful of brown sugar.

"That's a good analogy. I wondered if you'd like to take a walk with us before I pick up Katie," he said. "I want Jake to get comfortable with me first."

"Where were you planning to go?" Sunny wasn't sure Ash wanted to take the dog anywhere he'd end up needing a bath.

"Bush's Pasture Park shouldn't be crowded, but the trail can get muddy around the ball fields and in the woods," he said.

Sunny hadn't gone near Bush's Pasture Park since Tina's death. Her stomach knotted at the thought of it. "How about Riverfront Park?" she said before she thought about Ash's connection with it.

"That's an idea," he said after a moment. "The trail over the bridge is paved, and it's a couple of miles to and from Minto Brown Island."

"I don't want to go to Bush's because that's where Tina died. But I shouldn't have suggested Riverfront because of Amy." Sunny took her coffee to the dining table and sat.

"It's okay. Not your fault. We're both still trying to cope with loss," Ash responded. "I used to go to Riverfront Park every week so I could stand on the embankment close to where Amy drowned. It became an obsession that wasn't doing me any good. I had a few sessions with a grief counselor. He recommended I walk around the park itself and try to see the pleasure it gave other visitors. He went with me the first couple of times. I even got comfortable watching children ride the carousel, although I don't know if I could ever take Katie there again."

"Oh, Ash, that must have been so difficult for you." Sunny could only imagine. She had avoided driving on Mission so she wouldn't pass the intersection with High Street.

"Look, I know it's asking a lot, but after you were able to help Brad with his case, I'd really like you to go down the embankment with me and see if you feel any connection."

Sunny took a sip of her coffee. It tasted lukewarm and bitter. She stirred it vigorously and popped it in the microwave. "I've been thinking about that, too," she said as she waited for the coffee to reheat. "You and Schilling tricked me the other day, not telling me where we were going or why. You both gave me a test, like I'm a faker."

"I know. I apologize…"

"Ash, be quiet and let me finish." The microwave dinged. Sunny took out her steaming coffee. "Being able to give Brad useful information not only proved I had psychic abilities to a couple of skeptical cops, it gave *me* proof. This gift is real. New, and completely unexpected, but real."

"You've made me into a believer," Ash interjected. "Brad, too. You know that. You not only have Armenta's support, you now have ours, too."

"Which is such a relief, you have no idea." Sunny took a tentative sip of her coffee and found it delicious. "I think from this day forward I'd better start acting like this extra sense, or whatever it should be called, is an asset. I've been hiding from it because it frightens me, but I'm going to work through that, so I can be more help to you. Bring the earring and find out where we can get Jake groomed afterward. You can buy me lunch while he's getting bathed." She took another, bigger sip of coffee.

"Thank you." Ash's voice had a slight instability around the edges.

Sunny wondered whether he had been keeping a lot of emotion bottled up inside, and her heart ached for him. "What time do you want to pick me up?" she asked.

"Ten-thirty?"

"Sounds good." She took out a bowl and a box of cereal for a quick breakfast.

"Thanks, Sunny." He hung up.

CHAPTER THIRTY-TWO

THE EMBANKMENT at Riverfront Park was steep and difficult to negotiate. Sunny wondered how an abductor could have lured Amy down to the water or carried her without dropping her. Surely she'd have been screaming and kicking, unless she was unconscious.

"Are you okay?" Ash asked.

He seemed to be doing fine holding her with one hand and Jake's leash with the other. Mouth open and tongue lolling out, the dog enthusiastically trotted down the slope like he couldn't wait to swim in the Willamette.

"Hi, Mr. Haines," a man called.

Ash managed to stop their precipitous slip and slide. He looked toward a small camp of tents and tarps grouped on a slightly more level part of the embankment. "Hi, Pete."

"Haven't seen you around here in a couple of weeks," Pete said.

Sunny decided she wasn't going to fall if she turned to see who was speaking. The man walking toward them wore a fairly new coat, gloves and a bright blue hat. He didn't look like most of the homeless frequenting the downtown Salem area.

"I haven't been able to come," Ash said. "Too much going on."

"I've been wanting to thank you for the coat and stuff." Pete pointed to his jacket. "First time I've been warm and dry in a long time."

"You're welcome." Ash nodded. "Any strangers down here lately?"

"A couple." Pete slithered closer. "One wanted to join our camp, but we told him to go somewhere else. We've had trouble before with stealing."

"Who else came?" Ash asked.

"The other detective," Pete said. "Asking questions like, you know, you ask when you visit. He looked around with a flashlight, but I didn't see him pick up anything."

"Thanks again." Ash handed Jake's leash to Sunny. "I'm going to get rid of them for a while," he whispered.

Sunny watched him walk over to Pete and take an envelope out of his pocket. A few words were exchanged. Pete looked toward the encampment, where two other men sat on old lawn chairs. Ash gestured. Pete shrugged, then nodded. He went back to his companions. They argued between themselves while Ash made his way back to Sunny and Jake, then the two men joined Pete and they left.

"Where are they going?" Sunny asked.

"To eat," Ash said. "I gave Pete money and a watch. He agreed they'd all keep away from here for thirty minutes. They won't leave their camp unattended any longer than that. A lot of pilfering goes on, and more campers know they're down here since Amy's death." He took back Jake's leash. The dog wagged his long black tail.

"Then we'd better get to it," Sunny said. She took several steps, began to slide, and grabbed a sapling, but it slithered through her fingers like it was greased with oil. "Oh, no." She flailed her arms as she slid toward the water.

Ash grabbed her. "I've had a lot of practice down here. Have you ever skied?"

"No." She held tightly onto him as she tried to keep her footing.

"You need to stay side-on to the slope," he told her. "And don't let go of me again. The water's only five feet deep here, but that's deep enough to give you a good soaking."

After Sunny followed his instructions, she felt less likely to fall into the river. When they arrived at a more level area, she stopped and let go of his arm. "You'd better give me that earring now," she said.

Ash slowly took his arm away. "Are you sure you're not going to fall?"

Sunny wished she could dig her toes into the bank. Her ankles hurt from trying to maintain her balance. "This is probably as good as it's going to get." She held out her hand. "Let's get this over with, before Pete and his friends come back."

Ash took the little bag out of his coat pocket and handed it to her. Feeling nothing, she took the earring out of the bag, held it tightly in her palm and closed her eyes. Water lapped; a cool breeze touched her cheeks. Sunny tried first to concentrate on the earring, then when that failed to produce any results, clear her mind. The pain in her ankles radiated to her calves. A sense of profound sadness enveloped her. She abandoned her meditation.

"I'm sorry, Ash," she told him. "Neither of us will gain anything from standing here. You need to stop coming down to the water. It's only prolonging your sadness. What I'm feeling is you, grieving for your daughter."

CHAPTER THIRTY-THREE

ASH BROUGHT them along the shoreline to the Willamette Queen's dock, an easier route except for the mud. There he stopped to look at the peacefully flowing river.

"This is the first time I've been back here in a couple of weeks," he told Sunny. "I haven't visited Amy's grave, either. I felt guilty about that when we arrived." He turned to face her. "What you said, about letting go of that routine, I realize now that isn't abandoning Amy. Life will never be the same without her, but if she was old enough to understand, she would tell me I have to go forward, if not for my own sake, then for Katie's. Katie still has a full life to live, and it should be a happy one, not overshadowed by her sister's death."

Sunny saw the pain in his eyes. The deep lines around his mouth. The ache in her chest felt like a heavy weight. "We all have to move on," she said. "It doesn't mean we're forgetting our loved ones. It means we're learning to cope with their loss. I'm coming to understand that, too. Tina wouldn't want me to stay in a vacuum, and neither would Amy want that for you. We'll always carry them with us in our memories, and we'll always remember the joy they brought into our lives."

"That's pretty profound." A smile took the sadness from his face. "Wonderfully so."

He took her hand in his, warmth and strength flowing from him. Sunny suddenly felt awkward. "Come on," she said. "Jake needs his walk."

The dog's ears pricked. He barked once. Ash's smile widened. "Okay, boy, you can pull us up the steps. There are a lot of them."

Jake lunged. They ascended so rapidly, Sunny left her breath behind halfway to the top. Ash released her when they arrived on the footpath. They both took a few moments to recover before walking past the building housing the Carousel, around the huge EcoEarth Globe, which seemed to harbor a wide variety of enticing scents for Jake to explore, then across the white suspension bridge separating the park from a causeway linking it with Minto Brown Island. Finally, Jake stopped to check out the vegetation at the edge of the trail, and both Sunny and Ash sank onto a bench to rest.

"More exercise than I've had in far too long," he said, stretching out his long legs. "Jake'll have me back in shape or kill me by the time his owner's ready for him to go home."

"I've neglected my exercise routine since moving to Salem, too." Sunny was appalled at how quickly she had tired. "I've got to join a gym."

"That makes two of us." Ash grimaced, like he didn't find that a pleasant thought.

A couple of dog-walkers passed by, greeting Ash, Sunny and Jake as though they were all members of an exclusive club.

"Are you going to give up trying to help me find answers to Amy's abduction and death?" he asked after several cyclists sped past them, followed by a small group of runners.

"No, of course not, but going back to where it happened wasn't helpful, even with that earring," she said.

Ash sighed. "I was so hopeful." He got up. "Let's go back. Jake's got a date with the groomer, and while he's getting his TLC, my car needs detailing. There's a Mexican restaurant close-by. We can rest and eat lunch."

Disappointment radiated from Ash. Sunny took his arm as they retraced their steps. Perhaps, she thought, her job was over. She felt the strength of Ash's forearm beneath her fingers, and watched Jake happily trotting along beside them, ears flopping rhythmically. The day almost seemed normal. To anyone passing by, they must appear to be a couple walking their dog. Appearances, Sunny thought, could be very deceiving.

As they approached the Peter Courtney bridge, Ash's cell rang. It was Brad Schilling, updating them on the Bigelow case. With no one else around, Ash put him on speaker-phone.

"The next-door neighbor confirmed pretty much everything Sunny said," Brad told them. "We brought in a cadaver dog. It alerted in the back yard. A team's digging right now. While I wait, I had to call you. Sunny, your help has been invaluable. I want to talk to you both about this more...one minute..." He paused. "They're telling me to get back outside. I'll be in touch later."

Ash put his phone back in his coat pocket. "Damn," he said softly. "Sounds like the Bigelow family's going to get their child back, but not how they and everyone else involved with this case, would have wanted."

Sunny fought back tears. "I feel so conflicted. Such a terrible thing... their waiting may be over, but their grieving..." She couldn't finish her thought. "I wish I could get answers for you."

"You can't control this gift," Ash interrupted. "I understand that. If you could, then you would have given me the answers I need." He took her hand and squeezed it lightly. "Thank you for all you've tried to do for me, and for what it looks like you've done for the Bigelow family."

Jake barked and wagged his tail.

"I agree," Ash told him. "If we don't get a move on, you'll miss your appointment, and I'll have to bathe you in my tub, which will lead to me cleaning the entire bathroom as well. Not happening."

He dropped Sunny's hand but offered his arm, which she gladly took. They walked briskly back to the Range Rover.

"Can Katie and I still come to the shop?" he asked. "I'd like to continue as your handyman, and Katie loves to visit Armenta."

"Of course. But we should work out some sort of a payment plan for your services."

"All the cookies we can eat?"

"Deal."

She wanted to give him a hug, but she didn't feel either of them would be comfortable with that degree of closeness.

CHAPTER THIRTY-FOUR

ARMENTA HAD an enthralled couple in her arbor. Every time she gave a prediction, muffled *oohs* and *aahs* floated over to the counter.

Sunny tapped Watcher on his talons. "More satisfied customers," she whispered. Watcher's steely gaze remained fixed on a display of dreamcatchers. "Am I being too flippant for you?" she asked, raising her eyebrows and wiggling them. She knew she should be doing something constructive, like dusting merchandise, but that day, she didn't feel productive. She stifled a yawn and checked her watch: 3:00 PM on a Wednesday, traditionally their slowest day, and both cold and rainy. One of those outlier days in spring when the Pacific Northwest demonstrated that summer wasn't as close as the calendar indicated.

Katie skipped up to the counter. She had returned to school the week before after wearing her parents down with complaints of being bored and lonely. That afternoon, a parent/teacher conference had conflicted with Caroline's last Physical Therapy appointment. Katie had begged Ash to leave her with Sunny and Armenta.

Although Caroline's injuries had healed well, she still suffered from recurrent back pain that had delayed her return to work. Katie said her mother was no fun to live with, and wished the custody arrangements were reversed. Her father's home was far more appealing, especially since Jake the dog's stay had been extended due to his owner's continued health issues.

"There's a man in the back of the shop who wants to buy the big buddha," Katie told Sunny. "I told him I would get you."

"The big one?" Sunny whispered. "Did he look at the price?"

"Better than that. I *told* him." Katie smiled her sage smile.

"You're a great saleswoman," Sunny told her. "Isn't she, Watcher?" She tapped his talons again.

"I know; it comes naturally." Katie giggled. "Watcher and I can take care of the register until you get back."

Sunny took a quick look at the arbor, where Armenta's clients were nodding profusely. The woman picked up her purse from the floor. "I don't doubt you can handle the register," she told Katie in an undertone, "but if you do need help, Armenta will be available in a couple of minutes."

As Katie clambered onto the stool they kept behind the counter to put her at face-level with the customers, Sunny walked briskly to the very back corner of the shop. A tall, thin man dressed in a black coat stood contemplating the large statue.

"I understand you'd like to purchase the medicine buddha?" she asked.

He turned slowly and gave her a smile that only lifted the upper left corner of his mouth. His sallow complexion and hollowed cheeks brought the word 'cadaverous' to Sunny's mind. But apart from having some sort of facial paralysis and being a good 20-30 pounds under-weight, he looked well-to-do. Beneath the heavy woolen coat, he wore a shirt with a crisp white collar and a black tie. A slight odor of mothballs indicated the coat had recently been packed away, either in a trunk or a closet, which seemed strange. Any long-term resident would have transitioned to a raincoat before Memorial Day had come and gone.

Perhaps he had only recently come to Oregon, she told herself. Maybe he was decorating a new home for himself or someone else. Otherwise, why would he want a big, heavy medicine buddha? Wouldn't he want, like anyone else who came into the shop, the jolly laughing buddha with the fat stomach people loved to rub for luck? She looked at his sallow complexion again. Perhaps he really did need a medicine buddha after all.

"Your little salesgirl already gave me the price," he said. "I wondered if that was firm, or you would be willing to entertain a slight discount?"

His voice sounded velvety. It tried to wrap itself around Sunny, but she resisted. She wondered how often he had used its soft qualities to get his way.

"How slight?" she countered. "Our prices are usually firm."

"But you also don't usually have customers who are willing to pay three hundred dollars for a buddha that looks like it hasn't moved from this spot in a long while, do you?" That uneven smile again.

"That's a two-hundred-dollar discount," Sunny said. "That's too low."

"Hmm…" The man tapped his front teeth with his left index finger. The nail was long and well-manicured. A ring glinted. A large black stone topped by a white skull.

Onyx, Sunny thought. She wondered what stone had been used to form the skull. The mothball fragrance was becoming overpowering. She stifled a sneeze.

"I would be willing to pay the full price if you can deliver it at no charge," the man said. "It is heavy and difficult for me to transport. You see, I have a problem with my spine." He waved one hand in the direction of his back.

Sunny wondered whether she could ask Winston the glazier to deliver the buddha once he got off work. Even if she had to pay him $50, she'd still come out ahead. Winston had become a fairly regular visitor to the shop, and had made a couple of deliveries for them after-hours. Armenta said he didn't mind doing them favors because he liked the free lunches she made for him, but Sunny thought he was shy and working up to asking her out on a date.

Whatever the reason, she'd never asked him to lift heavy merchandise like the statue. Prior deliveries had been for a local little theatre company. They bought costumes and props for some of their productions, and none of them ever seemed to have a vehicle large enough to accommodate the load once the boxes had been packed.

"Let me see what I can do," she said. "I have to make a call. We don't usually deliver."

"You should offer that service. Some of your merchandise is cumbersome to transport," the man said.

He spoke like he came from a different era, or perhaps he was from another country, Sunny mused as she walked back to the counter. She told the receptionist at Capitol Glass she needed an estimate on changing out a friend's window, and the friend lived in Winston's service area. It was a little white lie she hoped wouldn't backfire, but she didn't want Winston to get into trouble for taking personal calls during his workday. He never seemed to have his own cell phone. Sunny felt like telling him that if Katie could have a burner phone, surely he could get a cheap pre-paid, too.

Katie returned to the back of the shop. Sunny knew the customer couldn't abscond with the heavy buddha under his coat, but there was plenty of other merchandise he could stuff into his pockets. Katie had proved to be an excellent floor-walker. She had been coming to the shop at least two afternoons a week, while Ash pursued what always turned out to be dead-end leads from dubious tips left at an online site dedicated to Amy's case.

Despite Sunny's invaluable assistance in the Bigelow case, the perpetrator's capture had been publicized as the result of stellar investigative police work and the invaluable assistance of the elderly neighbor. The previous week, after an expensive and fruitless search of a pond on the outskirts of Salem, Ash decided he was done with following up on bogus tips.

Armenta brought her middle-aged clients to the counter. She sold them two prayer bracelets and an amulet to be placed under the marital bed "to bring a speedy result to their desire for a child." Sunny hoped they wouldn't try to sue the shop if a miracle didn't happen, but the couple readily paid for everything and even took away a crystal statue of a fairy that had been lingering in a display for months.

"Why does it smell like mothballs in here?" Armenta whispered, after she waved the couple out the door. "Is it that man? Why has he been hanging around the back of the shop for the last thirty minutes?"

The phone rang before Sunny could give Armenta the good news that she may have just sold the largest and most expensive item in the shop. She hoped Winston was returning her call and held up a finger for Armenta to hold her thoughts. Winston cheerfully agreed to bring his pickup over to transport the buddha. He had a friend who could help, and yes, they could take care of the delivery for $30 each, as long as it was local. That would pay for pizza and a couple of beers before their pool tournament. He got off at 4:00 PM.

Sunny could have kicked herself. She had no idea where the customer lived.

"I'll find out." Armenta sailed off, her long garments trailing behind her.

She was back in less than a minute. "Oak Grove," she said, wrinkling her nose. "But I don't know if those boys *should* deliver."

"I know the area," Winston said when Sunny told him. "Out in the country, on the way to McMinnville. It won't take us long."

The customer had followed Armenta.

"They can pick it up from here around five o'clock," Sunny told him.

"Very agreeable." Again, he gave that disjointed smile. He took out a business card and slid it across the counter. "All they will need."

Sunny saw his name was Vincente Valderos. His address and phone number were printed below the title 'Antiques and Curiosities Dealer.' He pulled out a credit card and laid that on the counter.

Sunny confirmed the details with Winston, rang up the sale and asked Valderos to complete the transaction on the pad. "I never seem to adjust to this way of doing business," he said. "It was so much more personal when one had to sign in ink."

"You can't stop the march of progress," Armenta commented. She was leaning on the counter where the amulets lay in rows. "Can we interest you in anything else?"

He turned toward her, noticed Watcher and stepped back so quickly, he bumped into Katie, who had been watching him with great interest.

"That's our protector," Katie said. "His name is Watcher."

"I see." Mr. Valderos nodded. "Quite daunting, isn't he?"

Sunny noticed a fine sheen of sweat covering the man's face. The credit card hadn't been declined, so his apparent discomfort wasn't due to a lack of funds. Perhaps he was too hot in his coat or the odor of moth-balls was getting to him, too.

"Would you like a glass of water?" she asked.

His eyes widened momentarily, and Sunny noticed his pupils were mere pinpricks. "No." He sounded affronted. "Thank you," he added. "You are very kind, Ms. Kingston."

"You know my name." Sunny was surprised. She'd slipped into Tina's shoes without fanfare.

"I do." He returned his credit card to a jacket pocket.

Watcher was looking over his shoulder at Mr. Valderos. Sunny glanced at the gryphon's wings, which seemed to have lengthened. When she looked back up, Watcher had turned to completely face Mr. Valderos, who was intently buttoning his overcoat. He doffed his hat to Armenta, Katie, and then Sunny. Not once did he look at the gryphon.

How could he *not* look? Sunny wondered. People might be surprised, even shocked by Watcher's stony presence on the counter, but they never ignored him.

"I will expect the delivery at, say, six o'clock?" Mr. Valderos backed toward the door. Somehow, he didn't run into anything behind him. Sunny thought that a little odd in the cluttered shop, like he had some sort of an internal back-up camera.

"Sounds about right," she said, forcing a smile. "Thank you for your business."

"I will be back," he said. "There are other things here that interest me."

Sunny didn't like the sound of that. "Come here, Katie," she said, beckoning. "I'd like you to help Armenta rearrange the amulets."

"Ooh, okay." Katie scampered behind the counter. "I've always wanted to touch them."

"We'll have to find one for you to wear." Armenta looked at Sunny over Katie's head, and her gaze was troubled.

The little bell over the front door tinkled. When Sunny looked, Vincente Valderos was nowhere to be seen.

CHAPTER THIRTY-FIVE

WHEN ASH ARRIVED to pick up Katie, he heard all about the big-ticket sale and the strange customer. He took a sip of the Darjeeling Armenta had poured for him, then held up Vincente Valderos's business card between two fingers. "So, you want me to do a background check on this guy?"

Sunny nodded, her mouth filled with the last bite of the peanut butter and banana sandwich she had shared with Katie. She swallowed, but the peanut butter refused to go down, and she had to encourage it with a sip of tea.

Armenta placed a large oatmeal raisin cookie on the plate next to Ash's cup. "I made Winston and his friend wear amulets and swear they wouldn't take them off until they left the client's house," she said.

The corner of Ash's mouth quirked. "Since you two are obviously freaked out, did you also ask them to call after they made the delivery?" He picked up the cookie and bit into it.

Sunny watched his energetic munching suspiciously. She wondered if it had more to do with controlling a desire to laugh than satisfying a sugar craving. "I hope you're not trying to make light of this," she said, not attempting to hide the rebuke in her tone.

"I'm learning not to make light of anything associated with you two or this shop," Ash reassured her. He pointed toward his cup. "You make really good tea, Armenta. I never was a fan before. Coffee all the way."

"You also drank a lot of bourbon," Sunny muttered.

"I heard that." He jerked his head in his daughter's direction and gave Sunny a warning look.

"I did tell them to call," Armenta said.

The shop phone rang. Armenta picked up the extension and gave the usual greeting about the shop being the best in Salem for all things metaphysical. Then she listened for a moment.

"I see," she said. "Well, you'd better come here and tell us all about it. I have cookies." She paused again, listening. "Oatmeal raisin or chocolate chip," she told the caller. "And soda. I know you don't like milk or tea, Winston." She paused again. "Thirty minutes? Come to the delivery door and ring the bell."

"Where's the delivery door?" Ash looked around. "I only see the side door that goes into the alley."

"It's on the other side of the shop." Sunny took her empty plate to the sink.

"We needed a ramp," Armenta told him. "Tina didn't want goods coming through her apartment. There wouldn't have been room to bring something as big as the buddha through here, either."

"Makes sense." Ash nodded. "But it's too well disguised, and you should have an exit sign there, in case of fire."

"That's what the fire marshal said." Armenta shrugged. "Tina hadn't gotten around to it."

"I'd better take care of that, then." Sunny felt overwhelmed at the prospect of something else that needed to be done. *More* expense. But then she reminded herself they had not only gotten the enormous buddha off the inventory list, but she had $440 to hopefully cover the cost of the sign.

"You'd better have an alarm installed for that door, too," Ash said. "The downside of showing customers where the back door is will be giving them a second way to get out of the shop without paying for their purchases."

Sunny groaned. "You really did work in the robbery division, didn't you?"

Ash grinned. "I really did."

"I can see I'll need to sell a lot more big-ticket items if you stay around here much longer, making suggestions to improve security." She grudgingly returned his smile. "I know you're trying to make us safer as well as protecting the merchandise."

"You'd better believe it." Ash looked at his watch. "Katie, time to pack up your stuff. We need to get home. You can take a bath while I make supper."

"Okay, Daddy." She dutifully began loading her schoolwork into her backpack.

Ash stood up. "I'll check into this guy," he promised, placing the business card in a jacket pocket. "I'll be back tomorrow to take a look at your delivery door. Probably around lunchtime. I'll make a few calls in the morning." He helped Katie zip up her jacket before putting on his raincoat.

"Thanks, Ash." Sunny followed them to the front door.

"Make sure you lock up well," he told her. "Especially since those guys are using the delivery door."

"I will." Sunny held the front door open. "See you tomorrow."

Katie reached up on tiptoes. "Kiss," she said.

Sunny bent down and felt soft lips on her cheek.

"'Bye, Sunny," Katie said.

"'Bye, Katie."

Sunny noticed Ash's smile had reached his eyes. Something she hadn't seen before. Her heart contracted. "Take care, you two." She added a silent wish for their continued safety.

"We will." Ash took Katie's backpack and offered her his hand.

Katie took it. "What's for supper, Daddy?"

"A surprise." He shook his head when she frowned. "Don't worry. It'll be a good one."

Sunny wondered whether he'd serve tomato soup and grilled cheese or fried egg sandwiches. Katie had told her those were her father's two meal choices for nights they got home close to her bath-time. Other evenings, he'd make macaroni and cheese from a box or order pizza. She felt glad Katie had finally returned to school, where she was sure of a meal that included the four food groups.

After she waved goodbye and locked the door, she took a moment to look over the state of the shop. Not *too* untidy, she told herself. If she started cleaning up and reorganizing, she would have to stop for Winston's report on the delivery, and she didn't want to miss one word of that. She sneaked a look at Watcher. Head down, he appeared to be sleeping. If he was off-duty, then everything must be okay.

She walked back through the shop and turned off the light panel before joining Armenta at the sink. Armenta washed, and Sunny made short work of drying. The delivery door's bell rang.

"I'll go." Armenta trotted off.

Sunny brought two sodas from the refrigerator to join the waiting tin of cookies already on the table with plates and paper napkins.

"You wouldn't believe what we saw," Winston announced as he followed Armenta into the apartment. "Would they, Ben?" he asked his friend.

"Oh, hell no," Ben said. "It was like a friggin' movie set in there...for a horror show." He grinned. "It was goddamned awesome."

CHAPTER THIRTY-SIX

"We drove through a vineyard," Winston said. "Up to a big pair of gates with a security system. I had to say who we were, and there was a camera, too. The gates opened, and we drove up a hill to the house."

"Which was a mansion," Ben interjected. He took a swig from his soda. "Like one you'd see on TV, in a horror movie."

Sunny wondered how many times he was going to emphasize the horror movie concept. "Turrets?" she suggested.

"Nah. Lots of leaded windows and chimneys," Winston said. "Those ornate chimneys that you see…"

"…in horror movies." Ben took another cookie.

"Those leaded windows," Winston said. "We don't see those often, anymore. People want solid panes of glass. Easier to clean."

Sunny wanted to hear more about the interior of the house and its owner. "So, did he have a butler, or did Mr. Valderos open the door himself?"

"Double doors," Ben said around a mouthful of cookie. "And he opened them wide. Had to. Otherwise we couldn't have gotten the statue inside."

"He wanted it in the front hallway," Winston said. "I don't know why. It took up a lot of space. We had to move a couple of chairs and a table to put it against the wall."

"What was the house like inside?" Sunny asked.

"The other rooms were really dark, like all the curtains were pulled across the windows, except for one. That had a weird green light coming out of it."

"The staircase was huge." Ben waved his cookie, as though to impress his audience with the sheer size of what he had seen. "Halfway up, it split in two. But both sides were completely dark at the top."

"Interesting," Armenta said. She brought two more sodas from the refrigerator. "Did he have any antiques that you could see? His card said he's an antique dealer."

Sunny wondered whether either Winston or Ben would know an antique if they saw one, but Winston, working as a glazier, at least knew about leaded windows.

Winston shrugged. "The chairs and table were big and heavy. They had to be old. I've seen stuff like that in old people's houses when we put in new windows. We didn't hang out and chat, if that's what you're asking, and he definitely didn't encourage us to look around. He thanked us for coming and gave us both good tips on the way out. He'd already closed the doors before we got off the porch."

"I saw someone watching us from upstairs when we arrived," Ben said. He put down the cookie, and his eyes lost their sparkle of excitement. "I can't seem to remember what that person looked like." He frowned. "My memory of the inside of that house is fading, which is really weird." He looked at Winston. "Is that happening to you, too?"

Winston's brow wrinkled with concentration. He rubbed a hand over his chin. "I remember everything about the drive up to the house and Mr. Valderos opening the doors and telling us where to put the buddha. But except for that green light, I can't seem to remember anything else clearly until we were back in the truck."

Sunny saw the confusion on his face. She looked over his head and didn't like what she saw when she caught Armenta's eye.

"Good thing you both wore your amulets," Armenta said. "Now, I think you'd better keep them on for a while. Don't take them off for any reason until I tell you it's okay to do so."

Ben stopped munching the last cookie. "You want us to wear these to bed? When we take a shower, and ..."

"Yes, Ben. Yes to all of it," Armenta interrupted. "Don't ask questions," she added, when Ben opened his mouth to comment further. "Be glad you got a big tip. Put it into a savings account. Don't spend it on anything right now."

"You're making me think I shouldn't have asked them to make that delivery," Sunny said.

Armenta made some dismissive little noise partway between a snort and a throat-clearing. "They'll be fine." She looked at the two young men, both staring up at her like she had taken their birthdays away. "I'll tell you when you can spend the money," she said. *"We'll* tell you," she corrected. "We want to make sure it's not counterfeit or anything."

"Oh." Both men looked relieved. "But why do you want us to wear these amulets all the time?" Winston asked.

"Don't question me on that."

The look Armenta gave them made Sunny feel very glad it wasn't directed at her. She watched them shrink back. Ben's cookie dropped onto the table. Armenta poured two small cups of green tea that Sunny didn't remember her brewing.

Armenta set the cups in front of Winston and Ben. "Drink," she commanded.

"I don't like tea," Ben protested. "Especially something this green."

"Drink it," Winston said, picking up his cup. "I've gotta take the truck back. My boss said it was okay for me to borrow it, but I don't want him seeing me bringing it into the yard at nine o'clock when he reviews the security footage tomorrow. He'll wonder what I was doing with it. I told him it was a local delivery for a friend." He drank the tea in one gulp and then shuddered. "Ugh."

Ben still looked mutinous, but he picked up his cup, gave it a disapproving look, and then followed his friend's example. He put the cup down. "That's the worst-tasting thing I've ever had in my life."

"I'll let you out the back door," Armenta told them. "You'll want to get the truck back to the yard and go home."

"Yes." Winston stood up.

"You know what to do," Armenta said.

Ben nodded. "Take back the truck and go home."

"Wear the amulets until you tell us to take them off." Winston drew his from under his sweatshirt and fingered it.

"Don't spend the money yet," Ben added.

They followed Armenta out of the apartment. Sunny watched, fascinated. They looked like sleepwalkers. She went over to the table.

"Don't drink that," Armenta called.

Sunny took the lid off the pot. Green tea started swirling. She hurriedly replaced the lid and left the pot and the two empty cups on the table. She washed the empty cookie tin and the plates while she wondered what was in that green tea.

CHAPTER THIRTY-SEVEN

WHEN SUNNY TURNED on the overhead lights the following morning, she saw Ash standing outside. She deactivated the alarm and unbolted the door.

He held up a large paper bag. "Bagels, cream cheese and lox," he announced. "There's also a donut for Armenta, and one to hold for Katie after school."

"Thank you." Sunny took the bag and opened the top. Tempting aromas of warm bagels floated out.

"I remembered no onion or garlic," he said. "Which cut out the everything bagel you really like."

"Sadly." She gave him a mock pout. "Can't repel the customers with bad breath that can't be tamed by mouthwash."

"Maybe I should have brought garlic to hang around everyone's necks, though," Ash said as he followed her through the shop toward the smell of fresh coffee. "I found several postings about your big purchaser last night." He pulled back the curtain and motioned her to go ahead of him into the apartment. "A couple included publicity shots from various gallery events or auctions. That's one creepy looking dude." He waved at Armenta, seated at the table with a cup of tea. "Good morning. I brought you a raspberry-filled donut."

198

"Good morning, Ash." Armenta watched Sunny pull a smaller bag from inside the big one and place it in front of her. "Have a seat, and thank you." She opened the bag, and her long nose practically disappeared inside it before she pulled out the donut.

"Valderos *is* creepy." Sunny set the bagels, cream cheese and lox on the table. "Coffee?" she asked, lifting the full carafe.

"Please." Ash watched her pour him a mug and place it in front of him. "Those eyes of his…I swear he looked like he was on some heavy drugs. But the news reports definitely didn't make him sound like an addict." He paused and rubbed his chin. "He'd have to be a really high-functioning one," he continued, as though he'd stopped sitting on the fence and made a decision about Valderos's habits. "He deals only in high-end merchandise, and his clients swear by him. Not just with testimonials. Interviews with news media. Never any with him. Always someone else talking about how he found what they had been searching for unsuccessfully, like he'd conjured it up." Ash poured creamer into his coffee.

"He can conjure all he wants with that buddha," Sunny said. She brought plates, knives and napkins to the table. "It's been hanging around here for a long time, hasn't it?" she asked Armenta.

Armenta swallowed a bite of her donut. "Two years. Tina said she took it on consignment but the owner died and the family didn't want it back, so here it stayed, waiting for the right buyer."

"Any buyer." Sunny looked at the bagels. "Which one do you want?" she asked Ash. "You brought them; you get to choose first."

He smiled. "You know I bought the pumpernickel for you. Go ahead and take it."

"Thank you. I hope you know you're much appreciated." Sunny took hers and passed him the Asiago cheese.

Armenta had almost finished her donut. "I'll open the shop," she said. "Don't rush. You two have things to talk about." She popped the last piece into her mouth and stood. "I'll take my coffee out front." She left.

"She ate quickly." Ash spread cream cheese on his bagel and took a sliver of lox.

"She likes to read the cards before we have customers," Sunny said. "Sometimes she tells me what she found, but only if the reading was good. I told her not to tell me if the reading's bad. I still don't believe in a lot of this metaphysical stuff." She shrugged, unsure how to put her feelings into words. "But I'm not such a skeptic these days. I've seen too much, felt too much, to dismiss everything the way I used to."

She thought of Tina, warning her best friend not to push away something because it wasn't grounded. Earthbound, she'd called it. How much had Tina really known? Had she actually seen her own death?

Sunny felt goosebumps rise on her arms. "It's cold in here." She got up and turned up the dial on the wall heater.

"Valderos's credit is good," Ash said. "He looks legit. Creepy as hell, but that's not a crime unless he's up to something I didn't find. I hate not being able to access all the data I used to have at my fingertips. You want me to call PPB? Talk to a couple of my buddies?"

"No." Sunny still felt cold, but she sat back down and picked up her cup. "His card wasn't declined. Winston and his friend, Ben, didn't disappear into thin air, and they told me Valderos tipped them generously, on top of what I paid them. We'll probably never see him again, anyway."

Ash had finished his bagel. He leaned back in his chair. "What's Valderos's home like? Some place the Addams Family would be happy?"

Sunny had to smile. She enjoyed Ash's down-to-earth sense of humor. "Just about, to hear Winston and Ben talk, even though they only got as far as his entrance hall. They said that was enormous. Valderos wanted the buddha left there, even though it didn't fit in with the rest of the furniture, so maybe he's redecorating." She shrugged. "It's his home. He can put anything he wants in there." She poured herself a second cup of coffee. "Want a refill, Ash?"

"No, I'm good. I had two cups at home, bought another when I picked up the bagels, and now I drained this mug, too. Old habits die hard. It's true what's said about cops and coffee." He grinned at her when she sat back down.

"I need a lot of coffee this morning, myself." Sunny tried to suppress a yawn and failed.

"You didn't sleep well again?" His dark brows drew toward each other.

Sunny sighed. She hadn't planned to complain about her lack of quality sleep, but why try to hide it? "No, and it wasn't the moon shining through the skylight, either. I had weird dreams. Watcher was flying around the ceiling. When I woke up, I halfway expected him to still be up there."

"Are you absolutely sure you don't want me to take that gargoyle somewhere and dump him?" Ash asked. "He'd fit right in at Pioneer Cemetery. Those old Salemites would love him."

"No way." She had to laugh. "The shop wouldn't be the same without him. Since he's been on the counter, we haven't had the problems with shoplifters that we used to. A couple of guys came in yesterday, took one look at him, and left. I was glad to see them go. Covered in tats. Biker jackets. Chains. I wondered what they wanted in here. Then I decided my imagination was too vivid for my own good."

Sunny couldn't decide whether the image of Watcher flying around Pioneer Cemetery at night was more troubling than the two would-be customers who looked like they belonged in a biker gang.

"He hasn't lived in Oak Grove very long," Ash said.

Sunny left disturbing thoughts of biker gangs performing satanic rituals in the woods of Minto-Brown Island Park and pulled her concentration back to Ash. "Who hasn't?"

"Your Mr. Vincente Valderos."

"He's definitely not mine." She shuddered. "Perish the thought. How long has he been living there?"

"Two months. He'd been a resident of New York City for so long, none of my research gave the actual date he moved into a brownstone in the East Village. Anyway, he suddenly sold it and moved here. He bought an old winery with a house that had seen better days. One of the early would-be vintners had spent a lot of money renovating and enlarging it. Big ideas for destination weddings and receptions, corporate retreats, that sort of thing.

"Trouble is, that owner had no idea how to grow grapes, much less turn them into wine. He left the place in shambles after a couple of years.

By the time Valderos arrived on the scene, pigeons were roosting in the attic. Water damage all over the inside, according to a local realtor's report, but that didn't put off Mr. V. He sent in contractors and brought a vintner over from Europe. Got the winery operating and opted to repair instead of gut the house. He had a separate tasting room built at the edge of the grounds, close to the vines. He keeps the house closed to visitors. Still runs his antique business in New York, but remotely. He participates in sales online and has become something of a recluse. He's about to launch his first Pinot, according to local sources."

"If you got all that information without using any of your contacts at Portland Police Bureau, then I would hate to think what you could have found out about me," Sunny said. "You probably know the date of my last dental cleaning."

"Maybe." He started gathering up dishes to put into the sink. "I've got a meeting with Brad Schilling in thirty minutes. I'd better get going."

"Leave those dishes for me," she said. "I'll take care of them during our lunch break."

"Okay." Ash rinsed off his hands.

"There's been a new lead?" Sunny asked when he didn't elaborate.

"I doubt it, or he'd have told me over the phone." He dried his hands on a dishtowel. "I wish you'd have another vision. One that would be more helpful." He carefully draped the towel over its drying rack next to the sink. "I still worry about Katie when she's at school. And now Caro's feeling better, she wants to move to the coast. Get away from everything. She got a good offer from a realty group in Coos Bay. They sell properties all the way down to the California border and up to Florence."

Sunny was horrified. "But that'll take Katie away from you. Coos Bay's a long drive from here."

"I know." Ash pushed his chair closer to the table and leaned on the back of it. "But if it would keep Katie safer, how can I make things difficult for Caroline?"

"You can't." His pain was palpable. "Ash, I'm so sorry."

"I'd better get going." Emotion rippled through Ash's voice. "I'll take the alleyway." He unbolted the door.

"Call me or come over later if you need to," she said.

Without responding, he walked outside. Sunny took the few steps needed to get to the door before it closed behind him.

Ash turned, deep lines of worry around his mouth and eyes. "Thank you. You're a good friend."

"You, too." She forced a little smile of reassurance.

Ash walked rapidly away.

Sunny closed and bolted the door. She thought of him moving to Salem so he could be close to his daughters. Would he now have to follow Katie to Coos Bay?

"Sunny." Armenta's voice wafted in. "Can you come here?"

Sunny hoped she wasn't being called to handle a disgruntled customer. When she walked into the shop, it looked deserted. "Where are you?" she called.

"Right where the buddha used to be."

Armenta didn't sound like her usual self. Sunny hurried to join her. Armenta was holding the flashlight they usually kept behind the counter.

"I'm not so good with runes," she said. "They were Tina's forte. They're more open to interpretation than the cards, and I already got a bad reading from those. I think this is another warning."

The buddha had left an imprint on the floor. Runes were placed in the center of the indentation.

Sunny felt really disturbed at the prospect of Tina's spirit returning to the shop. She wondered if that was the reason she couldn't seem to get warmed up. She'd heard spirits left cold spots.

She wished she had read up on runes and rune magic, instead of taking Tina's pile of books off the coffee table and storing them under her bed. Maybe that's why she felt cold all the time. She shivered as a draught slithered down her back.

"So maybe my dream about Watcher flying around the ceiling wasn't really a dream after all," she said.

The hair on the back of her neck bristled, and she felt someone eyeing her. Reluctantly, she turned to see who it was.

Watcher was facing them, his wings spread.

CHAPTER THIRTY-EIGHT

Awed by the incredible sight of the gryphon's full wingspan, Sunny blinked. In that infinitesimal moment, Watcher returned to his normal pose, facing the center of the store with his wings furled.

"Sunny, can you keep focused on the runes?" Armenta sounded irritated. "Watcher's not going anywhere."

Sunny decided she must have been hallucinating again. Reluctantly, she turned her attention to Armenta and the runes. "I had something in my eye," she said.

Armenta harrumphed.

Sunny wondered whether she needed a medical appointment. A check-up. Maybe even a consult with a neurologist. She could have a brain tumor...

"I asked you to come here and look at these runes," Armenta said, her voice filled with rebuke. "What do you make of them?"

"I've got nothing," Sunny told her. "I still haven't gotten around to studying runic symbols."

Armenta grunted her disapproval.

"I'm sorry," Sunny said, not feeling sorry at all. "I've been too preoccupied with getting the shop's finances out of the red so we both have an income."

"Fair enough." Armenta nodded. "We'll move on from that discussion for now." She tapped a finger against her gold tooth before pointing a foot toward the first rune. "They're more difficult to read than the cards, and to me, less reliable. Tina studied. She cut the divination down to a fine art." She gave Sunny an unmistakably stern glance. "You *do* need to crack those books. Tina might have left notes in them. She was always scribbling things down on scraps of paper or the backs of store receipts."

"You want me to bring in the runes book she left on the table? Would that help?"

Armenta grunted again. "Not sure." Her face scrunched up in concentration. Finally, she expelled a long breath and took a step forward. "I'll give it a try. For one thing, these *are* Tina's, so I'm at least familiar with them. I don't see the velvet bag she kept them in, but these are definitely her Elder Futhark runes."

"How many were in the bag?" Sunny looked around, unsure whether she should be looking for a tiny bag or something that would carry a large amount of the little stones.

"Twenty-four," Armenta said. "Without the blank that's usually included. Tina maintained the blank should never be used. She said it muddied the waters even more." She stroked her chin, the numerous rings on her fingers glittering fiercely.

"Then the bag isn't small," Sunny said. "What color velvet?"

"It *is* fairly small, but we don't need it right now." Armenta circled the runes. "We only need to concentrate on these. Let's see." She pointed an index finger at them. "It's a five-rune cast. There are also three rune and a nine-rune casts that she used, but I remember she said this cast is more centered. Tina also only used the ones that face upward, which these do. She told me in this cast, the divination flows from the center. The two to the left show what happened in the past to influence the present. The two on the right show what can happen in the future."

Sunny stepped closer and squatted to take a better look at the small golden designs on each rune. "I wonder what problem these are honing in on? Since they're placed where the buddha was displayed, you think it has to do with our inventory or maybe the cash flow?"

"I very much doubt that." Armenta tapped her tooth again. "That's too concrete. You have to look at the abstract and try to define the meaning."

Sunny thought about telling Armenta she just seen Watcher spread his wings, but decided not to distract the seer. "Okay, so let's go really abstract. Yesterday, a very creepy man came in here and bought our biggest and most expensive piece of merchandise. Let's assume he's involved somehow with this reading."

Armenta's intense expression softened slightly. "All right."

"And let's assume I'm involved, because I'm the one having the visions."

Armenta actually smiled. "Good observations. Perhaps this reading will give you insight into your visions. Usually, runes are cast in answer to a question, but in this case, we don't know who cast them. The only visitor we've had since yesterday evening was Ash. We know he didn't come back here, but let's assume he's involved somehow."

Sunny had a horrible thought. She looked around. "Forget interpretations, Armenta. If we don't know how the runes got here, how do we know someone else wasn't in the shop?" She pulled out her cell. "I'll call the police. We must have had another break-in. The alarm system must have malfunctioned or been tampered with..."

"Calm down." Armenta took Sunny's phone out of her hand. "There wasn't a break-in. No one else has been in the shop. Well, let me correct that...no *person* has been here. As to which spirit visited, I would probably say it was Tina."

Chills crept up Sunny's back. "A ghost? In the shop last night while I was trying to sleep?"

"Not everything in this shop is an object," Armenta rebuked. "I told you things come and go here."

"I was hoping more for the 'go' part of that statement than the 'come.'" Sunny glanced around. "Are we alone right now? Can you tell?"

"You have nothing to worry about." Armenta took Sunny's hand and gave it a squeeze, her grip warm and comforting. "At least, not from anything that lives here or visits on a regular basis. If anything that isn't friendly tries to approach, then I know a lot of ways to expel it."

"So, what did you sense about Mr. Valderos?" Sunny asked.

"That man, if he even is one, isn't the topic of conversation for this moment." Armenta shook Sunny's hand before releasing it. "We're about to interpret these runes."

"Very well, but don't think we're *not* going to discuss whatever is coming and going around here and what you think about Mr. Valderos, in case yesterday wasn't the first and last time we're going to see him. If you've got doubts he's human, I need to know that, and how to deal with him."

"Those are topics for our lunch break." Armenta tapped her watch. "We open in ten minutes. Let's get on with this reading."

"Fine." Sunny would much rather pick up the runes and forget reading them, but she knew Armenta well enough to understand her assistant wouldn't allow that to happen. "Let's get this over with, then."

Armenta turned her attention back to the row of stones. "We already agreed the reading is for you. You're the one having visions, which you find troubling, so that should be what this casting is about."

"Why don't we skip over the past and present and concentrate on those two runes on the right, so I know what help I'm supposed to get?" Sunny asked. "Then we can have a quick cup of coffee before unlocking the front door."

"Oh, Sunny." Armenta rolled her eyes. "No short cuts, remember?"

"Look, I really don't need or want a reading about my past. I know I made mistakes. My present is here in this shop with you." She waved at the runes. "So why *not* focus on the future?"

"You'd better be glad one of those runes isn't *Uruz*, the wild ox, although you act like one sometimes." Armenta sounded like she wanted to gnash her teeth.

"Oh, that's just rude, Armenta."

Armenta's hand shot up like a traffic cop at an intersection. "Don't interrupt me. The past is the *Nauthjiz*, which means need. It also means delays, resistance, confusion and conflict. But it also means facing fears. Tina told me that, and it does fit your circumstances, doesn't it?"

Sunny nodded. She had to agree. A little quiver of uncertainty gained a space inside her. She looked at the rune and tried to memorize its graphic.

"The next one is closest to the present," Armenta continued. "Let's see...*Eihwaz*. The Yew tree." She gave a small smile. "That one's easy to interpret...strength, motivation. Setting your sights on a reasonable goal."

"Reasonable? I wouldn't call taking on a metaphysical shop without any suitable skills a reasonable goal," Sunny grumbled.

Armenta's reprimanding frown was extremely effective. Sunny closed her mouth, but she still felt mutinous, and a little afraid. "The future?" she asked, pointing to a rune almost resting on top of the one in the center.

"I'm not sure I remember what this one is." Armenta frowned.

"Well, you're not going to guess about my future; I'll get the book."

Sunny shot a fast look at Watcher before turning up the center aisle. Head down, he appeared to be sleeping. She pulled the book on runes from under her bed and jogged back to Armenta. They had five minutes to opening, and she could see two cars outside already.

As she walked up to her assistant, the book flopped open, as though a breeze had passed across it. She found herself looking down at the very rune they had wanted to name correctly. Trying to ignore the chills that felt like icy fingers on her spine, she read: "*Perthro*. A secret. Hidden occult abilities. Initiation. Determining your path." She took a moment to look at the interpretation if it was upside down. "The reverse is stagnation and loneliness. Well, I don't want that in my present *or* my future."

"I remember it also means fertility." Armenta grinned. "Good to know you have it."

"Don't laugh at my expense," Sunny said, but she cracked a smile, and the chills left her spine.

"Okay, that's the present. Now, on to the future." Armenta moved over to the last two runes. She pointed to the first one. "This is the help you're going to get. *Algiz*. The Elk. Protection. A shield."

"Good enough. I'm going to be protected."

"Or you will be the protector. Remember, the runes are open to interpretation."

"I'm going to interpret this as a blanket protection, then," Sunny decided. "That's enough divination. Time to open the shop." She closed the book and wondered if Watcher could use those huge wings to fly with a bag of runes in his talons or his beak. "If you'll unlock the door, I'll open the register."

She bent to scoop up the runes. "Maybe you can figure out a new display for this area, so it doesn't look like a large bare spot in the shop?"

Armenta grabbed Sunny's arm. "There's one more rune to interpret. A little further into the future."

Sunny didn't want to hear any more divinations that morning. She straightened up. "I've heard enough, and I believe the future can always be changed."

"Our actions can't always be changed, Sunny." Armenta's voice was uncharacteristically soft and gentle. "Some things are inevitable."

"Like Tina's death?" Sunny didn't try to disguise the sharpness in her voice.

Armenta didn't seem to feel the impact of Sunny's agitation. "Yes, dear, unfortunately," she said. "The domino effect. One has to fall in order to set the others in motion."

"I don't like that rule." Sunny needed to be able to target her anger. "Who decided that?"

"Sometimes, it's better not to ask too many questions," Armenta peered down at the runes again. "The lighting's so poor back here, I can't make out the last one."

"I can describe it to you." Sunny leaned forward. A slight breeze stirred her hair. The book's pages were fluttering again. She watched as the fluttering stopped at another page. It showed her the same graphic as the last rune on the floor.

"What does it say?" Armenta asked, like she already knew the book had opened to the correct page. "Read it aloud."

"Hagalaz," Sunny read, hands trembling so badly, the print kept jumping around. "A change, or a transformation." She tried to stop shak-

ing, but the more she tried, the worse the trembling became. "Be prepared for crisis. Oh, dear."

"There's more," Armenta said. "Read on."

"A...a...good outcome...can be achieved with growth of the spirit." Sunny needed to take a breath. "There's something about mystical forces."

The book fell to the floor and slammed shut.

"Well, that seems to be the end of the reading." Armenta scooped up the runes and dropped them into a pocket in her skirt. "I'm sure the bag will turn up." She walked away, leaving Sunny behind. "I'll open the front door. We've got customers waiting."

Sunny wanted to leave the book right where it was, but she didn't want a customer tripping over it, or worse, opening it. Who knew what could happen? she asked herself as she scooped up Tina's book and took it with her to the counter. Watcher glared as she passed. After she placed the book on a shelf under the register, she looked at him again. He was attentively watching Armenta greet the customers. Sunny wondered whether 9:00 AM was too early to start drinking something a lot stronger than coffee.

By noon, they were both ready for a break. Walking into the apartment ahead of Armenta, Sunny saw Tina's books neatly stacked on the coffee table instead of under her bed. On top of them sat a royal blue velvet pouch. Without asking Armenta, Sunny knew it had to be the bag containing the other 19 runes.

CHAPTER THIRTY-NINE

Brad Schilling took a sip from his cup and looked across his cluttered desk space at Ash. "Sorry for the quality of the coffee, but I'm sure you've had worse."

"Maybe, but not by much." Ash put down his cup.

Brad rubbed a hand over his chin. "Budget restrictions at work. Buying cheap and in bulk."

Ash noticed the detective had grown a goatee. Although mostly dark, it included a couple of white hairs. He wondered whether the stress of police work was responsible.

"I reviewed all the security footage again. I reinterviewed staff and volunteers from the carousel and sternwheeler. I've bought more coffee and sandwiches for the homeless in that area than some of the local organizations. I know you've been using Pete as an informal watchdog and informant, but from what you've told me, he hasn't learned about or seen anything remotely suspicious apart from the usual scum trying to steal from the campers."

Ash leaned back in his chair. "Even I am beginning to wonder whether I'm one of those deluded parents who won't accept the truth." He looked across the desk. Schilling was leaning back, too, his fingers steepled. "You want me to stop chasing a non-existent killer, don't you?" Ash said, figuring he already knew the answer.

Schilling rubbed his goatee again. Ash waited. He wasn't going to make it easy for the detective.

"When I got through interviewing those staff and volunteers, a couple of them called to complain. I got my ass chewed." Brad drummed his fingers on the desk. "Meeting Ms. Kingston...Sunny...I personally believe there could be another child in danger. But without confirmation from another source, if I want to keep my job, which I like a lot, I can't meet with you in an official capacity again about Amy's case."

"I understand," Ash said. He did. If he was in Schilling's position, he would be giving the bereaved father the same spiel.

"Look, if Sunny gets something more concrete, like a vision of the perp, call my cell immediately."

"I will." Ash stood and held out his hand. "Thanks for all you've done."

"This has to be hell." Schilling got up and shook hands. "I can't even imagine what you and your family are going through."

Ash hoped Brad never had to find out what hell was really like. "Caroline's talking about moving to the coast and taking her mother and Katie with her," he said.

Brad's eyebrows rose. "I thought she had a great career in Marion County."

"Too many memories here, she said. And she's worried about Katie's safety. I had to tell her about Sunny and Armenta before Katie gave Caroline her own version."

Brad smiled briefly. "How did she take that?"

"As badly as you think. Maybe worse."

"Does she believe Sunny's clairvoyant, or whatever the correct term is?"

"She doesn't want to, but she's not taking any chances. Katie's never alone. The dog's still with us. Jake's owner isn't ready for him to go home yet, so Katie gets to go into the back yard with him. Any freedom's better than none, she told me. Caro's got her sleeping in what used to be a sunroom attached to her bedroom. She decked it out with new bedding and furniture, but Katie hates it. She said she has no privacy, and her mother snores."

Brad followed Ash to the door. "Moving away wouldn't necessarily protect Katie if she's really in danger," he pointed out. "But Sunny didn't specifically name Katie when she said the perp took the wrong child. You and I have agreed the prediction could be about any one of those other children at the field trip that day. I can't alarm any of the kids' parents or the school staff based on a psychic's vision."

"I know." Ash shook his head to clear the whispers gathering in his mind. Those quiet voices told him Katie was the target, not another child from the outing. "Katie said she saw nothing unusual, nor anybody who looked suspicious, either before or after Amy's death. She was supervised at all times both at home and school. I asked her to go back a couple of months before Amy's death. That's wasn't easy for either of us."

Brad walked Ash to the elevator. "I hope everything works out for the best," he said when it arrived.

"We're all hoping for that," Ash said as he stepped inside.

CHAPTER FORTY

NEXT DAY, an intriguing invitation arrived, hand-carried by a tall, thin man in a black suit who drove a black limo with tinted windows. Sunny opened the envelope, remarking to Armenta on the flowing copperplate script detailing the store's name and address.

"People don't write like that anymore," Armenta said. "My father spent hours perfecting his penmanship, but now computers and smart phones are used almost exclusively, writing skills have taken a backseat."

"Katie's handwriting isn't bad," Sunny said, only half-listening. She had drawn out a white card with a black border. The printed invitation requested Sunny's attendance at a private wine tasting at Valderos Vineyards, in honor of their new Pinot Noir the following afternoon. A handwritten note asked her to bring a guest. Suggested was, 'Your policeman friend.'

Sunny had no idea how Vincente Valderos knew about her friendship with Ash Haines. She felt sure Winston or Ben would have mentioned Ash's name coming up during their delivery of the medicine buddha.

Armenta took the invitation and studied it. "Oooh, a visit to the creepy vintner's winery. What could go wrong with that?" She gave one of her dry-leaf chuckles.

"Shut up," Sunny said, but she laughed, too, relieved to break the tension she'd felt after Ash's revelation about Katie possibly moving to the coast. "I'll go only if Ash can come. I'd love to see Valderos's home, even if it's from the other side of the vineyard."

Armenta pointed to the address. "Ash still has Valderos's business card, but I'm pretty sure that's where we sent Winston and Ben, so the tasting room must be close to the house. You'd better take Ash, otherwise the shop will be mine, all mine." Her laugh turned into a disturbing cackle.

"Now *you're* being creepy." Sunny pulled out her cell phone. "I'm going to text Ash. I hope he'll go. It'll give him something else to do than worry about Katie moving to Coos Bay." After sending the text, she quickly updated Armenta on what Ash had told her.

"I'll read his cards." Armenta bustled off to her arbor.

"I hope it's a good reading," Sunny said. "Ash doesn't need any more bad news. I know neither of us wants him to leave, but he won't have any reason to stay."

"That might not be true." Armenta ducked under the arbor's canopy.

Sunny wondered what Armenta might be thinking. Maybe she'd already read Ash's cards without his permission. Permission was something Armenta routinely ignored.

Sunny's phone beeped, signaling an incoming text. Ash was intrigued with Valderos, and Sunny wasn't going anywhere near the creep's house without back-up.

Sunny thanked him and asked for a 4:00 PM pick up. She got a thumbs-up in response.

The bell over the shop door rang three times in rapid succession. Several customers began browsing. More came in soon after. The morning flew. Armenta did three readings, Sunny sold two of the larger gargoyles and four of the windchimes that tinkled so beautifully in their new display whenever the front door opened. Several of the most expensive amulets were also selected and a variety of other items filled customers' baskets. Sunny saw sales tipping heavily into the profits column of her ledger and hoped the trend continued.

At 1:00 PM she locked up, placed the 'Closed for Lunch' sign in the window and joined her assistant at the kitchen table. "How was Ash's reading?" she asked.

Armenta poured homemade mushroom soup from her flask into a bowl. "Complicated. I'm going to do another reading and consult the crystal ball."

"What about the runes?" Sunny asked.

"Those are your territory." Armenta waved her spoon at Sunny before plunging it into the soup. "You'd better start studying. You'll need to be proficient in the near future."

"Did you read my cards, too?" Sunny scooped a spoonful of peanut butter from the jar and spread it on toast.

"Didn't need to," Armenta said. "Your involvement with Ash was what complicated his reading."

CHAPTER FORTY-ONE

THEY CLOSED the store at 2:30 PM, so they could have tea and a sandwich before Sunny got ready for the winery event. She changed clothes three times before choosing a denim jacket over a black dress with a pencil-thin skirt, long sleeves and a scooped neck. If she saw women who were more formally dressed, she'd leave the jacket in the car. She opened her little bag of costume jewelry and took out a string of fake pearls she'd received as a gift many years before.

"Wear this, instead." Armenta dangled a pendant on a thin gold chain.

"It's pretty," Sunny said, cupping the pendant. "Is it yours?" Then she looked closer. "That's an evil eye."

"Yes, it is, and no, it's not mine," Armenta smiled. "I got it for you. It's been blessed."

"Has it?" Sunny had no idea who would have done the blessing or why, but the pendant was far prettier than the pearls.

"I texted Ash to remind him to wear his amulet. I hope he does."

"I'll check before we leave. In case you need to give him another one for today." Sunny slid her feet into black high-heeled shoes for the first time since taking over the shop.

"I can't give him a different amulet; it won't have been blessed." Armenta, who never seemed to be worried by anything, looked anxious.

"You want me to call him now?" Sunny pulled her cell out of her black evening purse.

"No...that might make him leave the amulet behind." Armenta helped Sunny into her jacket. "Men are funny that way. They don't like women telling them what to do."

"Don't I know *that.*" Sunny thought of Mark. "My ex was always arguing with me over stupid little stuff."

"I never married," Armenta said. "I was too busy learning my craft."

"For which I'll always be in your debt," Sunny said quickly. Sometimes Armenta still annoyed her, but without her assistant's Romani blood and knowledge of the occult realm, Sunny knew she would have floundered in Tina's shop.

"We both know that's not entirely true," Armenta said, echoing Sunny's thoughts. But her worried frown softened. "Let me put the necklace on for you."

Sunny ducked down, so Armenta didn't have to stand on tip-toe. The necklace felt surprisingly warm on her bare skin. She wondered whether Armenta had kept it tucked away in her pocket all day.

Ash arrived in his black Range Rover at exactly 4:00 PM. Sunny watched him get out and check his suit, like he might be looking for tell-tale signs of his recent smoking habit. The suit actually had a good cut and fit him very well. He definitely didn't look anything like the disheveled man who had first walked into her life.

Sunlight glistened through swinging tree branches across the street. It was one of those blissful spring days that fooled residents into thinking it was really warm until they stepped outside to find a chilly breeze blowing. Sunny suddenly felt under-dressed.

"You'd better take a coat." Armenta had Sunny's London Fog raincoat draped over her arm.

"Thanks, Armenta."

As she took the coat, Sunny was glad she had kept some of her high-end clothes after her marriage and her job both ended. Friends had convinced her that donating her suits to Dress for Success was a better option than throwing them into a dumpster. She had also listened to them when they advised her to keep a couple of the dresses she'd worn to evening events as Mark's wife. One of them was the simple but elegant black dress Mark had liked so much. Sunny put on the coat and buttoned it. She cinched the belt tight.

When her divorce became final, she had vowed never to think of Mark again. But she'd found it impossible never to talk about or think about her ex. Especially after he'd called to give his condolences for the loss of her best friend, she reminded herself. He'd even offered financial assistance. She wondered what sort of spell he must have fallen under.

"Go on," Armenta urged. "Don't keep Ash waiting."

Sunny shook off her unwanted introspection. "I'm going, already. Don't forget to set the alarm before you leave."

"I won't forget." Armenta gave Sunny a little push. "I was alone for three weeks after Tina died. The shop didn't burn down, and no major merchandise got shop-lifted."

Sunny felt really guilty. She stopped and turned before stepping into the parking lot. "I didn't mean to sound like I thought you couldn't handle the store for an hour and a half."

Armenta was already closing the door. "Everything here will be fine. Have a good time, but make sure you stay close to Ash."

"I don't think Mr. Valderos is going to drug my Pinot Noir and spirit me away somewhere," Sunny said. "And he'd have to slip a very big mickey into Ash's glass to knock him out. Ash would be sure to taste it."

The breeze decided stirring tree branches wasn't enough of a thrill. It slid around Sunny's legs and stirred Armenta's flowing ankle-length skirt. Armenta patted it back into place while Sunny repressed a desire to shiver.

"He might be more interested in Ash," Armenta said. "That invitation asked you to take him along."

"Ash told me he has a gun locked in his glove compartment," Sunny whispered. She tucked her purse under her arm.

Armenta gave a loud snort. "That won't help when you're both inside the tasting room."

"Armenta, you've given us charms. We'll be fine." Sunny wasn't sure who she was trying to convince more with that remark.

"Go on, then. But don't brush off my concerns when you don't know who or what you might be dealing with." Armenta closed the door.

Sunny walked over to Ash.

"Hi. You look nice." He gave her a quick smile that hinted at embarrassment. "Not that you don't usually," he added. "I should say you look extra nice today." He opened the passenger's door and handed her up onto the side step.

"Well, thank you, sir." She dropped her purse on the seat, held onto her skirt and slid in. "Such chivalry."

"I don't want you getting mud on your dress. I didn't have time to get the car washed." He closed her door and walked around to the driver's side.

Sunny wondered what could possibly have kept him so busy over the last 24 hours. Katie was spending the week with her mother and attending school. Then she remembered Ash had gone to see Brad Schilling. She put aside all thoughts of chiding him in a friendly manner about his lack of time-management skills and wondered if he'd tell her about the meeting.

But Ash said nothing as they drove across the bridge into West Salem. And his silence continued during a short drive on Highway 22 to an intersection with Oak Grove Road. When he turned right, they passed a cemetery. Sunny wondered who would want to purchase a winery located close to internment plots, but she held that thought. She'd never asked where Amy had been buried. She glanced at Ash, but his face was expressionless.

"You look like you know where you're going," she said as they passed through pastoral countryside.

"I've programmed the GPS," Ash said. "Since the vineyard's fairly new, I only got a general location. I figure there'll be a sign. Did the invitation give directions?"

Sunny fished it out of her purse. "It says to follow Oak Grove Road, and it's two miles past where the blacktop ends. We're to take a left at the sign."

"Okay."

She suddenly realized she hadn't asked him a very important question. "Did you get Armenta's text about wearing the amulet?"

"I did." He pointed toward his chest. "It's under my shirt. Damn thing felt like it had been stored in a freezer when I put it on. I almost took it off again, but…well, I didn't."

"I'm wearing an evil eye," Sunny told him. "Armenta's convinced Vincente Valderos is going to do something to one of us that doesn't involve introducing us to his Pinot."

"I've thought of that possibility, too," Ash said. "I'm not drinking his brew. I'll tell him I'm taking medication, but I'll buy a bottle for later."

"He might think that's rude."

"I don't care what he thinks." Ash had a grim downturn to the corner of his mouth. "After what you and Armenta told me about him, I don't want you drinking his wine, either. I'll distract him if he comes to the table, so you can toss it somewhere, like a plant pot. Otherwise, it'll have to get spilled on the floor. If we sit outside, it'll be a lot easier to get rid of." He glanced up at the sky. "Not sure that'll happen. It's getting pretty overcast."

"Ash." She had to laugh. "Armenta's worry seems to have rubbed off on you. Honestly, you could probably drink an entire bottle of his wine and not feel any effect."

"Is that a jab at my drinking habit?" He sounded more than a little defensive.

"No, silly, that was a joke." She looked over at him, but Ash wasn't smiling, even a little. That was disturbing. "Do you think he'll try to poison us? Why would he do that?"

"I'm not taking any chances," Ash said. "Why would he extend an invitation that specifically included me? How does he know we're friends? Did you tell him?"

"No, of course not. We only haggled over the price of the buddha." She wanted to ask Ash why he'd think she'd chit-chat about her private life with a new customer and specifically list the limited number of people she knew in the Salem area. But she decided a sarcastic response would only lead to a silly argument that had nothing to do with the real reason both of them felt on-edge and snippy.

"We're both tense," she said. "I'm blaming Armenta. Valderos was strange, but he didn't feel threatening. He's probably an eccentric antique dealer trying to make his new business successful. Maybe he'll have the buddha in the middle of the tasting room."

Ash's mouth curved upward. "That would be a real conversation-starter."

"It would." Sunny relaxed back in her seat. "I'm going to try the wine. You can tell him you're our designated driver and sip bottled water if you're going to continue being as suspicious of his intentions as Armenta."

"Now that's a great suggestion." He gave her hand a gentle pat. "Sorry I'm being a grouch. Schilling told me he's done trying to find reasons to continue investigating Amy's death as suspicious. He pretty much told me to accept the coroner's verdict. The vineyard shouldn't be much further. We've passed signs for two wineries already."

"Valderos didn't mention you by name," she said. "Maybe he doesn't even know about Amy. The card just said 'Policeman friend.' Armenta swears she didn't tell him anything about you, and she was in her arbor most of the time he was there."

"Maybe Armenta said something she doesn't remember. Was she alone with him at any time?"

"Only when she went to ask him where he lived, but she's got a mind like a steel trap. She doesn't forget *anything,*" Sunny didn't attempt to keep the irritation out of her voice. "Let's change the subject. I don't feel like arguing with you over what is probably nothing. If Armenta hadn't insisted on putting charms on us, do you really think we'd even be having this conversation?"

Ash shrugged. "Maybe not. In fact, I'd probably be pleased to go out for something social and adult for a change."

The GPS told them their destination was in three miles.

"How's business?" Ash asked.

"Well, that's a real change in subject, but thanks for asking." Sunny took a couple of deep, cleansing breaths. The irritation with Ash subsided. "It's surprisingly good," she told him. "I put in a big order this morning to replenish stocks of our most popular merchandise. Now the buddha's out of the way, there's room to rearrange and add more shelving."

"You should have offered Valderos an even better deal if he took that gargoyle off the counter, too," Ash said.

Sunny's irritation kicked back up a notch. "I don't know why you get so worked up about Watcher. He's completely harmless. As you said, he's only a step above a garden gnome."

Ash's mouth twitched. "Now look who can't take a joke."

"Oh, you." She laughed, relieved to break the unexpected tension between them.

She looked out the side window and was enchanted by the rich agricultural scenery flashing by. "It's so lovely out here," she said. "I should try to get out of the shop more often."

"It's a pretty day, despite those clouds," he agreed. "When it's cold and raining, the Willamette Valley's not so inviting."

"I particularly love to see the vineyards." She looked at her watch. "This seems like a long three miles. Are you sure we didn't miss the turn-off while we were bickering?"

Ash checked the GPS. "Nope. Another mile." He pointed to trellised rows of grapevines flowing back for what looked like hundreds of acres. "Those must be Valderos's."

As if on cue, a sign with an arrow pointing left announced the Valderos Vineyards tasting room. They turned onto a narrow, graveled track that climbed a hill between rows of vines.

Ash had to maneuver the Range Rover over several large potholes. "He's not going to attract many visitors if he doesn't maintain the entrance."

"You've got that right." Sunny held onto her purse as they bumped over yet another pothole. "Why wouldn't he fix the access road?"

She wondered whether the tasting room was going to turn out to be an old barn with a hole in the roof, but she didn't voice her concern to Ash. He might want to turn around, although she doubted the big SUV could accomplish that without taking out both the fence and a significant number of vines.

"Maybe he's offering his wine dirt cheap." Ash deftly turned the wheel to avoid yet another pothole.

A steep curve appeared ahead. Sunny hoped they wouldn't encounter any other vehicles. There really wasn't room for more than one car. Ash continued to navigate his way through muddy and pocked terrain that was steadily deteriorating in drivability.

Finally, they bumped and jolted their way into a forecourt. Ahead of them, a barn-like building sported a sign identifying it as the Valderos Vineyards Tasting Room. No holes in the roof. Sunny allowed herself a small sigh of relief.

A number of other cars, trucks and SUVs filled all the parking spaces closest to the tasting room. A covered walkway led from the parking lot to the front door of the tasting room, dark green and black striped canvas flapping in a strong breeze.

Ash got out. "Wait for me to come around and help you."

Sunny opened her door and saw the side-step silently sliding out from beneath the chassis. Before it covered the ground, she saw muddy tracks and potholes filled with murky water. With Ash's help, her feet landed on dry land. She took his arm and they picked their way across the lot.

"I'm not impressed so far," Ash said. "If Valderos's access road is any indication of the way he operates his winery, then his vintage won't be worth drinking. I'm glad I didn't have time for a car wash; the Rover's filthy." He opened the tasting room door and strains of a cheery Viennese waltz drifted out. "Okay, that's better." He ushered Sunny inside.

At least they hadn't been greeted by Chopin's Funeral March, Sunny thought. As her eyes adjusted, she became both relieved and enchanted. Softly diffused light from a thousand tiny bulbs winked above their heads. A domed ceiling soared above an enormous tasting room lined on both sides with banks of windows. Beneath their feet, a burgundy runner beckoned them forward. On both sides of the runner, tables for two made the cavernous space more intimate. She felt Ash's hand on her back, firm but gentle as he guided her forward and closed the door behind them.

At the far end of the room, a spectacularly arched window gave an uninterrupted view of a flagstone patio peppered with groups of umbrella-shielded tables. The furniture looked to be heavy wood, with burgundy seat-cushions on the chairs. Beyond the patio, a manicured half-moon lawn led to neat rows of trellised grapevines flowing up a rolling hill to a mansion overlooking the vineyard. The mansion itself appeared to be in need of some TLC, with missing shutters and two paint colors visible in several places. Sunny wondered whether Vincente Valderos had put all his efforts into turning the winery into a profitable venture before renovating his home, but if so, why hadn't he thought visitors needed and deserved a smooth ride to the tasting room?

All the outside tables were empty. As Sunny watched, soft shades of green and brown on the hillside became subdued by wisps of fog. The hovering clouds were descending, bringing rain to pepper the windows. A ribbon of mist floated around and between the patio furniture. Black umbrellas bearing the Valderos Vineyards name fluttered forlornly.

Looking around the interior again, Sunny wondered why no one had come to greet them. She thought she saw waiters moving between the bar and the tables, many of them occupied by what looked like couples. But the overhead lighting seemed to have dimmed, and she couldn't distinguish more than indistinct shadows.

"I bet they all have a bottle of his Pinot Noir," Ash whispered in her ear.

"Shut up." She stifled a nervous laugh. "After our drive through the vineyard, I'm really shocked at how beautiful this building is inside."

"It certainly is, Stan," Ash said, mimicking Oliver Hardy perfectly.

"You have hidden talents," she told him. Feeling the need for strong, human contact, she took his arm and gave it a light squeeze as she urged him forward on the burgundy runner. "Let's go find our host."

CHAPTER FORTY-TWO

VINCENTE VALDEROS suddenly materialized from the gloom. He hailed Sunny and Ash as he strode toward them, a burgundy-lined cape flapping around his calves.

"Ms. Kingston, so delighted you could come." His long strides matched his imposing height. He made short work of the distance. "And you must be Detective Haines." He beamed a welcoming smile at Ash as he took Sunny's hand in his. "So lovely to see you again," he told her. "Thank you for accepting my invitation."

Much to Sunny's relief, he didn't kiss her hand. But he held it an overly-long moment while he stared into her eyes, the smile continuing to play around his lips. Sunny thought his complexion looked waxy, like he'd just come from a dipping session at Madame Tussaud's.

Valderos slowly released her hand to shake Ash's. "Delighted to meet you, sir. How was your drive?"

"Muddy." Ash disengaged Valderos's hand. "Thank you for the invitation. I've retired from police work, so I'm now *Mr.* Haines."

"Ah. I see. Well, are you a wine connoisseur, Mr. Haines?" Valderos continued to smile like an indulgent uncle.

"I wouldn't say I'm a connoisseur of Oregon wines, but I've sampled my fair share, and I know what I like," Ash said.

"How about you, Ms. Kingston?" Valderos took her hand again. "Let me call a waiter to escort you to a table." He waved his free hand while tugging her forward with the other.

"Even less of a connoisseur," she said, taking a couple of ungainly steps to maintain her balance. "I usually get my wine at the supermarket." She was still holding Ash's arm, which made for an awkward little tug of war on Valderos's part.

When he realized she wasn't going to stop dragging Ash along, he reluctantly released her. "Perhaps you will both be pleasantly surprised today when you sample the Pinot Noir of Valderos Vineyards," he said.

"Perhaps." Ash didn't sound convinced.

Valderos heard that hesitation. "Are you truly convinced you won't like my vintage?" he asked. His smile looked considerably thinner.

"I'm ready to make a comparison with the other vineyards in Oak Grove," Ash said. "The soil and the climate in this area differs slightly to that of the Dundee Hills, or so I've been told."

"Those legendary micro-climates I've heard so much about." Valderos didn't actually sneer, but the corner of his mouth barely lifted.

Sunny found herself honing in on their host's eyes. Half-closed, it was difficult to make out their color, let alone know where he was looking, or, more importantly, who he was looking at. Her purse slipped from her shoulder. She quickly caught the strap and readjusted it.

"Come," Valderos said. "Let us *all* go to a table." He snapped his fingers, and a man dressed as a waiter hurried over. "We will sit in front of the terrace," Valderos announced. "But not in the sun. I have an allergy, you see. That is why Oregon's wet climate so agrees with me." He drew Sunny's arm through his. "I hope you don't mind if I escort her," he said over his shoulder to Ash.

Ash said he didn't, even though he very much sounded like he did. Sunny was about to remark that since it was raining, it didn't matter where they were seated. But as they followed the waiter toward the patio, she saw the weather had cleared as fast as it had clouded up, and the sun was making inroads through dwindling amounts of resistance.

The waiter brought them to a shady corner close to the panoramic view outside. Another waiter appeared with a tray holding a bottle of wine and three glasses. He uncorked the bottle and deftly poured generous servings for them all. A third waiter arrived with a dish of mixed nuts and a pair of nutcrackers.

"I have been told that in this area, nuts are used interchangeably with crackers," Valderos said. "I do not personally care for crackers, and hazelnuts are native to Oregon. You will, of course, tell me if you have a preference for those little dried pieces of bread."

"Nuts are fine for me," Sunny said. "Ash?"

"I never eat dried bread with wine." Ash's deadpan face looked a little put on.

Sunny hadn't been entirely truthful about her knowledge of local wines. She had even owned an Oregon wine passport in the days before her marriage. She picked up the Valderos Vineyards Pinot, sniffed, swirled, and allowed time to exhale the aroma clinging to her nostrils before taking a sip. The wine smelled and tasted noticeably oaky, which she didn't care for, but it also had an unexpected smoothness, without the overpowering tannins that would have rendered it undrinkable. Underwhelming, she decided. And a touch vinegary.

Both men watched her put down the glass, select a couple of hazelnuts and a large brazil nut. She easily cracked the hazelnuts, but the brazil nut's shell was as tough as it looked. After an initial attempt, she used all her strength. The nut flew out of the nutcracker's jaws. Valderos caught it.

Sunny couldn't believe her eyes. She knew her mouth had dropped open and closed it.

"Great catch," Ash said. "Did you play short-stop for the Yankees recently?"

Valderos laughed. He cracked the nut effortlessly using only his hand and returned it to Sunny. "No, but I wouldn't have minded the position."

"Where exactly did you come here from?" Ash asked.

"I have been traveling for several years. No fixed address, as you say." Valderos picked up his glass and swirled the wine around. Sunlight glinted through the liquid. He quickly put the glass back down. "And how do *you* find my Pinot Noir, Mr. Haines? Does it compare favorably with my fellow Oak Grove vintners?"

Ash picked up his glass and slowly swirled the wine around. Sunny thought he was stalling, but since they were nowhere near any potted plants, and he hadn't used the designated driver card, he was either going to have to at least take one sip or perform a parlor trick to make his wine disappear.

Ash sipped. He appeared to be savoring the taste. Finally, he swallowed. Sunny realized she had been holding her breath and let it out slowly.

"Interesting," Ash said.

Valderos picked up his glass again, gave it a perfunctory sniff, then swallowed the contents in one gulp. "Very refreshing," he remarked. "How do you find yours, Ms. Kingston?"

Sunny sipped again and wondered whether she should risk offending Valderos with the truth. Should she tell him it was subpar? Insipid? She tried to think of something pleasant to say about the bouquet. What if he became so offended he stopped the check and told her to arrange to take back the buddha?

She decided to take another sip before making a decision that could jeopardize her financial plans for the next month.

"I am very sorry for the loss of your daughter, Mr. Haines," Valderos said.

CHAPTER FORTY-THREE

ASTOUNDED BY THE sudden turn in their conversation, Sunny almost choked. She grabbed a couple of napkins and covered her mouth while she coughed.

Valderos signaled a hovering waiter. "Water. Immediately." The waiter ran off.

"I'm okay," Sunny managed between coughs.

The water arrived in a carafe, along with three small glasses. Ash took the carafe from the waiter and poured Sunny a glass. While she drank, the waiter replaced the napkins before leaving. As Valderos watched the proceedings, he twirled the stem of his wineglass.

"I'm surprised you heard about my daughter," Ash said when calm had been restored. "I thought you had only recently moved to Oregon. Am I mistaken?"

"You are not, Detective."

"As I told you before, Mr. Haines will do fine."

Valderos inclined his head. "Perhaps by the time you leave here today, we will all be on a first name basis."

Sunny couldn't see them getting chummy enough for that, but kept her thoughts to herself.

"Ms. Kingston has a gift," Valderos said. "A new gift. One she is unable to successfully control. Isn't that correct, Ms. Kingston?"

When he looked at her, she finally saw his eyes. The irises were a murky gray. Horizontal black slits replaced round pupils. She tried to look away, but their gazes remained locked. She wanted to get up and bolt out of the building, but found herself unable to move. "Yes," she mumbled, her lips stiff and partially numb. "That's true. I can't."

She wanted to tell Ash she was terrified, but the words wouldn't form. Valderos's hand was on top of hers as it lay on the table, next to the cracked brazil nut. She wanted to take her hand away, but it wouldn't cooperate.

"I have decided to assist you with your problems," Valderos said. "Since Ms. Kingston is the vessel, she is the one to whom I will give my support. Mr. Haines, you are her protector. Her partner. You will be charged with keeping her safe while she works." His hand slid across hers, coming to rest on her fingers.

Sunny was able to turn away from Valderos to see Ash's reaction. He seemed frozen in place, too, but he returned Valderos's gaze unwaveringly. While Ash may not be exhibiting fear, Sunny knew Valderos must have sensed her terror. Her stomach contracted painfully. She felt queasy and slightly lightheaded.

"You both have a very long road to travel together," Valderos continued. "It will be fraught with danger and dark forces. But you can find your daughter's killer, Mr. Haines, with Ms. Kingston's help. This I promise you."

His hand covered hers again. Her hand warmed in response, then began tingling in an extremely uncomfortable manner. She wasn't sure whether she was feeling nerve pain or pins and needles from the pressure Valderos was exerting. She wanted to tell him to release her, but as the uncomfortable feeling progressed up her arm, she completely lost the ability to move.

"In return," Valderos continued, still keeping his attention on Ash, "you will have to continue to assist others in finding closure for their own misery." He returned his attention to Sunny. "That is the price of my help. Do you both accept?"

He released her hand, and the trancelike state zapped away. Sunny gasped to fill her empty lungs.

"Who the hell *are* you?" Ash was on his feet. He tried to tug Sunny out of her chair, but her legs were too cold and stiff.

"Sunny, snap out of it," Ash urged. "We have to go."

He put his hands under her armpits and yanked hard. Sunny remained anchored to the chair. He tried to move the chair, but it wouldn't budge.

Ash finally lost his composure. "Let go of her, right now," he told Valderos. His voice shook.

"Sit down, Mr. Haines," Valderos responded. "Please." He gestured.

Ash abruptly sat, like he couldn't stop himself. "What are you doing to us? What do you want?"

Valderos laughed, the sound as sharp as broken glass. When he looked at Sunny, his eyes still had putty gray irises, but with round black pupils.

"Are you the Devil?" she asked.

"Not *the* Devil." He shook his head. "Do you seriously think The Master would interest himself in taking on an Oregon winery with a bad vintage?" He laughed again, this time short and rapid, like a barking dog. He looked at Ash. "Yes, I know my wine is inferior." He snapped his fingers. "Wilhelm, will you please bring me a clean glass? I wish to partake of the excellent Willamette Valley wine Mr. Haines had in his Range Rover's trunk."

"You had one of your minions break into my trunk?" Ash sounded furious.

"Of course not." Valderos watched the waiter take the cork out of a bottle and pour a full glass for Valderos. He took a sip. "Stellar," he said. "I must hire their head vintner to improve my own label."

Another waiter cleared the table and set two clean glasses in front of Sunny and Ash. The first waiter poured Ash's wine into both glasses.

"I didn't leave my car unlocked," Ash said.

"Do you believe my powers would be insufficient to open a trunk lock?" Valderos motioned with one hand, and the bottle floated up. He motioned again. It poured more wine into his glass before lowering back to the table.

"That's one hell of a parlor trick," Ash said.

"That's nothing." Valderos motioned again, and the sunny day turned dark and menacing. "Would you like it to rain?"

Sunny found her voice. "No. You don't need to do anything else to convince us, does he, Ash?" She hoped they were going to make it out of the tasting room with their lives.

"No," Ash said.

The sun returned outside, a warm yellow glow spreading across the patio.

"Do try your partner's wine, Ms. Kingston," Valderos said.

Sunny obediently took a sip. "Oh," she said. "That really *is* good." She tried to smile, but her mouth wouldn't cooperate. She still felt icy cold and partially numb.

"If you're not the Devil," Ash said calmly, as though nothing unusual had gone on between them, "then who or what are you? Some sort of fallen archangel? After what you've shown us, you're definitely not a regular human being like either of us, although I suppose Sunny isn't really that, either."

"I agree with you, Mr. Haines; Ms. Kingston is not. As for me, well, I do not feel either of you need to know anything more about me right now. You can speculate all you want, but your detective skills will not serve you well where I am concerned. You will have to form your own opinion as to what I am, what Ms. Kingston is, and where you want to fit into our relationship, if we move forward with my proposal."

"Make a deal with who, or what?" Ash asked. "I'm not signing over my soul, if that's what you're asking. I'm planning to see Amy again in the afterlife."

"Ah, the afterlife." Valderos nodded slightly. "The ultimate goal. But before that, you still have many years to live, and you would prefer to live them knowing your daughter's killer has been brought to justice, would you not?" He leaned forward.

Sunny instinctively leaned back. She reached for Ash's hand and found his seeking hers. As they held onto each other, Valderos raised an index finger. His putty-colored eyes slid from one of them to the other.

"Think it over," he said. "I will come to the shop for your answer.

Tomorrow. Six o'clock." His lips drew back into an unsettling grin. "When the sun goes down. My allergies, you understand."

He clapped his hands. Everything went dark.

CHAPTER FORTY-FOUR

"WHAT THE HELL?" Ash felt the steering wheel beneath his hands. The Range Rover's headlights pierced late afternoon twilight and showed a sign pointing left to McMinnville and right to Salem. He glanced quickly at the passenger's seat and felt reassured to see Sunny sitting beside him.

"Are you okay?" he asked.

"I think so." She stirred in the seat. "How did we get here? And where are we?"

Ash peered out his side window and saw another sign, illuminated by a spotlight. That one said, 'Thanks for visiting Valderos Vineyards,' and asked them to come again.

"Looks like we're at the end of the exit road from the tasting room," he said. "Did we...did you..."

"Yes. Get us out of here!"

"You bet."

Ash made sure they weren't about to be hit by another vehicle before turning onto the paved road and hitting the gas as hard as he thought safe.

"We shouldn't talk about anything that happened at that winery until we get back into town," Sunny said. "This isn't the time for distracted driving."

"Agreed."

She turned on the radio and tried several stations before turning it back off. "I don't remember how I got in the car," she said.

Ash couldn't help himself. "What happened to us not talking about the winery visit until we get back to Salem?" he asked.

"I'm too rattled to sit in silence." She hunched down. "He wants an answer to what tomorrow? Whether we're willing to sell our souls?"

"No," Ash said. "What he wants is for us to commit to helping others in the same situation I'm in. Fine for me to decide whether to get sucked into his scheme, but not you. I don't want you involved."

"Ash, without me, neither you nor Valderos has anything. I'm the vessel, remember? The one with the visions. What I got from him is he'll help me control them so I can use them effectively in the search for Amy's killer. In return, we have to help solve more murders. What a lovely thought." She shivered. "I think he mentioned the number ten, but I'm not sure of that."

"Why would he want us to agree to do that?" Ash forced himself to concentrate on the road. His thoughts kept wandering around in a disconcerting manner. "What's in it for him?"

"I don't know." Sunny drew up her coat collar and shivered. "But whatever it is, he wants to use us to get it."

Ash flipped on the heater. "He said he doesn't want our souls, and for no good reason, I kind of believe that. What do *you* think? You're the one with all the insight."

"I've still got training wheels, Ash. Armenta's been trying to coach me, but I've been very reluctant to learn anything." She rubbed her face with both hands. "That was obviously a big mistake. But as far as believing anything Valderos promised?" She shook her head. "I wouldn't trust anything that man said, if he even *is* a man."

Ash felt a chill so deep, his bones ached. Sunny turned in her seat to face him.

"Do you think he's a demon?" she asked. "He said he wasn't the Devil, but what else is he? Did you see his eyes?"

"Yeah." Ash tightened his grip on the steering wheel. It felt good to clutch something solid. "Christ, they were scary."

Sunny laughed. A nervous bubble that ended as abruptly as it had started. "I felt really glad I was wearing that charm."

"I know what you mean. I never believed anything to do with witch-craft...the occult." He remembered scoffing, and felt ashamed. "If I hadn't listened to Armenta and worn the amulet..." He was having trouble articulating his thoughts. He glanced over at Sunny. Her hands were clasped in her lap; her head lowered. His own discomfort was instantly pushed aside. He took one cramping hand from the wheel and laid it over hers. "Are you crying?" he asked, and was surprised by the raw emotion he heard in his voice.

"No." She sat up straight and stared through the windshield at the gathering darkness beyond. "Wondering what he wants in return, and why."

They drove several miles in silence except for the whisper of the Range Rover's engine as the SUV ate up the miles. They encountered no other vehicles. The moon rose to cast a pale silver light over the rural landscape.

"I want to get control over my visions and help you find Amy's killer," Sunny said as they made the turn onto Highway 22. "Armenta knows a lot, but she's not much help with the visions. She did bring me out of the trance the first time, though. I don't know what would have happened if she hadn't been there...I kept drifting back." She shuddered. "And she had to help you bring me back from the one I had at your house. If I go asking for help with visions around the Salem community, I may end up doing a stint in the State Hospital. People will think I'm delusional."

Ash gently squeezed her hand. "I'll never let that happen. I'm your protector, remember?"

"Are you sure you want that role?" She sounded on the verge of tears. "You can't endanger yourself. Katie needs you."

Ash locked eyes with her briefly, her face a pale oval in the lights of oncoming traffic. "I know she does. I'll keep us safe; I promise. All those years in law enforcement taught me well."

"Ash..."

"Sunny," he interrupted, pre-empting her concerns. "I took an oath to serve and protect. Retirement doesn't mean I don't intend to continue keeping that pledge." He took a deep breath, pent-up emotion sweeping through him. "My life changed for the better the day I walked into your shop, even though I've always believed the occult's hogwash. Christ, I just had a meeting with something I'm sure wasn't human, and I felt protected because Armenta made me wear an amulet."

"Oh, Ash." Sunny drew in a deep, shuddering breath.

"It's true." Ash patted her hand before returning his to the wheel. "I feel at home with you and Armenta, even when I'm drinking strange herbal tea that's brewed from god knows what. And Katie loves to visit. You and Armenta feel like family to us."

"A very dysfunctional family."

Ash felt Sunny's smile in the darkness. "That doesn't matter," he said. "I've yet to meet a normal family. Frankly, I don't think one exists."

"Could we stop off somewhere and get a drink before you take me back to the shop?" Sunny asked as they crossed the bridge from West Salem and joined a stream of traffic leading into the well-lit and busy downtown core. "Non-alcoholic," she added. "Coffee or soda."

"Definitely. And we'll pick up dinner, too. Let's eat together, so we can talk about whether we're even going to consider asking Valderos any questions tomorrow afternoon before I throw him into the parking lot and lock the door."

"Trouble is, I don't think any number of locks would keep him out," Sunny said.

Ash had to agree.

CHAPTER FORTY-FIVE

Tɪɴᴀ sᴀᴛ on the end of Sunny's bed. "So, what have you decided to do?" she asked.

Sunny rubbed her eyes and decided she must be having a waking dream. She peered at the clock on the nightstand: 2:00 A.M.

"You're not dreaming," Tina said. "I've waited too long to talk to you already. It's been so busy around here, I haven't been able to successfully manifest."

Tina wasn't outwardly terrifying. She looked pale and had a slight shimmer. Sunny took several deep breaths. Tried to calm her galloping heart and think rationally. If the visiting spirit turned threatening, she doubted locking herself in the bathroom would stop Tina from drifting in through the keyhole. She would have to escape out the back door, and she wasn't going to run around the neighborhood in her pajamas. She'd have to put on her slippers and robe.

"Life goes on, Tina," she said, relieved to hear the quiver in her voice was minimal. Congratulating herself for not panicking, at least for the moment, she sat up. "Are you one of my visions?"

"No. I have nothing to do with your visions." Tina sounded tired. Even a little aggravated. When she shook her head, her dark hair slid across her shoulders. "If I could help you control the visions, I would have done so by now, don't you think?"

Tina leaned forward until her face was only inches away from Sunny's. Sunny forced herself not to recoil. She told herself that Tina would never try to hurt her. There had to be a reason for her friend's nighttime visit, and appearing open and receptive would be the most sensible course to take, while she tried to garner as much information as possible.

"I don't know what I think half the time," she told the ghost. "Armenta says things come and go around here. She's right. There's a stone gryphon I swear flies around when we're not looking, and there's a cat that suddenly appears, stays for a while, then disappears for days, sometimes weeks. Now you're sitting on the end of my bed. When I first took over this shop, I thought I must be out of my mind, trying to step into your shoes. Now, either I've already lost my marbles or there's a lot you didn't tell me before you died."

Tina nodded. Sunny thought the light shimmering around her was like soft candlelight. But even though Tina *looked* increasingly solid, Sunny didn't want to try a touch-test. Tina could disappear, or worse, turn into something that wasn't so pleasant to talk to in the middle of the night. Sunny felt like Alice, having a conversation with one of the creatures in Wonderland.

"If I'd tried to tell you then, would you really have been ready to listen?" Tina asked.

She sounded like she was in one of her preachy moods. Sunny had never liked those when Tina was alive, but decided not to risk angering the apparition by pointing that out. "No, I don't suppose I would." She forced a smile.

Tina didn't return it. In fact, her face seemed to be fixed in one expression. Kind of...neutral. Sunny swallowed the lump in her throat. She had to keep panic at bay. "But the visions...did you know I was going to have those?" The tremor in her voice had grown stronger. *Damn.*

"I knew you were so resistant, only a severe shock would bring down the wall you had erected to keep your gift locked away."

"Is that why you were killed right in front of me? Tina, that's too awful." Sunny felt choked with anger. "What I have isn't a gift; it's a curse. It doesn't help anything. All I see is what *was.*"

"You can speak for the dead," Tina said. "That's your gift. You don't have clairvoyance. You have the means to bring justice to the ones who died. The ones who are lost."

"Oh, my god." Sunny covered her face with her hands as blood drummed in her ears. "Those poor souls in the woods."

"Yes," Tina said. "There are so many."

Tears welled up. *Buddy. The little girl who had called out. The people whose voices had carried to her on the cold, sharp wind. The one who was found in the back yard of that abandoned house.* The task was over-whelming.

"It was my time," Tina said. "It wasn't your fault. You have nothing to feel responsible for. I wanted my death to have meaning, and this was the way."

"I don't know if I can accept that," Sunny said.

"You will in time, if you allow yourself to open your mind. Interpret things in a different way."

"That's *exactly* what Armenta said about the runes. Your runes. Did you cast them?"

"I did. With great difficulty. But it was a triumph after months of breaking things and being unable to show you I'm still here until I finish my purpose."

"What purpose?"

"You don't need to know."

"Tell me about the runes. We tried our best to read them, but Armenta wasn't sure…"

"You were supposed to study the books. I left them for you. Armenta was only to act as your guide." Tina sounded irritated. Her aura had darkened.

"She's been trying, but I haven't been a good student." Sunny felt Tina's displeasure radiate like a blast of very warm air. She tried smiling again, but her lips trembled too badly.

"I had more faith in you," Tina said. "It appears I was mistaken."

Sunny slid her feet into her slippers. Tina didn't react, so she put on her robe.

"It has taken a lot of effort to assume a form you recognize," Tina said. "I had to learn to move solid objects first. Everything fell to the floor. That startled customers. I think I lost you a few during that phase. Then I couldn't seem to get past the floating mist density. Very annoying."

Annoying? Sunny bit her tongue to avoid commenting pithily on that observation. "Pretty darn scary for all of us," she said. "Not just the customers."

The sudden crashes, the shifting misty forms, were all explained. Knowing what had caused a large portion of the incidents was a relief. But Tina's growing displeasure had teacups rattling in the dish rack, and the chairs around the table began scraping their way across the floor.

Sunny decided she needed to divert Tina's attention from her short-comings. "Is the cat a spirit, too?" she asked.

The rattling ceased. The chairs stopped moving.

"He is. He came with the shop."

Suddenly, the cat jumped onto the bed. Tail high, he stepped over to Tina's side. She smiled at his raised face, and her aura lightened to a golden glow. "He only appeared to me at first, then later to Armenta as well. I think he searches for his owner, who never materializes. There are no other spirits in the shop."

Sunny felt profoundly relieved. "He almost knocked me off the ladder one day," she said, watching the cat's pleasure as Tina stroked his sleek black coat.

"The day you had a vision and Ash walked into the shop," Tina said.

"Yes. You were floating around, I take it?"

"I don't 'float around' all the time." Tina sounded defensive. "I'm bound to you until something happens to release me. I'd like to be released. Being around the living but unable to communicate effectively isn't a rewarding existence. All I ever do is scare people."

Her aura had darkened again. The shimmer was gone. The cat jumped off the bed and disappeared. Sunny wondered whether he'd become as frightened as she felt by the abrupt shift in her friend's mood.

"You're the first one who hasn't reacted that way," Tina said. "I thought I'd try materializing to Armenta, but she ignores me completely. Sometimes, I think Katie sees me, but I haven't tried talking to her. I don't want to frighten her. She's been through enough, already. I thought I'd try Ash next. He's so earthbound, though, I think he'd dismiss me like he does everything else metaphysical."

"Should we hold a séance or something? Maybe get a priest to exorcise you?" Sunny couldn't think of anything more helpful to say. She was still wondering why Armenta ignored Tina, and why Katie hadn't mentioned seeing a shadowy figure in the shop or the apartment.

Tina folded her arms across her chest. Her glow intensified. To Sunny, it felt like staring at a burst of sunlight. Half-blinded by the glare, she looked away.

"Now you're just being mean," Tina said. The clock on the bedside table crashed to the floor.

"Tina, it's the middle of the night," Sunny reasoned, hoping the glow would return to a shimmer. "I should be scared out of my wits, but I'm so tired and wrung out from a visit with Vincente Valderos, the guy who bought the buddha, that all I want is for you to drift off to wherever you hang out when you're not misting around the shop, so I can get some sleep."

Tina's glow deepened from yellow to orange.

"Maybe we can talk more tomorrow evening?" Sunny added. "Before I go to bed. That would be better, if it's all the same to you. I'm not at my best in the middle of the night." She managed a nervous laugh.

"I came here to help you make a decision." Tina's aura began to pulsate.

"I can't make any reasonable decisions at two in the morning. Really. I need my sleep, Tina," Sunny pleaded, "even if you don't."

Oops. Bad idea. Sunny swallowed with difficulty. The aura had red tinges.

"If...if you can't help me control the visions," she babbled on, nervously watching the colors around Tina deepening to a fiery sunset, "then I don't need you to stay earthbound for me." Sunny hoped she sounded as passionate as she felt. "Ash and Armenta both watch over me. The gryphon seems to want to do that, too."

The glow slowly returned to yellow. Tina remained at the end of the bed. Obviously, she wasn't taking the hint about leaving.

Sunny decided to change the subject. Maybe to a more neutral subject. "Do you know anything about the gryphon's history?" she asked. "I named him Watcher."

"I thought you wanted me to leave." Tina sounded petulant.

Sunny was tired. She didn't feel like arguing with a spirit or the result of a nightmare. "Don't be so annoying."

That time, Tina's response was a pair of raised eyebrows. And her aura was almost back to a shimmer.

"You want to help me, then help," Sunny urged. "What's Watcher's story?"

Tina's eyebrows lowered. "He's a protector," she said. "He came on consignment at the same time as the buddha. The owner told me he was brought over from France many years ago by someone with ties to the French nobility. I don't know anything else. I didn't do any research on him. He always seemed to be glaring at everyone, so I put him up on that high shelf, where you discovered him and brought him down. He seems very attached to you."

A sudden crash startled Sunny. She was flat on her back, staring up at the moon through the skylight above her bed. She sat up. Tina's apparition was gone.

No alarms were ringing. Sunny wondered whether she had dreamed everything, including the noise that startled her awake. She looked for the bedside clock. It was on the floor, face up. 4:30 AM. She was not only lying on top of the covers, but wearing her slippers and robe.

She stopped long enough on her way into the shop to grab a trekking pole from one of the coat hooks opposite the refrigerator. She flipped on the entire panel of switches to illuminate every corner of the shop. Nothing looked disturbed until she reached the counter. A display of cheap charms lay on the floor, but could they really have made such a noise when they fell? Sunny asked herself. Then she looked at the completely empty counter and realized something much bigger was missing.

Watcher.

CHAPTER FORTY-SIX

ASH AWAKENED TO CRYING. Amy's crying. He threw off the covers and sat up on the side of the bed, coming face to face with her.

She wasn't crying anymore. But her lip trembled, and her cheeks sparkled with tears.

"What's wrong, baby?" he asked. Then he blinked, rubbed his eyes, and blinked some more. Amy was dead. She couldn't possibly be standing beside his bed.

Yet she was.

Her favorite thumb was in her mouth, and her blonde hair hung in wispy curls over her shoulders. She wore a pink nightdress he knew had become too small for her. She was also wearing a pair of fuzzy slippers with bunny rabbits at the toes, their ears flopping onto the carpet. Long ago they had become worn through and trashed. And she was holding a teddy bear that had been left behind somewhere on a trip to Lincoln City when she was two years old.

"What the hell?" Ash said aloud. "You're not real. This has to be a nightmare."

"Daddy," she said.

It was definitely Amy's voice.

"Daddy, why can't you catch the person who killed me?" she asked around the thumb.

Ash had no answer for that. He was rapidly coming to the conclusion he'd lost his mind while sleeping. He tried pinching himself, which was definitely painful. He opened his nightstand drawer and took out a flashlight. When he shone the beam at Amy, she didn't move. She didn't blink, either, not even when he reluctantly directed the light at her eyes. Expressionless, she continued sucking her thumb. She'd quit doing that when she was three years old. Ash didn't believe in ghosts. He didn't believe in waking nightmares, either, yet he had to be having one. He tried to stand, but his legs wouldn't support him.

"I'm going to lie back down and close my eyes," he decided aloud. He looked at Amy, or whatever was passing as Amy. "I'm going to ignore you," he told her, his heart contracting painfully. He desperately wanted to play into the hallucination. More than anything, he wanted to take her in his arms and hug her. But his analytical mind told him she wasn't real, and he shouldn't give her credence.

He managed to get his legs onto the bed, but it wasn't easy. Amy leaned over him. He felt no warmth, no breath, even though her lips were partially open. He could see one baby tooth was missing, top right, next to the thumb. *Had she lost any baby teeth before she died?* He couldn't remember, and that saddened him. Amy took her thumb out of her mouth, a thin line of spittle attached. Ash watched, fascinated.

"You could catch him," she said, her face only inches from his. "You and Sunny."

"Leave me alone," Ash commanded, raising his voice slightly while hating himself for using what Caroline had dubbed his 'authority voice.' He hoped it would have some effect on the apparition.

It didn't.

Amy remained. She was sucking her thumb again, but at least she wasn't crying.

"I'm going to close my eyes and count backward from ten," he said. "You'd better be gone by the time I get to one." Inside, he cringed at the anger in his voice. "Go to your own bedroom. Go back to sleep."

He squeezed his eyes shut and listened as his heart hammered.

"Goodbye, Daddy," he heard. "You help Sunny. Remember, you can catch him if you do."

Ash slowly and silently counted back from ten, sweat running down his face, before opening his eyes.

Amy was gone.

Tears joined the sweat. He pulled the pillow from under his head and laid it over his face. He didn't want to admit it, but he had to...for the first time in his life, he was in waters so deep and uncharted, fear wasn't an adequate word for what he had experienced. He touched the amulet resting against his chest and wondered whether he'd soon need a lot more than that to go up against whatever was about to be unleashed on them if they didn't agree to Valderos's plan.

He threw off the pillow, sat up and put the flashlight back in the drawer next to his handgun, which he figured to be the least-effective weapon in his arsenal. With sleep the last thing on his mind, he turned on all the lights in the house, brewed coffee, and settled down to watch reruns of old sitcoms. Dawn couldn't come fast enough.

A crick in his neck awakened him to the Today Show at 7:00 A.M. He was still on the couch, covered by the blanket from his bed. He wondered if he'd started sleepwalking. Finding the remote beneath him, he pushed the power button, but the TV didn't turn off. Annoyed, he threw off the blanket and sat up.

Watcher stared at him from the coffee table.

"What the hell?" Ash asked.

He swore the gryphon's feathers rippled slightly in response.

CHAPTER FORTY-SEVEN

"I'M COMING OVER," Ash said when Sunny answered her phone.

Sunny's attention went from Armenta stirring a pot of oatmeal on the stove to the clock. It was 7:10 AM. Even before she asked, she thought she knew the answer: "Did you have any visitors last night?"

"Yes. Two. I'm bringing your gargoyle." He hung up.

"OMG," Sunny groaned. She put down the phone and covered her face with her hands. "Ash has Watcher."

"Have another cup of coffee." Armenta filled Sunny's mug. "You'd better get dressed and brush your hair if you want to see him again after this morning."

"You'd be looking like this if you'd had Tina sitting on the end of *your* bed in the middle of the night," Sunny grumbled.

"Well, I didn't." Armenta returned to stirring the oatmeal. "But I knew something had happened even before you called me."

"I'm sure you did."

Taking her mug with her, Sunny opened the closet in the bed alcove. She pulled out black pants, a black sweater and a fake sheepskin-lined denim vest. Good enough for a visit from Ash, closely followed by opening the shop and trying to appear alert and friendly for the public, she thought as she rummaged around in a drawer for underwear that had disappeared under a tangle of nightclothes.

After showering and blow-drying her hair, she added makeup to minimize the shadows under her eyes. Surveying herself in the mirror, she thought her appearance still rivaled Tina's ghost.

As she straightened her bed, she heard a knock at the kitchen door, followed by Armenta's greeting and Ash's deep voice. He had a nice voice, she thought. Well-modulated, and without any hint of a regional accent. He'd never volunteered much information about himself, but she had researched him online. She knew he had attended Harvard Law School, graduated with high honors, but left a prestigious law firm in Boston to join the Portland Police Bureau. She pulled back the curtain and joined them in the kitchen.

"You need coffee and breakfast," Armenta told Ash as he took off his hat and coat.

"Thanks." He hung his wet outerwear on a hook by the door. "It's raining hard out there, again."

Watcher was perched on the kitchen counter. "Any idea how he turned up at your house?" Sunny asked as she sat at the table. "Did Katie hide him in her backpack? If so, how could she lift him? We all know how heavy he is."

"And good morning to you, too." Ash sat on the stool next to her chair. He gave her a thorough once-over. "You look about as bad as I feel," he said, replacing her empty mug with a full one. "I woke up in the middle of the night to find Amy standing beside my bed with her thumb in her mouth. After she disappeared, I couldn't get back to sleep, so I made coffee and turned on the TV. Next thing I knew, I woke up on the couch with the opening credits for the Today Show and found your gargoyle sitting in the middle of my coffee table."

"I got a visit from Tina last night," Sunny said. "After she left, there was a big crash. I went into the shop to investigate and Watcher was gone. Nothing else seemed to have been taken. There were no broken windows. What's going on?" She looked at Armenta.

"Don't expect answers from me." Armenta poured oatmeal into three bowls. "I slept like a rock." She set bowls in front of Sunny and Ash.

"But when I got up at five this morning, my tarot cards were spread out on the table. I got a reading that there's trouble ahead, so I came here as soon as I got dressed." She sat down opposite them, pushed the sugar bowl and coffee creamer toward Sunny and the milk toward Ash.

Sunny needed energy from somewhere. She dumped two heaping spoonfuls of sugar onto her oatmeal. "Tina was here at two o'clock." She exchanged the sugar bowl for the milk carton. "When I woke up on top of the covers with the bedside clock on the floor, it was four-thirty."

"Amy was standing by my bed at four-thirty." Ash stirred his oatmeal. "You think those visits were related, Armenta?"

"Had to be." She pointed to a dish of blueberries. "Antioxidants. You both need them. Now eat. I'm making more coffee."

Ash dropped several blueberries onto his oatmeal while Sunny sat contemplating the bowl Armenta had placed in front of her. She had never thought oatmeal had an enticing look, smell or flavor. But she was hungry, so she added a handful of blueberries and covered the entire concoction with a thin layer of creamer. Maybe, she thought, that would make it more appetizing than milk.

Armenta stirred maple syrup into her own oatmeal. "Tina wanted to help you make a decision," she told Sunny. Then she pointed her spoon toward Ash. "I bet Amy told you that you could solve her murder if you helped Sunny. I think Mr. Valderos had more than a little something to do with those apparitions. He wants you to take him up on his offer, so he tried tipping the scales in his favor."

Ash frowned. "You think he was able to send them? How much power do you think the guy has?"

"I think he has a lot. Don't you?" Armenta raised an eyebrow. "Yesterday, he gave you several small examples. Last night, he might have come himself, manipulating spirits already adrift. He'd have had more trouble getting into Amy's character than Tina's. It's been a long time since he was young...if he ever was." She wrapped both hands around her coffee mug before taking a sip.

Sunny digested the idea of Vincente Valderos in her bedroom. Not a pleasant picture.

"That's a horrifying thought," Ash said, echoing Sunny's troubled musing. "Although it makes sense in a weird way. Amy was wearing clothes she'd outgrown and carrying a toy that'd been lost years ago. But why would he bring the gryphon with him?"

"I'm sure he didn't," Sunny said. "I think Watcher flew over to protect you."

"And left *you*? I can't see that." Ash hadn't touched his coffee or his oatmeal. He leaned back in the chair and ran a hand across his face. "I've never felt more like a drink and a cigarette than right now."

"You promised Katie you'd stop smoking, and the last thing you should be drinking this early in the morning is hard liquor," Sunny told him. "Drink your coffee and eat your oatmeal."

"Yes, Mother." Unexpectedly, he gave her a half-smile and raised his mug. "Cheers. You want me to sip or drink it straight down?"

"Children, children." Armenta waved her spoon at them both, like she was a conductor trying to regain control of an orchestra. "No squabbling. You've both got to make decisions by what time today?"

"Six, if Valderos is on time." Ash put down his mug. He drew the oatmeal toward himself, stirred the blueberries around and grimaced. "I hate oatmeal."

"You need it this morning," Armenta said. "Don't argue with me. I put a spell on it."

"You're joking." He didn't sound like he doubted her.

"Just eat the oatmeal," she told him. Then she gave Sunny a hard look. "You, too."

Sunny ate everything. Ash did, too.

"You want me to lick the bowl?" he asked afterward.

"This isn't the time for sarcasm." Armenta snorted. "You still don't completely believe, do you? Even after you had to bring Watcher back from your house."

"I believe enough that I burned a smudge stick in my kitchen sink before coming here, and I ate the oatmeal," Ash said. "Did you really put a spell on it?"

"No." Armenta got up and cleared the dishes into the sink. "I wanted to see whether you were able to move out of concrete thinking into abstract." She grinned when Sunny couldn't hide her surprise. "I took psychology classes a few years ago to help me with my readings. You know, hone them down to be more specific." She emptied the carafe into Sunny and Ash's mugs. "Now, what did you two decide to do? Are you taking Valderos up on his offer?"

Sunny looked at Ash for some indication that he'd made a decision.

Ash shook his head. "No decisions made here. Valderos wants something in return, and it's got to be something big."

"He said he doesn't want our souls. That's the biggest 'something' I can think of," Sunny said. "But he wouldn't get specific yesterday, so we've been left to speculate. What *I* want is to help you find out who murdered your daughter, Ash." She felt unsure how he'd react to her reservation, but it had to be said. "I'm just not sure how far I'm willing to go to do that."

"Sunny, I wouldn't ask you to do anything that puts you in danger. In any way. Make no mistake about that." Ash swirled the remaining coffee around inside his mug and watched it circle the china, like he was as uncomfortable with the situation as she.

"You have to be specific in your demands if you choose to negotiate," Armenta said. "I should be with you at the meeting. Demand it's here. Then I can prepare. There are protection spells."

"He said he'll come to the shop. You think he'll be driven here in that big black limousine or materialize?" Sunny felt cold chills ripple up her back. Valderos might be lurking somewhere inside the shop at that moment. She doubted he'd be anywhere near Armenta, however. She fingered the evil eye and wished she hadn't taken it off before going to bed.

"Maybe he'll send Tina or Amy again." Ash stared across the table at Armenta. "What do you think? You're the one with all the experience."

"No telling." Armenta took off her apron and hung it up on the peg next to Ash's raincoat. "I do think you two should stay together today. Don't let him come at you separately. And don't agree to change the meeting place. I can't prepare adequately otherwise."

Ash nodded. "I'll stay here. You've got some rearranging to do in the shop now the buddha's gone. I'll move shelves and help with the displays."

"That would make the reorganization a lot easier as well as keeping us together." Sunny took her empty mug to the sink. "I was going to ask Winston to stop by after he gets off work. Now I won't have to."

"We can close early." Armenta looked disapprovingly at Sunny's barely-touched oatmeal. "I'll start by cleansing with sage."

"If he does try to move the meeting somewhere else, I'm not going back to the winery, much less his house." Sunny shuddered at the thought. "So creepy. I don't know how I slept at all last night."

"We'll tell him it's here or nowhere," Ash said. "Screw him."

"I'm going to open the store." Armenta bustled out.

"I'm sorry I got you involved with Valderos," Sunny told Ash.

"I'm not. I wouldn't dream of leaving you and Armenta to cope with him by yourselves. When I met him yesterday, I thought he embodied the true meaning of the word sinister. Did he feel like that to you when he came to the shop?"

"Not as pronounced. Maybe because he was out of his element. Or there were too many good vibes and tokens in this shop."

"All the more reason to make sure the meeting takes place here."

"Yes." She nodded. "We'll have Armenta and Watcher. Tina, too, unless he really did manage to use her last night. I can't see her letting that happen, unless it was against her will. Of course, I don't know if spirits have the ability to resist anything."

Out the corner of her eye, she noticed a long black tail waving around. She turned her head in time to see the tip disappear under the curtain closing off the apartment.

"There's that damned cat." She jumped up. "I'm going to catch up with it this time."

She sprinted over to the curtain and pushed it out of her way. No tail. No cat. All the lights were on, and the shop appeared to be empty. She heard Armenta shuffling cards in her arbor.

"Well, double damn," she muttered under her breath. Her phone rang in her pocket. She pulled it out and looked at the screen. The caller ID showed a name she hadn't expected to see again: Mark Kingston. Her ex. What could he possibly want?

"Hello," she said.

"Sunny, what's going on? Someone sent me an old accident report on Tina. Why didn't you call? I'd have come to the funeral; sent flowers. Given my support. I'm so sorry for your loss. I know how much Tina meant to you."

He sounded genuinely distressed, which was a bit of a shock. Sunny couldn't remember him being that upset about their divorce.

"And then I saw in the obituary that you were taking over her shop," Mark continued. "That old store you thought was a waste of her time and effort? Why...you need money? I'll make you a loan. No strings attached. Pay me back whenever you can."

Sunny spotted a long black tail waving close to the counter.

"I'm fine, Mark," she told him as she hurried toward the front of the shop. "Tina's death was a terrible shock, but I'm working my way through my grief by taking care of her legacy. I'm remodeling and changing a lot of the merchandise. Things are going well. I don't need..."

She was about to say she didn't need anything from him, least of all his money, but she'd promised herself she wouldn't turn into a nightmare ex who couldn't be civil if she ran into Mark somewhere by accident.

"I don't need any help, I promise," she assured him. "But thank you for asking, and for calling with your condolences."

The tail was now heading for the open area the buddha had occupied. Sunny wondered why she could still see it over the top of the shelves. How tall was that cat, anyway?

Maybe it was floating around, she thought. "I have to go, Mark. I have customers," she told him.

"I understand."

But he didn't say goodbye, and he didn't hang up.

The cat's tail had disappeared. Sunny was standing in front of a wall. She hadn't seen a feline leaping over any racks. Peering up, she looked through the shelves of gargoyles. Only their eyes stared back at her. None of them had been displaced to make room for a cat.

"Well, hell," she said, then cringed. Of all days to mention that word...

"Sorry?"

"Oh, Mark, not you. I've got to go. Thanks for calling." She hung up before he could respond.

"Okay, what do you want to do with this space?" Ash asked from behind her.

Sunny wondered whether she jumped as high as the cat must have done to perform another disappearing act.

CHAPTER FORTY-EIGHT

Ash spent the morning dismantling, moving and reassembling display racks. Then he brought unopened boxes from the storeroom and neatly stacked them according to their lot numbers. Sunny was able to use the inventory sheets for orderly unpacking.

While she worked, the aisle closed off with a length of yellow ribbon and a sign announcing the arrival of new merchandise, a steady stream of customers came into the shop that afternoon. Armenta kept busy with tarot card, palm and crystal ball readings. Ash manned the register as though he had always been behind a counter. Sales were plentiful.

At 3:30 PM, Sunny finished her display, removed the yellow ribbon, and stood aside as shoppers enthusiastically looked over the new merchandise. She watched a lot of it go into baskets before she joined Ash at the counter. She took over the register and Ash bagged purchases until 5:50PM, when the last customer left the store. Sunny closed the register and began tidying up the area in front of the counter. She noticed Watcher's steely gaze was directed at the front door.

At exactly 6:00 PM, Vincente Valderos strode through the front door. All lights dimmed, and the locks shot into place behind him as soon as the door closed. Ash came to stand behind Sunny, his hands on her upper arms. She wondered whether he had plans to push her aside if Valderos did anything remotely threatening.

Armenta emerged from her arbor. "Tea?" she asked.

Valderos turned his attention to her. "Yes, thank you, Ms. Kaslov." He gave her a slight bow.

Sunny sneaked a look at Watcher. His head had turned toward the newcomer.

"We'd better go into the apartment, then," Armenta said.

"Lead the way, Ms. Kaslov." Valderos gave his thin, crooked smile. His eyes glinted in the low light.

Sunny wasn't sure fitting all of them into the confined space of the apartment was the best idea, but drinking tea while standing at the counter didn't sound like a good alternative.

"After you, Mr. Valderos," Ash said. It was a command, not a request. Valderos hesitated only a nanosecond before following Armenta, his cape rippling behind him.

Sunny found the wavelike motions of the cape mesmerizing. She jerked her attention away to see if Ash had noticed the cape, too, but his gaze seemed to be fixed on the back of Valderos's head. He took her hand and gave it a light squeeze before ushering her ahead of him. Sunny's heart was beating a loud tattoo she hoped wasn't audible.

Armenta filled the kettle and set it on the stove. She took a square tin out of her big purse and opened it, releasing heady aromas of sugar and spices.

"Oatmeal raisin," Armenta announced. "In your honor, Mr. Valderos. The raisins. What some grapes become that are not processed into wine." She pulled out a chair next to the stool she usually occupied "Have a seat."

"Would you like me to take your cape?" Sunny offered. She wasn't sure whether she wanted to touch the cape or not. It seemed to have a life of its own as it continued to sway gently, almost hypnotically.

"No, thank you. That will not be necessary." Valderos pushed the cape back from his shoulders and sat.

Ash pulled out the chair farthest away from Valderos. "Why don't you sit here?" he suggested to Sunny.

She realized she couldn't see what the cape was doing from that seat and accepted his offer. But she felt a mixture of relief and cowardice to see Ash take the stool, placing himself right next to Valderos. Armenta brought cups, saucers and napkins from the counter.

She held out the tin to Valderos. "I baked them from scratch this morning. Brown sugar and steel-cut oats."

Valderos took one of the oversized russet-hued cookies. "They look delicious. Thank you." Without taking a bite, he placed his cookie on the napkin Armenta had given him.

"Don't wait for us," Ash encouraged their guest. "Armenta's cookies are too good to hang around for long. I eat more than my fair share whenever I visit." He took one and bit into it, munching loudly.

Sunny thought of the Mad Hatter's tea party. Not the first time she had imagined being in Lewis Carroll's book, she thought, unsure whether she felt amused or appalled. She wondered whether the next time she blinked, she'd find Watcher sitting in the middle of the table instead of the cookie tin, or at the head of the table in place of the March Hare.

"So, what have you both decided about my offer?" Valderos asked.

"You're pretty direct," Ash commented. He finished the cookie and took another.

Sunny realized they had worked through lunch. Ash must be really hungry, she thought, even as she wondered why her mind was wandering off the subject at hand. Perhaps she was feeling the effects of low blood sugar. "Can I have one of those?" she asked.

"Sorry." Ash passed her the tin.

"No point in beating around the bush," Valderos said. "What is your answer, Mr. Haines?" He leaned forward to make eye contact with Sunny. "Ms. Kingston?"

Sunny swallowed the entire piece of cookie she had just bitten off. As she tried not to choke, she felt a strange tingling in her scalp, like static electricity. Unable to speak, she shrugged, hoping that would suffice.

"You can at least wait until you've got your tea," Armenta reprimanded.

She filled the pot with hot water. Steam rose into the air, and a fragrant aroma wafted across the table after she heaped several spoonfuls of leaves into the water and stirred gently before placing the lid on the pot. She added a cozy, padded and decorated with what she had told Sunny were embroidered sprigs of Jasmine. Armenta had also added a Peace Lily to the center of the table that morning, for positive energy, she said. Sunny saw Valderos give both the plant and the cozy a couple of sideways glances while he appeared to be concentrating on his yet-untouched cookie.

"Are you going to let that steep for ten minutes?" he asked when Armenta sat. "I'm a busy man, Ms. Kaslov."

"Is that what you are?" she asked. "A man, I mean. Men love my cookies, but you haven't even tried yours."

Valderos glared at her. Armenta stared right back, unblinking. Sunny watched, awed by Armenta's unflappable calm. She knew she would have been sweating if he'd looked at her with the same blazing intensity.

Valderos abruptly broke eye contact. "I already told Ms. Kingston I am not the Devil," he said, his tone dry. A slight quirk appeared at one corner of his mouth.

"*A* devil. *The* Devil. There's a difference we are all aware of," Armenta responded. "Usually, when someone like you makes an offer such as the one you made my friends yesterday, something is required in return. Usually, that is something significant and very unappealing to mere mortals."

"Ah, but Ms. Kingston is no mere mortal," Valderos responded. "She has special powers."

"Powers you would like to tap into," Armenta said.

"This is a negotiation, Ms. Kaslov. Between Ms. Kingston, Mr. Haines and myself."

"No negotiations are going to happen without Ms. Kaslov," Ash responded, his voice calm but his jaw noticeably tight.

Armenta picked up the pot. She poured tea into four cups. Green tea. Sunny fervently hoped it wouldn't start swirling. Perhaps it was benignly herbal instead. She could only hope.

"Drink," Armenta encouraged.

Valderos took his cup in hand and sipped. "Very good," he

commented. "Do I detect laudanum?" He smacked his lips. "Perhaps not. There is no bitterness."

"I'm not trying to poison you, if that's what you're thinking." Armenta lifted her own cup and took a sip. She didn't elaborate on what variety of tea she had used.

Sunny chanced a look inside her own cup. Nothing swirled, spun or churned. She sipped. It tasted like the regular herbal tea Armenta brewed frequently. She allowed herself a little sigh of relief she hoped no one else heard.

"I prefer English Breakfast," Ash said. "I'm not much of a fan of green herbal tea." He took a sip, grimaced, and set down his cup. He took another cookie.

"So, we are ready to negotiate?" Valderos asked. "My expertise can be shared with you, Ms. Kingston. I can enhance your powers. You will be able to assist Mr. Haines more effectively in the search for his daughter's killer. You have been experiencing difficulty controlling your visions."

"How do you know that?" Sunny made no attempt to smooth the sharpness from her voice.

"I know much, Ms. Kingston." Valderos took another sip of the tea, but his cookie remained untouched.

"What *are* you?" Ash asked. "And why do you care about whether my daughter's killer is found? What's in it for you?" His hands clenched into fists. "You'd better stop hinting around and lay everything out or I'm throwing you out of here. On your ass." His elbows locked, and his chair grated against the floor as it moved away from the table.

"You will not be able to get physical with me, Mr. Haines, but I appreciate the effort. You are an adequate protector for the three women in your immediate circle. I am including your daughter, Katie, of course." The glint in Valderos's eyes brightened.

"You leave Katie out of this," Ash warned.

"Ash," Sunny pleaded. She laid her hand on his forearm and felt the muscles relax slightly.

"More tea, Ms. Kaslov?" Valderos raised his index finger slightly.

The pot lifted and poured tea first into Armenta's cup, then into Valderos's. He looked at Ash and Sunny. "Would you both like more?"

Ash cleared his throat. His Adam's apple bobbed. "No, thank you. That's a good magic trick."

Sunny realized her hand was still on Ash's arm, and she was squeezing hard. She quickly let go. His hand dropped from the table, clasped hers and held it. She wasn't sure whether the contact was for her benefit or his. Perhaps for them both. She thought she detected a slight tremor through his wrist, but wasn't sure whether he was shaking, or she was.

Valderos had the quirk back at the corner of his mouth. "I have a proposition for both of you," he said. "If you like it, then you will agree to it, and we will move forward. If you do not, then the visions will continue to be troublesome and without resolve, Ms. Kingston, and your daughter's killer will not be found, Mr. Haines. I guarantee that, unfortunately. The perpetrator of the crime will remain unpunished."

"How can you know that?" Ash was on his feet.

"Sit down, Mr. Haines. There is no need for drama." Valderos made a sweeping motion with his hand.

Ash sat. He looked a little bewildered to be back in his chair. The color left his face.

"Are you okay?" Sunny took his hand and felt coldness seep into her skin.

Ash wasn't answering her.

"What did you do to him?" she asked Valderos. "Stop it, immediately, or I'm not going to even consider your proposition."

"Very well." Valderos motioned again.

The color came back into Ash's face. His hand warmed. "I heard you both, but I couldn't move or speak," he said, his voice alarmingly weak.

"Don't try anything like that again," Sunny told Valderos.

"You are very strong, Ms. Kingston." He gave her the thin smile. "I am going to like working with you from time to time."

"I'm sure I won't reciprocate that feeling." She gave him the strongest glare she could muster. He stared back with those putty-colored eyes, the pupils narrowing to slits.

"Lay your cards on the table," Armenta said. "I hate lengthy meetings almost as much as you seem to, Mr. Valderos."

"Very well." He stopped staring at Sunny.

She felt like a heat lamp had been turned away.

"I am in a little trouble," Valderos said. "I have actually been in that little trouble for a while now. In my frame of reference, it is a really long time, but that is not the issue. You want the short version. I am in disgrace. I have been informed I can regain favor by performing some…" he grimaced, "…beneficial deeds. Like the one I am offering you, Ms. Kingston, and you, Mr. Haines."

"I can fall for you helping Sunny gain control over her visions," Ash said. "But I don't see how you're going to help me solve Amy's murder. Are you going to give me the killer's name?"

His voice continued quiet and weak. The staccato thump of Sunny's heart increased again.

"Nothing that simple, Mr. Haines," Valderos said. "You will have to agree to assist Ms. Kingston with bringing resolution to others in your situation as well as yourself."

"If that's all you want, then I could agree to that without all the theatrics," Ash said.

"Careful," Armenta cautioned. "Remember what I told you both before he arrived."

"You advised them not to agree to any false promises, Ms. Kaslov. For a human, you are indeed a wise and prudent guide. But I will not harm any of you. I need Ms. Kingston and Mr. Haines to succeed, so I can regain favor and return to my previous position. For me, living here and having to operate a business is pure hell."

"Your Pinot Noir reflects that," Ash said.

He was playing with fire. Sunny tightened her grip on his hand.

Unexpectedly, Valderos laughed. It was a resounding laugh that echoed around the apartment. "You are unafraid of me, Mr. Haines. I appreciate your spirit. But be careful, as Ms. Kaslov counsels. You do not want to anger me."

"Don't threaten. That's not the way to gain favors around here." Ash rapped his knuckles on the table. "I want you to tell us in plain English what you want to give us and what you expect in return. You said you don't want our souls. What else is in it for you?"

"Very well." Valderos pushed his empty teacup aside. He leaned forward, hands clasped and forearms resting on the table. "There is only one catch to me endowing you with improved investigative powers, Mr. Haines, and you with clearer visions, Ms. Kingston. There is nothing for you, Ms. Kaslov. You have already chosen your path. I could not offer you anything you could possibly want, except, perhaps, peace of mind with this transaction." He leaned back, picked up the cookie and took a bite. "Delicious, indeed. You see, I eat and drink like the rest of your species." He looked down, brushed crumbs from the front of his black suit jacket and shook his cape again.

Sunny watched, wondering whether he was going to perform another illusion or something far more sinister. But he appeared relaxed as he drummed the fingers of one hand on the table. His nails were slightly long and well-manicured. She noted they tapered to a sharper point than she had noticed before. She tried not to stare at the six fingers.

"You will have to agree to descend one step," Valderos said. "Only one. And you can ascend that step again when you have completed your tasks."

"What steps are you talking about?" Sunny thought she knew, but she needed her fears confirmed. "And how many tasks? Are we talking two tasks or two hundred?"

"Ten tasks." Valderos surveyed his fingers, like he was checking his manicure. "If you wish to continue after that, you will have no further debt that has to be repaid."

"What kind of tasks?" Ash asked.

Valderos stopped studying his cuticles. "You must solve ten homicides as a team. Within Oregon. You are not being asked to travel throughout the globe."

"Are we talking individual murders? Cold case crimes?"

"I do not know what cold case crimes are." Valderos looked genuinely confused. "They must be crimes that have remained unsolved despite all efforts by law enforcement, family, friends and community.

Like your daughter's, Mr. Haines. There are many more. You should have no trouble finding and solving ten of them."

"Is this in addition to nailing Amy's killer?" Ash asked.

"Yes." Valderos nodded. "Solving her crime is my gift to you. I have to give you something with high stakes, or you would not be interested."

"And what do you get out of this?" Ash asked. "Whose good graces are you trying to get back into?"

"That is none of your business." Valderos stopped lounging and surveyed them all with his slitted eyes. "Any of you. Now, or in the future." He stood up. "You have twenty-four hours to think about my offer. Remember, you are only agreeing to go down one step until you have solved those ten murders."

"Down one step to where?" Sunny felt a chill come over her like a smothering icy blanket. "Are you talking about Hell?"

"It has many names, Ms. Kingston." Valderos's cape began undulating in a slightly erratic manner.

"Let's not mince words," Ash said. "Call it like it is in these parts. Hell. Down below. The fire and brimstone place."

Valderos shrugged. "Whatever you want to title it."

"I'm not agreeing to take any steps down toward the toasty zone," Ash said. "Count me out."

"Not even to bring Amy's killer to justice? Not even for your own peace of mind and the safety of your other daughter?"

"What the hell do you know about Katie's safety?" Ash sounded horrified.

"You throw that name around very freely, Mr. Haines," Valderos said. "Your other daughter is safe for now, but she knows something of which she is unaware. Amy's killer suspects this. He will come after her, Mr. Haines. Mark my words. I never lie."

"Interesting you say you're always truthful," Armenta said. "That's not typically a trait for demons."

"I am not your common demon, devil or anything else you are familiar with," Valderos said.

"Oh, so you're special," Sunny said. "A truthful something from down below." She tapped the floor with her foot. "Or a charlatan who's trying to get us to do his bidding."

"Oh, please." Valderos rolled his eyes. "Do I really have to perform another so-called magic trick to get you to believe me? To cooperate? I was hoping to avoid the theatrics. They tend to frighten mortals to death, and they give me indigestion."

CHAPTER FORTY-NINE

ASH WANTED to grab Sunny and Armenta as soon as the words left Valderos's mouth, but he felt like he was moving in slow motion. Valderos raised both hands and what looked like an electric charge flew from him to Sunny. The impact pinned her to the back of her chair, her blonde hair streaming behind her. The effect only lasted a breath of time, and then it was over. Ash opened his mouth and gulped in air. He felt like he'd been in a vacuum. Sunny's gaze meet his. Her eyes glinted, like Valderos's.

"What did you do to her?" Ash pitched himself at Valderos. *To hell with the consequences,* he thought as his hands fastened around the man's throat.

He found himself back in his chair and had no idea how he had gotten there.

Valderos straightened his tie. "I warned you not to get physical, Mr. Haines."

Ash's hands hurt. He brought them up from his lap and stared, horrified. The skin was blistering on all his fingers. His palms felt as though he had touched an open flame.

Valderos waved one hand, and the burns disappeared. "My gift to *you,* Mr. Haines. If you attempt anything similar again, I might not be so generous."

"Ash was trying to protect me." Sunny's voice quivered. "He wanted to know what you did to me."

"I gave you the insight your gift lacked." Valderos shook out his cape. "I will return tomorrow."

"Wait!" Armenta stepped forward. "You didn't tell them how they can ascend that one step, and if there are seven steps in total, or only two. I have heard, and read, many books that disagree on the number."

"Whatever you believe." Valderos brushed tiny shimmering specks from the cuffs of his suit jacket. "I am not dictating the number of steps that exist. I am only telling you that you will descend one of them if you accept my offer."

"Then how do we get to back up?" Sunny asked. "And how will we know that we have?"

She had gotten to her feet, but she didn't look very steady. Ash tentatively gripped the arms of the captain's chair, felt no pain through his hands, and stood.

"Consult with Ms. Kaslov or a priest if you want more answers." Valderos sounded irritated.

The apartment felt hotter suddenly. Alarmed, Ash tried to divert Valderos's attention from Sunny. "Did you send Amy to me last night, and Tina to Sunny?" he asked.

"Perhaps." Valderos shrugged.

"Don't do it again," Sunny said. "If you do, any deals we make are off."

Ash tried sending her a cautionary look, but she was intently watching their visitor. He couldn't believe she would risk antagonizing Valderos further by issuing ultimatums. She was in no position to dictate anything, he thought. Neither was he. Neither was Armenta. That man, or whatever he was, had control of them all.

"Very well." Valderos bowed slightly to Sunny, then to Armenta before inclining his head briefly toward Ash. With that, he turned and strode away, his cape flapping behind him like a ship's mainsail.

Armenta followed close behind.

Ash grabbed Sunny's arm. "Stay behind me," he told her, but she shook him off.

"Don't try to order me around," she said. "You're lucky you didn't make him angrier. What were you thinking? My god." She grabbed his wrists. "He burned you without even touching you."

A beating of wings and a bit-off oath from Valderos sent them rushing into the shop.

Valderos cowered, one arm thrown protectively over his head. Above him, Watcher circled, wings beating rhythmically, long tail flapping, talons extended. Armenta held the front door open. Valderos charged through it.

Ash couldn't help himself. "See ya,' Vinnie," he called.

"Good grief, don't bait him." Sunny pushed Ash behind a display rack.

Armenta closed the door. Watcher returned to the counter and shook his wings before folding them neatly across his back. His tail slid across the glass counter before curling around his feet.

"Christ, I need a drink," Ash said to no one in particular.

Since Sunny was still holding his right arm, he took a look at his left hand before rubbing it across his face. Even the pink tinge had faded. Ash wondered whether he was in the middle of a waking nightmare, much like the one he'd experienced the previous night.

"I could do with a drink, too," Sunny said from beside him. "My head hurts."

Armenta trotted swiftly past them. "I have a bottle of brandy in my purse," she said.

"Of course you do," Sunny muttered. "You have anything and everything in that purse." She tugged Ash's arm. "Come on. Let's fortify ourselves before something else happens."

CHAPTER FIFTY

"I'm not waiting for him to come here," Ash said after he'd finished a juice glass filled with Armenta's brandy. "I'm going to confront him at the vineyard. Just not today." He held up the glass for a refill, but Armenta put the bottle back into her purse. He looked at the cold green tea in his cup and felt queasy. "Can I have a cup of coffee?"

"You're not a fan of green tea, are you?" Armenta took the cup away. "Coffee for you, too, Sunny?" She placed the cup in the sink and took the coffee carafe from the draining rack.

"Yes, please." Sunny rubbed her hands together. "I need to warm up. Ever since Valderos did whatever he did, I've felt cold to my core."

Ash brought the afghan from the couch and wrapped it around her shoulders. When she looked up at him, her eyes glinted. Startled, Ash backed away. He collided with the end table beside the couch. A lamp toppled off and landed on the floor.

"Careful," Armenta said, coffee scoop in hand. "That lamp's an antique. I think it belonged to Tina's grandmother."

"I'm sure it's okay," Sunny said. "If it isn't, no great loss. It's really ugly and much too big for the space."

"If I broke it, I'll either fix or replace it." Ash put it back on the table, but couldn't straighten the bent shade.

"Tsk, tsk." Armenta sank the scoop into the coffee canister.

Ash decided to address the elephant in the room. "Armenta, you must have noticed. Why are you ignoring it?"

"Ignoring what?" Sunny frowned. "Did something else break?"

"No." Ash strode over and picked up the carafe. "Well, did you?"

"I did." Armenta calmly took the carafe out of his hand. "But I don't think anyone else will, except maybe Katie." She turned on the water and began filling the pot.

"See what?" Sunny was running both hands over her face. "What did he do to me? Did he give me purple splotches or something?"

"No, child." Armenta turned off the water. "Go into the bathroom and look in the mirror, but don't turn on the light."

Sunny scrambled to her feet and ran into the tiny bathroom. A piercing shriek followed. The bathroom light flickered on. A moment later, she came back into the kitchen and leaned against the wall. "I don't feel so good." All color had drained from her face.

Ash brought her over to sit at the table.

"My eyes," she said. "What did he do to my eyes?"

"He enhanced your powers," Armenta said. "I can sense it. He's given you an enormous gift."

"What if I don't want it?" Sunny rubbed her eyes with the heels of both hands. "It'll be a little difficult to explain to people. What am I going to say? 'Oh, don't worry about the gleam in my eyes; it's a natural phenomenon. You know, like some people have crooked teeth.'"

"I don't think you have to worry about that," Armenta said. "I'm more worried about the 'one step down' bit that came along with the gift."

"Yeah." Ash's stomach tightened at the thought. "He said he was going to give me something, too, but the only thing I got was a brief stage-four burn to both hands. Scared the crap out of me."

Armenta shook her head. "He also gave you what he said he would, along with that very graphic warning."

"What? The promise of exceptional detection skills? I don't feel the need to buy a deerstalker hat and go detect anything."

Armenta's eyebrows drew closer. "Not even in your daughter's case?"

"I've tried, believe me. But everywhere I went, Schilling had already been there. There aren't any new leads to follow."

Armenta pushed the button to start the coffee's brewing cycle. "I know you keep the earring in your pocket. Take it out."

Ash dug in his pocket and brought out the little Ziplock bag. He held it up. "I went into every shop in Salem. No one remembered selling anything like it."

"But you didn't go *outside* Salem," Sunny said.

"I didn't. I thought this was a dead-end. You've handled it several times without getting a vision." Ash felt defensive. Angry. Like the two women were accusing him of giving up too quickly.

"Yet you keep it with you," Armenta said.

"I couldn't risk having a chance meeting or seeing someone wearing something similar." Ash knew he was snapping at them, but he didn't care.

"Give it to Sunny again. Let her hold it. This time, she may have a revelation."

"You said Valderos enhanced my powers," Sunny said. "What use is that for finding out anything from the earring? Isn't clairvoyance only for the future?"

"Not always, and I didn't specifically mean clairvoyance." Armenta sat down and took the bag from Ash. She opened it. "There are more forms of psychic ability than that. A gift such as yours can also reveal things from the past. "Open your hand," she told Sunny.

"You've never given up, Ash. You've always felt it's a clue." Sunny held out her hand. "Okay, I need to find out whether Valderos really gave me more than a fright and a pair of really sparkling blue eyes. This is the perfect opportunity. Let me try again."

Ash barely dared to hope that Valderos had sharpened Sunny's skills. He found it difficult to breathe as he watched her fingers close over the earring.

She placed her right hand on his arm. A tingle shot all the way up to his jaw. "Dallas," he said.

"Yes." Sunny nodded. "We'll go together in the morning."

CHAPTER FIFTY-ONE

THE ROCKS and Crystals Shoppe stood at the corner of a nondescript mini strip mall. When Ash parked in front of the store, he wasn't sure it was worth going inside. A small neon sign in the window sporadically declared it was open, although poor interior lighting threw that into doubt.

"It doesn't look very inviting," Sunny said. She opened her door. "Armenta said she thought it had closed last year. The owner was really old and in ill-health."

"Maybe you should stay here," Ash cautioned. "I'll come out if I need you."

"Are you afraid my glowing eyes will scare whoever's inside?" She grinned at him before hopping out of the SUV. "Cheer up. I'll be better than a flashlight, and we might need one of those. Good grief, it's dark in there."

Her attempt at levity did nothing to alleviate Ash's misgivings. He remained sure his determination to prove Amy's death was no accident had unduly influenced Sunny and made her vulnerable to Vincente Valderos.

If he hadn't gone into her shop, Ash said to himself. If he hadn't picked her up from the floor and carried her, swooning, into her apartment. If they had both ignored Armenta's questionable delusions. The If-list in his head went on and on.

But Sunny would have met Valderos anyway, Ash reasoned. Valderos would still have gone into the shop to purchase the buddha. But then he had to wonder how Valderos knew of the buddha's existence. Questions without answers. Questions that might never be satisfactorily answered before more strange events occurred. He stepped out of the Range Rover and watched Sunny give him a reassuring smile before they closed their doors and he locked the vehicle.

Ash had never been one to spend much time considering whether there was an afterlife and where he'd end up if there was one. Everything had changed after Valderos left the store, his cloak flapping behind him, as Watcher the granite gryphon circled overhead. The impossible had become the incredible truth.

Armenta had been so worried; Ash had no doubt they were all in danger. At least Katie was safely at the coast with her mother and grandmother. But he wondered whether he was being delusional, thinking Lincoln City was a safe zone. Valderos might well be able to cast his net as far as he wanted. Hell, Ash thought, feeling irony at the word he'd chosen to use, the other side of the world might not be far enough away.

"Come on, Ash," Sunny said, giving his arm a gentle shake. "Let's be hopeful."

Ash reluctantly peered through the front window. He couldn't see anything beyond a display of dusty crystal balls. "I can't stop worrying, and with good reason. Maybe the owner *did* die. Maybe the shop really *did* close. Valderos could have arranged something to trick us."

"Come on, Ash. We'll be okay." Sunny tugged him to the front door. "Armenta read the cards this morning. I cast Tina's runes. I've been studying the book. Both readings were positive. Armenta said we have to keep on this path. My enhanced instincts are telling me the same thing."

Her fingers closed around his wrist, and a sense of peace flowed through him.

"Okay." He took a deep breath. "Let's do this." He halfway expected the door to be locked, but when he pulled the handle, it opened. A fusty smell wafted out. A mixture of familiar odors Ash now recognized as sage, myrrh and lavender vied with musk and decay. The odors were much stronger than the other metaphysical stores he had visited. He stopped to sneeze.

Sunny slipped past him as though drawn by some invisible force. Ash quickly followed. The door closed behind him, and a set of bells jingled from above. Sunny disappeared into the gloom. He paused on the threshold and squinted, hoping his vision would adjust before he felt compelled to use a flashlight.

"Good morning," a voice called from somewhere ahead.

Female, Ash thought, *with a clear, high voice.* His vision cleared, and he peered around. The interior was incredibly crowded, dark and dingy. He spotted Sunny at the counter. She'd moved quickly and purposefully around a clutter of shelves, baskets and miscellaneous piles of merchandise at floor level.

Ash worked his way through a maze he suspected was designed to detour customers through as much merchandise as possible before arriving at the counter. He dodged around and ducked under wind chimes, dream catchers, and crystal chakras, light catchers and prisms, some of which hit his head. In fact, some of them seemed to start swinging right before he reached them. By the time he joined Sunny, his head was sore.

"May I help you with a selection?"

A woman sidled toward them. She wore an orange and yellow kaftan beneath a deeply-fringed turquoise shawl. A pink and orange scarf twisted around her head concealed her hair. Gold hoops dangled from her ears, and silver bracelets jangled on her wrists. Fetishes and charms adorned several long, gold necklaces.

"I'm Serenova Shappasian." The woman smiled, exhibiting gold incisors. "I own the shop. Lovely, isn't it?" She swept an arm around, bracelets chattering excitedly. "You'll find everything you desire."

When she came under the subdued light of a single bulb hanging over an extensive jewelry display, Ash realized that despite her voice, she was an older woman. Thin, angular, and with a pointed chin.

"You do have a lot of merchandise," he agreed.

Sunny held up a pair of earrings. "These look similar to the one you have, Ash. Can we compare?" She laid the earrings on the counter. Her eyes glimmered in the low light as she looked at him.

Ash's mind wanted to wander away, perhaps taking his body with it. He pulled himself together, took the earring out of his pocket and laid it next to the others.

"Very similar." Sunny pushed Ash's earring toward Serenova Shappasian. "Is this one of yours?"

Serenova also had a pair of glasses dangling on a chain around her neck. She placed them on the end of her nose and studied first the earring Sunny had indicated, then the pair.

"This may be one we have sold," she said, pointing toward the lone earring. "I believe we had several similar pairs last winter. Exceptionally fine work. Let me look. Our local suppliers are asked to send images of the items they would like to place with us. If I know it's something that would sell here, then I have them bring those items to the shop before I purchase or take them on consignment. I always want to see if what they sent me accurately depicts the quality." She walked to the other end of the counter and brought a large book from beneath the register.

Ash took the earring he had found. Sunny brought the other pair. Serenova snapped on a banker's lamp, illuminating the book. She leafed through pages covered with images of jewelry and spidery handwriting.

"Ah, yes. Sebastian Poole made those." She slid the book toward Sunny and Ash. "Now, let me see who purchased them." She brought out another book.

Ash looked at the photographs, and his wandering attention snapped back into its rightful place. Three pairs of earrings from the same designer, one set identical to the earring he'd found in the mud at Riverfront Park.

"Yes, here it is." Serenova brought over the other book and tapped it. "A Mister Clive Pritchard. He paid cash. Visiting from Reedsport, I think." She took off her glasses. "I told him he'd driven a long way to visit a metaphysical shop. That's why I remember him. He had business in Salem. Something he had to take care of. I warned him the earrings didn't have any backs to hold them in his ears. He didn't want to purchase those separately. He told me he didn't have any more cash, and he had forgotten to bring his debit card." She frowned. "I thought it a little strange, making a trip like that without making sure to bring a card for expenses, then purchasing a pair of earrings, but..." she shrugged, "...to each his own, after all."

"Do you remember what Pritchard looked like?" Ash tried to keep the excitement out of his voice. He was out of practice maintaining a poker face, and he'd been waiting too long for any positive news to come about Amy's case. He saw speculation in Serenova's eyes as she stared up at him.

"I do. My store doesn't get that many out-of-towners. He was about your height." An ornate ruby and gold ring glinting on her index finger as she tapped the ledger entry again. "There's a crystal hanging to the left of you. It never sells, but it's useful for judging a customer's height."

Ash looked to his left. Sure enough, a large pink crystal hung close to his ear.

"He had dark curly hair and thin eyebrows. Washed-out blue eyes. I couldn't tell you what he was wearing. I study faces, not clothing. Some dark outfit."

"How about his voice?" Sunny asked. "Low, high?"

"Low." Serenova closed her book. "When I bought this place from the previous owner, she told me to keep the ledger. She said one day it would help a person in need. She was right."

"Thank you." Sunny slid the earrings toward Serenova. "We'll take these, and a couple of your smudge sticks."

Serenova rang up the purchases, wrapped everything separately and placed them in a small paper bag with a jute handle. As she passed the bag to Sunny, their fingers touched. Ash saw both women look startled.

"Your power is very strong." Serenova's voice had become soft and breathless. She turned toward Ash. "You're her partner, aren't you? Take very good care of her."

"I do. Well, I try to." Ash attempted a chuckle, but it strangled in his throat.

Sunny took his arm. "We have to go. Thank you again, Serenova."

"You're most welcome." The woman smiled. "Please come to see me again."

277

Ash pulled out one of his new business cards and placed it on the counter. "Call if you remember anything else or the guy comes back."

Serenova looked at the card. "Investigations," she read. "What kind?"

"The needed kind," Ash said.

Sunny tugged on his arm, and he let her hurry him out of the shop. "What's going on?" he asked.

"I had a revelation when her hand touched mine. He must have handled those other earrings. He's after Katie." She bit her bottom lip. "That description she gave…Armenta told me a guy came into the shop the other day and was asking our regular customers a lot of questions. I thought Valderos might have sent him, but the man's description fits Clive Pritchard."

"I told you to get security cameras," Ash said.

"I can't squeeze anything else out of the budget this quarter." Sunny sounded irritated as well as anxious.

"Katie's safe in Lincoln City for now," he assured her. "No one outside the family knows she's there except you and Armenta. You're with me, and Armenta's putting so many spells around the shop, even Valderos will need to be invited inside." Ash unlocked the Range Rover. "I should call Brad Schilling, but he'll say I'm crazy if I tell him he needs to bring in Clive Pritchard based on what we learned from Serenova. It's not enough."

Sunny worried her bottom lip as she fastened her seatbelt. "So frustrating, but I know you're right. What do you want to do?"

"Well, I can tell you one thing…Caroline won't be receptive to coming back from the coast so I can stake out her house and follow Katie wherever she goes. Caro would be even less receptive to me hiring a couple of former Portland detectives to do the job." Ash backed out of the parking space, but hesitated before turning onto the street. "But why would Pritchard target Katie? Caroline and I already talked to her several times about whether she had seen or done something she hadn't told us about, and she swore she hadn't."

"What if she didn't know she'd seen something she shouldn't, though, Ash? Maybe she didn't know what she was looking at, but Pritchard doesn't want to take the chance that someday she *will*."

Ash had a feeling of urgency. Something was telling him not to spend another moment in Dallas. So far, Sunny's predictions had been correct. If Pritchard was hunting for Katie, he might be aware school was out for the summer, and if he had found out where Caroline lived and worked, he'd be heading for Salem, if he wasn't already there.

"Screw worrying about whether Brad is going to tell me I'm crazy; I'm calling him," he decided. He reached for his phone, but it was already ringing, and the car's system picked up the call.

"Mr. Haines, this is Serenova," a hesitant voice said. "I made a mistake when I said that customer was from Reedsport. He was from Newport. And after you left, I saw he was in my store again yesterday afternoon. He bought a pair of earrings and some other items from my assistant, including a book on spells. She was alone in the shop while I had a dental appointment, and she forgot to enter his purchases in the ledger. She just called to apologize and tell me what he bought. He said he was on his way back from Salem. She said she didn't like him, and she was very glad when he left."

"Thanks," Ash said. "Thanks a lot, Serenova. You've been really helpful."

Instead of turning east out of the parking lot, he turned west.

"We're going to Lincoln City," Sunny said.

"You bet." The urgency inside Ash grew into a gnawing in his gut. "I'm calling Caro first, to find out where they all are. Chances are, she's working. Maxine's always out doing something, and she may or may not have Katie with her. Caroline hired a housekeeper to take care of Katie while she's out selling real estate. After that, I'll call Brad and convince him he's got to talk to the cops down in Newport and Lincoln City. Let's hope this guy gave Serenova his real name."

"I'll call Armenta." Sunny dug her phone out of her purse. "She needs to close the store."

Ash swerved around a delivery van. Sunny grabbed the dashboard. "Please be careful," she said. "The last thing we need right now is an accident."

"I know." Even while his foot ached to push down on the accelerator,

Ash kept to what he felt was a reasonable speed as they headed back to Highway 22.

"Valderos is coming back at six," Sunny said. "What are we going to do about him?"

"We'll deal with him later." Ash heard Caroline's crisp tones as her voicemail picked up the call. "Damn, damn, damn," he said. "Caro, call me back immediately. This is an emergency."

"She's probably showing a home," Sunny said. "Armenta can call Valderos and tell him we'll have to reschedule. If we get struck by lightning after that, well, I hope we see each other wherever we end up."

Ash thought of his years with PPB. "In my case, that may be somewhere you don't want to go."

Sunny gave him a reassuring smile. "I very much doubt that."

CHAPTER FIFTY-TWO

BRAD SCHILLING WAS all business when he returned Ash's call. "Clive Pritchard's got a record. I talked to the shop owner in Dallas, and the description her assistant gave matches his mug shot. He lives in Newport now, but a year ago, he was living and working in Salem. He was a carpenter on one of the new condo towers going up close to the river until he got fired for stealing. He was already in the system for beating up his girlfriend outside a bar. She pressed charges. He was overheard telling her she'd be sorry. When she failed to turn up on the court date, charges were dropped. Her landlord said she'd cleared everything out of her apartment and must have left town. Sounded reasonable that she'd want to get away from Pritchard. We may have made a mistake, closing that case so soon. We're trying to get in touch with family, to see when they last heard from her."

"Newport's an easy drive to Dallas or Salem," Ash broke in. "Passing through Lincoln City."

"If Lincoln City PD's unable to make contact with someone at your ex's house, they'll send an officer to make a wellness check," Schilling said. "That's the best I can do right now. The threat's too vague and based on information that's not going to hold up with my supervisors."

"I know, damn it." Ash felt Sunny's hand on his arm. He glanced at her concerned face. "Did you have another vision?"

"What?" Brad asked.

Sunny shook her head.

"Sorry," Ash said. "I was talking to Sunny."

"Where *are* you two?" Brad sounded suspicious.

"On route to Lincoln City. Sunny's trying Caroline's cell, but so far, it's gone straight to voicemail."

"Ash, I know you're really worried, but you and Sunny shouldn't get in the middle of this." Brad's tone was crisp and authoritative. "LCPD touched base with another agent at the real estate office. She said Caroline had a full afternoon, including showing a large home to out-of-state buyers with a big budget. She may have turned off her phone."

"Where the hell is Maxine?" Ash felt a rush of anger. "Caroline made the worst decision ever, taking Katie to the coast."

"Hold a moment." Brad could be heard speaking with someone in an undertone. "Okay, Ash," he said, "we got in contact with Maxine Hildebrand. She's stopping at the outlet mall to pick up a few things for Katie before they go home. She turned off her phone for a hair appointment. She has Katie with her." He sounded annoyed. "Apparently, Mrs. Hildebrand had rescheduled her appointment three times already. The salon said they'd charge her if she cancelled again, and your ex-wife said she couldn't take Katie with her and leave her in the car all afternoon. The detective who spoke with Mrs. Hildebrand said he had trouble getting her to stop talking once she did pick up."

"Typical for Maxine," Ash said. "And she probably lied about the cancellation fee. Damn those two women. You can see why they aggravate me."

"I feel for you," Brad said. "I'm buying flowers for my wife on the way home." He sighed. "Hold another minute."

Ash listened to a second brief and well-muted conversation.

"Mrs. Hildebrand said there's no need for a wellness check, and LCPD isn't going to argue with her," Brad said when he came back on the line. Are you still going to Lincoln City?"

"We are." Ash felt like calling Maxine himself and chewing her out, but knew that would only make her dig her heels in even deeper. There would be no wellness check.

"I tried Katie's burner, but she's not answering her phone, either," Sunny said.

"Can you send Pritchard's mug shot?" Ash asked Brad. "I don't want to risk assaulting a gardener or maintenance guy when I arrive."

"Will do," Brad promised. "Be careful. If you see anything suspicious, call LCPD and let them handle the situation."

"I will. Thanks, Brad." Ash figured Schilling had to cover himself on a recorded line. They both knew Ash wasn't going to stand around and wait for help if he saw anyone in danger.

They had rejoined Highway 22. As they headed toward the heavily-forested Coast Range, Ash dreamed up a couple of satisfying scenarios where he told Caroline and Maxine exactly what he thought of them before walking out the door with Katie. He'd get total custody and only have to see his ex-wife and her mother on special occasions.

Sunny broke the tense silence and brought Ash back to reality. "I'm scared for all of them," she said. "When I touched your arm, I got a flash of someone being really frightened."

"Do you know who?" he asked as they took Highway 18 and passed the casino at Grande Ronde.

Ash's phone beeped. Sunny picked it up. "I think it's the mug shot you wanted."

"Take a look," he said. "Maybe it'll trigger something for you."

She stared intently at the image. "I'm not sure this is the man I saw in my vision," she said, sounding disappointed. "You?" She held up the phone.

Ash took a quick look and saw a dark-haired man who was probably in his early to mid-thirties. Mug shots always seemed to bring out the worst in people, he thought. Maybe it was the lighting, or the reality of knowing they were getting booked. It showed in their eyes and their mouths. But even with those drawbacks, Pritchard didn't look like someone capable of murdering an adult, let alone a child.

"He's not ringing any bells for me," he told her. "And I'm pretty observant."

"Give me the earring," Sunny said.

Ash dug the little plastic bag out of his pocket and handed it to her. Sunny pushed up the cuff of his denim jacket. Then she took the earring out of the bag, held it in one hand and placed her other hand on his bare arm.

Ash felt such a heavy jolt, he momentarily lost control of the wheel. He heard the crunch of gravel beneath the tires as low-hanging tree branches hit the roof and scraped the right side of the vehicle. He cursed as he fought to bring the big SUV back onto the road. Mud and gravel flew. They bumped over the uneven shoulder before he regained control and took them back onto Highway 18.

He gave her a quick glance. "Are you okay?"

"I think so. I jammed my elbow." Sunny winced as she ran her fingers over it. "Really sore, but I don't think anything's broken."

"I'm surprised we didn't get into an accident," he said. "It felt like you shot me with a taser."

"That hasn't happened before," Sunny said. "Has to be another side-effect of Valderos's supposed gift. Does your arm hurt?"

"My wrist's still tingling, but apart from feeling like I stuck my finger in a light socket, everything else seems normal. Did you get anything?"

"Glimpses," she said. "I don't even know whether they have anything to do with today. I saw something hanging…flapping. Brightly colored. Maybe swirling more than flapping." She closed her eyes and concentrated, but no other images came to her. "I can't get a clearer picture." She glanced at her watch. "How much longer before we get there?"

"We're close to the outskirts of Lincoln City," Ash said. "Let's hope we're in time."

CHAPTER FIFTY-THREE

CAROLINE DECIDED she had really heard enough complaints from clients about rescheduling their appointments. She had canceled the rest of her afternoon showings after listening to Ash's alarming voicemails, and the call from Lincoln City's Police Department. No, Caroline thought, she definitely didn't want a wellness check. What would the neighbors think if they saw a patrol car parked outside the house?

She laid her cell on the glass-topped table, picked up her wine glass and took another sip. There was no need to worry, she told herself. The home security system was top-of-the line. She settled back to enjoy whatever uninterrupted time she had left to relax on the back patio and work on her tan before her mother and Katie came home from their shopping trip at the outlet mall. Katie was no fan of retail therapy, so Caroline didn't expect to have more than 30 minutes to herself.

She hiked up her skirt, exposing her thighs, and stretched out in the recliner. Beyond the stone wall, she heard muted sounds of the surf below. The only thing she didn't like about her cliffside house was that waist-high wall, which she planned to replace with glass for an uninterrupted view of the ocean. Her mother had tried to persuade her to leave the work until fall, but Caroline wanted to get the house on the market before all the visitors departed at the end of the season. If the house sold as quickly as she hoped, they'd rent a property outside of Coos Bay until she was sure she liked her new job. She drank to a smooth transition and finished her wine.

Inside the house, a door crashed and she heard voices, one of them Katie's piping tones, which grated on Caroline's already-frayed nerves. Katie wasn't usually excited about much, she thought, pulling down her skirt. She got up and walked inside. Bags were scattered across the coffee table and the couch. "What's going on?" she asked her mother.

"We found everything we needed for Katie in one store." Maxine put down her purse and fluffed out her hair. "I went for a new style and color. Like it?" She turned her head side to side.

"I do." Caroline said, although she wasn't sure she liked her mother's auburn highlights. Katie was jumping up and down on the seat of a recliner. Caroline gave her a disapproving look. "Did Grammy give you too much sugar?"

"I did not," Maxine said,. "But another stylist took her into the break-room, where there was birthday cake. She had two pieces, didn't you, Katie?"

"I did. And two glasses of fruit punch, too." Katie jumped off the recliner and pulled a rainbow-hued swimsuit out of the nearest bag. "Look, Mama." She held it up and waved it around. "Isn't it pretty? Would you like me to model it for you?" Without waiting for an answer, she scampered off.

Maxine kicked off her sandals. "I'm exhausted. We bought far too much, but everything fit, and I wanted to get her home before she broke something."

"Sit down, and I'll get you a glass of wine," Caroline said. "I'm sorry the housekeeper couldn't stay to babysit."

"That makes two of us." Maxine sighed. "I'm going to take these bags to Katie's room. Then I'll join you on the patio. I'm going to encourage her to lie on her bed and read a book. Hopefully, she'll fall asleep, so we can have an uninterrupted talk about your plans for the future."

Caroline didn't want to discuss her plans with her mother until she'd made a few more decisions about how to handle Ash's visitation rights. He wouldn't be able to drive down and take Katie back to his home for a weekend. It was much too far. She didn't want him to think he was going to sell his house and move close to them again. Caroline wanted distance between them. She opened the refrigerator and took out the open bottle of Chablis, filled a glass for her mother, another for herself, and thought she had better take a box of crackers outside to munch on.

The doorbell rang when she was inside the walk-in pantry. Caroline wasn't expecting anyone. Neither, as far as she knew, was her mother. She grabbed two boxes of crackers and closed the pantry door behind her. Surely the police hadn't ignored her refusal and sent some officer to do that wellness check?

"I'll get it," her mother called. "It had better not be the police. You told them not to come. Don't they ever listen?"

"Don't open the door," Caroline said, alarm filling her. "Mother, don't open the door!" She dropped the boxes, ran out of the kitchen and through the living room to see her mother falling to the floor in the front hallway. A man stood in the open doorway. Caroline paused and stared. Suddenly, she realized who he was and why he was there.

She found it difficult to breathe. Her phone was on the patio. If she could get to it, she could hit 911 before he caught up with her. She could only hope that Katie would remember their teachings about safety and what to do in case of a home invasion. Ash had insisted on it. She screamed, not out of terror for herself, but to alert her child.

She continued to scream as she turned and ran. She ran faster than she ever had in her life. Out the patio door. Across the flagstones to the table. She knocked over her empty glass, which hit the ground and shattered. Broken glass sprayed Caroline's lower legs and feet. She barely noticed as she reached for her phone.

He was faster than she imagined. His fingers closed around her wrist even while she used her self-defense training to stomp on his feet. She needed to turn around to knee him in the groin or gouge his eyes, but she couldn't move. He had her pinned against him, and neither arm nor hand was within biting distance. He lifted her effortlessly and carried her, struggling and wildly kicking her legs, to the retaining wall.

"Tell me where she is," he said. "Tell me where she is, or I'll throw you off the cliff."

CHAPTER FIFTY-FOUR

NEITHER ASH nor Sunny spoke as they drove through Lincoln City, the Pacific coming into view as they passed a beach access point before climbing a hill that left the tsunami-zone behind. Ash followed a narrow road that wound between homes that increased in size as they drove further up a steep slope. Sunny rolled down her window to inhale scents of surf and pine.

At the end of the road, a narrow drive led to a sprawling white two-story home with a wrap-around deck and a three-car garage. A dinged-up white Nissan Stanza was parked haphazardly at the front steps. The front door stood wide open.

Ash pulled in behind the Stanza. "Stay here, lock the doors and call 911," he ordered. He leaned across and opened the glove compartment. It held only paperwork and a tire gauge.

"What the *hell?*" Ash turned toward Sunny. "I know my gun was in there. I cleaned it this morning and put it in there." He sounded completely shocked.

Sunny didn't know what to say.

"Did *you* do this?" He accused, anger deepening the ridges around his mouth.

"No, of course not," Sunny said. "Ash, I don't have *that* much power.

HEATHER AMES

If I did, I certainly wouldn't use it to take away your chance to defend yourself and your family."

He didn't look convinced. "I'm trying to prevent someone dying," he said through clenched teeth. He opened his door and got out. "When you make that 911 call, report a home invasion in progress, and tell them there's an unarmed, retired detective on scene. Make sure the dispatcher knows my name, and that I'll be in the house." He gave her a piercing look. "Don't let me down." He quietly latched his door and moved warily toward the house.

Heart pounding, Sunny climbed into the driver's seat, locked the doors and dialed 911. As the phone rang, she watched Ash run in a crouched position to a set of windows close to the front door. After taking a quick look into the house, he flattened himself against the wall and moved over to the doorway. A dispatcher came on the line, identifying herself and asking the nature of Sunny's emergency.

Sunny parroted the instructions Ash had given her. He had left his keys in one of the cupholders. She picked them up. No pepper spray or anything else useful, like a Swiss Army Knife. She made a fast check under the seats, coming up with nothing but fast-food wrappers and empty soda cans.

"Are you still on the line?" the dispatcher demanded.

Ash had disappeared from view. "I am," Sunny told the woman. "Mr. Haines went inside the house."

Her heart accelerated to a painful gallop. The heat inside the closed vehicle became stifling. Ignoring Ash's instructions, she partially lowered the windows. A strong breeze kicked up dust and sand around the vehicle. She closed her eyes and tried unsuccessfully to channel Ash's feelings. But as she used the deep breathing and mind-clearing tactics she needed to free herself from her own frightening thoughts, mists gathered around the periphery of her awareness.

She found herself standing on a large stone patio, surf crashing onto rocks far below. Two people struggled, one wearing the brightly colored skirt she had seen fluttering in one of her previous, much briefer visions. She heard the woman scream as the man bent her backward over a wall at the edge of the patio. Sunny struggled to escape the vision's clutches.

A woman's voice kept calling her, the tone more and more demanding. The mists whirled away, and she was back in the driver's seat of Ash's Range Rover. The demanding voice belonged to the LCPD dispatcher.

A compulsion to be inside the house swept over Sunny. She ignored the dispatcher's summons and opened the door. She had to warn Ash. He had to save the woman on the patio from certain death. As she ran toward the house, she heard piercing, terrified screaming, too high-pitched to be coming from a woman.

Katie!

Sunny ran inside and stopped, horrified. Close to the open door, she saw a motionless woman sprawled on the floor. An older woman with auburn streaks highlighting light brown hair peppered with silver.

Maxine.

Sunny made a split-second decision. There was nothing she could do for Katie's grandmother at that moment. But seeing her on the floor slowed Sunny's precipitous rush. She advanced far more cautiously. A quick glance down a hallway to the left showed it was empty. Farther along, an open door led into an empty home office. The screaming grew louder.

At the end of the hallway, she arrived in a living room with a massive stone fireplace and floor-to-ceiling windows. A small figure stood pressed against the glass, blonde braids trailing across her shoulders. She barely took time to draw breath before one pealing shriek came on the heels of another.

Sunny ran to her. "Katie, it's Sunny."

She tried to pull the child to her, but Katie resisted, mouth wide open, tears streaming down her face. She screamed again and pointed to the window. Sunny looked outside and saw a woman she realized must be Caroline. Wearing that same brightly-hued, flowing skirt Sunny had seen in her vision, Katie's mother struggled with a man who had her pinned against a wall at the far end of the patio. Ash fought to pull off her assailant, while Caroline beat at him with her hands and flailed her legs.

Their valiant efforts weren't enough. The man bent her backwards over the wall. Sunny knew what came next. She forcibly turned Katie away from the window and held her tightly. While the child trembled and sobbed against her chest, Sunny watched the horror unfolding beyond the glass.

The assailant lashed out, viciously kicking Ash, whose leg buckled. Continuing to hang onto the man, Ash started to go down. His weight caused the attacker to stumble and loosen his grip. Caroline's feet left the patio. The pain of being bent over the wall must have been excruciating. Sunny wanted to close her eyes, but she couldn't stop watching.

Ash fell to the ground and brought the assailant down with him. But the damage had already been done. Caroline's entire torso had already gone over the wall. Her skirt flapped in the wind. A sandal came off one of her feet.

Sunny watched in horror as Caroline's legs followed her billowing skirt over the wall. As though part of a vanishing act, Caroline Barlow Westmont Haines completely disappeared from view.

CHAPTER FIFTY-FIVE

"HE TOLD her if she didn't give him Katie, he was going to throw her into the ocean," Maxine said. She winced as a paramedic tended to the large lump on her head. "Caroline refused; fought him back." She gave Katie a squeeze as they sat together on the couch. "Your mother's always been courageous, Katie. Now, she's an even bigger heroine than Nancy Drew."

Katie struggled to free herself. "Grammy, I don't know who Nancy Drew is, and you're squashing me," she complained. "Please let me go. I want Daddy to hold me."

Maxine looked down at her granddaughter's face, streaked with tears. "Your daddy has to stay with the police right now."

"Perhaps Katie can help me make coffee?" Sunny suggested. "You'd like some, Maxine, wouldn't you?"

Maxine grimaced as a dressing was applied to her head. "I'd prefer a brandy."

"That's not advisable, ma'am," the paramedic told her. "You should see your own primary care physician or go to urgent care, since you're refusing to let us take you to the ER."

"I told you already, I'm fine," Maxine snapped, but when she tossed her head in defiance, she groaned and closed her eyes. Her face, already pale, went chalk white.

"Do you need to lie down, ma'am?" His fingers went to Maxine's wrist.

"No, but I am a little dizzy," Maxine admitted. "Perhaps coffee *would* be a good idea."

"A glass of water would be a better choice." He placed a dressing over an abrasion on her elbow.

"It's coffee or brandy," Maxine declared. She released her granddaughter to brush his hand away, even as he tried to attach tape to the dressing.

Katie rushed over to Sunny, grabbed her hand and tugged hard. "Let's *go.*"

Sunny, relieved to leave Maxine in professional hands, allowed Katie to drag her through a spacious dining room into a kitchen that rivaled any she had seen on TV shows. She wondered whether anybody actually cooked in it as Katie led her to a coffee-maker that appeared to dispense everything from hot water and simple drip coffee to coffee pods and cappuccinos, complete with frothed milk. The behemoth almost made her volunteer to pick up an order from Starbucks, but she managed to detach the carafe, fill it with water and with Katie's help, locate coffee and filters.

"Is Mama dead?" Katie whispered. "I saw that man trying to throw her over the railing before you made me look away. If she was alive, they'd let me see her, wouldn't they?"

Sunny agonized. It wasn't her place to tell Katie anything about the fate of her mother, yet the child was too smart to be brushed off by pacifications.

"Your daddy will come in soon and let us all know what happened," she said as she pressed the button to start the brewing cycle. "Your mama's being taken care of by paramedics, like the one who's with your grandmother. I'm sure as soon as she's able to see you, your daddy will take you to her."

Sunny honestly wondered whether she was telling Katie the truth. But she'd seen Caroline move, so she knew Katie's mother had survived the fall, which thankfully hadn't sent her hurtling over a cliff. But whether Caroline was stable enough to see her daughter before going to the hospital was less certain. Worried that her face would reveal her reservations about Caroline's fate, Sunny kept her back turned to Katie and watched as coffee begin to drip, then run into the carafe.

"I hope they don't forget about me." Katie's voice wavered.

Sunny turned to see Katie's bottom lip quivering. Tears filled the child's eyes and spilled onto her cheeks. "Oh, Katie." She crouched down and wrapped her arms around Ash's daughter. She inhaled scents of strawberry shampoo from Katie's hair and something floral from a dryer sheet on her clothes.

Only warm feelings swept through Sunny. Nothing negative. Nothing troubling. "Everything's going to be okay," she said.

"How do you know that?" Katie sniffled against Sunny's neck.

"Because I do. That's my job," she said. "Well, my job when I'm not taking care of the shop," she clarified.

Katie pulled away and gave Sunny a hard stare. "Armenta told me she reads cards to help people find their way when they feel lost. She said you sometimes see things without needing cards or the runes you've been studying."

Sunny silently thanked Armenta's preparation for unusual happenings in The House of Serenity. She wasn't sure Ash would approve, but one thing at a time. She saw a box of tissues on the kitchen counter, pulled out two and handed one to Katie.

"Why don't you blow your nose and help me set up a tray so we can get the coffee into the living room?" she suggested as she carefully dabbed tears from Katie's cheeks.

"Okay." Katie blew her nose and went into the laundry room.

Sunny heard water running.

"I've thrown away my tissue, and I'm washing my hands," Katie called.

Sunny allowed herself a smile of relief and opened the pantry, finding a tray on the bottom shelf. She placed it on the kitchen table, easier for Katie to reach than the breakfast bar.

Together they placed cups, saucers and spoons on the tray. Taking care of the simple task seemed to calm them both, although a disturbing rerun of Caroline going backwards over the wall continued to play in Sunny's mind. She held herself together for Katie's sake, forcing her hands to go through the motions of opening a large container of cream and giving Katie the simpler task of spooning brown sugar into a delicate porcelain bowl decorated with forget-me-nots. Katie spilled some and tried to sweep it into a neat pile at the corner of the tray.

"Don't worry about that." Sunny placed her hand on Katie's head for a moment, the softness of the little girl's hair bringing tears to her eyes.

Caroline had been fighting like a tigress when they arrived. Sunny hoped the man Ash had tackled so ferociously was telling the police everything they needed to know, so Katie wouldn't need to be questioned. She knew everything could have ended horribly if the police hadn't arrived so promptly. But she still wondered how Caroline had avoided falling down the cliff. Had her vision been wrong?

Katie threw her arms around Sunny's waist. "I love you, Sunny," she said. "Please don't leave me with Grammy. She gets so hysterical."

"Oh, my sweet." Sunny didn't know whether to laugh or cry. Feeling shaky, she sat on a chair and held Katie against her. "I won't." She leaned close to Katie's ear. "Whenever you need me, I'll be there for you," she whispered.

"Thank you." Katie hugged Sunny's neck and kissed her cheek.

Sunny blinked back tears. "We'd better get our coffee into the living room."

Katie nodded, brow furrowed. "Grammy shouldn't be left alone or she'll get herself a brandy, even though the paramedic said she shouldn't."

Sunny smothered a smile and added the coffee pot to the tray before picking it up. "I'm right behind you."

Katie skipped over to the pantry and grabbed a packet of chocolate chip cookies. "Someone might be hungry."

"Someone might," Sunny agreed, giving Katie a conspiratorial wink. "Would that someone be you?"

"Maybe." Katie smiled. She picked up a handful of napkins. "For the crumbs," she explained.

"Any time you want to talk, call me on your burner phone," Sunny told her.

"I will." Katie's eyes might be bloodshot and her nose reddened, but her mouth was firm, and her chin squared. She resembled her father when he was firmly debating his point of view. "I'm going to be strong for Mama and Grammy," she told Sunny. "For Daddy, too. He and Mama fight over everything, but he still loves her in his own way."

"I'm sure he does," Sunny agreed, although she thought Katie was over-simplifying her parents' relationship. She watched the little girl scamper off toward the living room.

She stayed behind to clean up most of the sugar spill with a paper towel and pour Katie a glass of milk. Voices drifted to her, one of them Ash's deep, calm tones. When she took her tray into the living room, she saw him sitting at the opposite end of the couch to Maxine and holding Katie on his knee. Katie was brandishing a chocolate chip cookie.

He gave Sunny a brief but reassuring smile. "Katie told me you made coffee together," he said when she placed the tray on the table in front of him. "Thank you."

"I had to do something to keep busy." Relieved he seemed to be none-the-worst after fighting the intruder, she returned his smile.

"Katie got to wave goodbye to her mother before they loaded Caro into the ambulance, didn't you?" he asked his daughter. Katie nodded, her face grave. "Maxine has a friend coming to take her to the hospital for a check-up," he told Sunny.

Maxine looked mutinous, but all she said was: "I take cream in my coffee. A splash."

"We're taking Katie back to Salem with us," Ash said. "I've given my statement, and LCPD knows where to find us. I told them you took care of Katie and didn't see anything."

Relieved, but more than a little worried about how they were going to manage a meeting with Valderos after everything that had happened, Sunny poured three cups of coffee, adding the splash of cream for Maxine and a more generous serving for herself and Ash.

"Maxine?" She held out one of the delicate china cups and saucers Katie had insisted were the right ones to use.

"Grammy," Katie prompted, when Maxine continued to stare ahead.

"What? Oh, yes, thank you." Maxine blinked rapidly. "I was lost in thought. I do hope Caroline is all right. She said her back hurt."

"Maxine," Ash cautioned with a glance toward Katie, "Caroline is going to be okay. She's getting the best care."

"I'm sure she is." Maxine sat up straighter. "Your mother is a tough woman, Katie," she said.

"She is." Katie nodded vigorously. "Really tough. Isn't she, Daddy?"

"Yeah. That's a good description of her."

Maxine glared. Ash shrugged his shoulders. The tension in the room actually dropped a notch or two.

"Good thing you decided not to go to the hospital," Maxine said. "That probably would have sent her blood pressure up."

"Undoubtedly."

"Daddy. *Grammy,*" Katie shook her head.

They all managed to laugh, although Maxine's and Ash's both sounded a little forced. The slightly strained atmosphere continued until they left with Katie and her belongings for the drive back to Salem. Sunny felt that managing to part from Maxine in a positive manner after seeing Caroline almost plunging to her death was a minor miracle.

"Is Katie asleep?" Ash asked Sunny after they were back on Highway 22.

She turned and checked. Katie was breathing quietly and evenly, her head leaning against a big teddy bear she had insisted on bringing with her. The bear was the latest present from her mother, she had told Ash. His name was Edgar, and he wore a jaunty yellow polka-dotted tie.

"I got the story from the Lincoln City detective," Ash said in a slight undertone. "Why Amy was abducted."

Sunny watched scenery flash by as Ash gave the details. She wanted to interrupt several times, but he needed to talk, so she kept quiet while the story unfolded. She felt angrier and more resolved as every minute and every mile passed. She had wondered what she was going to say to Valderos. Now, she knew.

CHAPTER FIFTY-SIX

"So, let me see if I've got this straight," Sunny said. "Caroline left Katie in the car while she showed a house to a client. Katie saw the guy taking photos on his cell while her mother was accessing the lock-box." She glanced back at Katie, but she still appeared to be sleeping.

"Yes. Caroline said she couldn't find a babysitter on short notice, which is bull…" Ash bit off the curse, glanced in the rearview mirror and lowered his voice. "I've told her countless times to call me if she needs a sitter on short notice. If she had, then maybe Amy would still be alive."

"Oh, Ash, you can't go there." Sunny felt his anguish. "Caroline almost paid for that mistake with her life. She refused to tell Pritchard that Katie was hiding, even when he threatened to throw her off a cliff."

"I know." Tears glistened on Ash's cheeks.

"Do you want me to drive?" Sunny asked.

"No. I'm okay."

He didn't sound anywhere near okay, but Sunny wasn't going to insist she take over the wheel. He wasn't driving erratically, and she thought that perhaps having to maintain his concentration was actually helpful to him.

"Let's talk about what happened after Pritchard took those photos," Ash said.

"All right." She waited.

Ash's mouth turned down. "Two days later, he took some girl there, used the code to open the lock box, assaulted and murdered her, and left her body on the deck. She was found the next time the house was shown, which wasn't until the following weekend."

Sunny hoped she would never get a retroactive vision of that crime scene.

"Katie told Caroline about the client using his cell to take pics," Ash continued. "They both thought he was taking shots of Caroline, not the lock box. Caro was so worried she'd lose her real estate license for giving what I'll term special favors to the guy while they were in the house, she kept quiet about it. Since she was doing a favor for the other realtor and left Lincoln City the following day, she didn't hear about the murder." Ash's voice held an undercurrent of fury. "She confessed to leaving her daughter in the car for close to an hour. She bought Katie an ice cream sundae afterward and said if she ever said told anyone, she'd never see me again. Katie believed her."

"How did Pritchard know Katie was in the car?" Sunny interrupted. "If he saw her, wouldn't he have been more careful about taking photos of Caroline opening the lock box?"

"Caroline thinks he spotted Katie when she drove away. Katie complained the car was hot, rolled down the back window and stuck her head out. But he must have only seen a child with blonde hair." Ash stopped speaking to concentrate on safely overtaking an old green sedan laboring up a steep incline in the Coast Range.

"Where was Amy that day?" Sunny took a sip from one of the bottled waters Katie had insisted they bring for the trip back to Salem.

"With Maxine. Amy loved going to the beauty salon with her grand-mother. They always went to the outlets afterward, too." He smiled briefly. "They were a pair of shopaholics. Katie, not so much, although she'll spend hours in a bookstore, and she loves your shop."

Sunny could only imagine Maxine's grief at losing her little compan-ion. "Maxine must miss Amy terribly," she said.

Ash nodded. "Yeah." He didn't elaborate.

Sunny decided keeping their conversation to the facts would be less stressful for him. "Okay, so I can see why Katie didn't want to go with Maxine and Amy, but why did Caroline wait until the last minute to find a babysitter?"

"According to Maxine, Katie and Caroline were planning to go to the beach, but Caro got a call from her realtor friend, begging a favor. She must have believed he was just a looky-loo when she arranged the walk-through. Agents know when a client's really interested in buying. The ones they think aren't seriously committed get a quick tour. Since Caroline wasn't the actual agent, she would only have given him an agency card to follow up if he was really interested. But when they got inside the house, something changed her mind."

Sunny's stomach churned. "It's like fate intervened."

She stared out the window and wondered whether the other realtor would have been so eager to grant those 'special favors' to make a sale. Perhaps Caroline's behavior had actually saved her from becoming a victim. Or maybe Pritchard hadn't planned to murder anyone. Maybe when he returned to the house with that girl, what he thought was going to be consensual turned into a violent encounter. But then he went on killing, like he didn't care how many people he murdered to cover his tracks, she reminded herself.

Tall trees flashed by in a mesmerizing pattern of light and shadow as sunlight glinted through their branches. Sunny felt herself beginning to drift. Mists billowed at the periphery of her mind. She had no intention of tapping into Pritchard's psyche or his victim's. She quickly pulled her attention back to Ash.

"I've never believed in fate," Ash said. "But now, I'm beginning to feel there has to be some sort of grand plan for all of us."

"Maybe there is," Sunny agreed. "We can try to cheat our destinies, but do we really succeed? How would we know if we hadn't?"

"Those are questions you should be asking Armenta," Ash said.

"Maybe." Sunny decided to shelve that discussion. "Didn't Pritchard leave DNA behind that could have linked him to the girl's murder?" she asked. "I've watched a lot of reality cop shows on TV. His prints would be in the system if he already has a record."

"After he murdered her on the deck, a couple of strong storms blew through. Unless they had also touched surfaces inside the home that he hadn't cleaned, there wouldn't be much left to find."

"So how was the house linked to the crime?" Sunny asked, making sure she kept her voice lowered, in case Katie suddenly awakened.

"A TV reporter decided to do an investigative series on unsolved crimes from Florence up to Lincoln City. She picked those parameters because both coastal towns get a lot of tourist traffic, which she was using as an angle. She started with Lincoln City, and the unsolved murder of a young woman that had become linked to a home that was for sale. Apparently, a friend of the victim remembered an off-hand remark about a date the girl was planning with a new boyfriend.

"Pritchard must have seen the broadcast and gotten spooked. The detective I spoke with thinks he tried to contact Caroline, only to find out she wasn't available. I'm sure her friend was reluctant to say she'd blown off a potential sale and had a friend cover for her. When Pritchard finally tracked Caroline down, he must have seen her with Amy and figured she was the child he needed to get rid of." His voice cracked. "Katie had a bad cold and was staying with me to keep her from giving it to Amy. She missed school for over a week." He glanced at Sunny. "Fate again, huh?"

"Oh, Ash." The pain on his face threatened to break her heart.

Sunny ran her hands through her hair and found it sticky with salt. She looked back at Katie. She was still sleeping. Edgar's black plastic eyes stared straight ahead. His tie was crooked.

Ash's phone rang.

"Ash, Caroline's in surgery," a female voice said.

"Hello, Maxine," Ash responded. "I'm sorry to hear that. Her back injury was serious, then?"

"Yes, they have to do a fusion. What a heroine she was when that man came to the house. She protected Katie and me..."

"Maxine, get real," Ash snapped, his cheeks reddening. "Caroline's behavior resulted in Amy's murder. And all three of you would have died today if help hadn't arrived."

"My daughter made a mistake." Maxine's voice had turned to ice. "Haven't you ever made any mistakes? Oh, yes, there was that affair you had."

"There's a lot of blame to go around, Maxine. I'm not going to argue the finer points of our marriage and divorce with you. When Caroline's well enough, we'll get together with our attorneys and revisit her plan to move Katie to Coos Bay."

"I was able to talk to her before she went into surgery." Maxine sounded like she was trying valiantly to keep calm. "Caroline suggested you to keep Katie until she's completely well. That could take months, and I have no doubt you'll be very relieved to send her back to us after that. You always were the parent whose career came before marriage and children."

"This is not the time to insult me, Maxine." Ash ended the call.

Sunny decided Ash didn't need any comments from her while he simmered down. She watched as the heavily-wooded mountainous terrain gave way to fields of crops, fruit orchards or further away, up gentle slopes, vineyards. Traffic became heavier after they passed the turn-off to Independence, a picturesque little town on the other side of the river from Salem. The Willamette River sparkled into view shortly afterward.

Sunny checked the time. "We're meeting with Valderos fifteen minutes after we get back to the shop," she said.

"Yeah, we are." Ash sounded surprisingly calm. "What do you want to do about that?"

Sunny didn't think she could have regained control of her own emotions that quickly. She wondered whether it was some sort of male mind-control thing.

"It's more a case of what are *we* going to do," she said. "If Valderos hadn't enhanced our powers, today might have ended very differently." She took a deep breath, unsure how Ash would take her decision. "I'm going to accept his offer. With this gift, I could help so many people."

Ash's eyebrows rose. "Suddenly, you're ready to accept a gift that sends you into a trance and scares the hell out of you?"

Sunny had to smile at both his shock and his choice of words. "Look, what happened today was horrible, but it could have been so much worse." She tried to speak as carefully as possible. "Caroline will be okay." The corner of his mouth turned down. "Come on, Ash, be generous. She's the mother of your children."

He shrugged. "I'm not feeling very charitable toward her right now. It wouldn't matter if she'd had ten of my children and was supporting me financially; I'd still be pissed."

"Okay, let's leave your hostility alone for now. You tell me how, when the police ask for more details, we're going to explain getting to Lincoln City in time to save Caroline's life and very probably Katie and Maxine's, too?"

"Deduction," Ash said. "We have to get our story straight, but I want to protect you from the cops and the press."

"The detective in Lincoln City is going to want to talk to me," Sunny said. "He's not going to take your word that I didn't see anything. Katie knows I was in the house, and so does Maxine, although she didn't until she staggered into the living room. She saw my glowing eyes. Right now, she may think she was imagining that, but as she calms down, that could change."

"The glow's not as noticeable," he said. "And I'm not just saying that. I think it's wearing off. By the time you have to talk to anyone else about this afternoon, it might be gone. If not, we'll find you some tinted glasses."

"I think it's time I embraced not only my gift, but my ownership of the shop." She ignored his grunt. "What have I got to lose? I may even attract more customers to the shop. And hopefully, the skeptics in both Lincoln City and Salem police departments will think I'm either a bit eccentric or I'm whacked. Eccentric's okay with me. It works for Armenta. But as I've told you before, I'm not too keen on being called a nut-case."

"I'm worried the skeptics and non-believers will try to hurt you," Ash said. The harshness had left his voice. "There are always those who want to destroy anything they don't understand. You could be in danger if word gets out that you have visions."

"I know, but word getting out might bring more grieving people to me who need closure, like you and your family. If I've been given a gift that could help those in need of answers, I'd be selfish and cowardly to hide it."

She felt the need to touch Ash, like that would somehow calm him. She closed her fingers around his wrist and felt a radiating warmth spread across his cold skin.

Ash took several deep breaths. His shoulders relaxed. "You've got some mojo," he said. "The bitterness I've felt for so long...it's fading." He shook his head. "I'm not sure if I'm relieved or resentful."

"Be relieved. Much better than resentful." She squeezed his arm. "Let the past go, Ash. It's time for you to heal."

Her fingers tingled. She released him and looked down, expecting to see some visual evidence of her power. But her hand looked the way it always did, and her fingers were still covered with paper cuts she'd gotten at work instead of any evidence of Valderos's intervention.

"When this first happened to me...when I took over Tina's dream...I thought it would never be mine," she told Ash. "I was sure I would never understand how she felt about her own psychic gift, the shop, and Armenta. Now, I can't think of my life without them."

"And me?" He sounded hesitant.

"Without you, I couldn't have done anything to save Katie or Caroline. You *are* my protector, as Valderos said."

"We're a team, then?" Ash held out his hand.

Sunny slid hers into a warm and comfortingly-familiar grip "We are."

"He told us it's one step down toward Hell, remember?" The pressure from his fingers increased. "Unless we negotiate, like Armenta said."

"You think she's right? We don't have a clue who or what we'll be trying to bargain with. He might turn us into toads."

"Maybe." Ash gave a quick smile. "But from what I heard, Valderos needs us to help him regain favor. That should give us some leverage, don't you think?"

Sunny thought about their previous conversation with the reluctant winery owner. "It's worth a try."

"But whatever we agree to, we need it in writing. I think when you deal with someone you suspect could be a demon, you have to do that."

"Ash, did you go to parochial school or something?"

"Something like that." He grinned.

"That's good, because I definitely don't have any expertise with striking bargains when the other party might not be human."

"We'll figure things out together." He released her hand before turning into the parking lot outside the store, two spaces away from a black Lincoln Navigator.

"Must be him," Ash said.

Katie popped up from her nap. "Are we there, yet?" She yawned widely. "How are you, Edgar?" she asked the bear. "Did you nap, too?"

"He didn't. He kept a close eye on you and acted as a pillow," Sunny told her.

Katie saw the shop, brightly lit under graying skies. "Oh, good." She unbuckled her seatbelt and threw open the door. "I'm hungry, and Armenta always has the best cookies."

Before Ash could stop her, she had run into the shop with Edgar under one arm.

A man in a black suit opened the back door of the Lincoln. Vincente Valderos stepped out. He nodded toward Ash and tipped his hat to Sunny. "Ready?" he asked. "You've had a demonstration of the powers today."

"We have." Ash placed his hand in the small of Sunny's back.

He guided her over to the front door, where Valderos's chauffeur waited. When he opened the door, Valderos stepped inside first. Sunny caught a whiff of something like charcoal or woodsmoke when she passed the unblinking and expressionless chauffeur. The interior of the shop smelled strongly of sage.

Valderos coughed, then sneezed. "Shall we have tea?" He pulled a large white handkerchief from his pocket and dabbed his nose. "Perhaps with some of Ms. Kaslov's excellent cookies." A lazy, lopsided smile barely lifted the corner of his mouth and did not touch his cold, putty-colored eyes. He returned the handkerchief to his pocket.

Watcher flapped his wings as they passed the counter. Valderos shied away, his cloak billowing into widely-flowing ripples. The gryphon screeched, the sound both piercing and bone-jarring.

Sunny took Ash's hand as they followed their would-be mentor into the little apartment. Katie lay sleeping on the bed with Edgar in her arms. Armenta drew the curtain across the alcove and pointed toward the table, where a china teapot sat, a thin ribbon of steam rising from its spout. Ash seated Sunny and placed himself between her and Valderos.

Armenta opened a large tin and offered its contents to Valderos. "Would you like a Snickerdoodle with your tea?"

"Excellent." He took one and bit into it, munching loudly. "Now." He put down the cookie and pulled a large, rolled-up parchment from beneath his cloak. "About the contract." He placed it on the table. "Let's discuss details."

Sunny ran her fingers over the necklace Armenta had given her. She saw Ash had pulled the amulet from beneath his shirt. Armenta poured tea and set the first cup in front of Sunny, who glanced down and saw it swirl once before settling. She took a large sip, almost burning her tongue, but the tea seemed to sharpen her senses.

"Drink," she told Ash. "Green tea's really good for you."

He took a small sip, scrunched up his nose in disgust, then took a larger one. "We've got reservations," he told Valderos.

"Humans always do." Valderos finished his cookie and took another. "But I'm sure we can work things out. I'm reasonable."

"Good," Ash said. "Because we bring special gifts. We had those before you came on the scene."

Valderos laughed. "I look forward to working with both of you."

"About that one step down toward Hell," Sunny said. "We want that taken off the contract."

"It's only a small step." Valderos pouted. "The smallest, in fact. I have to have something. You can't have all the perks and none of the disadvantages."

"Have another cookie, Mr. Valderos," Armenta said.

"Yeah, Vinnie, have two." Ash leaned back and folded his arms across his chest. "We plan to drive a hard bargain."

A crash from the shop made Valderos jump. Sunny heard a loud yowl, followed by flapping that seemed to come from somewhere a lot closer than the counter.

"Ms. Kingston," Valderos said. "I must insist you keep your pets in line."

"As long as you remember to behave," she told him, getting up. "I have no control over the phantom cat that prowls around here, and Watcher, for your information, is no pet."

She walked over to the heavy curtain, which stood wide open. Wings flapped again inside the shop, and Sunny saw a long black tail swish back and forth between two rows of shelving.

"Play nice," she said before partially drawing the curtain. But she left a space she thought Watcher could easily negotiate if it became necessary.

When she returned to the table, she noticed Valderos had indeed taken two cookies. He looked even paler than usual.

Ash finished his tea, and Armenta poured him another cup. Sunny felt an aura of calm encircle her. *Tina,* she thought, and she smiled.

THE END

ACKNOWLEDGMENTS

ACKNOWLEDGMENTS

Thanks again to Pacific Online Writers Group (POWG) members Bonnie Schroeder and Miriam Johnston for their support as well as their insightful critiquing during an extraordinary year when a global pandemic affected everyone's lives.

To Jenn Oliver for making my words look good on the pages with her excellent formatting skills.

And to my readers, whose support is always much appreciated. The first book in this new series takes us all on a very different journey. One I hope you will all enjoy reading as much as I enjoyed writing it.

ALSO BY HEATHER AMES

Brian Swift & Kaylen Roberts mystery/suspense series

Indelible (Book 1)

A Swift Brand of Justice (Book 2)

Swift Retribution (Book 3)

Suspense

Night Shadows

Romantic Suspense

All That Glitters

Contemporary Romance

The Sweetest Song

Upcoming Books 2022/2023

Brian Swift & Kaylen Roberts series - Book 4

Ghost Shop series - Book 2

ABOUT THE AUTHOR

Heather Ames has enjoyed a nomadic life, living in 5 countries and 7 states. Currently, she lives in Salem, Oregon, where after a long career in the healthcare industry, she has finally achieved her dream of writing full-time. She is a past finalist in Romance Writers of America's prestigious Golden Heart contest, and while living in Boston and Los Angeles, she took classes in TV production. She wrote, produced, directed and edited two documentaries, one of which was nominated for an award.

She currently moderates a highly successful online critique group that has been exchanging manuscripts for over ten years. She can be found on Facebook, LinkedIn, Instagram, Twitter, Goodreads and Pinterest, as well as her website heatherames.com and has been affiliated with Sisters in Crime, Mystery Writers, Willamette Writers, the Electronic Publishing Industry Coalition (EPIC,) Alameda Writers Group and Romance Writers of America. She served AWG twice as a board member as well as host and moderator for the Fiction Special Interest Group, and was a coordinator for several of RWA's local and national conferences. She is currently a board member of Portland Oregon's Harriett Vane Chapter of Sisters in Crime and an active member of both Northwest Independent Writers Association (NIWA) and the Salem chapter of Willamette Writers.

Made in the USA
Middletown, DE
31 July 2021